THE OA

THE OA

Alasdair Wham

Greenan Publishing

THE OA

First published in Great Britain in 2024 by Greenan Publishing, Ayr

ISBN 978-0-9933400-4-8
Copyright 2024

The moral right of Alasdair Wham to be identified as the author of this work has been asserted in accordance with the Copyright, Design and Patents Act. 1988.

This work is a work of fiction. Names, characters, businesses, organisations, places and events are either the product of the author's imagination or are used fictitiously. Any resemblance to actual persons, living or dead, events or locales is entirely coincidental.

A catalogue record for this book is available from the British Library.
For information, please contact info@geenanpublishing.co.uk

Also by Alasdair Wham

Fiction

Machir Bay
Bac Mor
Devil's Cauldron

Non-fiction

Ayrshire's Forgotten Railways
Dumfries and Galloway's Lost Railway Heritage
(both published by Oakwood Press)

This book is dedicated to Isla, Emily and Lucy.

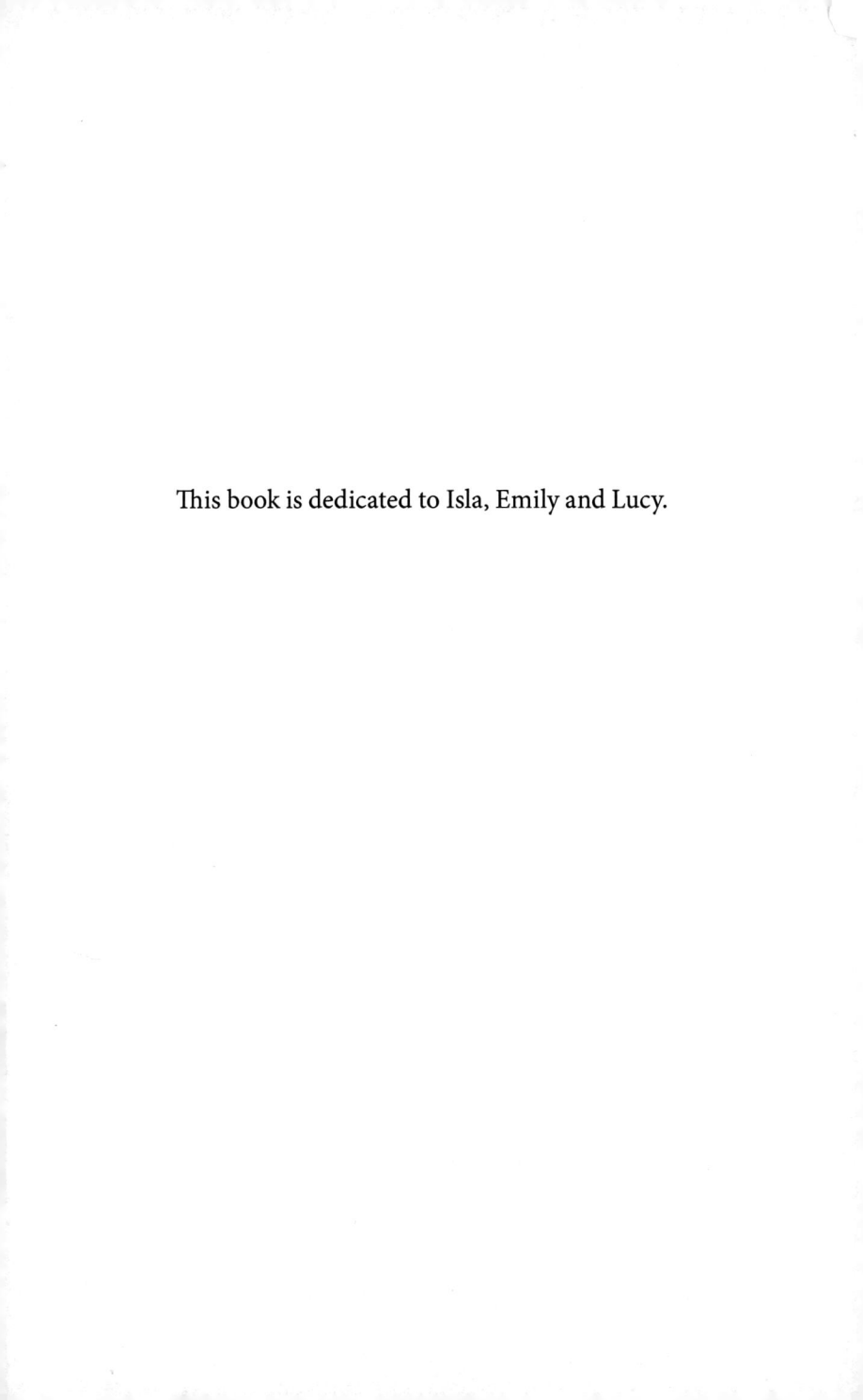

1

'Laphroaig, Lagavulin, Ardbeg.' The sudden pronouncement jolted Henry, who was driving, alerting him that his mind had wandered again. He automatically gripped the steering wheel while checking the road ahead. They had been travelling for a few hours, having left Glasgow early, and conversation had been slow, to say the least.

'What was that, Alan.'

'Laphroaig, Lagavulin, Ardbeg. They are distilleries on Islay.'

'I know that,' he replied, maybe too sharply.

'I was thinking about our trip.' That was not a surprise, Henry mused. 'There's a path now, the Three Distilleries Trail, starts at Port Ellen, a tourist route that links all the distilleries in that part of the island, starting with Laphroaig. We can get a bus from Bowmore to Port Ellen and spend the day visiting the distilleries. Better get a taxi back,' he added, a smile flickering as he spoke. Henry's brother-in-law, Alan Wright, was a successful financial director of an electronics company in his early fifties, his hair primarily grey, a mature adult in other words. Yet, he appeared to have caught a bad dose of Islay whisky fever.

'Okay, I am up for that,' but inside, Henry groaned. Whisky was not his passion, although he wouldn't miss the opportunity to visit a few distilleries. After all, it is what you did on Islay, the whisky island on Scotland's west coast. When Hazel, his sister-in-law, discovered Henry was visiting the island on business, she encouraged him to stay longer and take her husband. Henry had wanted to visit to take in the beaches, breathe in the fresh air and find peace and solitude. If only that was possible. It was still all too raw, probably a mistake; Mary had been dead only a few months. His emotions were still all over the place, his attention distracted by random connections that led to precious memories and sudden upwelling of emotions. Memories were all that he had left, and he had to nurture them even if, at times, they were painful. If he was still, he could sense Mary's presence and even remember the floral perfume she always wore. For a second, he couldn't remember its name, felt panicky and then the name returned – Libre by Yves St Laurent. You have to fight to hang onto memories.

Ahead lay the small Argyllshire town of Lochgilphead, a brief stop for petrol and then the final section of the A83 to the terminal for the Islay ferry. He glanced at the car clock; they were on time.

The car filled with petrol, they continued their journey, crossing over the westerly end of the Crinan Canal, then hugging the western side of Loch Fyne, tree-lined slopes to their right, the loch reflecting the clouds that hung above it, a mixture of darkness and light.

Henry kept his thoughts to himself, pleased that Alan was not wanting to talk. Usually, he would be in his campervan, he thought, Mary by his side, plotting an excursion, happy in each other's company, especially after his sons had left home. He couldn't go near the campervan, locked and abandoned on his driveway – too many associations. At least he had been at home the day Mary complained of indigestion, which suddenly developed into a heart attack, and an ambulance was summoned. She never had a day's illness before. He remembered the bewildered look on her face, the shock for both of them. Of course, he blamed the pressure they were under when he was forced to leave the police, their anger, and the sense of injustice. He realised he was gripping the steering wheel tightly, his knuckles white. He tried to relax, breathing slowly as the doctor had suggested to regain composure.

'Do you want to visit all the distilleries?' he probed, anxious to deflect his ruminations, trying to be friendly.

'A good number.'

Henry found himself laughing, slightly forced but at least he was making an effort. 'I'm looking forward to sampling them, or at least some of them.' Alan was okay; they had just never been that close, but he owed a lot to Hazel, and the support she had given him in the last few months. Bringing her husband was payback.

The journey eventually took them down the hill into Tarbert, a small but active fishing port. In the last few miles, the sun had broken through the cloud cover shining on the harbour, two sides lined with houses, tenements and sheds, fishing boats and leisure craft in the harbour. The sea intruded on both sides at Tarbert, almost making the Kintyre peninsula an island. In the past, Vikings could haul their boats the short distance between the harbour at Tarbert and West Loch Tarbert to avoid the long and dangerous detour around the Mull of Kintyre further south.

The road swung sharply west, after the Coop store on the corner, soon after reaching the town and, after a few miles, reached West Loch Tarbert, the ferry terminal for the Islay ferry. And then, in the distance, he saw the MV *Finlaggan* edging slowly up the loch towards the ferry terminal with its twin brightly painted funnels overlooking an exposed car deck at the rear.

Henry turned into the ferry terminal, crossed the narrow causeway at the entrance and joined the queue, waiting to show their tickets at the ticket booth and be directed into line.

Once parked, Henry switched off the engine and twisted in his seat watching the MV *Finlaggan* approach, much larger now. 'There you are, the ferry that will take you to whisky heaven.' For a second, Alan's lips pressed together, and there was a flicker of irritation, as if he didn't want to be patronised, before he got out of the car to watch its arrival. After a minute Henry joined him, standing on the large rocks that had been dumped to form a barrier at the edge of the waiting area and breathing in the sharp sea tang.

The ferry manoeuvred beside the terminal, the bow doors opened, the ramp lowered, and a few tankers disembarked. Standing beside Alan, Henry overshadowed his companion and was undoubtedly a lot bulkier. 'Whisky for the warehouses in the Central Belt,' he stated as the tankers drove past, 'most leaves this way, I believe, limited storage on the island.' He remembered a colleague, a whisky fan, saying it spoiled the romantic notion of casks maturing by the wild Atlantic Ocean. An industrial estate in deepest Lanarkshire was the reality for the tankers' precious liquid to be discharged into casks to mature.

Twenty minutes later, they were driving onto the ferry and with the mezzanine deck filled with cars and raised, they were directed towards the rear of the ferry on the exposed section just behind a black Ford Galaxy with its tailgate open, a man hurriedly searching for something in the luggage compartment. The inside was crammed with cases and metal boxes. The deckhand stopped them until the man hauled out a slim case, and three others joined, all casually dressed in work trousers and black jackets. They looked like engineers arriving to carry out maintenance.

With the tailgate shut, the deckhand motioned Henry forward to within inches of the Ford Galaxy. Both Alan and Henry got out of the car swiftly to avoid being trapped by other vehicles arriving beside them. They left the vehicle deck, climbing up the steep stairs and into the lounge area, already busy, where they bagged two seats and settled down. Henry suddenly felt lonely again, another wave of despair overwhelming him. He and Mary had a routine on ferries, deciding who got the coffee and then settling down with a newspaper or book of puzzles to spin away the time or watch the changing scenery. But he also felt guilty. Alan sat mutely beside him, beginning, Henry thought to surmise that he was if not unfriendly, then his fellow traveller was certainly distant. For Mary and Hazel's sake, he had to make an effort. He got up, smiled at Alan, asked what he wanted, and headed to the cafeteria to wait in the queue for a coffee as the usual pre-sailing briefings were issued over the tannoy. Shortly after, Henry could hear the bleeping sound accompanying the vessel's door being shut, and the scene out of the windows changed slowly as the MV *Finlaggan* reversed away from its berth. He watched the screen display on the nearby wall-mounted monitor where the ferry's location on a map could be followed. The coffee lifted him, and the two talked about their plans. Alan relaxed as they talked, now more about Islay than whisky.

The crossing was popular and to keep their seats, they took turns to go up to go to the deck above where the Mariner Café was located for some food. Alan went first, leaving Henry to look around to assess his fellow passengers, routine for this ex-detective. He found himself looking at one middle-aged woman talking to her husband. She reminded him of Mary. The woman noticed his gaze and scowled. Henry closed his eyes; it was easier. Eventually Alan returned clutching a miniature of Caol Ila twelve-year-old. The first of many, Henry assumed.

Food was Henry's passion as his girth showed. No more Mary to keep an eye on what he ate and impose a diet when his weight ballooned, and he was, he confessed, taking advantage of that. Comfort food, he felt good after eating. He climbed the stairs to the restaurant passing the table with the four men from the Ford Galaxy now peering at the laptop screen, his suspicions confirmed. They weren't whisky tourists.

'I'll have the curry and a portion of chips,' he stated, and he watched the assistant serving as the items were placed on the tray and as he approached the cashier, he grabbed a can of Coke and a Danish pastry. He sat at an empty table and poured the curry over the rice when a voice interrupted.

'Pleased to see you, Mr Smith,' and Henry looked up to see Charlie Smith, carry out coffee in one hand. Shoulder-length hair, now greying, balding on top, the familiar smile exposing a missing eye tooth and a misshapen nose, the result of an altercation with a brick wall, was all too familiar to the ex-detective. The shared surname was the source of much banter back at the station. Morton one of his former colleagues, would wind him up. 'I see your brother's in trouble again,' a frequent comment on a Monday shift as Charlie was usually arrested for an inept burglary. Henry paused fork raised halfway to his mouth.

'Charlie, what brings you here?' An edge of suspicion in his voice. Here was a memory he didn't particularly want even though he had a surprising soft spot towards Charlie. He wasn't the hardened criminal type, more one of life's losers and he ensured a successful arrest when business was slow.

'Nothing bad Mr Smith, just visiting my daughter, Sammy, and her partner. They live on the island. Nice to see you – long time. I am a reformed character.' I've heard that before, Henry thought – until the next time but that was someone else's problem now. Henry didn't feel like offering an explanation for his recent absences.

'Take care then, Charlie,' and Henry stuffed the forkful of curry and rice into his mouth, ending the conversation.

'I'll see you around,' and his namesake walked away, crumpling his coffee cup and joining the line waiting for food.

Having finished eating, Henry returned to the deck below and re-joined Alan who was completing a crossword. He looked up. 'Oak barrel used for storing whisky, four letters.'

Henry paused not quite hearing the beginning.

'Cask,' stated Alan with a broad smile.

Henry held his hands up. 'Good one,' and then taking the opportunity, he continued. 'Alan, I am finding life hard. Too many memories. I was down the A83 six months ago with Mary. Give me space, and I will try and cheer up.'

'It's okay Henry, Hazel, and I were talking before we left. It must be hell. She didn't want you doing a trip on your own, so early. We get on well, and I want to support you. It won't just be about the whisky, honest.'

Henry's eyes filled with tears, a common occurrence these days, and he bit his bottom lip. Kindness crucified him.

The conversation did turn again to whisky, but that was now safe ground for both of them.

Looking out the window, Henry could see that the ferry was reaching open water, and he glanced up at the display screen. The vessel was beginning to turn.

'Let's get some fresh air,' he suggested and they got up, abandoning their seats, climbing the stairs and out onto the deck. A cold wind snapped at their faces, but they were rewarded with a view of the island of Gigha, basking in the afternoon sun as the ferry turned west. Changing their position, they could see ahead to Islay and, further north the long island of Jura, with the Paps of Jura and their scree-covered summits glistening in the bright light.

'This is what I need,' Henry muttered, receiving a reassuring smile from his partner. They watched the scene as slowly the ferry edged towards the islands. There were also hills to the north but they couldn't identify most of them. Northern Ireland stayed stubbornly out of sight to the south, masked by a haze.

Islay and Jura gradually parted to reveal the Sound of Islay, the throbbing sound of the engines increasing as they fought against the strong tides which swept down the Sound. A white lighthouse surrounded by a low stone wall appeared to their left, moor on both sides, the Paps beginning to fill the horizon. They walked to the rear, overlooking the exposed part of the car deck, looking down on their vehicle and the Ford Galaxy, which Henry noted had a built-in satellite dish on the roof. Definitely, engineers, he concluded.

The engine tone changed again, a different beat and Henry glanced at his watch. Port Askaig could not be too far away. A RNLI lifeboat station appeared and a house partly hidden by trees. Then the *Finlaggan* started to swing around exposing a concrete ramp on the Jura side with a narrow single track road meandering way from it. A small ferry was approaching the ramp. He was about to suggest they went inside when the tannoy announced that all car passengers were to return to their cars.

Soon, they were leaving the ferry past the local hotel and lifeboat station and winding up a very steep hill.

'I would hate to be a cyclist attempting this,' muttered Alan as they reached the top, speeding away as Henry shifted up gear. Signs appeared for Caol Ila, Bunnahabhain and Ardnahoe. Alan read them out with a big smile on his face. 'From what I have read, we will need a car to reach them.' Soon, they were passing through the small village of Keills, slowing down through the village, with the Paps of Jura looming large in the rear-view mirror the sun shining on them reminding Henry for some reason of large dragon's teeth.

A convoy of cars and trucks before them and to their rear gradually spacing out as they approached Bridgend, and then they were heading towards Bowmore; they soon reached their destination, a self-catering house almost across the road from what looked like a former bank building.

'Here we are,' stated Henry and after entering a code on the keypad, he retrieved the key, and they were inside.

'You take the room with the double bed,' suggested Alan, and he didn't need to explain why. Unpacked, Henry opened the sliding doors to the rear, and they were standing on a patio protruding into Loch Indaal. 'Brilliant, eh?' Henry stated, sitting on one of the patio chairs. 'Another distillery across the loch?' he pointed across the loch to a white building with warehouses behind.

'Aye, Bruichladdich, one of my favourites.' They both laughed.

'Just like the others, then.' Henry riposted. The mood was improving.

...

Later, freshened up, they strolled along Shore Road to Morrison Square in the centre of Bowmore, looked up the hill towards the famous Round Church, noticed the distillery by the shore and then walked down to the small harbour.

'So quiet and peaceful, but time for something to eat and a beer,' and Henry started towards the Lochside Hotel, which he had noticed earlier. The hotel was busy, but they got served quickly and then moved to the bar for whisky sampling.

The two chatted, cementing their relationship and making plans. Henry did his usual people-watching. Mainly families, a couple by the window having what looked like a date night and another couple in the corner, the woman sulking. Then there was the third pair, a mismatch he surmised. A striking woman with a prominent aquiline nose and long blond hair pulled back over her ears, revealing long golden earrings that ended in a point and what looked like a pricey dress with a Paisley pattern, her shoulders draped with a pastel pink cardigan. Bizarre to Henry were the trainers she wore, which were undoubtedly very expensive but clashed with her otherwise elegant appearance. Opposite sat a young man with a bob of brown hair, leaning forward, listening, casually dressed. 'Sophisticate and the kid,' mused the ex-detective. The woman was pointing to an iPad and pointing at something on the screen. The man leant further forward and touched the woman's arm. The woman smiled, and their heads moved together. Henry turned away. Voyeurism wasn't his scene.

Alan butted into his observations. 'The first distillery tomorrow will be Laphroaig, so I suggest we sample several drams, starting with the older ones. You don't leave the fine wine to the last.' Henry agreed. The whisky was peaty and burnt his throat, but after a couple, he didn't notice. Later, as it got darker outside, they finished and wandered back to their house, discussing the merits of the individual drams.

Henry made himself a coffee and wandered out to the patio, the night air quite chilly with a breeze from Loch Indaal. Across the loch, along the coastline at Bruichladdich, a few lights shone underlining the scattering of houses. Alan joined him as they surveyed the scene, sensing Henry was thinking about Mary again and hung back.

Suddenly, there was a bright colour flash to the south over the harbour and a headland, reaching high into the sky. Colour cascading, expanding green and luminous. Startled, Henry grabbed Alan, pulling him inside and banging his elbow on the open patio door. The display lasted about a minute, as if a giant Roman Candle had been set off, but there was no accompanying pressure wave.

'What was that?' Alan shouted as the colour faded, leaving an afterimage burnt into their retinas for several seconds.

'I haven't a clue, but I was expecting a pressure wave, as I thought something had exploded,' he stated, explaining his reactions honed during service in the police force. He knew quick reactions saved lives. Henry was now in police mode, examining the alternatives. It wasn't an explosion, too big to be a firework or a meteorite, or he would have seen it streaking across the sky. As he rubbed his elbow, he had to admit he was puzzled.

'I think it was several miles away south of the headland. No doubt we will be hearing more about it in the morning.' Still rubbing his elbow, Henry pulled the patio doors shut as they retreated inside.

2

'Hello, I'm Jean; so pleased that you came across,' stated the elderly white-haired woman, her hair tightly permed. The couple stood awkwardly at the door. He was heavily bearded, a head taller than his partner, quite bulky, but mostly muscle, she suspected. 'Here, I'll take your jackets. Wet night.' Jean helped his partner off with her jacket, revealing a short white dress that would attract attention. Nice legs, I had pins like that once, Jean remembered. She was probably in her late twenties, slim and with blonde hair with a side parting. The woman looked at her lover, and he nodded. First impressions, they were still unsure of themselves. Jean waited as the man took off his jacket and handed it over. 'Here is a bottle of wine. Nice of you to invite us.'

'Bill,' she shouted, 'where are you?' She tilted her head towards the woman and winked. 'Too busy talking.'

A balding man appeared, looking flustered, similar in age to Jean. 'Pouring wine, dear,' by way of explanation and stopped when he saw the new arrivals, he added smiling, 'I'll take your jackets and put them upstairs. Gosh, they are damp; still heavy rain? Thanks for the wine,' and Bill took it from the woman carefully. The man nodded before Bill climbed the steep stairs from the narrow entrance hall, slowly with their jackets and wine.

'If you follow me, I'll introduce others from the cul-de-sac and a few friends.' Jean stated. 'If I can remember their names. I am not that good with names. It's Claire, isn't it,' and the girl nodded, 'and Paul.' Paul gave a slight smile masked by his bushy beard. 'I'll introduce you to everyone.'

Pushing open the lounge door, Jean took them in. Faces turned towards them. There were about six couples and an elderly, white-haired and stooped guy who stood up with some discomfort, leaning on a stick and shook Paul's hand. 'I often see you first thing in the morning, from my window, as you are leaving for work. I live around the corner. We've never talked. Pleased to finally meet you.' Paul appeared thoughtful before smiling broadly, revealing a bottom row of uneven teeth. 'I am always half asleep first thing.'

'I'm Claire,' the woman announced, looking around the room, 'Paul's new partner. I've only just moved in.' Most of the guests knew that from the expressions on their faces and were intrigued as to what happened to the last partner.

A bold statement, Jean thought, laying claim to her man, maybe not a shrinking violet after all, as she poured each a large glass of Merlot and pointed to the crisps and canapes. 'Help yourself,' she added. 'Now let me see if I can get everybody's names right.'

As Bill returned to the room, Jean had finished the introductions, often fumbling. Bill cleared his throat, getting everyone's attention before beginning. 'I'm pleased that you could all accept our invitation. Some of you didn't have far to go, just as well on a night like this. Thought that a wee social would help us to get to know our new neighbours and, of course, we can't forget our good friends. No excuses, you know where we are now,' and he pointed at a couple standing by the front window and laughed. 'Not so long next time, eh.' He continued, 'As you might know, we moved from Fife to the west end to be nearer our son, and guess what? He got a promotion and has moved south. Still can't see our grandsons.'

'The same thing happened to us. Children,' stated a middle-aged woman snorted while sitting on the sofa. 'Inconsiderate,' she concluded.

'But we are enjoying exploring Glasgow. Lots to see and do.' That was the signal that the hidden microphone would pick up. In his tiny earpiece, there was a slight vibration. To Bill, his message had extra meaning.

Jean surveyed the scene. With luck, everyone would mingle, and Bill poured more wine for their guests. 'Supper is prepared for later when we are all sozzled,' she declared to encourage them.

The doorbell rang, Jean rushed to the door, and she could be heard welcoming more new arrivals. She returned and introduced everyone again, pleased to see Claire and Paul talking to a couple. Paul, perched on the arm of the sofa, was talking to a male neighbour, and Claire, head bowed, was engaging with his partner. Bill was still doing his waiter bit, joking and ensuring everyone was mixing. So far, so good.

Then Julie, one of the more inebriated guests, tripped and stumbled. Her wine glass spilt wine over Claire's dress. Jean watched with horror and rushed over, grabbing Claire and propelling her towards the kitchen, mopping up the wine with paper towels. The soaked dress clung to her body, revealing her panty line. 'So sorry, there should be no problem,' hoping the hidden microphone would pick up the emphasised 'no problem'. Adding, 'I am sure we can remove the stain,' relieved to feel the tiny vibration in her earpiece.

'Don't worry,' said Claire, 'you are both so kind. I'll just nip across and change. I won't be a minute.'

Looking out the kitchen window, Jean saw that it was still raining. 'Bill,' she shouted, 'get the umbrella and escort Claire to her house.' Bill immediately appeared looking flustered. 'Okay, dear.'

Paul appeared puzzled by the turn of events, but the older man grasped his arm. 'I hear you work at Wilson's. I had a friend, now retired, who worked there. I bet it has changed.' Paul responded, leaning towards the man to reply much to Jean's relief and handed Claire the house keys as she passed by. Panic over.

Bill grabbed a golf umbrella from the brolly stand by the door, fumbling with the button. The umbrella opened, blocking the small entrance hall. 'So sorry,' Bill muttered, red in the face. He collapsed the umbrella and opened the front door, a chill wind blowing in. The two of them crossed the road, the rain heavier than ever, Bill sauntering the pair of them, huddling under the umbrella until they reached Claire's house. Bill waited as she unlocked the door. 'Can I wait for you inside, dear,' he added. Claire smiled sweetly as she stepped in. 'Of course. I'll nip upstairs and change. I won't be a moment.' and she almost ran up the stairs. With relief, he saw no sign of disturbance in the downstairs lounge and open-plan kitchen to the rear. There was a TV in the corner on a glass unit, a satellite box on a shelf underneath, an easy chair and sofa, and what looked like a drink cupboard. No photos but two paintings, one abstract and the other of an unidentifiable scene. All very normal. Bill held his breath until he saw a torch flash at the kitchen window.

Five minutes later, Claire ran down the stairs in an equally short dress, yellow, this time with an embroidered petalled flower on her right side. 'I only do short,' she laughed, adding, 'this is Paul's favourite. Let's get back to the party. It's so good of you to arrange a gathering for the neighbours.' She took Bill's arm as they walked back. Bill felt lightheaded, not that he had had any wine. It was simply relief.

There were approving glances at Claire's dress as they returned. The wine was beginning to work.

'Supper in twenty minutes,' Jean declared. 'Another lovely dress, dear, although I suspect you would look good in anything.' She noticed Paul smiling, probably thinking of later.

The windows were steamed, the kitchen door open to let out the heat, empty plates were strewn around, and people were still drinking. The Merlot had gone early, a pity since it was Jean's favourite, and she could do with a drink. The first guests left about eleven, and eventually, Paul caught Claire's attention and motioned his head towards their house. Claire was busy talking to a couple in the kitchen but nodded in return, and a few minutes later, they moved towards the door.

'I'll get your jackets,' Bill shouted, manoeuvred past them, and headed upstairs. He brought down the jackets, helping Claire with hers. She rewarded him with a cuddle and kiss, leaving him red-faced. Paul shook his hand and thanked them, and they staggered slightly, hanging onto each other as they walked back to their house. Bill shut the door and gave the thumbs up to Jean. 'Now for a glass of wine,' he stated.

...

Minutes later, there was a rap on the back door, and Jean rushed to open it. 'All clear,' she stated, 'did you get a fright, Roddy?' as she ushered him in.

Roddy nodded furiously, water droplets cascading from his mop of red hair and what might become a beard. 'I got soaked waiting out the back of their house. I just got out in time when I got Imran's message. I had just finished fitting the gadget in their bedside digital clock and raced downstairs. No telephones in the house must use mobiles, so I fixed the other transmitter inside their DVD when I returned. They probably never use it anyway.'

'Bill's good at delaying tactics. Do you want a glass?' Roddy nodded again as she held up a bottle of red wine. 'Sorry, Merlot's finished.'

Roddy sat on the sofa, the older man joining him, his stick on the floor beside him, no longer needed. 'Jack, you are looking sprightlier. It must be the wine.' Jack winked at him. The group looked at Roddy expectantly. He savoured the moment, his face lighting up with a smile, tugging on his gold earring.

'I found his passport,' which got the group's attention.

'And?' Jean queried impatiently.

'Paul Hogg Russell, born 22nd May 1992, place of birth was Helensburgh.'

'We'll run checks on that. Been abroad?'

'Yes, Slovakia and Estonia and probably other places.'

'Interesting.'

'I photographed everything.'

'Good boy,' exclaimed Bill.

The lounge door opened, and they were joined by another tall, gangly, heavily bearded colleague who had to duck his head as he entered to avoid bumping it. Jean looked serious. 'Any success, Imran?'

Imran beamed. 'I got hair samples from both jackets, so we can run a DNA profile. The wine bottle should give us fingerprints.'

'And the wine glasses?' he asked, and Jean pointed to two glasses already in a sealed plastic bag.

'Glad the comms worked', Imran added, turning his attention to Roddy, 'I think I won the battle of the beards with our friend Paul, and you're a poor third.' There was a broad smile as he teased his colleague. 'I've connected the listening devices you fitted, so we can hear everything they say in the bedroom or downstairs. I wondered what they are doing now,' and he tapped his phone. They all listened in to hear romantic murmuring. Imran pressed pause. 'Wasting no time. Too much information. I'll check the recording tomorrow and discover if he uses a different language when aroused. The cameras upstairs are recording their house 24/7. We'll soon build up a profile of their activities.'

'So, we are set up. Swan will be pleased,' Bill declared, no longer acting as an old man, standing erect, assuming group leadership.

'Claire is his new woman.' Jean chipped in, and Jack agreed. 'I heard her say she has been with him for only a few weeks. Nice girl, hopelessly in love. She's from Paisley, and they met in a bar in Glasgow. Works as a PA in a lawyer's office.'

'Any information on his ex?' Jean asked.

'When I was searching the drawers in his bedside cabinet, I found a picture in a face-down frame of Paul and what must be his ex. I photographed it.'

'Oh good, that should be helpful, but not very romantic to hold onto it,' stated Jean. 'Did anyone pick up anything about the ex from the neighbours?'

'Her name is Helen, and she was blonde and good-looking. It must be his type. Friendly but gave little away, unsure where she worked,' Jack added.

'Oh, one further thing,' Roddy stated, 'tell me if I am being misogynist, Jean, but there was a chess board set up a game in progress in one of the spare bedrooms. I presume that it is Paul's.'

'I'll let you off on this occasion.'

'Anyway, I took a picture of it.'

The team went silent. They all knew someone who would have been interested in examining the chess match.'

'Hopefully, she'll be back soon,' Bill declared after a few seconds, breaking the silence. The team looked awkward, avoiding Roddy, sipping their wine, each with their own thoughts.

3

The patio chair squeaked as Henry sat down, adjusting his position and placing his coffee mug and bacon rolls on the glass-topped circular table. The morning was bright, the water lapping gently around the protruding patio area. He deliberately smiled. Mustn't appear morose, he thought, as Alan joined him on the patio carrying a roll, a banana and a glass of orange juice. 'Great day for our trip,' he stated, eyebrows raised.

'We have over an hour to wait for the bus, so I'm enjoying the tranquillity and the views.'

The western shore of Loch Indaal was basking in the sunlight, cottages sparkling in the early sunlight, with the small communities of Bruichladdich and Port Charlotte visible.

'Picture perfect. This was why I came.' Henry added quickly, 'and all that is missing is a dram.'

'At nine in the morning, you must be desperate,' and they laughed.

To the south, over a headland, were the rugged cliffs of the Oa, hazier, wisps of mist lingering.

'I wonder what we witnessed last night,' as his view reminded him of last night's incident. 'It was strange. Something flared up just over that headland. No doubt people will be talking about it.' Henry rubbed his elbow almost subconsciously, now embarrassed by his overreaction.

Each was still finding their way, anxious not to upset the other. 'I was too slow to react,' Alan noted. 'Blame the whisky. I didn't hear any explosion.'

They sat for a long time, taking in the scene before getting up and packing for their day out, each carrying backpacks, whisky purchases loomed, Henry wearing a sun hat to shield his balding head. They wandered along Shore Street past the Lochside Hotel and reached Main Street, passing the Coop, before reaching the bus stop.

Alan glanced at his watch and stopped. 'Time to call inside? he asked, pointing towards a whisky shop.

'Let's explore Shaun and Nora's Whisky Emporium', although it sounds more Irish than Scottish.' Alan tried the handle, but it was locked. But inside, he spotted a man walking towards the door, tying on a green apron adorned with the shop's name and unlocking it.

'Our customers are queuing up today. Just what I like. We can't open to ten by law, but we are only two minutes away. In you come. I'm Shaun Byrne, the owner, and you are most welcome,' and he waved them in. 'Looking for anything special?'

'Passing time until the bus comes,' Henry stated, sounding colder than he had intended, 'but it is Islay, so I am sure there will be plenty of whiskies to tempt me.'

'Indeed, a full range from each of the island's distilleries, and we don't forget our neighbouring island of Jura, including special releases on the top shelves of rarer bottlings. We even have some Campbeltown bottlings and a few from across the country. Something for everyone. But as you say, it is Islay, so we specialise in whiskies from this wonderful island.' Henry guessed Shaun was just over five feet, but his personality filled the shop, and his enthusiasm lit up his face.

'No Irish?' Alan enquired.

'Ah, sir, you have detected my accent. There is no demand here. Bushmills and Jamesons can be bought elsewhere. We have only been open a few months and are doing well.' Henry was enjoying his sales patter. Shaun talked a good game.

'And no extra 'e' in whisky,' Alan added.

Shaun laughed. 'No. It might upset the locals.'

Henry wandered over to a display where bottles were perched on glass shelves, turning a bottle round to see the price and coughed when he did. 'That's steep,' he exclaimed. Shaun watched him and adjusted its position when Henry put the bottle down.

'That's a rare Bruichladdich. It should be on the top shelf. I sold two bottles last week. Whisky clubs often jointly buy a bottle to spread the cost, and everyone can then sample a few drams without costing a fortune. Creates memories. And then most foreign tourists don't travel to the island to leave empty-handed. But you both sound Scottish. Where are you from?'

'Glasgow,' Henry muttered. 'Edinburgh,' Alan added, glancing at his watch.

'How long are you here for?'

'Until the end of the week, maybe longer.'

'Pleasure?'

'And a little business,' Henry replied. 'We better go, but we'll pop in again.'

'Visiting the distilleries in the south,' and Alan nodded, 'following the whisky trail.'

'Please return. You'll be most welcome; hopefully, you can sample some of our drams from independents that the distilleries might not sell. No shortage of whiskies to try.'

'We could have busted the budget before we had reached our first distillery,' Alan claimed as they stood at the bus stop joining the short queue. 'Difficult choices lie ahead. Hazel threatened me not to overspend.' Then Alan noticed Henry biting his lip. Best not to mention other halves.

They paid their money and found spare seats. The bus moved up the hill, passed the Round Church and headed south.

'Did you notice anything unusual about Shaun? Henry asked, more to pass the time.

'Small, Irish, moustache didn't suit him,' and he paused.

'What about the scar on the neck?'

'I didn't see one.'

'He exposed a scar on his neck when he adjusted the whisky bottle I had examined. Either an operation for a blocked carotid artery or someone has slashed him. Some ugly stitching. Probably late forties. He would be unfortunate if it was an operation. Anything else?'

Alan shook his head.

'He was very nervous and kept glancing in a security mirror at someone in the back shop.'

'What security mirror?'

'Top corner above the shop window. A woman was standing in the back shop, probably Nora, but you can't make assumptions, and she wanted him to get us out. She was of a similar age, with a narrow, pointed face and black hair cut short. When we left, he locked the door.'

'Eyes of a detective. What does it mean?'

'Probably nothing, and you don't have much time to decide if you are investigating a crime. I tend to absorb and observe all I can, not be judgemental and think about it later. Sort out what might be relevant and what isn't. I would have been slightly suspicious of them. The pair have probably just had an argument.'

'As an accountant, I would have been worried about how they could survive, charging the prices that they do.'

The bus headed south on what the islanders knew as the Low Road, slowing at the bridges where the road narrowed slightly, crossing open peatland. They passed the airport, where a small private plane was parked in the corner nearest the road. Then, over by the sea, a Royal Navy Helicopter stood, blades drooping, unattended. To the south was the headland that was the Oa, protected by cliffs, windswept and exposed and, after many emigrated, sparsely populated.

With some sharp corners, the bus finally reached Port Ellen, passing the island's maltings, a tall ugly building at the start of the village, and they were dropped off near the Post Office. They walked down to the pier where the ferry terminal was located to have a look and walked back beside the pontoons, admiring some of the yachts. They collected juice, walked through the village, and headed past the primary school, the playground busy with kids playing and the start of the Three Distilleries Whisky Trail.

Ahead a mile on was Laphroaig Distillery, reaching warehouses beside the footpath first and then the entrance to the distillery among trees. They stopped, sipping more juice before wandering through the woods to the car park and the visitor entrance. Tourists were photographing the iconic name displayed in large letters on the warehouse wall on one side of an attractive small bay.

'They say that whisky tastes better at the source. We better find out,' and Alan led the way into the visitor centre. Henry bought tickets for the next tour in half an hour, and they waited outside in the sun. 'This is our whisky heaven,' Henry declared, choosing his words carefully.

'And this is only the first distillery,' came the reply.

After the tour of the malting floor, the stills and the warehouse, they enjoyed a dram, chatted with other visitors and watched in amazement as a Danish tourist went crazy in the shop, ringing up a four-figure total before hauling his purchases out to a campervan like a Viking raider dragging away his loot.

They continued on the trail another mile to reach Lagavulin, another distillery displaying its name on a warehouse wall and set in an attractive bay with the ruins of a castle overlooking the sea. Lagavulin had a different charm, but the whisky was equally enjoyable, even if their discernment was now slightly blurred.

They were weary and glad to get a snack and coffee by the time they reached Ardbeg at the trail's end. They skipped the tour for another day but bought a dram. Close to the sea, empty casks were stacked on their end, some rims filled with rainwater. The scene again was iconic, and as they climbed a few steps, they found themselves overlooking the sea. The distillery name was again boldly displayed on a white wall in large letters beside a small pier where the puffers once serviced the distillery.

They sat tired but content, Henry's eyes drooping in the hot sun, wanting a cold beer. After a while, reluctant to leave, they phoned for a taxi and waited in the square beside the warehouses milling with people. It took twenty minutes before their taxi arrived, and a woman taxi driver looked out for her fares.

'I'm Mary; back to Bowmore?' she enquired as they got into the taxi. 'You both have a good glow – whisky or the sun?'

'A mixture,' Henry declared, pleased to be in the relative cool of the vehicle as he slumped in the front seat. They sped past the distilleries and soon reached Port Ellen, heading back to Bowmore.

'I'm going by the Low Road, past the airport. There's lots of activity today. I think it's after that bright light last night. They're searching for something. I saw one of the helicopters hovering above the cliffs on the Oa. Apart from the whisky, the island is usually very peaceful. Maybe they laid a display on for yourselves,' she added teasingly.

Henry, slumbering, sat up as they approached the airport, alert. There was still very little activity on the tarmac. Towards the sea, he could see a helicopter and some people around it, like stick men, in the distance. But over the Oa, Henry spotted another helicopter hovering. He knew little about the Navy, but two helicopters in one area suggested something potentially important.

'You saw the light display?'

Mary nodded. 'I was bringing a party back to Port Ellen, and the sky lit up. Fairly sobered up my guests, I can tell you. It looked like it was somewhere beyond the campsite, just about where the helicopter was hovering. It took some time to fade and hurt my eyes.'

'What do you think it was?'

'Lot of talk, everything from an alien invasion to something running aground. The waters in the North Channel, between here and Northern Ireland, are chockful of ships and submarines, all playing a game of chess. The Russians are trying to latch onto our submarines as they leave the Clyde. I have a nephew in the Navy, and he tells me what he can. But here we are more concerned with whisky.'

A voice from the back muttered. 'I prefer whisky.'

'Good choice,' the taxi driver replied, 'earns me a living.'

The conversation faded as they reached the outskirts of Bowmore and headed down towards the harbour. 'Where exactly is your house?' Henry gave directions.

'Oh, Betty's place. Nice and clean, isn't it, and great views.'

'We're very pleased with it.'

'You would have had a good view of the fireworks last night from the rear of the house.'

'We did, but like you, I have no idea what it was.'

They paid up and got back into the house. Henry immediately went to his bed and slept for a few hours.

4

Henry left Alan at the house, planning to visit the local distillery and the whisky shop. Hopefully, he told Alan he would be back by lunchtime. Henry drove towards Port Ellen, passing the airport again, window open, enjoying the fresh air on another bright morning, nursing a sore head from yesterday's whisky sampling. He watched a plane landing on the tarmac, the morning flight from Glasgow. There was no sign of a helicopter, but a large tent, boxes stacked beside it, had been set up closer to the sea, so the Royal Navy was probably still around.

The road was long and straight, if not bumpy, as it crossed the peat moorland. As he approached Port Ellen, instead of turning sharply left as the bus did the day before, he drove on and quickly reached another road, and as instructed, he then turned right. There were several houses surrounded by woods. As he emerged from the woods, he saw a narrow road on the left winding past a cemetery leading down to a beach. He examined the steep hillside to the south and spotted a larch-framed house built into the hillside with a turf-lined roof. A narrow tarmac road with passing places wound up to the house. Impressive, thought Henry, but too modern for his taste.

When he arrived at the house, he reached a parking area surrounded by a low stone wall and noticed a garage to the side. Large tinted glass windows extended from the roof line to near the ground, with a porch area in the centre. The house was recently built with a narrow flower bed along the front, showing only a few small shrubs. As

Henry exited the car, the front door opened, and a young man smartly dressed in black trousers and a white shirt and tie stood waiting.

'Mr Smith, please come in. Sir Angus will be able to see you shortly; I'm Murdo, his assistant,' and Henry followed Murdo into a long, narrow lounge sparsely furnished with two parallel long black leather sofas with a semi-circular table in front of the window with a telescope perched on it. On the inner wall was a large abstract painting which dominated the wall to the right side of a log burner, with logs stacked neatly to the other side of the painting. 'Can I get you a coffee?'

Henry nodded, 'Black with cold milk and two sugars.' Murdo retreated, having shown the detective to one of the sofas. Intrigued by the view, Henry stood up and walked to the window. Beneath him was a sandy bay, and on the far side, the village of Port Ellen, the straddle of houses he remembered from the day before and the ferry terminal. There was a square white lighthouse on this side of the bay. Looking north, he could see the Paps of Jura over a wooded area and a helicopter hovering. The aircraft suddenly rose up and headed directly over the house, the noise deafening before it passed heading towards the sea.

'I don't know what they are searching for, but they are persistent.' Henry spun around to see Sir Angus dressed in tartan trousers with a green velvet jacket over a white open-necked shirt. Sir Angus walked towards Henry and shook his hand, smiling warmly. Certainly not underdressed, Henry mused.

'Now part of Islay legend is that several years ago, a local fisherman netted a bright yellow mini-submarine belonging to the Royal Navy. I bet that you are thinking of a Beatles tune at the moment. All together now.' Sir Angus laughed, which was infectious, and Henry broke into a wide grin. 'Initially, the Navy denied it was theirs, so it ended up as a tourist attraction at a local distillery, complete with a special bottling released by the distillery. They are good at special bottlings on Islay – any excuse. Later, much to their embarrassment, they claimed it back. I don't think that they want to make the same mistake again. Presumably, the Navy's presence is linked to the other night's fireworks. They are searching for something, and there are many caves in the sea cliffs around the Oa to explore.

'That is not why you are here, but I'm glad you could come. I hope you are enjoying your visit.' Sir Angus pointed towards one of the sofas, and Henry sat down, sitting opposite as Murdo appeared with coffee and shortbread, serving Henry first and withdrawing from the room as he finished.

'A good lad, he and his wife, Fiona, tend to my needs here. They are both local. I like to give employment to locals. I now spend most of my time here. My wife, Veronica, is away on holiday, which is maybe fortunate as it allows me to discuss freely my problem with you. Indeed, there is now an additional issue I would like you to attend to. You come highly recommended for your discretion and skill in tracing missing persons. Let's get down to business.'

'A little background first. My great-grandfather, Walter Gillies, was brought up on the Oa, the peninsula to the south, on a farmstead near Glenastle Loch. Hardly anyone lives there today, just a few farmers and RSPB wardens, but I did buy the old farm as a family memento. Over 800 people were trying to make a living out of the land in my great-grandfather's time. The landowner, John Ramsey of Kildalton, encouraged many to emigrate to Canada. He even paid for their passage on the SS *Damascus*, which sailed from Glasgow in 1862 before arriving in Quebec. Most of them ended up in Simcoe, Ontario, and their descendants can still be found today; some still come back to trace their roots. Ramsey even visited them there to see how they were getting on. Walter was just ten, but he didn't like Canada. Winters were too cold. He couldn't settle and returned to Scotland as a young man.'

'Walter got a job with the Caledonian Railway, became a bookkeeper, and met Martha. Family legend says it was on a train. Martha's father ran the Dalkeith Investment Trust, and after they were married, he joined and in time, ran the trust. Our family have run the company ever since. I am currently the managing director. Now, I want to retire and live permanently in Islay. It must be in my blood, but I feel I belong here. Walter's grave is in the cemetery below.'

'Now, here is my problem and where you come in. People know that I am wealthy. I live a good life and support charities, but some always want a slice of my cake. Scammers and the like. Sometimes, it seems that the past can come back to haunt you. As a student at Aberdeen University, I had an affair with a Chemistry undergraduate, Lesley McKenzie. Lovely girl. We had good times, but her family were not supportive, and after a silly argument over politics – she was very left-wing – we parted.'

Henry sat impassively, absorbing what was said, hesitant to pass any judgment. He hadn't gone to university, but similar temptations are part of everyone's life, and he was fortunate to meet Mary early. Quickly, he blanked thoughts of her, but Sir Angus was observant and saw the fleeting expression on his face, not sure how to interpret it, but continued on.

'Lesley got pregnant and had to drop out of her course. I didn't know this until recently,' and he pulled a letter from his pocket and handed it to Henry. It was a single sheet, creased and badly typed, slightly yellowing.

"I'm your son, Kevin. Lesley was my mother. You have never acknowledged me. While you have your riches, I live in poverty, and I had to watch my mother die when I was too young. Some attention from you would have helped, and some money would have made life more bearable. I want to talk with you. I'll be in touch soon. I know where you live."

'When did you receive this?' Henry asked.

'Some time ago, but I recently got a phone call backing it up.'

'Did you recognise the voice?'

'No.'

'This is threatening. Have you considered calling the police?'

'Yes, but I don't want them involved. I don't want Veronica to know.' Henry was sure that wasn't the whole story, but he went along with it. 'If this is true, I will help him. I am an honourable man, but it might be a scam. Could you check it out? Track him down and report back to me.'

'I can do that, but I need more details, especially about Lesley, place of birth, age. Things like that.'

'I'll provide all the details that I have.'

'I'll start on my return from Islay. You have read my terms?'

'Good man, that would be excellent. I accept your terms, and your deposit will be transferred into your bank account today.' He straightened himself, finishing his coffee, relieved that he had unburdened himself.

Henry sat still, waiting for the extra task that Sir Angus had hinted at.

Sir Angus pointed at the large canvas on the wall. 'This a painting by a local artist, Jenny McDougall, who is becoming very famous and collectable. Art is one of my passions. She lives in a converted cottage a few miles south of here, on the Oa. I commissioned her to do the painting, which is of the area,' Sir Angus paused, noting Henry's reaction. 'I love abstract art and try to collect it, although I know it is not to everyone's taste. Her work is part of my pension pot, although I would be loathed to ever sell it.'

'Jenny is married to Peter Meldrum, and they are a well-known couple on the island despite being only in their twenties. They used to live at Machir Bay and moved to the Oa last year, fortunate to get planning permission to renovate a crumbling cottage with a bit of land. They are also quite notorious because of a run-in with a criminal gang passing drugs from Ireland to the mainland via Islay. They were innocent victims, although one of Peter's ex-girlfriends was involved. Almost lost their lives. A couple of years ago, there was a lot of talk about it. Some people remember Jenny as a young girl, living in poverty, and sadly resent her rise to fame and fortune instead of acclaiming her incredible artistic gifts. Peter was a whisky ambassador for one of the distilleries on the island. Now they are involved with controversial plans for starting a micro distillery on the Oa. Many locals feel that there are already too many distilleries on the island and don't want another one. Others wonder how they can fund the plans, even though it is on a small scale – boutique size. The Oa is a special unspoilt place. However, I support them, and their proposals are modest.'

'I can't comment on their relationship, but I have noticed that Jenny has been struggling with her health recently. She is under a lot of pressure to meet deadlines. Creativity needs to be nurtured, not pressurised, and the poor girl struggles.'

'The other night, Peter did not return home. We don't know where he is. He was having a meal in Bowmore with one of the leading investors. Jenny's confidence is shot to pieces, and she believes that Peter and Cash, that's her name, short for Cashelle, I believe. Not a bad choice of name for an investor,' and Sir Angus raised his eyebrows. 'Jenny believes they are having an affair and are still on the island. It would finish Jenny to have the police involved. The publicity and subsequent gossip would destroy her in her present state. Can you speak with her? See if you can help.'

It was inconvenient and unfair to Alan, and he wanted to explore more of Islay. Henry was unsure and fidgeted on his seat, face blank.

Sir Angus saw the expression on the ex-detective's face.

'It would be a big favour to me, and I will pay handsomely if you can help. At least please meet with Jenny, and you will understand my concerns. I am very fond of her and Peter. Can I add, in confidence, that on the night Peter disappeared, when I was returning home, I saw Peter and Cash in a white van parked on the High Road, the back road to Bowmore. They appeared in good spirits. Jenny's fears may be correct.

'Any more details, like registration. Even on Islay, there will be many white vans.'

After a few seconds, Sir Angus shook his head and added, 'Probably by its size, a Ford Transit.'

'Where exactly did you see them?'

'Next to the road that leads to Duich Lots. The van was parked on the side of the road.'

'This was the night of the bright flare?' Henry asked, checking the timeline.

Sir Angus nodded. 'However, I can't see any possible connection.'

'Good, I wouldn't know how to deal with alien invaders.'

Sir Angus laughed. 'Good man, then you'll do it.'

Henry replied, 'Yes.' He knew the pain of losing someone, even if it was only temporary for Jenny, he hoped. Here was a chance to help someone who was struggling. Mary would have supported him. He could always buy Alan a special bottle of whisky as compensation. There were many to choose from on the island.

'I'll phone ahead and alert her then,' Sir Angus added, 'good man.'

5

Henry drove back the way he came to the outskirts of Port Ellen and followed the signs for the campsite at Kintra. Several tents were pitched among the sand dunes, a stiff breeze blowing in from Loch Indaal with one exposed tent flapping in the wind. There were even a couple of campervans, which would have been his choice. There was a Royal Navy Land Rover in the car park, a reminder that this was near the location of the mysterious flare. Past the farm buildings, he followed a narrow forestry trail leading up a hillside, winding past a wood. After a mile, he spotted a newly cut track across a peat bog, pools of water on each side heading back towards the loch. A brightly painted white stone cottage was not far away, partly concealed by a ridge. Across a yard from the house was a wooden barn in poor repair, missing several wooden panels with rusty metal work exposed. As he drove closer, he saw that a conservatory had been added on the west side of the cottage overlooking the loch.

Parking the car, he got out. Expecting fresh air, he was surprised to detect a faint burning smell and saw the remains of a shed, only a few burnt stumps remaining in a sea of grey ash. The wind was spreading wisps of ash around as he watched. Inside the barn was an elderly Golf and a new Land Rover Discovery. Henry continued towards the small porch and rapped on the door. Immediately, he could hear excited barking. A minute later, the inner door was tentatively opened, and a woman appeared. Her green eyes looked dull, her buzzcut, making her hair bristle. She held back an excitable Border collie. Henry tried to conceal his surprise at her appearance.

'I'm Henry, Sir Angus sent me,' and he tried to smile reassuringly. She un-snibbed the porch door and ushered him into the cottage in silence.

The interior was messy, with picture frames stacked against one wall and piles of un-ironed clothes perched on chairs and a table. She seemed to be moving and thinking slowly, and Henry guessed she was on medication.

'I'm Jenny,' she finally stated as the dog started to lick the detective's hand.

'Nice dog,' Henry stated, trying to break the tension as Jenny cleared washing off a chair to make space for him, and he sat down, the dog nuzzled against his leg.

'As a boy I had a collie who had a blue eye. He was a lovely dog. What's your dog's name?' and for the first time, he saw the flicker of a smile on her face. 'Jodie,' she replied. Henry looked around, noticing a picture of a married couple, presumably the Meldrums, and another of two boys, but the photos were too far away to identify. Henry was frustrated at his declining vision.

'Can you help find Peter?' Jenny's voice was low, barely audible, an anguished plea for help.

'I will try my best.' Mary would have expected nothing less. Henry felt her presence.

'When did you last see him?'

'The night before last. He didn't eat as he was going out for a meal with Cash Elliot.'

'Sir Angus mentioned her. And he has not been back since?'

Jenny lowered her head and nodded. 'I've not been myself recently, the pressure of work and I'm struggling to complete some commissions.'

'Sir Angus rates you very highly. When people appreciate your work, it adds pressure to keep up standards. Success can be stressful, but many would love your talent.'

Jenny looked, her eyes glistening. 'Thank you.'

'Is Cash involved with the distillery project?'

Her expression changed, tightening, and she breathed in deeply.

'The company she works for are willing to put up the finance, or most of it, to build a small distillery, starting off producing gin to finance its development. Peter is very excited about it. After leaving his job in the whisky industry, he needed a new challenge.'

'But you are not so sure?'

Jenny grimaced. 'It's a big task, and that woman has swayed his head. Clever, speaks six languages, upper crust, not his type.'

Henry heard the door suddenly being opened, and in rushed a young boy home from school, throwing his bag on a chair and rushing over to his mum, giving her a hug. Jenny gripped him tightly, kissing him on the forehead.

'I forgot that there was an early closure today. Ben, we have a visitor – Mr Smith.'

Ben stared at Henry. 'I saw you passing the school the other day.'

'Well done,' Henry replied, 'you'll make a good policeman when you grow up.' Ben appeared delighted.

'Cops and robbers are his latest passion. It makes a change from dinosaurs.' Henry laughed.

'Wait a minute, and I'll get him a glass of milk and a biscuit,' Jenny disappeared into the kitchen with Ben. She returned a few minutes later. 'He's watching the TV in the kitchen.'

'Good, I need to ask a few questions. I am not on the island too long, but most missing person enquiries are resolved quickly. One obvious question: why don't you involve the police?' He wanted to hear her answer.

'People talk about us. How can I make so much money? The truth is that Peter got left money by Catherine Robinson, Jason's mother.'

'I see two boys in the photo over there. Ben and Jason?'

'Yes, but Jason didn't settle; he's at school in England,' stated firmly as in don't go there. That was one fault line, mused Henry.

'Some would love to see us in trouble. Anyway, I'm sure that Peter is with Cash. And they are still on the island. I have been down at each ferry departure. They weren't there. Agnes, at the airport, confirmed neither had left by plane.'

'Where can they be staying then?'

'That woman was staying at a fancy lodge on the Islay estate. I drove past, and she had left; her posh sports car had gone. It's a red Porsche. She described it as vintage,' and Jenny snorted in contempt. 'Little room for two in the back.'

Henry ignored the barb. 'But he never returned?'

'He's hiding. I own half the field out back and won't allow the project to start.'

'Don't jump ahead of yourself. There is still hope.'

Jenny's eyes immediately filled with tears.

'Have I your permission to speak with friends.'

Jenny nodded vigorously, and Henry took out a small notebook.

'Malcolm Baxter, who is off the island but very close to Peter, keeps in touch. He's a sub-editor at the *Strathclyde Evening Echo*.'

'I know Malcolm, he covered several cases I worked on.'

Jenny appeared surprised for a second and then realised how their paths might cross.

'Then there is Ronnie. He lives in Jura and runs a boat hire company.' Jenny's expression froze. 'Maybe they left by one of his boats.'

'Possible, and I will check. Anyone else?'

'Elaine Soutar often helps him out. She's happily in a relationship. You could contact Susie, Malcolm's sister; she always has her ear to the ground and is working at a craft shop in Bowmore. They sell some of my work. She might know something, although she denied that when I phoned.'

Henry wrote down the contact details, gave Jenny his phone

number, and asked a few more questions. 'Are you on social media?' Jenny nodded. 'I have a page for the business and a personal one, so does Peter.'

'Any details for Ms Eliott?' Jenny rummaged in her handbag and handed over a card. 'Thanks,' and pocketed it. 'Contact me immediately if he returns. Can I see a photo of Peter?

Jenny collected the wedding photo.

Henry immediately recognised him. The Sophisticate and the Kid from the Lochside Hotel. Peter was the Kid.

6

When her boss, Tom Paterson, walked in, Sally Rundell was packing parcels into a Royal Mail bag at the end of a long day, looking tired, a sheen of sweat on her brow.

'I would like to complete the holiday rota. Any dates yet?'

'I'll phone my sister in Yorkshire tonight. She's not been in and I'll get back to you tomorrow.'

'No mobile phones in Yorkshire?' His tone was edgy. 'Everybody needs a holiday, Sally,' he retorted as he left the small room, his tone meant to suggest frustration. Tom was a busy man; holiday rotas were a nuisance. This was not the first time that he had raised the topic. He couldn't understand Sally. She took no holidays unless forced to. Her sister in Yorkshire, if she existed, and Tom did wonder, never seemed to be in. Sally was attractive, probably in her mid-thirties and lived like a hermit as far as he could determine, enduring a long commute to live in isolation in a remote Highland village. Everybody to their own, he thought, and on the positive side, she was his best worker, reliable, conscientious and honest.

Sally packed up, ready for home. The route from Aviemore in the Spey Valley up to the remote village of Tomintoul was beautiful, unlike the backdrop of her youth. She marvelled at the scenery, often spotted deer enroute, buzzards floating on air thermals. The journey was fascinating, a balm to her soul, from the greenery around Aviemore to the heather-clad moorland and remote hills near her home. In winter, the road was frequently treacherous and icy, with snow drifts and corners having to be taken at a snail's pace, but she always made it to work on time, a source of pride.

The journey took her through Nethy Bridge, the forest village, with the woods soon left behind and replaced by exposed moorland, the road climbing as she left the small community behind. Later, she was forced to slow as she navigated the notoriously tight corners at the Bridge of Brown, descending into the Glen where the river flowed. This section almost had a redemptive quality as she reached the valley floor before rising up again, like dropping to hell before rising again as she approached home, casting off the day's cares, resurrection complete. Sally passed several abandoned cottages, often thinking about the tenants forced to give up their struggle with the harsh weather and poor soil. It made her think about home.

With the outskirts of Tomintoul in sight, she pulled off the road at a disused quarry and parked. Glad the quarry was deserted, crows rising up, cawing on nearby crags disturbed by her presence, a taunting sound. She walked up the steep path to the viewing point, an artistic installation – a large metal cube with no front or back. She stepped inside and savoured the view of Glen Avon. As she practised her breathing, trying to control it, she relaxed. After a few minutes, Sally sat cross-legged, catching her reflection off the metalled sides, haunted images reflected to infinity, a form of eternal hell. Here was peace, how she coped momentarily away from the trauma which haunted her daily. Images slowly reappeared, as they always did, a nightmare haunting her. 'Oh, Clara,' she thought, emotion rising until she was overwhelmed and sobbed head down, her lengthy hair flopping like a curtain covering her face, shards of grey amongst the brown veil. Eventually, she stood up, emotion spent, wiping her face roughly with the back of her hand and trudging down to her vehicle. Looking in the mirror, she adjusted her hair with a brush, wiped away the trickle of tears and drove on to Tomintoul. The anniversary of Clara's death was always traumatic; the scene was impossible to forget, made worse because it was deliberate. 'Don't forget, don't ever forget'. And she hadn't, couldn't.

Returning to the village, she was composed and adept at covering her emotions. Tomintoul, the highest community in the Highlands, is a village based on a grid system by the then-landowner. A main street with two parallel roads and frequent cross-connections between the roads. Sally drove to the shop in the village square, collected shopping and then went to her bungalow looking out over open moorland to the east; savagely exposed in winter, but on this summer's evening, it was tranquil.

Inside, she lifted the post left behind the storm doors and made her way to the kitchen, discarding letters and an airmail letter on the kitchen table. Ming, her black cat, born of a nocturnal encounter in the village and welcomed as a stray, purred and rubbed her leg until Sally picked her up and stroked her. The cat fed, kettle on, she made a cup of coffee, took off her shoes and wandered to the bathroom, stripping off her clothes as she went and turned on the showers. Icy cold water soaked her, invigorating her. She dried herself with a towel and put on her bathrobe before entering the lounge. Finishing her coffee, she waited, Ming wandering into the spare room. Outside, she heard footsteps crunching on the gravel. The door opened slowly, and there was Ricky, eyes ablaze, casting nervous glances around the room before he quickly joined her on the couch, his kisses searching for her mouth, fumbling with his shirt. They were soon entwined, consumed with passion.

Ricky left half an hour later, going home to his wife, leaving Ming to re-join her on the sofa.

Sally sat still, reliving the experience. Lust might not replace love, but it helped her and took away her loneliness, even if it didn't help her feeling of self-worth. Eventually, she got up to make herself more coffee. It was then she remembered the post and casually lifted it. The letters were of no consequence, reminding her about renewing a direct debit and usual mail drops. She picked up the airmail letter and glanced at the sender's address. Her mood changed as she tore the letter open, her fingers fumbling. Anxiously, she read the letter with mixed emotions, more tears as she grieved for the past, but also understanding that the future could finally be different.

7

Henry parked his car at the top of the hill leading down to the harbour in Bowmore, close to the craft shop, a few yards away from the Round Church. There was a display of local crafts in the shop window, including two of Jenny's paintings on stands. A small plastic holder with details underneath each painting displayed eye-watering prices, certainly colourful but very abstract and not to his taste, thought Henry, as he pushed open the glass door, hearing a small bell ring. An assistant behind a desk was busy on the phone, but she acknowledged Henry with a wave. From Jenny's description of Susie, who she described as having a wild mane of black curly hair, he was sure that it was her. He took the time to look at the other crafts on display, from the good to the tatty, and stopped, wondering if there was anything suitable for Mary. Drawing a breath, he stopped himself from pursuing that line. The woman hung up the phone and rose from behind her desk, wearing a long black stripy dress, appearing like a zebra on steroids. Before she could speak, Henry stated, 'Susie, pleased to meet you.'

Susie looked surprised until the detective added, 'I've just come from Jenny's house, and she thought you could help,' adding, 'I'm Henry Smith; I don't know if she let you know about me.'

Susie shook her head. 'I spoke to Jenny yesterday. I couldn't help her but I am concerned. I don't know where he's gone, it's not like him.'

'You've known Jenny and Peter for years, and Jenny is distraught.'

'I know, but it will blow over. You know, men. He'll return once the lust burns out, more than my man did. He's still on the mainland; lucky he wasn't done for child abuse.' Her face changed as she spoke, her smile replaced with a grimace and tossing back her head, her curls fanning out. Jenny's depiction was accurate. He had met many bitter partners in his work, some never letting go.

Henry changed tack. 'I know your brother, Malcolm,' and Susie's mouth opened slightly and, sensing an opportunity, continued, 'He covered several criminal cases I was working on. Malcolm is very professional; you could talk to him confidentially, and it wouldn't be splattered over the front pages the next day. He's probably Peter's closest friend, and I hope to talk to him tonight. Is there anything that I can pass on?'

'Jenny has been worried for a while. Cash Elliot is beautiful in an alluring way, out of Peter's league in style. She also wants to drive the project and get brownie points from her bosses. Probably thinks that we are all simple on the island.'

'Peter and Jenny have been having issues. Jenny is very successful, but it comes at a cost. She's stressed out. I believe Peter feels neglected; a man thing, his pride hurt, so he wants to show he can succeed, too. And, of course, there is the money that Catherine Robinson left them. A recipe for conflict.'

'I should have asked Jenny, but what's the name of the company Cash works for?'

Susie looked away for a minute, thinking. 'Wheelan Investments, they act as angel investors, rip off merchants if you ask me.'

'Provide capital.'

'Yes, something like that.'

'That's helpful. Jenny believes that they are still on the island. What do you think?'

'Peter is well-known and would have been noticed leaving on a ferry or plane. He's probably still here.'

'Any idea where they might have a bolt hole.'

'She was staying at that fancy lodge near Bridgend. They might have some idea. It is all a bit blatant, not like Peter. Despite their differences, they do love each other. Peter is not like my ex.' Sourness spewed out of her again, but Henry believed her assessment was still valuable. Something out of character had happened.

'A final question.' Susie, by now, was more relaxed. 'Maybe it has no connection to my enquiry, but what caused Jason to move away?'

'Restless, like his mother, Catherine. He couldn't settle. They packed him off to a posh boarding school in England.'

'Did that cause ructions between the two of them.'

'I'm sure it did, but Peter agreed to it as he was worried. There was trouble at the local school.'

'Okay, thanks, you have been helpful, and I appreciate your time. If you hear anything, please let me know. Here's my card. We both know that Jenny needs help, and we don't know what has happened to Peter. We want him back.'

A young couple wandered in to browse the different crafts on display. Henry took the opportunity and left.

Henry called in at the Coop on the way back and got a copy of the local paper, always a good source of information. The headline was predictable. Mysterious flare spooks islanders, and underneath Royal Navy refuses to comment. He returned to the house and let himself in, calling for Alan. He was out on the patio, sipping coffee with a glazed expression. 'A good time at the distillery?'

'Wonderful tour. Great selection of different drams. I enjoyed myself.'

'I can see that.'

'Do I look that bad?'

'Let's say a strong coffee and a quick nap, and you will be fine.'

'I also went to the whisky shop again. They're very nice in the shop; let me sample some expensive drams. I bought an independent bottling of an eight-year-old Laphroaig. How did you get on?'

'I have now got two jobs. One I'll start on my return; the other is more immediate.' A good time to tell him mused Henry, and he explained about Peter Meldrum. 'I have a phone call to make,' and he left Alan. A few minutes later, he heard Alan stagger through to his bedroom and shut the door.

…

'Malcolm Baxter, here.' Henry introduced himself.

'Oh, yes, the Henderson case, I remember it. You got a conviction.'

'Yes, the jury didn't fall for his charms.'

'How can I help?' he sounded busy but curious about why the ex-detective was calling him.

'I am on Islay and spoke with Jenny Meldrum this morning. Peter is missing, maybe with another woman. Jenny is understandably distraught. She asked me to investigate. That's what I do now that I have retired. She gave me your phone number and permission to talk with you and your sister, Susie, who I spoke to earlier. Jenny is convinced that he is still on the island with her.'

'I see. How long has he been missing?' The voice was passive as he absorbed the information.

'Two nights.'

'The night of the big flare?'

'That news has reached you.'

'Half of Islay has been in touch. I have no idea what it was, and the Navy are staying mute. Can I say that I am both surprised and horrified by your news. Peter and Jenny have been through so much. My friend doesn't have a wandering eye, so that can't be the reason, so I am perturbed. Who is the woman?'

'Cash Elliot.'

'Oh, her.'

'You know her?'

'Peter has discussed her and her company's backing for his project. I think that he wanted to prove himself after leaving the distillery. I doubt they'll get planning permission for even a small distillery on the Oa. They struggled to get planning permission for their extension. But so many small distilleries are starting up, and Islay must be near capacity. I know Jenny was concerned about the project and their financial involvement and is already stressed out – and people believe that island life is stress-free.'

'Can you help? Jenny has tried his phone many times, but no reply. I'm sure he won't have it with him, so he can't be traced.'

'The paper's next edition is imminent, and I have to go, but I'll phone around later and see if anyone has seen him. I'll also run a background check on Elliot's investment company. Remind me of the name of Elliot's company?'

'Wheelan Investments.'

'Thanks. It's good that Jenny got in touch with you.'

'She didn't directly. Sir Angus Gillies, who I am working on for a different case, asked me to get involved. He is very supportive of her work.'

'I don't know him, personally. He arrived on the island after I left, but I hear he is a generous type, anxious to integrate into island life. The important thing is that Jenny accepted your help, and with your experience, you will find him if anyone can. I was going to fly to the island at the weekend when I have a few days off. My wife is visiting friends with Dylan. Hopefully, you will have found him by then. Keep me posted.' In the background, Henry could hear someone calling on Malcolm. 'I better go,' he ended.

Henry made himself a coffee, sat outside and browsed the local paper. It yielded little information he could use in his search, filled with speculation about the flare. In an unfamiliar place with few connections, he needed time to think and let his mind dwell on what he knew, hoping to find inspiration. One thing for sure, he much preferred this to touring distilleries. However, he knew someone close by who might disagree or maybe not, as he heard Alan go to the bathroom hurriedly again.

8

Cash clung to his body, arms wrapped around him as they huddled together in blankets to fight off the cold. He didn't feel comfortable but understood. Gone was her stylish appearance; now, he could see her white face even in the dim light, her face streaked with tears, her make-up spoiled. One earring was missing, goodness knew where, her hair tousled, the pink cashmere cardigan streaked with dirt, and her long dress ripped. The contrast was stark from their time at the Lochside Hotel. Her calm, commanding presence reduced to a sobbing hulk. Peter felt sorry for her and brushed whisps of damp hair from her face.

Peter felt little better, although, incredibly, he had more experience of situations like this. Indeed, he couldn't believe this was happening again, especially on Islay. What was it about him that attracted trouble? At least Jenny was not here. Thank God. He was terrified until he realised they weren't McGory's thugs on a revenge mission. Peter moved his body, freeing a hand to rub his cheek, where he could feel a lump emerging. Cash responded by clinging tighter. Any self-control was gone. How easily her veneer of sophistication could be stripped away, exposing primitive emotions.

'Who are they?' she whispered.

'I don't know. They have hardly spoken, so I can hardly even guess their accents.'

'What were they doing?'

'I wish I knew,' although he thought if I promised not to reveal what happened, maybe they would let us go, but that was naive.

'What are they going to do to us?'

'We'll only find out when they come back,' he stated, trying to be patient with her endless questions. Then he had a worrying thought, panic setting in. Maybe they won't come back. Perhaps they are abandoning us here while they get on with their business. Since their entrapment, he had heard no sound from above. They had been deserted, even if only temporarily. Cash sensed a change, Peter's breathing deepening as he fought to resist that idea.

'They are going to come back, aren't they?' she asked as if reading his mind.

'I'm sure that they will. We're on a small island. When people realise we're gone, they'll search for us.' At least he knew that he was still on Islay. There had been no boat trip. He had tried to memorise the route taken. After all, he knew every road and corner on the island. Best guess? Somewhere on the Rhinns. Ironically, he had been so close to his former home when it happened. Curiosity had got the better of him, and he would regret that for a long time.

Anxiously, Peter scanned the cellar they were in. It was small, lined with breeze blocks; the ground was hard earth, and there was a pile of discarded papers and what appeared to be clothes in one corner. He had heard rustling in the corner but had not commented, not wanting to alarm Cash further. A thin shaft of light pierced the gloom from the trapdoor. Peter's head had been covered in a blanket that smelt of dogs, dragged from a van and driven here before being propelled by two people to this cellar. The air had been cold, with a breeze probably from the sea, not that that helped much on an island to identify the location.

Then he heard a bolt being withdrawn, a whiff of damp air and then roughly, he had been lowered a few feet and then dropped to the ground, losing his balance and tumbling to the ground. Cash followed a minute later, trying to scream, but someone must have covered her mouth because it was short-lived, and she fell against him as the trapdoor was slammed shut and the bolt rammed home. No one spoke, which made the situation even more surreal and no less terrifying. Cash reached out, grabbing his arm and clinging to him, their eyes slowly adjusting to the dark. The height of the cellar made it more comfortable to sit down.

And that had been some time ago, probably many hours, although Peter had lost all track of time and hadn't been wearing a watch.

Peter was dozing when he heard footsteps above and two people whispering. Suddenly, he heard the bolt being moved, and the cellar lit up; a rat scurried into the corner. Plastic water bottles and what looked like packs of sandwiches were thrown down. By this time, Peter was struggling to his feet, dodging a metal pail and toilet rolls as he attempted to reach the entrance. He saw one figure's work boots and black trousers before the trapdoor was slammed shut and bolted. Peter screamed in frustration. 'Let us out,' but that was a forlorn hope. Cash shrieked at the top of her voice until he touched her mouth and hugged her. As she quietened, he shouted, 'People will be looking for us; let us out, whoever you are.' His voice echoed around the cellar, tailing off. He looked down in horror to spot a rat at his feet, nuzzling the wrapper of a pack of sandwiches. He grabbed the metal pail and hit it, finishing it off with his shoe, kicking its limp body away. By now, Cash was in hysterics, and he screamed at her, releasing some pent-up emotion. 'Shut up.' To his surprise, she did and sat down. Peter grabbed one of the water bottles, unscrewed it and gave her a drink. She glugged down some water, crawled swiftly to the far corner, and was sick.

They hadn't been abandoned, but neither did it look like they would be released anytime soon. For the immediate future, this was to be their prison, literally kept in the dark. Peter swallowed hard, fighting against the fear he felt of the unknown. A few hours ago, all the plans had been shattered, their future now uncertain.

9

Henry spotted the *Casablanca* from some distance as it manoeuvred into the harbour at Port Ellen before reaching the jetty, gleaming white in the sun. Alan was still hungover and only slowly followed his companion towards the boat, both clutching backpacks.

'Ronnie,' Henry shouted as a shaven-headed man appeared from the cabin sporting a long drooping moustache. Ronnie, deeply bronzed by exposure to sun and sea, waved them onboard.

'The sea is choppy today. Are you sure that you want to circumnavigate the Oa?' as Ronnie glanced towards Alan, who was very pale.

'Yes, it will be good for us,' Henry announced, not wanting to allow Alan the opportunity to back out.

'Okay, you better wear them,' and handed over lifejackets. 'The coastguard says that all restrictions near Kintra have been lifted. Plenty of scope for bird watching, and that's what you wanted?' he added quizzically.

Henry nodded. 'I always wanted to see a golden eagle and hear there are several pairs on the Oa. We forgot to pack binoculars, but you said you could supply them.'

'No, bother.' The two sat beneath the awning erected to the rear as Ronnie guided the boat away from the pontoon. Once past the many small islands and the lighthouse on the other side of the bay, Ronnie set course, made everyone coffee, and told them something of the history of the Oa. Alan started to recover as he drank the coffee and listened. Henry had given him no choice as he wanted to get a chance to talk with Ronnie, and this was the only way.

The *Casablanca* initially sailed past sandy beaches before sea cliffs were reached. Ronnie spotted many birds, handing over his binoculars to the two men. Alan still appeared white and drawn, only giving a cursory glance, the choppy waters making him nauseous. Ronnie just smiled, understanding his condition. The coastline was rugged, with rocky promontories sticking out and narrow ravines in between. It was hostile territory for even the few hardy sheep they saw munching grass on exposed ledges. In the choppy sea, water surged up narrow gullies, leaving thin lines of spume at the far end, which appeared like the top half of a rictus grin as the water receded. This was too much for Alan, who curled up on the rear bench in a foetal position.

Ronnie gave up on Alan but called Henry forward. 'Look up there,' and Henry saw a tall monument perched near the cliff top. 'That's the American Monument to the 550 American soldiers who died near here. We're entering the North Channel, a hotly disputed stretch of water even today with the Russians trying to track our vessels, but during the First World War, U-boats swarmed here and were able to torpedo SS *Tuscania* about seven miles offshore. That and the sinking of *Otranto* further along the Islay coast at Machir Bay were the biggest loss of life at sea incurred by the Americans in the First World War. The coastline was littered with bodies. You could imagine how difficult it was to retrieve bodies on the Oa. The islanders were highly commended for their efforts. It must have brought the reality of war home to them.

Henry studied the monument through the binoculars. Mainly made of local stone, according to Ronnie, perched on top of the 400-foot cliffs. He shuddered at the cataclysmic events and their aftermath. Alan got up was sick over the side and then lay down on one of the benches that ran along the sides of the boat, trying to sleep, clutching his backpack as a comforter.

'What about the *Empire Constellation*? It sank off Machir Bay during the Second World War?' Henry had done his homework. It was an excellent opportunity.

'A few people ask me about that and what happened to the gold on board. Is that why you were so keen to speak with me?'

'Not quite. You're busy, and I needed to talk with you.'

Ronnie's eyes narrowed. 'Most of the events, especially recently, are in the public domain. The gold has gone.'

'It's not the gold I am interested in, but what has happened to Peter Meldrum.'

'What do you mean?' his voice rose slightly in pitch, alarmed at the detective's declaration.

'Peter is missing.'

'What,' Ronnie appeared surprised, baffled, then concerned. 'What's happened to him?'

'I don't know, and that is why I had to speak to you and hiring your boat allowed me to get your full attention. Jenny has asked me to find him,' which wasn't entirely accurate, but he wanted to avoid complications. 'I'm retired but have a business searching for missing people and was on the island.'

'On the night of the mysterious flare, he didn't return home and hasn't been seen since.' Ronnie nodded; he had heard about it, and by now, most people had. Henry was convinced by Ronnie's reaction that he knew nothing.

'Jenny is very concerned and believes he's staying on the island with a Cash Elliot.'

'Listen, I don't know how much you've discovered about Peter and his run-in with the drug gang, but our relationship cooled since McGory, the drug gang leader was killed on Jura. We occasionally meet for a drink, but I had to put my wife first, and he believed I had put his family in danger. He was correct; I was in an impossible position, but it turned out okay; fortunately, I even saved his life in the end.'

'Maria, who is my wife, was blackmailed because her sister, Hanna, was being trafficked into this country and was being used as a sex slave, heavily drugged. What we did freed her from McGory's clutches, but she was hollowed out, no longer the same person. Hanna returned to Romania, where she is being looked after. Sadly, Maria went back to see her about a year ago and has not returned.'

'I'm sorry to hear that. It must be difficult.'

'Yes, it is, but I am also sorry to learn about Peter. I hope he hasn't found another woman; Jenny relies on him so much. But where is he?'

'That's what I have to find out. Any ideas?'

'I'll ask around.'

'Have you seen a red Porshe around the island? Cash drives one.'

'No, I haven't.'

The *Casablanca* sailed round the Oa, Alan still slumbering, with the occasional groan, with Henry and Ronnie left to their own thoughts. Ronnie pointed out sea arches and numerous caves, and he was pleased to share his local knowledge; it earned him a good return. They passed a farmhouse with a barn beside it. Both looked in bad repair near the cliff top but saw little sign of habitation besides a few ruins and finally turned into Loch Indaal.

'This area was restricted until yesterday,' Ronnie stated, breaking a long silence. There are many caves, which I presume they were searching for something.' He pointed out a sea stack known as the Soldier's Rock. 'It must have been here that the flare happened, not far from Jenny's house, which is hidden from this angle by a ridge on the clifftop.'

'What do you think the flare was?'

Ronnie shrugged. 'No idea.'

Henry was scanning the coastline, more out of curiosity, not sure that he knew what, if anything, he was looking for. Ronnie manoeuvred the boat very close to the shore, leaving the engine idling. In his youth, Henry could have jumped the gap, but not now.

'You want to know more about Peter. Tell me, what do you see?' Ronnie pointed to bushes by the entrance to a cave.

'That looks like blackness on these bushes. Burnt?'

Ronnie laughed. 'I bet that confused the Navy boys, but it is a black mould found where whisky is produced. It is known as distillery fungus or *baudoinia compniacensis*. It forms when ethanol combines with moisture in the air, and a fungus feeds on the sugar in the alcohol. It's why the distilleries on the island have to keep painting their warehouses, and some of the houses nearby complain about their houses needing to be cleaned repeatedly. Peter told me, I hope I got the pronunciation correct.'

'An illicit still?'

'Yes. There were once many on the island and all over Scotland. But there is a story behind this one that involves Peter and Sir Angus Gillies, no less. Have you heard of him?'

Henry nodded.

'They decided to experiment with distilling whisky and make their own, a harmless hobby but strictly illegal. Small-scale stuff, no threat to any of the distilleries. I went along once, but it was not really my scene. The fumes in the cave were overpowering. The spirit produced was alright; they even had small casks to fill the raw spirit Peter must have procured from one of the distilleries. We are talking about a year ago, so it couldn't be classified as whisky yet, not that they would sell it. It was just for their own amusement. Rumour has it the customs got a whiff of it, and Sir Angus was warned. Anyone else would have been charged, but he got away with it. No doubt plenty of influential contacts helped. They removed the equipment and casks to a cellar in his house. You should see his wine cellar.'

'The distilling was another example of Peter's restlessness; after all he went through, he couldn't settle. Probably PTSD with both of them. I was the same, but I got counselling. Maria didn't, she refused.' There was regret in his voice.

'It was Sir Angus who put me in touch with Jenny.'

Ronnie thought for a minute. 'That makes sense. It is the sort of thing that he would do, he means well. He is also very well connected in political circles; some very important, top cabinet people have stayed with him on the island. He is a good host, it just a pity that his wife hates the island.'

Alan started to stir, sitting up stiff after sleeping on the bench, and Ronnie made more coffee for them all. 'Thanks,' Alan muttered, 'I think that I will stay off the whisky for a while,' he muttered, looking more himself, colour returning to his cheeks.

'Do you want me to head back now,' Ronnie suggested, and Henry agreed. The primary purpose of the trip was to discover what Ronnie knew. He had achieved that. They traversed the coast back into the North Channel, and then Ronnie shouted, 'Above the farmhouse, do you see it?' You're in luck, an eagle.'

Henry grabbed the binoculars, focussing in the direction indicated.

'It's above the farmhouse. Press the image stabilising button,' and Henry found the creature hovering. Its size was impressive from a distance, with its wings stretched out as it floated. Dark brown with lighter feathers and brown plumage on its neck.

'It's large. Incredible.' He handed the binoculars to Alan, who seemed much more alert. He found the bird quickly. Suddenly, it plunged towards the moorland, and Alan tried to follow it. He handed the binoculars back to Henry.

'You guys were talking about a red Porsche.'

The detective nodded. 'Well, there's one beside the farmhouse. Is that the one you were searching for?'

Henry snatched the binoculars and pointed them towards the farmhouse, a two-storey harled building, its walls, once white, badly needed repainted. Beside it, there was a carport, its perspex roof sagging and parked underneath was a red car. Ronnie joined him in studying the scene. 'It's definitely red,' he proclaimed, and it does look like a sports car. Can't be sure, however.'

'The location is remote, unlikely to be found. I wonder if Peter and Cash are there. Time to pay a visit.'

'Maybe not at the moment. We're being watched. I just saw sunlight glint off binoculars. Upper window to the left. Get under the awning.' Ronnie returned to the cockpit and throttled the engine, taking it further out. 'My old friend,' he murmured, 'what are you up to. Why would you take an upper-class girl to a place like that? If you want a dirty weekend, why in an almost derelict farmhouse.' He turned to Henry. 'I'm worried something isn't right.'

'I've suspected the same. If that is the Porsche, someone has probably dumped it there.'

Henry remembered Sir Angus's claim about seeing the couple near Duich Lots. They are in trouble, but why? What had they done?'

10

The group sat quietly around a semi-circular table, the only sound the slow swish of the fan on the ceiling. The room deep in the bowels of the building, as usual, was too hot. They were all watching the large screen on the wall for signs of life. Bill sat impassive, but his left hand revealed his inner tension as it slowly clenched and unclenched. Jean leant forward while Imran's long legs were out to the side of the chair, crossed at the ankles. Roddy was the most composed, sitting still, tugging at the beginnings of a scraggily red beard as if trying to encourage it to grow. The screen flickered into life, and there he was, Swan. Domed head with only wisps of hair, the eyes scrutinising the scene, enjoying his grip on the assembled team. A grey figure, drained of colour, reminding Roddy of the Big Brother figure in Orwell's book *1984*. Appearing from a remote location added to the sense of his power. His eyes were deep-set, cold orbs at the end of a tunnel, shielded by bushy eyebrows, a tangled mass of grey and white, projecting a fierce look. Roddy focussed his thoughts as he noticed Swan's gaze sweep over him.

'I'm sorry that I can't be with you personally. Update me, Bill.'

Bill looked down at the iPad before him, clearing his throat, used to Swan's clipped tones.

'Paul Russell left home after midnight, a day after the party. Our listening devices heard no conversation between him and his partner that suggested he was leaving. The camera in our house picked up his departure. He was wearing an anorak, jeans and a baseball cap and was carrying a black bag. He has not returned, and that was a day ago. His partner was alarmed when she realised he had gone in the morning, shouting for him, suggesting she didn't expect his departure. After attempting to phone him a few times, she gave up, throwing something as we heard a glass break. His phone must have been switched off or left behind. Later, she called a friend, worried.'

'Imran can provide more information,' and Bill turned to the bearded man beside him, who sat up, bringing his legs underneath the table.

'Following the usual procedures, I studied local CCTV footage. I picked him up a few hundred metres away on Main Street. It was the middle of the night, and only one other person was around. They approached each other and swapped supermarket bags at the last minute. They didn't appear to acknowledge each other, and the swap was very smooth. Russell then turned left down Cook Avenue, a residential street and out of range of cameras. It looks like a classic dead drop.'

'Disappeared?'

'Yes, I am searching other cameras to see if I can pick him up. So far, no success.'

'It might be worth asking residents in the street if they saw something unusual. It means legwork, but we have little to go on. The other person?'

'I've tried to trace him, but he also vanished.'

'Keep searching for both.'

Swan's attention switched quickly. 'Jean, what do you have?'

'Russell's DNA strongly suggests ethnic Russian. Ninety-five per cent confident and no record of fingerprints on any database.'

'What about his partner, Claire?'

'DNA, fifty Scots and Irish, typical west of Scotland. No suspicious circumstances. Someone that he has picked up after the previous woman left.'

'Anything on her?'

'Name, Helen Burns, has appeared in voters' role for the last few years. She and Paul set up a house together, not married. No DNA. Border Force recorded her leaving for Cyprus a month ago, and no trace of her after that. Passport records give the date of birth as 2nd April 1994.

'A double plant, and she has probably been recalled. I wonder why, but instruct Border Force to alert us if she tries to return.'

'Roddy.' Despite expecting to speak, he felt his body surge with nervous energy.

'I have found a birth record for a Paul Hogg Russell. The same birthday and parents match on the birth certificate and passport application. Died as a young boy and was buried near Aberdeen. Like Russell, Helen Burns has also taken someone's identity. This time, a girl killed in a car accident with her parents at age three. Both have been tomb-stoned, the identity of the dead children stolen.'

'We could do with the help of Ash.' Heads were lowered, avoiding Swan's gaze, but he acknowledged their reaction. 'I accept your feelings, but holding an inquiry is standard practice. Ash is part of that inquiry but remains a valued team member, even if she is not officially active. Roddy, you are close to her.' There was little that Swan didn't know, but he still felt himself squirm, tugging at his gold earring, feeling uncomfortable. This was personal. 'Please visit and suggest that it would be helpful for her to use her open-source contacts to trace Paul Russell and Helen Burns.' Just like that, thought Roddy, now he dictates my personal life.

'My information is that Russell is a Russian sleeper inserted several years ago. Not the type trying to inveigle himself into our society and build relationships with influential contacts – not an Anna Chapman, in other words. Kept in reserve for particular circumstances. Whatever these are, we must find him and discover his mission. He poses a threat.'

'Imran make sure that the face recognition cameras can identify him. We might be lucky they cover busy places like bus or railway stations. Roddy, we need to contact Claire; if she doesn't contact the police, make some excuse. Get her permission to search the house, the bins, etc. Quiz her; she might have some helpful information.'

Swan addressed the team again. 'The information that enabled us to identify Paul Russell is very sensitive. I can't divulge much more. The fact that the result was positive gives credibility to the rest of the testimony. We need to catch Russell. Bill, keep me updated. Good luck, everyone,' and the screen went black. No one spoke for a minute, half expecting he was still listening. Bill broke the silence. 'We have our instructions.' Turning to Roddy, he added, 'I am sorry that you are placed in an awkward position, but please pass our love to Ash. Let's go, folks,' and he stood up.

11

'Good morning; we've come in response about your missing partner. I'm PC Sarah Mullen, and this is DC Roddy McNeill.' It was a small lie for the latter, but it saved further explanations, and no one wanted to alert Claire to her partner's true identity.

'Oh, thank you. I'm so worried,' she ushered them both into the lounge. The room was familiar to Roddy, but in daylight, it appeared different. Roddy was more aware of the patterns on the lounge suite and the colours in the kitchen to the back.

'Call me Sarah. When,' and she glanced at her notes, 'did Paul leave?'

'Some point during the night, the day before last.'

'Monday?'

'Yes. I heard him get up and go to the toilet. He was in a while. I went back to sleep, and he was gone when I woke around four.'

'You must have been alarmed.' Claire nodded, gripping a handkerchief in her hand. She had been crying and appeared drawn without make-up, unlike the pictures Roddy had seen of her.

'Sometimes, when he can't sleep, he sleeps downstairs on the sofa.'

'You thought that was the case? And you've had no contact since?' Claire looked down, biting her lip.

'You can't think of any reason?' Claire shook her head again, too emotional to speak.

'He didn't appear different in any way?'

'We were very happy.'

'Have you tried to contact him?'

'Yes, but he doesn't answer his phone. His parents are dead, no other family.'

'There was no note left?' Claire shook her head more vigorously.

'Can I ask,' and Sarah was leaning forward warmly, 'were you having issues?'

'No,' and for the first time, Claire spoke strongly, 'we were getting on great. I can't understand what happened,' her voice cracked, and she bit her bottom lip again, causing it to bleed.

The police constable gently touched Claire's hand. 'I am sure that we will find him. Have you tried his work?'

'He didn't turn up. They're also worried. That nice man across the road, Bill, suggested I contact you.' Roddy suppressed a smile, knowing Bill was listening in.

'I'm pregnant. I didn't mean to be, but I am. I was going to tell him.' Roddy already knew. He had listened to Claire's tearful conversation with her mother earlier.

Sarah held Claire's hand while she sobbed. It was Roddy who spoke next.

'Sometimes people leave a note hidden. Can I have a quick look around the house?'

Between sobs, Claire murmured, 'Okay,' and Roddy got up as Sarah suggested that she make Claire a cup of tea and would then take more details.

'I'll start upstairs if that's alright,' Roddy waited for Claire to acknowledge his request and climbed the stairs. He quickly conducted another search of the room, but this time, there was less tension. He lifted a few books from the bedside table and flicked through them, looking for any notes. People often left a message if it had been a call for help, but he was not expecting any. He looked in the waste basket. Apart from cotton wool swabs used to remove make-up and damp paper tissues, the bin was empty. Why was he in the toilet for so long? Roddy wondered and checked it out. In the plug hole, there were several long strands of hair. He prised them out and bagged them. Maybe he had shaved his beard or cut his hair before leaving. The cameras didn't have enough clarity as he was hunched and wearing a baseball cap when he left.

Roddy hadn't expected to find much, so he checked out the other rooms, which had not changed from the previous visit. The chessboard was still set out, and for Ash's sake he photographed it again. He then returned downstairs.

'I'll just check in the bins,' he stated as he passed the two women on the sofa sipping from mugs of tea, thinking that Sarah's peoples' skills were first class. If there was anything to be gleaned from Claire, she would find it. Although a bit inexperienced, a person with a good future in the force he reckoned.

Out the back, only the blue paper bin had anything in it, which was disappointing and almost empty. He reached down among the circulars and local papers and spotted the wrapping for a small parcel. Lifting it out, he thought it would have contained only a small item. Still inside was some crushed paper used as padding. Nevertheless, he took a photo and saw that the postmark was Edinburgh. The sender's address was not on it.

Roddy returned to the lounge, caught Sarah's attention, and raised his eyes towards the ceiling, indicating that he had found nothing.

'I'm sure he will turn up, but can you give me a recent photograph. I'll log the incident,' and Sarah immediately regretted saying it like that. It sounded cold. 'I'll speak to the sergeant when I get back and if Paul has not returned by tomorrow, we'll pass on details and alert other stations, make a public appeal in time. In most cases, however, the missing person turns up safe and well, but please let me know if you hear from him in the meantime.'

As Sarah stood up Claire remained on the sofa, curling up, mug of tea on the floor beside her. 'Do you want me to speak to your mum? Get her to come over. It would be good if you had someone with you.' Claire shook her head again. 'I'll be okay.' Neither of them thought so, although only Roddy knew the true story. 'I'll phone back later and see how you are getting on,' Sarah added as they left.

'Poor girl,' Sarah stated as they walked to their car, 'her dreams squashed. Whatever Russell is up to, she didn't expect it.' Roddy stayed silent as they drove off. Imran was waiting in a car a few streets away, and Roddy changed cars, thanking Sarah for her efforts. She was too professional to ask about his interest in Claire.

They headed to Cook Avenue, ready to call on residents wanting to discover if Paul Russell had been spotted, even though it had been after midnight when most people would be in bed. Neither of them was hopeful, but Swan had spoken. It was a long street with terraced houses on both sides, which dampened their spirits further. At the far end was a busy road with a steady stream of traffic.

As it was during the day, many residents were not in, and they noted house numbers to call back later. Cars lined both sides of the street, even at this time of the day. The few they spoke to shrugged and offered no information. Imran turned to Roddy, exasperated. 'A waste of time,' and Roddy agreed.

'Five more houses, and we'll have a break. I noticed a nice coffee shop around the corner.'

'Any coffee shop would be good at the moment.'

Spurred with the thought of a coffee, they tapped on a few more doors.

'Two more to go,' Imram declared as they knocked on another door less than halfway down one side of the street.

'Good morning, we are investigating an incident that occurred the night before last - Monday. A person is missing. CCTV picked him up, turning into this street.' Imran stepped back, aware that his height often intimidated people.

'Jean, along the road, phoned to let me know that people were asking questions. I was asleep, like most people, but since you are here, can I make a complaint.' Roddy groaned inwardly, she didn't look like the sort that would hold back. 'Many students use this street to park their cars and walk to the local college. My husband often has to park on the next road. Two days ago, just before my husband returned, he was working late; it must have been about eleven. I was trying to get the cat in. A man parked in his space and was rude when I tried to explain that my husband parked there. He walked away and ignored me but must have returned in the middle of the night because his car was gone in the morning.'

'Describe him,' asked Imran, 'it doesn't sound like the man we're searching for, but I hate rudeness.'

'Certainly smaller than you,' and Imran smiled. 'Not difficult,' but the woman continued, 'clean shaven,' and she glanced towards them, 'like my husband. He scowled at me, muttered something rude and just walked away. Bernie wants a word with him.'

'Anything else? Roddy enquired.

'He grabbed a carrier bag from the back seat and walked off.'

'What colour was it?'

'Very dark, but it wasn't his bag I was concerned about,' she replied edgily.

'Can you remember the make of car.'

'I'm not an expert but my husband said it was a Vauxhall Astra.'

'Colour?'

'Blue. Are you going to do anything?' The woman was getting wound up.

'Not a lot to go on, but if you see it again, contact us at the station.'

'What about the student parking?'

'Complain to your local councillor.'

'Fat lot of use that would be,' and she turned away angrily.

They said nothing until they were back on the street.

'What do you think?' Roddy was the first to speak.

'I wouldn't like to bump into her again.'

Imran laughed. 'She doesn't like men with beards, and that's giving you the benefit of the doubt.'

'Probably coincidence, but then the dark bag and the car was gone in the morning. Maybe, our Mr Russell took it. And he didn't appear at the far end of the street. I'll check the CCTV footage for a blue Vauxhall Astra.'

'Time for that coffee you mentioned.'

…

The room was stuffy, as usual, and Imran reached up and pulled the cord to start the ceiling fan.

'Swan is unavailable, so I'll take the meeting,' Bill began. 'We have made some progress. Imran,' and pointed to his colleague.

'Our house-to-house on Cook Avenue showed unexpected results. One resident complained that an aggressive man had parked in her space. Seemingly, that is an issue on this street – blame students. He ignored the woman, something I wish Roddy and I had managed, she wasn't happy, but the man was carrying a dark bag.'

'Wow,' proclaimed Jack, who had missed the last meeting.

Imran shrugged and smiled broadly. 'However, my sceptical friend, we managed to follow Russell to Cook Street. Time 12.45am. The woman described the car as a blue Vauxhall Astra. One departed the other end of Cook Street five minutes later.'

'Furthermore, there is a camera not far from the end of Cook Street. We followed the car onto the Clydeside Expressway using CCTV footage. We're working on the registration. I managed one image of the driver. Facial recognition identifies the driver as Paul Russell without a beard.'

'I collected a hair sample from the sink in his house, and the

DNA matches. He shaved off his beard before leaving,' Roddy added.

'We have coverage of him exchanging a dark bag,' Bill turned towards Jack.

'Touche,' Jack proclaimed.

'Further, Russell received a small package postmarked Sunday from Edinburgh. I don't know the relevance of that, but it might have been a signal. There was nothing to suggest a sophisticated spy operation. Roddy has thoroughly searched the house. Russell was living off-grid, anonymously and has now suddenly displayed unusual behaviour.' Bill appeared worried.

'We've made some progress and are trying to trace the car. Whatever signal Russell received, he has sprung into action. The question is how do we find him, and what will he do next. I'm sure that it won't be to our advantage. I'll update Swan. Hopefully, Russell shows up on a camera somewhere. When we get the car's registration, we ask the police to help us trace it. Any questions?'

No one spoke. 'Good work, but as usual, we need more. Roddy, when are you going to visit Ash?'

'This evening,' but again, Roddy felt uncomfortable. Business and pleasure were not an easy mix, particularly when Ash was not at her best. It felt like an intrusion, and Ash could be sensitive. However, there were other considerations – national security. To Swan, it was a no-brainer.

12

Ash stayed in the centre of Glasgow, a modern building three stories high overlooking a thoroughfare. Poor soundproofing and the constant traffic noise made Roddy wonder about her choice, but Ash always made her own mind up. She also had pointed out to him that a shoe box on a modern estate with bedrooms so small that Imran couldn't stretch out in the second bedroom and had to sleep on the lounge floor was no better. Opinionated and beautiful, that was Ash for you.

Roddy called Ash on the intercom system at the entrance to the block and heard the click as the door unlocked. He took the stairs to reach her second-floor flat and rang the bell. Ash answered, wearing a long, patterned dress which showed off her figure to good effect, not that he needed further proof. Once the door was shut, the long lingering kiss made him feel welcome. The smell of exotic spices slowly cooking in a casserole from the kitchen area enticed him. He sat on the sofa, hoping that Ash would join him, but she went to check on the stew and then returned with a glass of wine for each of them before settling on the chair opposite. 'I need to keep an eye on the stew,' she uttered as if reading his thoughts.

'You looked tired. Been busy?'

'Usual stuff, mostly tedious procedural work. Imran and I knocked on the door of every house in what was a long street. In the end, it might be worth it. We'll find out.'

Ash slumped in her chair, avoiding his gaze. 'That seems attractive. I miss it.'

'It was bloody boring, to be honest,' and she laughed. 'We're searching for a Russian sleeper who has woken up just after we discovered him. Left his girlfriend pregnant and rode off into the night.'

'Charming fellow, I wonder if he plays chess. Can you trace him?'

'I know someone who could.'

Ash's face froze. 'Tell me you weren't sent by Swan.'

'He likes to think that he owns me, but he doesn't own this part, although, as usual, he is aware, he misses little.'

'We are all missing you and want you back. Any progress?'

'I was grilled yesterday by two faceless men who made the Gestapo look like pussycats. One had bad breath, and I am sure it was deliberate to wear me down. Two hours, two bloody hours of good cop, bad cop routine. And I am on their side, I think,' Ash blinked, her bravado slipping, holding back tears. Roddy's inclination was to lean over and hold her hand, but she was too proud and independent.

'Swan is missing you.'

'Oh, cheer me up,' she frowned, tugging at her braided hair. 'Roddy, I was in charge, and it was simple surveillance. I had instructed Benji to hang back; it was on the recording, and he dashed out, and a car ran him over. He was inexperienced and forgot his training. An accident shouldn't happen, and we are trained to avoid them. Blood, gore, ambulances, I can't forget and the man we were trailing disappeared. Total cock-up.'

'You're beating yourself up. Benji disobeyed your clear instructions.'

'Trying telling that to his young children,' and Ash firmly put down her wine glass, wine-swilling almost spilling, fighting temptation, not wanting to drink more. 'I was in charge,' the words spoken slowly to emphasise their import. There was a pause, then she added. 'I'll make the rice now, and then we can eat,' and she went to the hob, fighting to control herself.

Roddy knew Ash was on edge, her thoughts obsessively replaying the tragic events. He knew she had been offered counselling but refused it. 'I can cope,' she stated on more than one occasion. 'I've dealt with worse.' From what he saw tonight, he wasn't so sure. Being on her own, not allowed to work while waiting for the inquiry's outcome, was difficult.

Too proud, and Roddy feared that there was little he could do to help and was beginning to doubt that even their relationship might not survive the pressure. He sipped his wine thoughtfully.

They avoided discussing Benji during the meal and chatted about the team, laughing at their quirks and retelling stories. They were a close-knit group and needed to depend on one another. They moaned about Swan and yet still respected his role and authority.

At last, after another bottle of wine, her hand slipped across the table and grasped Roddy's. 'I'm glad you made it tonight; I've missed you.' That smile always won him over. There was hope.

Much later, Roddy stood by the window, which stretched from floor to ceiling, with a metal safety rail on the outside, a Juliette balcony, watching the brake lights of the vehicles on one side and the headlamps on the other. The sky was bright red, the light fading, and he knew he must return home.

Ash came out of the bedroom, glancing at a message on her phone. 'Pierre has conceded, checkmate. I can tell that he isn't pleased, but I am. A notable scalp.'

'How long did the match last?'

'Several weeks. We were well paired.' Online chess challenges were her hobby, and she was good.

'Before I forget, I was, shall we say, visiting a house, and he had a chess match set up in a spare room. I took a couple of pictures. I wonder if you could rate him,' and Roddy fiddled with his phone and air-dropped them to Ash.

'I'll look later,' and she kissed him again. 'I feel stronger; keep visiting.' She hesitated before continuing. 'We both know Swan. He'll want me to find out more about your suspect's background. "She can use her open-source friends,"' and she mimicked his voice.

'That was very good, but I won't tell him.'

'Send me the details, and I'll have a look. It will keep me busy until you return.'

'We all want you to return. The sooner, the better,' and with that, Roddy left.

13

Henry and Ronnie were concerned about Peter. Having spotted Cash's car and Sir Angus sighting them on the High Road, it was not clear what had happened to them, and they were both now worried. Ronnie berthed *Casablanca* and insisted on joining them as they headed towards the farmhouse on the cliffs above the sea. Henry drove fast, climbing up the hill towards the Oa plateau. They passed Sir Angus's house enroute, recessed in the hillside. For a moment, Henry remembered Arthur Conan Doyle's book *The Lost World*, a childhood favourite where intrepid explorers discover a lost world on a plateau surrounded by towering cliffs, a jungle where prehistoric creatures roamed. The Oa had a curtain of sea cliffs but no jungle. Instead, moorland, lochs, and abandoned shielings told of a landscape only partially claimed by humans, the rest having long since left, scrutinised by birds of prey from above.

As they drove past a loch, Ronnie pointed to a farm road, and Henry slowed the car, avoiding the ruts on the pitted track. Ahead was a small conifer plantation, and as they wound around the trees, Henry spotted the farmhouse, driving into the farmyard over a cattle grid, which rattled, no doubt alerting anyone who lived there. It appeared as if some of the cliff edges had eroded, leaving a jagged edge to the farmyard; pounding waves could be heard, the slapping of waves as they broke into gullies.

As Henry parked, Ronnie jumped out of the front seat, quickly followed by Alan from the back of the car. They had only covered a few yards before they realised the carport was empty. The car had gone. Ronnie ran around the back of the farmhouse, but there was no sign of the vehicle. By this time, Henry had clambered out of the car and joined them, looking around. The building was in an even worse state closeup. Window frames rotted, roof tiles missing, gutters overflowing with tufts of grass and net curtains flapping at an open window in the sea breeze. Not the place that Peter and Cash would have chosen for a lustful liaison, Henry concluded.

'I told you that someone was watching us through binoculars, so they must have moved the car. Probably hidden in the trees over there,' and Ronnie pointed towards the woods. Henry agreed, and Alan wandered off, checking behind outhouses.

The front door suddenly banged open, and a man came running out through a small porch, waving a shotgun. 'What are you doing here? He shouted angrily. His face was red and inflamed; he had bushy sideburns, long, unkempt hair, a torn tee shirt, and khaki shorts, walking with a slight sway as if one of his hips was causing him problems. 'This is my property. Go away, or I'll use this.

'Put down the gun; that doesn't help,' Henry exclaimed calmly, facing up to the man. 'Put down the gun,' he repeated, lowering his voice, not showing any aggression.

'You shouldn't be here.'

'Give me a chance, and I'll explain, but you shouldn't be pointing a gun at us. I was a police officer. I know you'll lose your shotgun licence if you act like this. We spotted a red car in the carport,' and Henry jabbed his thumb in that direction.

'So, you were the guys in the boat.'

'Yes, it belongs to friends of mine,' Henry replied.

'So where is the car?' Ronnie asked as the man kept waving the shotgun at the three of them with less conviction.

'Our friends are missing, and I can guarantee that if you don't tell us, police will swarm all over this place in the next hour.'

'Someone moved it.'

'Who?'

'None of your business,' he snarled at Ronnie.

'So, you were hiding a stolen car, not a good look,' and Henry took out his mobile phone. 'I've got a signal here, and he started tapping on the screen.

'Stop,' and he lowered the shotgun.

'What's your name?' Henry enquired.

'Ranald.'

'I'm Henry,' and he smiled encouragingly. 'When did the car arrive?'

'During the night. They woke me up.'

'A couple of nights ago.' Ranald nodded. 'What did they pay you?'

'Enough, none of your business.'

'Who were they?'

'I don't know, never seen them before.'

'Yet you accepted their money to leave a fancy car hidden, and you didn't know them. Pretty strange behaviour,' pausing to let the message sink in. 'We're searching for missing persons; their lives might be in danger. The police are going to be interested, and they'll keep asking questions. Arrest you if they are not happy.'

Ranald shook his head. 'They just said they wanted me to keep it for a few days. No questions. I was doing them a favour.'

'And made it worth your while. Where did you hide it?'

'They took it away.'

'Really.'

'A woman arrived an hour ago and drove off in it. Don't know where she went. Look around if you like, you won't find it.' More conciliatory, he added, 'I needed the money, don't think I did anything wrong.'

'The police might disagree. Who was driving the car on the night?'

'A man, never seen him before. They were in a hurry.' Henry glanced at Ronnie to see if he had picked up the implication. Cash was not driving her own car.

'There must have been another vehicle to take the driver away in. Did you see it?'

'There was a white van on the other side of the cattle grid.'

'What type was it?

'Quite big.'

'Recognise anyone in it?'

'No. They gave me some money and encouraged me to go back inside. Said they would collect the Porsche in a few days.'

'The woman who collected it today. Can you describe her? Young, old? Forties, fifties, younger?

Ranald paused. 'Maybe fifties.'

'Appearance?'

'Only glimpsed her driving away. Dark-haired.'

'Anything else?'

'Didn't have my glasses on.' Henry realised he would not get helpful information from Ranald or anything he could rely on.

It certainly didn't sound like Cash. Henry glanced at Ronnie, and he shook his head. They piled back into the car and drove away. In the rear-view mirror, Henry saw Ranald turn quickly and head towards the house, probably to tell someone about their visit. That meant someone would be alerted to their search for Peter and Cash. Unavoidable, but not helpful.

'Ranald was lying about not knowing the people. He changed his tune when I started dialling the police, believing my bluff. That likely means there is a mobile signal around here, and he alerted somebody to return. It took us two hours to get here, plenty of time to get the car taken away.'

'I'm now seriously worried about Peter. Who took the car away from them? Were they mugged? They were probably in the white van if Sir Angus is to be believed. We need to find them.'

'I think that we should call in and speak to Sir Angus. Confirm details about his sighting of Peter and Jenny on the road near Duich Lots. Do you know where that is, Ronnie?'

'Of course, but I doubt that there will be anything there. The croft dwellings at the Duich Lots are all ruins, someway off the road, and have been for many years. Let's call in on Sir Angus; I need to speak to him anyway.'

'Why?'

'I am meant to take out a friend of his fishing, and he is still to confirm the date.'

'Good, that gives us an excuse.'

They had almost forgotten about Alan, in the back, who had rarely spoken, content with listening.

'I think I know someone who fits the woman's description.' Ronnie twisted around quickly in his seat; Henry stared into the rear-view mirror.

'Nora, the woman in the whisky shop, might fit the description.'

Henry thought for a minute. 'You may be right. Well done, Alan.'

'I might have been drunk yesterday, but I had a long chat with her, and she asked lots of questions about you.'

'What did you tell her?'

'Not a lot. I didn't know about Peter and Cash but told her you were a retired detective working for Sir Angus. She appeared to know that.'

'I wonder who told her,' Henry replied.

14

It was now late afternoon as they reached the road to Sir Angus's house. One of the garage doors was open, revealing that the garage was the depth of the house. Henry wondered if Sir Angus was in, but Murdo came out to greet them as they parked. 'I didn't know that Sir Angus was expecting you,' which was a polite way of saying he wasn't. He retreated quickly, returned shortly, and ushered Henry and Ronnie into the lounge, Alan remaining in the car.

Murdo offered coffee, but they declined, and Henry sat down, Ronnie going over to the window to admire the view. The door opened, and Sir Angus, more casually dressed in chinos and an open-necked shirt, came in.

'Have you made progress, finding Peter?'

Henry shook his head, 'I'm increasingly worried about him.'

'Oh,' and he sat down, 'most unfortunate. Please tell me why,' and he acknowledged Ronnie, who joined them. 'Everything still okay for our trip,' he asked, and Ronnie muttered, 'Yes,' in reply.

'Good, good, and of course, you are a friend of Peter,' understanding why he was present.

'I spoke to Jenny, as you requested, who is extremely worried but is anxious to keep the news about Peter from spreading further.'

'I believed that to be the case.'

'I've begun speaking to friends. Hence, Ronnie is here. I thought we had discovered Cash's car,' and Sir Angus raised his eyebrows. 'But we were on Ronnie's boat and saw from the sea what we believed to be it in a carport beside a run-down farmhouse. It's quite distinctive. By the time we had berthed and driven to the site, the car had disappeared.'

'We were met by an eccentric man,' and Sir Angus interrupted, 'Ranald?'

'…with a shotgun. Not too pleased to see us.'

'Oh dear, I didn't know that he had a shotgun, probably wasn't loaded.'

'We persuaded him to lower it.'

'I own the farmhouse, I tried to get planning permission to refurbish it, but permission was refused; bats in the attic, I was told. I know he lives there, and I don't have the heart to evict him. I will speak to him. He makes a living of sorts working on local farms, general labouring, and he does some fishing. Sorry about him. However, you say that by the time you arrived, the car, the Porsche, had gone.'

'His answers were vague and evasive. He knew more than he was willing to admit. I believe that he was paid to hide the car. It was just unfortunate for him that we spotted it as we sailed past. We did see him looking at us through binoculars, and he had time to arrange for the car's removal.'

'Why would they leave the car there? Apart from being expensive and not the sort of car you leave abandoned, it doesn't make sense,' and Sir Angus moved his hands open, palms up and shrugged.

'It wasn't Cash who abandoned the car. According to Ranald, a man brought it to the farmhouse, if we can believe him. A white van was also there, and they drove off in the van. Could it be the same one you saw later at Duich Lots?'

'Now that is an interesting idea,' and he appeared animated, edging towards the edge of the sofa.

'Tell me more about what you saw as you drove past them at Duich Lots.'

'There is little more that I can add. Peter and Cash were in the front, Peter in the driver's seat. I just glanced as I passed. My impression was that they were cheery, nothing untoward.'

'Were they parked?'

'I thought so, but maybe they had just pulled over to let me pass them.'

'Anyone else about?'

'No,' and he shook his head firmly.

'It is strange that they abandon Cash's car in a remote location, let someone else drive it to that location and then travel in a white van somewhere else.'

'I agree, most strange.'

'It doesn't sound like the behaviour of a couple about to enjoy a romantic liaison.'

'What are you going to do?'

'I believe that I should be contacting the police. I suspect something isn't right.'

'I understand,' he paused,' but could you give yourselves another day. I am sure Peter will appear, even if there are issues with Jenny; he loves his son. I can't explain why they were in a white van, but they appeared in good form. Maybe they used the van to leave the island, less obvious than a fancy red sports car. I don't think we want to create a fuss and put more pressure on Jenny.'

Henry had already thought of that and had contacted Jenny without mentioning the white van. Jenny hadn't just been checking for the red car and had subsequently spoken to friends who worked on the ferry. Peter hadn't been seen and wouldn't have been allowed to stay on the car deck, so he would have been noticed in the lounges or decks. As far as he could tell, Peter was still on the island. Without suspicious circumstances, the police would not divert the resources to deal with what appeared to be a couple of romantic runaways. His instincts, however, suggested that something more was going on.

'Sir Angus, if I don't find him soon, I will be failing in my duty of care not to contact the police.'

'I'm also concerned,' Ronnie stated.

'Okay, I'm listening,' but he was thought Henry, wanting just a bit more time. The detective felt frustrated. Was there something that he was not being told? Ronnie shrugged, and they both got up

'Who is that outside?' Sir Angus asked, pointing towards Alan, walking up and down beside their car.

'That's my brother-in-law, Alan, who's accompanying me on the trip. Just stretching his legs.'

'I'm very busy,' and he stood up, meeting over. 'Keep up the good work, and I am sure the situation will be resolved.'

As Murdo showed them to the door, Alan stepped back into the car and was joined by the other two.

'Sorry to keep you waiting,' Henry said as he started the engine.

'No problem, but see, as you leave, look inside the garage. At the back is the vehicle we parked behind on the ferry.' Henry looked inside as he drove off and saw a black Ford Galaxy. Probably was the same one, but why would it be here.

Turning to Ronnie, he added, 'I noticed the vehicle on the ferry crammed with equipment and thought they were engineers working on the island. I can't understand why the vehicle is in Sir Angus's garage. Like many things, it doesn't make sense.' Suddenly, he felt tired. A straightforward task was beginning to dominate his visit to Islay.

'I don't know what he is hiding, but I found Sir Angus shifty, something he is not telling us. I am also worried about my friend. I spoke to Malcolm last night, and he's flying back tomorrow. Maybe we could meet up at your house.'

'A good idea, maybe together we can find Peter.'

Henry could hear Alan snoring from the backseat, but his observations had been helpful. He would only need to keep him away from the whisky.

15

Henry dropped off Ronnie at his boat in Port Ellen and arranged to meet the next day at the house in Bowmore where he was staying. They agreed to keep in touch if there were any further developments. A warm handshake concluded their parting, a shared conviction that they had to find Peter and Cash, certain they were in trouble. It had been a long day, combined with the fresh sea air, and Henry was yawning as he left Port Ellen. This time, instead of turning left and following the road past the airport to Bowmore, he drove along the High Road, from which you could reach Bowmore by a minor road at Laggan Bridge. Moorland stretched on both sides with scattered dwellings and the premises of a building supply company dotted with patches of isolated woodland. Several miles on, he saw the sign pointing to Duich Lots and stopped.

Many of the roads on Islay were like this: single track with passing places. Near the road junction for Duich Lots, there was enough room for vehicles to pass. Alan and he both got out of the car to look around.

'Something happened here,' Henry stated, 'and I am not convinced by Sir Angus's version. He says he saw the two of them parked here, but I feel he is spinning a tale, making their disappearance appear like a romantic affair. I don't know the motive, but he doesn't want the police involved. Cash's car was deposited in a remote area, where it was unlikely to be found. That troubles me. The two of them are then seen sitting in a white van here,' and Henry stalked around the area, scanning the ground and muttering to himself as Alan watched on bemused.

'Is there anything I should be searching for?' Henry shook his head. 'Why here?' he exclaimed, frustrated. He strode to the junction of the road that led down to the Duich Lots, a single narrow track cutting through moorland, with signs of peat extraction, stacks of cut peat left to dry. Peat was in great demand to feed the distilleries but also still used as a domestic fuel, and many islanders had the right to cut their own peat. Wandering down the road, he saw, in the distance, across the moorland, a row of bushes and trees that were growing beside a burn close to the broken-down ruins of a croft. He reckoned that not much of a life could be gleaned from this bleak landscape, which he considered harsh and unforgiving. In the distance was the airport and Loch Indaal, the sea shimmering in the sun. The moorland was brightening up as the sunlight spread towards him. He had to force himself to concentrate, but on what. Alan was walking about, but his efforts had little purpose without explicit instructions. Henry had been in this situation before, hoping that his thoughts and speculations were being processed in the other parts of his brain and a solution would eventually appear, or at least another piece of the jigsaw.

He retraced his steps, re-joined the High Road, and wandered along the road he had just driven, stopping where there was more space for vehicles to pass each other. The ground to the side of the tarmac strip was rutted where cars had pulled over. 'Why stop here?' he muttered to himself. There was a crushed beer can, an empty crisp packet flapping in the breeze, and a short distance on a discarded wiper blade. They appeared to have been there for a while.

Further on were several cigarette ends crushed in the ground, and he kicked the ground in frustration, turning around, despondent. An image of Mary flashed into his head, and he ground his teeth. As he turned around, he saw the sunlight had reached the road, showing how dirty his car had become after travelling on Islay's roads. He watched as Alan got back into the car and decided to have one final look around. Henry turned again and walked further, not wanting to give up. At times like this, he felt Mary's presence, still encouraging despite their separation. He noticed broken glass from a beer bottle reflecting the light, and he bent down, something catching his attention. Beside the glass was an earring, and he picked it up, examining it in the palm of his hand. Golden and long, ending in a point. It took a few seconds for him to make the connection. This was the type of earring Cash was wearing in the restaurant. Expensive, not an item you would casually lose. It couldn't be a coincidence, and he saw what looked like dried blood at the clasp, suggesting that the earring had been torn off. Close by, he noticed that tall weeds had been broken and grass trampled on, and then he spotted a pink button covered in dirt and prised it from the ground. A scene started to form in his mind, a possible scenario, not a good one. Something had happened here, probably a scuffle, and it had little to do with romance, confirming his fears that Peter and Cash were in trouble.

Alan powered down his car window as Henry approached the car and showed him the earring and button in his hand. 'I believe that this is one of Cash's earrings,' he explained, 'she was wearing this the night we saw them in the restaurant. The button also matches the cardigan she was wearing. There must have been a struggle.'

His companion drew back in his seat, frowning. 'I didn't expect an adventure like this when I accompanied you to Islay,' he smiled nervously, wondering where all this would lead. 'What are you going to do now?'

'We must find the couple.'

'I knew you were going to say that.' Alan shrugged and made no further comment.

'Let's get back to the house.' The familiar nervous tension was building in Henry. There was a puzzle to solve. Somewhere, he knew that Mary would be cheering him on. He pocketed the earring and button and got back into the car.

16

At Laggan Bridge, Henry turned left and took the back road down into Bowmore, reaching the Round Church and the graveyard overlooking the village. Even as his mind computed the latest revelations, he paused to appreciate the view over Bowmore and Loch Indaal. Whoever planned the village had done an outstanding job.

He eventually found a parking place on Shore Street, several houses away from their rented accommodation. Collecting their backpacks, they walked to the house. As he attempted to put the key in the lock, he noticed someone had tampered with it. On Islay, locking doors was not a priority, and it was a simple Yale lock, but it looked as if something had been inserted between the lock and the door jamb. Henry quickly unlocked it, revealing more damage, a splinter of wood. He entered the house, checking around. There was little apparent change, no wanton vandalism, which was a relief. A pile of magazines had been shifted in the lounge, leaving a strip with no dust on the glass surface. The door of the cabinet that contained board games for wet days and a selection of CDs was not shut properly. That wasn't how it was left. He strode into his bedroom, sensing that someone had been there. The top drawer of the bedside cabinet was slightly opened, a tourist leaflet he had picked up the other day preventing it from shutting. Henry was always meticulous about drawers closing, a trait that Mary ribbed him about. Inside the drawer was his notebook with the names and ideas about the investigation. He could swear that it had been examined as the spine had been forced back, the pages loose, probably to let a photo be taken. The picture of Mary and him at a wedding a year ago, which he always had with him, was untouched, and he breathed a sigh of relief. Some callous burglars would take items like this to add to the emotional impact of their efforts. The intrusion had been for a purpose.

Henry shouted to his companion. 'Everything okay in your room?' and heard a curse. Racing through, he saw Alan standing over a glass ornament which was broken and lying on the carpet.

'I don't know how this happened, and I suppose I will have to pay for it.'

'Don't worry, it is only an inexpensive knick-knack. Anything else disturbed?'

'Why?' and Alan looked anxious.

'We have been burgled.'

Alan crossed his arms, drawing breath. 'What next?'

'I'm sorry that the trip is not as you hoped. Do a quick check of your belongings, but I believe that they, whoever they are, knew about our investigation and were having a wee nosey about while we were out. Indeed, they may just have left, as they didn't attempt to clean up the breakage. Maybe we disturbed them,' and Henry strode to the patio doors. 'I locked them before I left, another of my habits; it's embarrassing if a police officer, even a retired one, is burgled.' He found the door unlocked, slid it open, and stepped out onto the patio area, checking left and right but seeing no one.

'They escaped this way.

'To a detective, this is very interesting, but it is probably very alarming to yourself. Not what you expect on Islay. They found my notebook, which would interest them, and have probably photographed each page. I'm sure that the break-in is related to our investigation. I'll put the kettle on while you check your belongings, but I am sure it was me they were interested in.'

Alan joined him shortly. 'At least they didn't take my whisky,' attempting a wry smile, he accepted the coffee and sat down. As he sipped the coffee, he added, 'I can see you are caught up in this missing-persons investigation; you're far more like your old self. Animated, even cheery. The distraction is helping you forget Mary.'

'Sad, isn't it, but I do feel more myself. But you are wrong about Mary. I feel her presence more strongly. She was always so supportive. She probably better understood the criminal fraternity than most people through me. Unless it was confidential, we shared everything.'

'So, what do we do now.'

'I'm hungry. I'll nip to the Indian restaurant and get a carry-out for us. There's a menu in the welcome folder; let me know what you want. Then I must phone Jenny and update her; she'll be wondering what's happening. Then, a bath and bed, I'm tired, it's been a long day for both of us. Tomorrow, we are meeting with Ronnie and Malcolm here after Malcolm arrives. But before they arrive, I want to visit the last name that Jenny gave me, Elaine Soutar, and see if she can add anything.'

17

Henry was up early, busy shaving as Alan emerged, appearing far brighter and with more colour.

'I spoke to Jenny last night; she is anxious but believes Peter is still on the island. I didn't say anything about finding the gold earring or pink button. I don't want to alarm her. I want to discuss that with Malcolm and Ronnie first. I'm going to visit Elaine Soutar and see if she has any fresh insights,' and left Alan phoning his wife.

Walking a short distance, he turned up Hawthorn Lane, a steep road and was out of breath when he reached the top. Turning left, he crossed the road almost opposite the police station, checking the number before he rang the bell. Eventually, an unshaven man in his pyjamas partially opened the door, sticking his head out.

'What do you want?' he said gruffly.

Henry realised that he had disturbed them. Not a good start, he mused, but time was tight. 'I'm sorry it is early, but can I speak with Elaine,' he handed over his business card, which the man took from him with suspicion.

He studied it and frowned. 'What's this about?' A woman's voice shouted from the top of the stairs. 'Who is it, Mick?' and Henry addressed them both. 'It's about Peter Meldrum.'

'Let him in,' she shouted, 'I'll be down in a minute,' and Henry heard noises from upstairs, and shortly, a woman wearing a loose-fitting blouse and jeans hurried into the lounge.

'You must be Elaine,' and the woman nodded, fiddling with her large-frame glasses and pushing them higher up on her nose. Mick stood back, not sure what to do.

'Is he okay? What's wrong?'

'Jenny asked me to contact you because he's missing.'

Her mouth opened in shock, and then her expression changed. 'But I just heard from him last night.'

'That's most interesting. What did Peter say?'

'He sent me a text inviting us to their house for dinner next week.'

'Can I see the text message, if you don't mind, because I'm surprised; he's been missing for several days now.'

'Mick, get my phone from upstairs,' and Mick rushed past Elaine.

Elaine grabbed the phone from Mick as he returned and searched for the message, fumbling with the phone. 'Oh, there it is. Strange, usually it shows up as 'Peter', but it's just a number.' Elaine handed it over to Henry, and he read the message and saw that Peter had signed it.

'Can you contact the number,' Elaine took the phone back, touched the number and held up the phone. There was no ringing tone.

'I thought that would be the case,' Henry explained.

'I'm staying just down the road, having come to Islay with my brother-in-law for business and a short break. To summarise quickly, I'm sorry to have disturbed you both so early, but I have another appointment this morning,' and Elaine flushed slightly, 'Sir Angus Gillies put me in touch with Jenny. It seemed Peter had gone missing the night of that strange flare. Jenny gave me names, yours included, to help me search for him, and I have been contacting them. I was burgled yesterday. I believe my notebook with your name and mobile number was photographed. I had ticked off all the other names. You were last on the list that Jenny wanted me to contact. Someone then texts you to make it appear that Peter is okay; the others would know he was missing already. Some people want to keep his disappearance a secret, including Jenny, or I would have probably contacted the police by now. I have to respect her view.'

'You think he's been kidnapped?'

Henry shrugged, 'I honestly don't know, but I am getting worried.'

'Oh dear,' and Elaine clasped her hand over her mouth as Mick returned to the room, now dressed, 'It's not these nasty drug dealers. They had such a hard time, you know.'

'I don't think it is. There may have been someone else with Peter.'

'Oh,' and Elaine pulled at her mouth. 'A woman?'

'Cash Elliot. I think so, although don't jump to conclusions. I believe Jenny is very hurt and had suspicions about the two of them, and would be embarrassed if word got out. I'm beginning to think that the situation is more complex.'

'I know who you mean. I've seen the two of them around in her fancy car. Aren't they working on a project together?'

Elaine glared at Mick. 'You didn't tell me.'

'I thought it was innocent.'

Elaine turned back to Henry, her voice more clipped. 'So where are they?' angry that her friend, Jenny, had been abandoned.

'Probably still on the island, but I don't know where.'

'I must phone Jenny, go see her.'

'That would be helpful; she's quite agitated,' wondering if that fully described her state.

'She has been for a while,' Elaine replied, 'very temperamental and struggling at the moment.'

'Have you any idea where they might be?'

The couple looked at each other, and finally, Mick said, 'No, but if we think of anything, we'll let you know. You mentioned Sir Angus. My cousin, Fiona, works for him along with her husband, Murdo.' For the first time, Mick smiled. 'Everyone on Islay is related or knows each other. I met her in the Coop on Tuesday. Some bigwig is arriving from London at the weekend. Sir Angus hadn't told her who, but he is very excited. He wouldn't want the police searching for missing persons on his island when he has visitors,' emphasising 'his'. 'It seems like that, the new Laird of Islay, Duke of Oa,' and he addressed the last comment to Elaine, who made a face in response, indicating she didn't quite agree with his sentiments.

'Can I add that Cash's red Porsche is missing although still believed to be on the island, and they were last seen on the High Road near Duich Lots by Sir Angus as he was driving home. At that point, they were sitting in a white van, probably a Ford Transit, which is odd. It's not the usual choice for romantic getaways. Any thoughts? If we could trace the van and I have no more details, we might find them.'

'Three thousand people live on the island, and many tourists, especially in summer. I work for the roads department, so I see many white vans. Vans are always arriving and leaving the island, and many local tradesmen use vans, but it would be good to get more details. White vans are common.'

Henry shrugged. 'Sir Angus was vague, even after I pushed him on it. I think he was distracted to spot Peter and Cash together in an unusual mode of transport.'

'Okay, better than nothing. I'll ask around.'

'That would be excellent,' and on that positive note, Henry stood up. 'Contact me immediately if you find out anything. And Elaine, it would be a good idea to visit Jenny, but don't tell her about the white van.'

18

When Henry got back to the house, Alan was waiting. 'I've been speaking to Hazel. She is, let me say, surprised at the direction our holiday has taken. However, she wants me to stay on and watch you. My wife is fond of you and pleased that I reported that you were more yourself. She wants us both to take care and for you not to allow me to overindulge.'

For a moment, Henry had expected Alan to say he was cutting the holiday short; instead, he felt gratified by his support. 'We'll make a good detective of you yet,' he said smiling, adding, 'observation is key, and you've shown that you can be observant. You know that you have made a difference. I find it exciting when you are energised in the throes of an investigation and want to solve it, but don't let me forget that this is a holiday.'

A knock at the door interrupted them. Henry went to it, ushered the two men into the house, and pointed to the patio area, where they joined Alan around the circular glass table. Ronnie was in his usual outfit of khaki shorts and tee-shirt, bulked out by muscles. Malcolm wore smart grey trousers, a light sports jacket, and an open-neck shirt, thinner than Henry remembered. After introductions, they settled with coffee and biscuits. Henry's impression of Malcolm was positive; behind the wire-rimmed glasses, he knew lurked an analytical brain, and he hoped that had not changed since they first met years ago at the murder scene. It was a bonus that he was back on the island to help with their quest.

'We're out here on the patio because I had the paranoid

thought they might have planted a bug as well as burgling our accommodation. We should be safe out here, and I did check.' The two visitors were shocked by his news. 'I would like to start,' Henry began, 'by recounting my experience from earlier this morning.' He talked about the alleged text from Peter how it linked to the burglary, adding that he felt he had disturbed the couple by arriving so early.

Malcolm was impassive, but Ronnie snorted. 'Mick and Elaine are one of the most lovey-dovey couples I know, but both will help if they can.'

'It's interesting what Mick says about his cousin, Fiona,' Malcolm stated, having reflected on what the detective had told them. 'Someone important must be due on Islay very soon.'

'And Sir Angus doesn't want anything to distract from the visit,' chipped in Ronnie.

'I agree. While we were at Sir Angus's house, Alan spotted in his garage the Ford Galaxy that we had parked behind on the ferry. We noticed it was stuffed with equipment, and the four men looked like engineers over to perform maintenance. Now, I suspect they were an advance guard preparing for a visit. Setting up communication equipment and preparing for some bigwig to arrive.'

'I'll try and check that out; Sir Angus has many political contacts, and given the advance party, it is likely to be a political figure of some standing. I can't imagine Sir Angus settling for anything less than a cabinet minister. My colleagues on the paper often get notice of ministers' diaries. Some are reluctant to reveal details for security reasons. However, politicians may tip us off if they want publicity for the visit, and most of them do,' he added cynically.

'Sir Angus doesn't want any trouble or anything to distract from the visit, but sending a false text does seem overkill,' cautioned Henry, 'and we mustn't assume that the text was created by Sir Angus or those close to him.'

Malcolm nodded. 'I spoke to Nick, a blast from the past.' He explained who he was as Ronnie wrinkled his nose. 'He's now retired and out of touch. Nick believes that when McGory was killed on Jura, his drug gang folded with him to be replaced by an Eastern European group, which I believe is even more brutal. I think we can rule out a revenge attack. We would probably have found a body by now, and why take the woman. Nick also stated that the 'Alan Siviter' app was no longer functional. But if not him, then who?'

No one could answer that, and after a brief pause in their conversation, Henry dug in his pocket and placed the gold earring and pink button on the glass-topped table. 'I found these at the road end to Duich Lots, where the couple were spotted in the van.' Henry pointed out, 'with what I take to be encrusted blood at the clasp. My observation of Miss Elliot during the meal at the Lochside Hotel is that she is a very sophisticated lady, carefully turned out. The earrings are expensive. What is one of them doing left on the roadside?'

'The pink button was probably torn from the cardigan she wore the night I saw her, matching the colour. Both items suggest a struggle. And what were they doing in a white van? Why did they abandon the Porsche? Ranald, not that I would believe much of what he says, stated that a man drove the car to the farmhouse and that the driver and others left in a white van. Nothing points to a romantic liaison, more an abduction. And that brings me back to Sir Angus. Why does he not want publicity? Is it to protect his friend, or is it something else?'

'I checked out what we had on file about him before I left the office. He appears genuine and very rich and is socially motivated to do good. I'll dig deeper and see what I can find and who his friends are.'

'Good, Malcolm.'

'Peter has spoken to me about Cash and mentioned the company she works for, Wheelan Investments. Before I came away, I phoned them on the pretext of wanting to write an article on the Islay micro distillery project. Cash is on holiday and won't be back until the end of the month.'

'When the police find that out, they would assume that Peter and Cash have disappeared together. Even if they started an inquiry, there would be no urgency. I know their approach and limited resources.'

'Hopefully, Malcolm's research shows up something, but there is another line of enquiry,' Ronnie suggested. 'Trace the white van. There can't be that many on the island. Malcolm, you know Jack White,' and Malcolm smiled wistfully, 'How can I forget a night to remember.'

'The same Jack now organises the loading for the ferries. If anyone can help us to identify the white van, it should be him.'

Malcolm laughed. 'My goodness, how people change. He's done well.' Turning to Henry, he added, 'a friend from our crazy days. Do you keep in touch with him, Ronnie?'

'I speak to him often, usually around the ferry terminal at Port Askaig, when I get off the Jura ferry, and he's hanging around for the next Islay ferry. I'll talk to him after this meeting.

'Good, Ronnie. One further thought, and again it was Alan who prompted this.' He acknowledged his travelling companion, sitting impassively beside him. 'Ranald described the woman who drove the Porsche away before we reached the farmhouse.' Henry stopped and then continued.' I am unsure why he would give an accurate description, but Alan suggested it might possibly be Nora at the Whisky Shop. It will provide us with an excuse to visit, won't it, Alan, but we are unlikely to buy given their prices.'

'I'll check their background out while I investigate Sir Angus.'

'As you are so well connected, Malcolm' and the statement had a hint of sarcasm from Ronnie, softened by a smile, 'can you give us any more information on the mysterious flare the other night.'

'I was getting so much hassle from locals that I did contact the Royal Navy at Coulport. They were embarrassed. They had lost contact with some top-secret surveillance equipment. It drifted to the shore, and the batteries caught fire. The remnants have been retrieved, I believe. So, definitely not aliens. The Royal Navy can be a bit careless; remember the Yellow Submarine incident. At least they realised that they had lost equipment and attempted to retrieve it quickly this time.'

Henry cut in. 'I don't think I could cope with aliens, so that's a relief. Should we meet at the same time and place tomorrow or earlier if we discover anything?'

Everyone agreed.

19

Ash flexed her hands together, hearing her tendons crack, a habit which she knew annoyed Roddy, but he wasn't there, and it was a part of her ritual before beginning work. 'Hey–Ho, off to work we go,' she murmured and settled back in her seat, typing fast on the keyboard. Soon, she joined the online Slack group she belonged to, an app connecting people to the information they sought by exchanging messages and files. The group of online volunteers were scattered around the world. Ash wasn't sure where they lived, their age or their gender. Life online was different, but she knew they shared her passion for searching for the truth by using information already out there. Open-source intelligence, or OSINT, changed the world, making it more challenging for individuals, companies or governments to conceal secrets.

Early success with Bellingcat, the forerunner of open-source organisations, proved they could pin down and identify suspects like the two Russians who had poisoned Sergei Skripal and his daughter, Yulia or who was responsible for the downing of Malaysian airline Flight MH17 over Ukraine. Checking feeds on Twitter, YouTube, Facebook, satellite images, and databases could reveal who was responsible. The truth was out there if you searched with intelligence and purpose. The two Russians responsible for the poisoning of the Skripals were traced using Facebook and databases, and their identity was confirmed as Russian agents.

Ash hoped to do the same by finding the true identity of Paul

Russell. Ash uploaded an image of Paul Russell and sought to discover similar images, adding that he was Russian. This was a reverse image search, and within minutes, Jules6324, a group member, had suggested further possible databases in that country that had been leaked over the years. These databases contained information on passports, telephone numbers, addresses, car ownership, and flight manifests. They were intended for use by corporations in Russia to complete background checks. Many of these databases ended up pirated. Frequently, they were out of date but could provide information about an individual before they had joined the army or a government organisation. Searches could be time-consuming, and the help of others was invaluable. Laptop nerds in her Slack group soon rose to the challenge; more signing on, and the quest was underway. Ash kept some details back, but others would have guessed what she was trying to discover. Here was a way that intelligence agencies could farm out work and save them time and cost, although they would deny it. Of course, when published, the counterfactual brigade sought to rubbish their work by muddying the waters and making counterclaims. Russia was one of the best at spinning alternative tales.

Retreating to her kitchen, Ash made herself a cup of herbal tea after several hours and practised some deep breathing exercises to help her relax. Refreshed, she re-joined the group and immediately saw a picture of Paul Russell as part of a school group ten years previous, found on an internet app translated 'classmates' in English. He was standing in the back row, taller than many of his fellow pupils, eyes looking skywards, much to the photographer's frustration, she presumed. A youthful version of the image Ash had been staring at earlier. The picture was taken at a school in northeast Russia, in a village called Apushka. This was encouraging, and underneath were the names of the pupils, which was a significant breakthrough. Paul Russell was really Denis Petrov. That information would do her reputation with Swan no harm. She thanked all the contributors. Armed with his name, others were searching different databases.

In 2015, he moved to Moscow to study English at a university, and his domestic ID showed a still youthful Petrov with a moustache and shoulders hunched. Then he seemed to disappear. No current passport was in his name, although one had been issued previously. His records were being deleted. This suggested involvement with the GRU, the foreign military intelligence unit for the armed forces. Petrov had turned up in the United Kingdom, living covertly as a sleeper. Russia had a history of planting operatives with borrowed identities who, it was intended, would live undercover, burrowing deep into the community they had adopted, making contacts, and rising through society. If lucky, some would meet future politicians and military figures and feedback information to the motherland; some might even influence policy in their adopted country. Sleepers were expensive to train, taking years to master dialects and cultural habits so that they would be taken for a local. The Russians invested heavily in the programme, setting up English villages where candidates practised how to order a pint, among other things. The UK was not the only country; every Western nation was targeted. In 2010 in America, many agents were uncovered, and their identity revealed by a source. Unbeknown to them, the activities of the sleepers were followed and filmed, and listening devices were even planted in their bedrooms. Eventually, ten deep-cover sleepers were exposed and exchanged for four people held in Russia. The pattern with Paul Russell was different, as apparently he had kept a low profile until he had been outed, which was a puzzle.

Pleased with her efforts, Ash glanced at her watch, realising that she had been working for ten hours. Ash felt more herself and, despite it being only six in the morning, phoned Roddy with the information. A tired-sounding Roddy answered, claiming that he was just about to get up but sounding pleased to hear from her anyway, which cheered Ash even more. They chatted, Ash passing on news of her discoveries, and just before she hung up, she proclaimed that he was a lousy chess player.

'I'm not up to your standard, but I'm not that bad,' he replied cagily.

'Well then, you're not observant,' claimed Ash, pleased to spin him along.

'Tell me, what did I miss,' but his tone was now one of amusement. He enjoyed bantering with Ash.

'The chess pictures you sent me. The second one had two extra pieces on the board. Paul Russell, or Denis Petrov, as we now know him, was fiddling with the odds. He was using an extra black king and a black bishop.'

'How strange.'

'Let's hope he is no better as a spy,' with that, she wished him well and hung up, heading for some well-earned sleep.

20

The day passed quickly for Sally, and the journey home was uneventful until the descent into Glen Brown, where she had to pull over to let a large campervan pass at one of the tight bends. Soon, she reached one of several abandoned cottages, its chimney stack standing proud beside collapsed walls. On the chimney stack, high up, someone had painted a Scottish saltire. Then she noticed a bunch of flowers sitting on top of the crumbled wall nearest the road. She braked hard, pulling over, the car driver behind forced to pull out, angrily repeatedly blaring his horn, the noise reverberating through the empty landscape. Fortunately, he drove on, leaving Sally to draw breath and slowly get out of the car, steadying her nerves. She approached the flowers with trepidation, lifted them off the wall, and detached the small envelope attached to them. There was no written message, nor did she expect one. The envelope only contained a small object, and she threw it into the ruins, its order delivered. She clambered inside the ruins until she got to the hearth and stretched above it, realising that she couldn't reach the loose brick, standing proud of the other bricks. Not the tallest person, she hauled a stone to the hearth over the hard ground through the nettles and brambles that had filled the former room, stood on it, prised out the loose brick, and dropped it. Reaching inside, she found a metal container with a screw-top lid inside a clear plastic bag. Tape had been bound around the container at the top. Carefully, she stepped back onto the ground, placing the bag down. Then she looked around for the brick and replaced it in the brickwork above the fireplace. Satisfied with her efforts, she picked up the plastic bag and returned to the car.

The rest of the journey home was sombre, and she repeatedly glanced at the package on the seat beside her. She knew this day would come, but the reality was still sobering. Back in her cottage, she fed Ming and moved about as if nothing had changed, but everything had. The food she kept in the fridge for her meal was untouched. Coffee was all she could manage. Later, she gathered a few clothes and toiletries into a sports bag. Ricky was not visiting until tomorrow, and he would wonder. It had happened before that she was unavailable, and he might be disappointed, but that was of little consequence.

Ming crawled on her lap, purring, and Sally gently stroked her. Now, this was a dilemma. Sally did care about the cat and couldn't just abandon it. Neighbours would want to know how long they would have to care for Ming and when she would be back; the answer was never. Sally sat for a long time, eventually putting the cat down on the floor and having a bath. Returning, she was still unsure, Ming lying on his side observing her, unaware. The innocence of animals, she pondered. Orders had to be obeyed, remember Clara. She screwed up her eyes, attempting to blank out the images burnt in her mind and made a decision.

Sally spoke to her boss the following day and requested the next two weeks off. It was short notice, she knew, but he was relieved that an obstacle to the holiday rota had been removed.

'You finally were able to contact your sister.'

Sally smiled as if agreeing and hurried to the counter where she served. Several people were already waiting, clutching letters and parcels. At the end of the day, she balanced the books and left forever.

21

'They're coming.'

Cash nudged Peter in the ribs, and he sat bolt upright, the blanket slipping off his back, startled, taking a second to remember where he was.

'Sorry,' Cash whispered.

'It's okay. I must have fallen asleep.' He massaged his neck as he crept forward towards the trapdoor. The shaft of light from the ill-fitting trapdoor was the only light visible. Overhead, he heard footsteps. 'Two people, damn.' Sometimes there was only one person. Their plan wouldn't work with two. Beside him, Cash scurried, like a rat, towards a gap in the skirting, over the ground, no pretence of ladylike behaviour left.

The bolt was slid open, and the light expanded rapidly, dazzling them, illuminating some of the corners of their prison, highlighting the grime.

'Don't look up. Head down,' the instructions stated fast, staccato, blurring any attempt at deciphering dialect.

'Bucket,' and Peter grasped the bucket by the handle and lifted it cautiously. He did not want to spill any of the contents over himself, conscious of a man to the side watching him as another man grabbed the handle. He knew to wait. They were being trained like performing animals. Footsteps retreated, and shortly after, he heard the bucket being emptied. A tap was turned on for several seconds, and the pail was returned wet.

'Head down,' the other man grunted and aimed a kick at him,

which Peter managed to avoid. The man who returned the bucket threw a towel into the cellar with a wet cloth and a small soap bar. As Peter scrambled to collect them, bottles of water and some packets of sandwiches landed beside him.

'Down,' shouted the other man, and Peter flattened himself on the ground as the trapdoor slammed shut and the bolt slipped in place. He and Cash floundered in the dark, collecting what had been thrown in, eventually retreating to the corner they now called home. Using the towel, which didn't smell fresh and the soap, they cleaned themselves as best they could and dried with the towel. Neither spoke as they did this. Then, quickly, they grabbed the packets of sandwiches, ripping off the plastic film and hungrily devouring the contents.

'Usually, I hate cheese,' muttered Cash.

'I have a chicken sandwich if you want.'

'I'll manage,' she replied, and they ate in silence, washing down the food with water. Their conversation in normal circumstances would be unremarkable, but in their present situation, it was surreal.

'It must have been hours since they last fed us. You fear they might abandon us,' and instantly regretted the statement as Cash whimpered in response. Peter was struggling, but given his prior experience with McGory, he could just about cope with what had happened. Cash had impressed after initially going to pieces. He had seen a more steely, determined side to her as she pulled herself together more like the ice-cool person she was during negotiations. Both of them, however, remained on a knife edge, with no control over what would happen next.

'Did you see anything,' he asked, changing the subject quickly.

'There is a breeze block wall with metal cladding above it. It all appears new.'

'Must be a cattle shed, but strange that there are no animals.' Their view of the world was so limited that they could only speculate.

'All I could see were black work boots and heavy-duty work trousers.

'They don't want us to see them,' and maybe we shouldn't, he added silently to himself, otherwise they might... and he blanked his thoughts. If he remembered correctly, he had read of a prison in Syria where prisoners had to squat all day and never look up at their captors for fear of a severe beating, even death. Their captives didn't want to be recognised. He shuddered. In the semi-darkness, their eyes having adjusted again, he sensed more than saw Cash staring at him.

Both of them were now caked in grime despite their efforts at washing. He slumped down, and immediately Cash settled beside him. He found her attention claustrophobic, but then so was their confinement.

Peter collected the empty sandwich wrappings and took them towards the trapdoor. Jenny would be proud of his housekeeping, he felt. The shaft of light illuminated the packaging, and he snorted. 'Reduced for a quick sale. Cut-price sandwiches from the Coop - they're taking good care of us,' he added sarcastically.

As he crawled back, Cash muttered, 'How much longer?' A frequent question. Then what? Peter mused, but he kept the thought to himself. They must have been here for at least two days. He didn't have a watch or his phone, which had been snatched from him, and they had been only too pleased to remove Cash's Rolex. The shaft of light at the trapdoor was a constant, suggesting that the cattle shed was lit up. With so little information, they could only speculate.

'No one will know that I am missing,' Cash stated. 'I was due to start annual leave.'

'I imagine many people will be wondering where I am. Jenny will fear the worst, and I hope our friends advise her to go to the police.'

'She is upset with you. As I have also disappeared, she will imagine we are together. Imagination can be a terrible thing.'

'Ben will be troubled, and Jason probably will not yet know about my not returning. What a mess.'

'Hopefully, someone discovers your car and wonders where you have gone.' They had recycled these thoughts many times, and neither felt the need to automatically reply. Mostly, they sat in silence, numbed by their predicament.

They had worked out a plan, but it would only work if one person turned up to attend to their needs. Usually, there were two of them, which was frustrating.

'We better prepare. Shorten your dress or hitch it up. I won't look.' In the gloom, it didn't really matter.

Surprisingly, he heard Cash shuffling about and her dress being ripped.

'See, it is now above my knees. Do you know how much the dress cost?'

'I would hate to think. I bet you'll start a new fashion on Islay, the ragged hemline look.' Her reaction was lost in the gloom.

'Fortunately, you were wearing fancy trainers.'

Silence resumed, leaving Peter to ponder why this had happened to him again. Who were they? What had they been doing when he saw them. Besides, he cursed his curiosity; would he ever learn. Feeling entitled to feel sorry for himself, he hoped that he would escape as he had the last time. Ronnie had saved his life then. Maybe Jenny had contacted his friends. They would rally to save him, but first, they would have to find him. A cellar beneath an empty cattle shed would not be the first place to search.

'Let's run over the plan again,' Peter suggested, 'we need to get it right the first time; we'll only have one chance.

'If one person turns up,' he started.

'I'll grab the pail, turn it upside down, and place it by the trapdoor. Yuch.'

'I'll jump on the pail, propel myself up and grab his leg as he lifts the trapdoor. I'll try and pull him down into the cellar.'

'I'll scramble past you.' she added.

'And if I am floundering, make your escape. I'll try and join you. I wish I could advise you on directions, but I don't know where we are. Avoid roads, try for any hills, hide if you must and try and reach a house where you can phone.'

'Stop, you make it sound as if you won't make it. I need you to be with me.'

'I'm just covering all options. Believe me, I want to escape as much as you.'

They sat waiting. Neither knew how long they sat there. Finally, they heard footsteps entering the barn. Both concentrated hard; it was vital to get it right. Two sets of footsteps. He nudged Cash.

'Not this time.' It had to be soon before they were too weak and before their captors had decided what to do with them.

22

The fan on the ceiling had stopped working, and someone had brought in a portable fan, which was only recirculating the hot air. Imran was absent, but the rest of the team had gathered. The mood had been lightened by the surprise appearance of Ash, who had been allowed to return to official duties. Even the stentorian gaze of Swan from the large screen did not seem so intimidating. Had there been a smile when he acknowledged her presence? If there had been, it was not there for long. As usual, business took centre stage.

'I can confirm from other sources that Paul Russell is Denis Petrov and has lived in this country for the last few years.' Swan only ever disclosed the minimum. There were things you didn't need to know.

'I am pleased,' Ash began, never one to remain silent, 'but I was concerned that we managed to identify him so easily. Could have been a set-up to confuse us.'

'You are correct, Ash; the enemy always wants to mislead us, and the Russians are good at that, but I am confident. No word on Helen Burns?'

Ash shook her head. 'I've been trying, but no breakthrough yet.'

'Keep trying, but we will need more help here,' he stated, looking at Bill. 'Not too many late nights, Ash. Remain sharp.' Like the others, Swan had noted that Ash was tired, her eyes red and watery; he missed little. The trouble was Ash's skill set; no one else could match her.

'What worries me about Denis Petrov is that his profile appears so low-key. He hasn't sought to penetrate any organisations or make contacts; neighbours know little about him, and work colleagues talk about a quiet, efficient, reserved worker. Most Russian sleeper agents attempt to infiltrate, inveigle themselves with strategically important persons, and win their trust. There are, nonetheless, some sleepers, 'konservys' the Russians call them or 'preserves' who make no such attempt but will remain dormant until war or some act of sabotage is required. I suspect Petrov belongs to the 'konservys', which makes his call to service worrying. We must find him and discover why he has been called into action. He is a threat to national security until apprehended. Where is he now?' That was a rallying call to those in the room.

Bill, as team leader, spoke up. 'We know that his car, a blue Vauxhall Astra, was found on a road near Falkirk High Station, roughly mid-way between Glasgow and Edinburgh. The station is on the main rail route between the capital and Glasgow, with four trains an hour at peak. Given that the station is just around the corner and he had just driven from Glasgow, we suspect he might catch a train to Edinburgh. Roddy discovered that Petrov had recently received a package from Edinburgh as he found the discarded wrapping, with an Edinburgh postmark, in the recycling bin at his house. Our colleagues have removed the car and are conducting a thorough forensic examination. The vehicle belonged to a Fred Hampshire, from Dundee, who sold it to a woman who paid cash a month ago. Hampshire could only give a hazy description of her. Backstreet dealer, the police will have words with him.'

'Imran has started to search through CCTV footage from the station site. We await further developments,' Bill stated, aware they needed more information. He tended to take the lack of progress personally.

Swan attempted to summarise. 'We have made progress,

particularly in identifying Petrov and his abandoned car. Face recognition cameras at railway stations and airports have been alerted to scan for him. He could be going anywhere. We need a breakthrough.'

That was stating the obvious Roddy felt. Like the others, he was frustrated, which was not unusual in this work. Ash's breakthrough, identifying Petrov, had given them momentum, and finding the car was a bonus, but ultimately, they didn't know where he had gone or why. A highly trained hostile agent making moves was not good news. Roddy looked across at Ash and caught her eye. Her smile was warm and friendly; she was happy to be back with the team. Hopefully, past events were now behind her.

23

Head down, Petrov descended the worn stone steps to the basement flat, the steps slippery after the recent rain. He rapped on the wooden door, aware that a tiny camera on the side of the door was observing his arrival. The door opened quickly, and he was ushered inside. A man of similar size and build stood back as he entered, and the pair hugged.

'So good to see you, Denis.'

'And you, Artyom, I didn't expect it would be you; it has been a long time.'

'Training days that seemed endless, I remember well. And here we are. Any problems in getting here?'

'No.'

'Good, come to the lounge, and we will talk, but first coffee.' Artyom disappeared along a narrow corridor, and Denis heard the kettle filling.

The lounge was dark despite the wall lights behind the sofa, casting a pallid shadow over the papered wall. A dark rug was spread over dark-stained wooden flooring between the sofa and two other chairs. Through lace curtains, Petrov saw a brick wall with more steps between the flat and the wall. Above that were iron railings, their green paint flaking. The room gave a sense of security despite the bleakness – no one could look in. Sniffing the air, Denis detected dampness; the property was pre-war, so that was not surprising.

Artyom came in with two mugs of coffee and handed over one of the mugs to his colleague. 'Don't expect homeland treats; everything is local. And no vodka,' he added.

'Stuart, isn't it?'

'That's correct, Paul,' and they both laughed.

'I am so pleased to meet you again, but we must never relax. I think in English now, always. There is no choice.'

'While making the coffee, I calculated that it was five years since the training finished, and it was tough.'

'Brutal,' Artyom testified. 'Now this. Did you ever think that you would get the call?'

'Many times, but latterly not so much. You settle into a routine, act out a lie and focus on not exposing yourself. So, it was a shock when the package arrived. Somehow, it was more low-key than I expected. You appreciate that people are working to set things up for you, and the brush pass was very well executed. Cars organised, I am treated well.'

Artyom nodded, stroking his unshaven chin, quietly assessing his colleague's emotions. 'We are trained for this eventuality; we'll follow orders,' he stated firmly.

Denis concurred, slightly alarmed that his colleague might question his dedication. That would be dangerous.

'So, you abandoned the car in Falkirk close to the railway station. If they traced your vehicle, they would imagine you took the train. Just now, they could be scrutinising CCTV footage. Keeps them busy,' and while the slight smile on his lips appeared distant, he seemed satisfied. 'We always must assume we are being watched. You picked up the next car...'

'And detoured here via the new road bridge and parked in a side street, a few miles from here and walked the rest.'

'You should be okay. Our Chinese friends installed all the face recognition cameras, an unbelievable security lapse. We arranged for the software to be adjusted to ignore individuals, which is very useful. You will still be captured on local CCTV but not with the face recognition cameras at bus stations, train stations and airports, making it much harder for them.'

'So, what is the situation that you want to use me for? I don't read about any increase in tensions between the two countries.'

'There is no increased tension, just the usual. We both seek to aggressively seek out weaknesses in the other for our own advantage,' and Artyom placed his empty coffee mug on the floor. Denis was aware of dark shadows under his eyes as he raised his head. Artyom was exhausted.

'There is one critical situation that you need to act on today,' he began launching in, not trying to finesse what he was about to say. 'One of our best-placed sleepers, who has excelled in penetrating high political circles, has been a fool and will be exposed for misdemeanours. If people dig into his background, they might find out the truth. It was him who contacted you, although you have never met him. Resources are tight in this part of the world, and we often have to double up. He was essential to our efforts, but no more.' Artyom stared at the floor again, then looked directly at Denis.

'He must be killed today. It will cause a scandal but appear innocent if you follow instructions. Unfortunately, we also need you to resolve another issue that worries us, but we will talk about that later. We will take you home after that, and you will be honoured if you are successful.'

Always the sting in the tail, Denis thought. The underlying threat if you failed.

'Tell me about today,' that was the correct response, and Artyom relaxed.

'His name is Felix Reeves, in this country a languages lecturer at Edinburgh University. He has been here a long time and got his degree at Edinburgh. Claims that he inherited a flat from a rich uncle. The apartment has wonderful views towards Edinburgh

Castle, you'll be impressed. He is well-known in social circles, and he arranges extravagant parties. Well-liked, people clamour for invites to them. Imagine the horror,' and Artyom snorted, 'if it was found out who was paying for them. The first minister even attended the last one. Imagine our frustration when we discovered he was fond of using prostitutes. Felix is being blackmailed and asked for money from us. He has been careless. Maybe he should have accepted the offer of a partner.'

'It doesn't always work out. I was glad when Helen was withdrawn; all we did was argue.'

'She was also glad, and what about Claire?'

So, they knew about her, hardly surprising. The level of supervision varied, but eventually, news got back to the authorities.

'Claire is naïve, innocent, and thinks she is in love.'

'That could be dangerous.'

'I won't be back. She will soon move on. Women in this country are different.'

'Maybe, but nobody likes to be left in the lurch.'

'Give me the details,' Denis demanded, cutting short the conversation. This dalliance would undoubtedly be included in his following report, but it would be of little relevance by then. All that would matter would be his performance over the next few days.

'Here is what you need to do, and you mustn't fail,' and any clubiness between the two had evaporated. This was business; this was for the motherland.

24

Petrov walked past the end of the cul-de-sac, carefully noting the street layout. A small privately owned park was opposite the front of the flats, entered using a keypad. Sitting on a bench was a young mother watching her toddler play. In one corner, a gardener was pruning roses. Beyond the road end were the Royal Botanic Gardens with extensive glass houses; Reeves's flat overlooked them. The flat was well positioned to see Edinburgh Castle perched on a volcanic outcrop dominating the city – a perfect position to control the surroundings and an excellent defensive position that Petrov couldn't help but admire. To the north was the shimmering Firth of Forth and the Fife coastline. The red sandstone-faced flats looked exclusive and would, he was sure, attract a hefty premium on Edinburgh's property market. I am beginning to think like a capitalist, mused Petrov, trying not to think of the brutalist concrete block he had called home as a child. Still, Felix Reeves had done well for himself, a nice place to live and central to all of Edinburgh's attractions. Petrov calculated that Reeves had been acting as an agent for over thirty years. It was an incredible achievement, but this was still a foreign country, and he must have felt lonely, unable to unburden himself and reveal his innermost secrets. Reeves had done so well and made so many vital contacts – a pity that he had spoiled it.

Not wishing to be seen loitering, Petrov walked away, baseball cap firmly on his head, until he found a small café where he had tea and a sandwich and mulled over what he had to do. He felt little emotion. After all, it was what he was trained for. Having paid up, he returned swiftly and walked to the entrance to the flats, some of the red sandstone frontage now in the shade, which suited him. Petrov checked the name and buzzed the intercom for Reeves's flat. There was a hiss of static, and a voice responded. 'Who is it?' The voice sounded tired.

'Timofey, it's Paul Russell here,' that got his attention. The voice rose an octave in response.

'Should you be here?'

'We need to speak. Let me up to your flat.' There was silence, a long pause, and then Petrov heard the electronic door lock buzz, and he pushed the door open. Inside, in the entrance hall, the air was cool. Mosaic tiles extended halfway up the walls, with the rest of the wall and ceiling painted in a neutral colour, all well maintained. In front of him was an old-fashioned lift with a metal cage inside a lattice frame. He pulled on the metal handle, the metal work concertinaed, and stepped inside, pulling it shut behind him. The last time he had seen such a system was in Eastern Europe, in a department store in Slovakia, if he remembered correctly. He pressed the button for the second floor, and slowly, rattling, the metal cage shuddered and rose sluggishly, eventually stopping, and he slid the cage door open. Reeves was waiting for him at his door, one hand nervously fingering the collar of his shirt, eyeing him anxiously, his hair uncombed. The effects of partying could be seen around his waist. Petrov had disturbed him, which alarmed him as he wanted Reeves alone. He felt the outline of the box in his pocket that contained the syringe and gestured for Reeves to move inside and join him.

'Are you on your own?'

Reeves didn't immediately answer, appearing shifty, before muttering, 'Yes, but I expect guests.'

That was a clever response, placing pressure back on Petrov.

Reeves ushered him into the hall and then the lounge, which looked over the Royal Botanic Gardens and beyond that Edinburgh

Castle. All the hall doors were shut.

'Have a seat, do you want coffee?'

'Yes, but I also want to admire the view, and Petrov strolled towards the large window. He detected a faint smell of perfume; someone had been here recently. Looking around, he eventually sat down, noticing the many framed photos of Reeves with politicians and celebrities. Reeves returned with a tray. 'Not sure if you take milk,' and he placed the tray on a small table beside Petrov. On the table was a laptop with the lid shut.

Sitting on the edge of the sofa, leaning forward, he asked, his voice sounding dry again, clearing his throat. 'Why are you here?'

'How many years have you been serving our country?'

'Thirty-four.'

'Do you ever yearn for home?'

'Constantly, but my needs are secondary.' Did Petrov notice a flicker of hope, Reeves's expression relaxing slightly, shuffling back in the seat. Maybe this visit was about an opportunity to return home, he hoped. But Petrov was listening intently, still unconvinced that Reeves was alone. They talked about being home, but Reeves was becoming more anxious again.

Noticing Petrov glancing at a framed photo, Reeves began, 'That is the French ambassador in this room at one of my soirees. Interesting man sees little future in relations between the EU and Russia. Of course, I fed that back to Moscow. I am famed for my parties and mixing with the elite. Jack Brown, the first minister of Scotland, was here last week and in the same room as the UK defence secretary. Not many can claim to have achieved that, sworn enemies that they are. I pick up small pieces of information and religiously report back.'

Petrov was unmoved; the guy was pleading for his life, unnerved by his surprise visit. Personal visits were never good news.

'Bathroom?' and Reeves told him it was the hall's second door on the left. Petrov got up and left Reeves on the sofa, still trying to figure out the reason for the surprise visit.

Petrov took out the syringe inside the bathroom and slipped it uncapped carefully into his pocket. He paused in the hall but could hear no sound, and then he walked back into the lounge.

Pointing out the window, he asked Reeves to describe what he saw. 'Is that the Royal Botanic Gardens?' he enquired, his tone gentle. Reeves got up warily and stood beside Petrov.

'There are important plant specimens...' he slumped as Petrov quickly plunged the syringe into Reeves's back, disgorging the contents. Reeves twisted towards Petrov, mouth open, shocked. His expression changed, eyes glazing, and he slumped slowly towards the ground. Petrov removed the syringe and carefully placed it back in its box, then checked the body for a pulse, but there was none. This was how the motherland treated traitors.

Pulling on gloves from his pocket, he cleaned up any signs of his visit. He took the tray into the kitchen and, finding a dishwasher, he set it up after placing the tray's contents and the tray itself in the machine. Switching it on, he listened as the dishwasher started its programme. Using bleach he found in a cupboard, he wiped surfaces, and then he sensed more than heard a movement. Racing into the hall, he saw a door handle halfway down, and he ran at it, forcing the door open. A young woman drew back, her mouth opening in a silent scream, her eyes wide, as she fell against a king-sized bed, cowering in fear. She was dressed to leave in a skimpy short dress, a denim jacket over her arm, clutching a purse. For a second, he thought of Claire and how he had used her. This girl appeared equally naive.

'Who are you?' he asked as he grabbed her, picking her up and twisting her body around, firmly positioning his arm around her neck until she coughed, choking, her body trembling with fear.

'Debbie,' came the strangulated reply. 'What are you going to do to me?'

And that was a dilemma. The drug that Reeves received would be out of his system in a few hours but was potent, a new nerve agent, paralysing the heart. There was none left. If he was to kill Debbie, he would have to use more traditional methods. Petrov was trained to do so, but another body found in the flat would complicate matters. As it was, police would assume Reeves had died of natural causes, at least until a post-mortem, when a vigilant pathologist might spot something awry and start asking questions.

'How much was he paying you?' Petrov asked. Her eyes wavered briefly towards the bedside, where he saw an envelope. He dragged her towards it and opened it with his other hand. Inside was a wad of notes. Reeves paid well, and he doubted if the girl was worth it. Then he noticed the tell-tale signs of addiction: needle marks in her arm. He opened the purse and found a calling card.

'Is this you?' he asked. The girl nodded.

Finally deciding what to do, he stuffed the card in his pocket. 'Take the money and leave. Don't speak to anyone. If you do, I will find you and kill you.' Petrov stared at the girl, emphasising the words, spitting them out. Debbie seemed paralysed until Petrov released her. She grabbed her purse and jacket and glanced at Petrov before snatching the envelope and racing past him. She quickly opened the flat door, and he heard footsteps retreating down the stairs.

This encounter changed everything; time was now vital. He returned to the lounge, stepping over Reeves's body, collected the laptop, and shoved it inside his backpack. He removed a dog-eared Ordnance Survey map from an inside pocket and stuffed it down the side of a cushion on the sofa.

Satisfied, he had one last look at the view and Reeves's slumped body and retreated into the hall. He shut the door to the flat, locking it behind him and drew breath. Strolling, he descended the stairs which wrapped around the lift, and left the building, head down, baseball cap firmly on.

25

'We came to Islay to explore the island and especially the distilleries. Let's do that this afternoon. Nothing much is going to happen, I suspect,' Henry suggested, aware he had probably ruined his friend's holiday.

Alan was sitting beside Henry on the patio, reading his newspaper, which he put down. 'Good idea.'

'I've heard a lot about Machir Bay and need some exercise. Kilchoman Distillery is next to it. If we have time, we can look at Bruichladdich on the way back.'

'Sounds like a good plan,' and Alan suddenly brighter, looked across the expanse of Loch Indaal at the distillery and warehouses at Bruichladdich.

Later, they drove to Bridgend and turned left, entering the area of Islay known as the Rhinns on the island's western edge, where the island is almost split in two by Loch Indaal and Loch Gruinart. Driving down the west side of Loch Indaal, they had a different perspective. They saw Bowmore from over the water, the distillery with its name prominent on its white walls and the Round Church on the hill. However, Henry, without glasses, assumed more than read the distillery's name. The loch was at its most tranquil, with the reflection of the village on the water clear. In the far distance were the sea cliffs of the Oa. Henry's thoughts turned to Jenny struggling to cope alone in her farmhouse, tormented by her predicament. Peter had to be somewhere, but where?

Alan nudged Henry, who lost in thought, had almost missed

the turn-off for the distillery. The next stretch was single-track, and Henry had to concentrate on watching out for stray sheep and other cars. The road climbed, and they were rewarded with views over to Loch Gruinart, a sea loch. Henry pulled over briefly to appreciate the scenery. As they drove on, Loch Gorm, the largest loch on the island, became their companion. On their left, they noticed building works at a farm – a house being demolished, barns being constructed, with the bleeping sound of diggers at work. Someone with a lot of money thought Henry.

Soon, they could spot the sea and a ruined church on a hill, and they passed the entrance to Kilchoman Distillery, a long road leading to the distillery with trees softening the view around the buildings. They left the road at a cluster of houses and headed down a dirt track to a car park. A fresh sea breeze blew in their faces as they exited the car. Clambering over sand dunes, they reached Machir Bay, a long strip of sand exposed to the sea. Only a couple walking their dog could be spotted; otherwise, they had the place to themselves.

Breathing deeply, Henry turned to Alan. 'Splendid isolation, away from everyone,' and they scrambled to the beach beside a stream. The waves were crashing against the remnants of what appeared to be a ship's boiler embedded in the sand. Water pounded the metalwork, and Henry heard a sucking sound as the water momentarily retreated before resuming the onslaught.

Inevitably, his thoughts turned to Mary, and he desperately wanted to share the experience. Alan interrupted his thoughts. 'Let's walk towards the rocks.' They started, leaving footprints in the damp sand, steep sand dunes to one side and the sea pressing in on the other. They reached the rocks and scrambled part of the way up a twisting path before stopping, looking along the length of the bay.

'Remember, Ronnie told us that two ships collided in a storm offshore during the First World War. The *Otranto* watch officer was confused, he said, about where they were and turned to port while the rest of the convoy turned starboard. Ronnie said that the captain of the *Otranto* watched in horror as the *Kashmir* carried atop forty-foot waves in a fierce gale loomed large and crashed into them. The *Kashmir* limped on, and despite a rescue attempt by another vessel, the *Otranto* drifted towards Machir Bay and floundered on an offshore reef. Of the hundreds still on board, few made it ashore. The beach must have been littered with the dead and the dying.' Henry studied his companion, impressed by his recollection of a day when he had been suffering a horrendous hangover.

Above the sand dunes, Henry spotted a tall cross marking the graveyard for some of the sailors; not far from the ruins of the church he had seen earlier, the rafters of the roof had long ago collapsed. Like many of the islands and Highlands, tragedy was never far from beauty. They wandered back to the car, now having the beach to themselves and drove to the distillery, parking in the car park. Henry immediately spotted three white vans side-by-side in the far corner. As they got out, Alan nudged him and pointed in their direction.

'The nearest one has got writing on its side. I'll check the other two,' and he strolled towards the parked vans. Henry checked them out and caught up with Alan. 'They all belong to an engineering firm. I think we can eliminate them from our enquiries,' he added, smiling. The policeman in him was not quite dead.

Settling at a table in the busy café, Henry sipped his coffee, relishing the cream sponge before him. Alan had left to study the display of whiskies.

'Can I join you briefly while your friend is away?' Henry looked up to see Charlie standing with a younger man whose forearms were covered in tattoos. Without waiting, Charlie sat down, flicking back his long hair, a mannerism Henry remembered from many interviews. The younger man also sat down.

'This is Drew,' Charlie explained, 'my daughter's partner.

Remember I told you that I was visiting them.' Henry nodded without any enthusiasm. Drew smiled wanly. The tattoos Henry noted were all about heavy metal groups. His tee shirt reflected his taste in tattoos, a skull with the group's name underneath. 'Drew works at Bruichladdich.'

'Aye,' he stated, 'I work shifts in the bottling plant. I was having my break when that big light appeared. Fair scared me. Wondered what was happening. My mates thought it was a missile exploding, but there was no sound.' Henry recollected his reaction and stayed mute, still embarrassed by his overreaction.

'I'm sure Drew would organise a tour for you and your friend if you wish.'

'That's kind. I don't know how long we will be staying,' and Henry noticed a flicker of a smile pass across Charlie's face.

'I just wanted you to know that I am reformed. I don't want you worrying about me,' or reporting you, Henry mused.

'I'm glad to hear that. Not everyone would be as understanding as me,' and he lifted his fork, wanting to start the cake.

'Drew worked as a builder on the island before the company went bust.' Henry put down the fork, hoping he wouldn't get the full life story, accepting they weren't going to disappear immediately.

'I worked on Sir Angus's properties, helping to build that fancy house of his near Port Ellen and his house and farm at Saligo.'

That intrigued Henry. 'I've been to his house; it's certainly impressive. I didn't know about the farm at Saligo. Where exactly is that?'

'Other side of Loch Gorm, next to the beach. I don't know if he got another builder to finish it yet. Drive towards Machir Bay and take the road on the right. Near a sharp bend, there's a gate. It's a short distance from the stumps of an old wartime radar mast.' Well, he did ask for exact directions.

From the corner of his eye, Henry saw Alan standing with a

bottle of whisky, appearing bemused, wondering what to do. Henry waved him across, and Alan joined them.

'This is Charlie. I told you about him on the ferry and his daughter's partner, Drew.' Alan smiled politely and sat down with his newly purchased whisky.

'Good whisky that,' Drew stated. 'I have a bottle at home, one of my favourites. I swop bottles from Bruichladdich with my mate who works here.'

'Good to meet up, Charlie and Drew,' Henry added. 'Enjoy your visit.'

'I will, Mr Smith and don't worry about me. Seeing wee Kylie's face, she's only two months old, has changed me.'

You protest too much, thought Henry, but he continued to smile as they got up and left them alone. Henry immediately picked up his fork and attacked the sponge.

'Charlie was one of your regulars?'

Through mouthfuls of cake, Henry murmured agreement. 'He hasn't changed much, but I can't imagine he will get up to much trouble here. Just let me say, old cynic, that I am not totally taken in by his doting grandfather routine. He did, however, or more exactly, Drew said something interesting,' and Henry filled Alan in. 'I think we should go home the long way.'

In the car, Alan pointed out a bird with red legs pecking about in the grass beside the car park.

'That's a chough, a bit like a crow. It's one of the few places you see them in the country. I read about them in one of the tourist leaflets.'

'Very good, Henry replied, amused, 'you learn something new every day.'

Henry retraced part of their route, cutting right before they reached the houses near Machir Bay and took the road winding around the loch, which appeared brown and brooding now that the sun had disappeared behind clouds. Close to cottages, the road turned sharp, and there was a farm gate. Henry pulled over.

'I want to have a peek at Sir Angus's other property, just curiosity.' They closed the gate behind and soon heard the natural rhythm of Islay life, the pounding of breaking waves on a shore. They stood on sand dunes above the beach. They watched the waves rolling in, crashing against the shore, in what was a more exposed beach than Machir Bay, the smoothed stones and twisted rock sculptures bearing testimony to the savage power of the Atlantic. They then wandered along the dunes, reaching an open space with scattered houses. In the distance was a row of ridged hills which reminded Henry of a building in Glasgow. He thought for a moment, a concert hall, the Armadillo, with its ridged back, like the Sydney Opera House. He focussed his thoughts and spotted a new farmhouse with a cattle shed beside it, close to the hills. They continued walking until they reached the farmhouse and noticed no one about. The house was still incomplete, the upper windows boarded, and the cattle shed appeared empty as they walked by, although the lights were on.

'Interesting, even Sir Angus can't get builders. He'll hate that, knowing the type of person he is.'

'You have mixed feelings about him.'

'Yes,' Henry replied, 'I can't quite articulate my feelings, but I have a hunch he is not as altruistic as he likes to make out.'

26

It was evening before Elaine Soutar had time to drive to Jenny's house on the Oa. She parked in the yard, surprised to notice the burnt-out remains of the shed and got out, greeted warmly by Jodie, the Border collie, who welcomed her, nuzzling against her leg. Alerted by the barking, Jenny stepped onto the porch and waved, but a quick glance informed Elaine that her friend was not in a good way, her face white, the torn jeans and faded tee-shirt and her slumped stance suggested a depressed figure. It was a couple of months since they had last met, and whilst Elaine had been very busy, she regretted not making the time to see her friend. The two hugged, and Elaine saw Jenny's eyes brimming with tears as they hugged each other.

'Come in,' Jenny said.

'I could do with a good cup of tea,' replied her friend as they entered the house.

'Good idea, I'll get the kettle on, and you go into the conservatory.'

Elaine sat on one of the rattan chairs and admired the view over the Big Strand, Islay's longest beach on the shores of Loch Indaal, the sun beginning to set. Beside her was an easel with an unfinished painting, which troubled her because she noticed the splotches of paint from the tubes of paints, which Jenny used for mixing, had dried. No work had been done on the painting for a while.

Jenny came through with two mugs of tea.

'Good timing,' she stated, trying to appear brighter, 'Ben's just away to his bed.'

'We had a visit from Henry, a nice man,' Elaine began. 'He told me what had been happening. Why didn't you call me?' And she took Jenny's hand, squeezing it gently. 'I want to help, and the thought of you here alone with Ben troubles me.'

Elaine released Jenny's hand and watched tears trickle down her friend's face. 'Tell me what's going on.'

'Where do I start? Jenny replied, dabbing her eyes with a paper tissue.

'Take your time.'

'People think that we live in some posh house up here, short of nothing, me making a fortune with my paintings. An idyllic existence. Life is never that easy. Few know that Catherine Robinson left us money, which has been a big help. Still, people think we benefitted somehow from McGory's death and illegal dealings. Go into Port Ellen or Bowmore, and people look at you, making me uncomfortable. Ben gets teased at school. Peter and I were traumatised by the dealings with McGory. He chased us to Mull and Jura, wanting us dead. I thought they would kill Peter, the scene etched in my mind, and we were lucky to survive. Both of us had counselling, which strengthened us as a couple, for a time, but...' and Jenny sipped her tea, her voice sounding dry.

'Life is never simple. Peter couldn't settle, and despite an offer to return to the distillery, he wouldn't – he was hurt as they believed the accusations against him. Men and pride, what is it about them,' and she dabbed her eyes again. He has been restless. Sir Angus and he got friendly, and you'll have heard about their exploits.'

Elaine nodded. 'I heard rumours.'

'Sir Angus used him, wanting to learn about distilling. A bored rich man, casting around for amusement. They were still trying last week, and that's how the hut burnt down. The fire could have killed Ben, who was playing outside. We managed to extinguish the fire and didn't need to call the fire brigade. That would have been really embarrassing.'

'My first thought was Jason had been experimenting. Where is he anyway?'

'Back at boarding school in England. Someone had a go at him in the playground, and he hit him. A teacher tried to break them up, and he attacked the teacher. Lost it. The psychologist was worried about suppressed emotions.'

'I didn't know.'

'Good, that is one rumour that hasn't got out yet. We talked to Jason, and he wanted to return to boarding school. We knew he had problems settling on the island, and he, too, was traumatised by past events. What a mess,' and she gave her friend a painful stare. 'I was sensitive to Peter's feelings. Jason is his son, after all. We talked with Jason, and he was determined to return to the boarding school; he has a good bit of Catherine Robinson in him, and we set it up. Catherine's money makes it possible, but Peter was dumped by it, quite depressed. I think he felt he was letting Catherine down. So was Ben; the two got on well.'

'We both tried hard, but we had been arguing a lot, even before that woman appeared. Sir Angus introduced the two of them. He fancied a project, a micro-distillery, near his home to show off to his friends. He set up a meeting with a company that could provide capital. It's what he does. I knew she was trouble from the beginning, although I always trusted Peter, who never had a roving eye. Somehow, the two of them clicked, long discussions and meals together. Peter denied everything, but you know a woman's instinct. They went for a final dinner to tie up their plans, or so they said. He promised to be back early. I had a bath and went to bed, waking up about midnight and discovering that he hadn't returned. I was worried,' and again turned to her friend, 'let me be honest, I was bloody angry,' she admitted. 'I got dressed, got Ben out of bed and strapped him in the back of the Land Rover. I drove to the fancy lodge she was staying in, and her car had gone. There was a white van outside, which drove off as I approached. The key was in the lodge door, and I went inside, but all her belongings had gone. They had already left.'

Elaine was intrigued by the sighting of a white van, remembering her discussion with Henry and asked. 'What do you think that the white van was doing there? It seems strange at that time of night.'

'I don't know. It was the Porsche I was looking for. The van was in front of her lodge but could have belonged to a neighbouring one. I don't think that it's important.'

'Can you recollect any details about it?'

'No, why?' and Jenny looked quizzical.

'It appears strange that it was there and drove away when the driver saw you.'

'Probably coincidence,' but Elaine wasn't so sure but didn't want to say much more until she spoke to Henry.

'Was it a local van?'

'Don't know, there was no marking on it,' and again Jenny looked at Elaine puzzled.

'What happened next?' Elaine asked, dropping the subject.

'I waited at the ferry the following day, but they didn't appear. I contacted my airport friend, who confirmed that neither was booked on a flight. Peter ran away with her, and they are hiding somewhere on the island. I've lost him,' and Jenny started to sob. Elaine comforted her, leant across, slowly rubbing her back.

The sighting of the white van alarmed her, but she wasn't sure what to say. That might worsen matters if she suggested that the missing pair were in trouble. They sat as the sunset turned the sky a deep red, and stars appeared. Slowly, Jenny regained composure, and Elaine made them more tea, which helped them both.

'I appreciate you coming to see me, but it's late, Mick will be wondering where you are.'

'I texted him while waiting for the kettle to boil.'

'All we have talked about is me. I'm sorry.

'That's what friends are for.'

'Any progress?'

Elaine's face lit up, and Jenny immediately warmed, a smile on her face. 'At last, I'm pregnant; the doctor has confirmed it. Early days, so, please don't tell everyone.'

Jenny's face sagged again, making Elaine ask what was wrong.

'I'm also pregnant. After one of our big arguments, we tried to make it up, and I wasn't careful. Even passion doesn't work for me. I haven't told Peter. I don't know how to tell him. Don't know what he will say. Life is a big bloody mess.'

They clutched each other, one relieved that she was finally pregnant and the other fearful of her partner's reaction.

'Have you seen the GP?' Elaine asked.

Jenny shook her head. 'I completed a pregnancy test, and it was positive.'

'Have you made an appointment?'

'I meant to.'

'Tomorrow, we will make an appointment, and I'll accompany you, even come in with you if you wish, after you drop Ben off at school. You must be seen and tell the doctor what is happening. Everything, do you understand? You need support. I must leave now, but I'll return tomorrow.' Elaine looked directly at Jenny to reinforce the message, and she responded, inclining her head. The two of them hugged before Elaine left.

27

Henry and Alan wandered around to Shaun and Nora's Whisky Shop the following day when the shop was open. Inside, behind the counter, was a young man who was checking a delivery note but put it down and gave them a welcoming smile.

'Shaun and Nora away?' Henry asked.

'You know them?'

'We've spoken briefly.'

'They won't be in for the next few days.'

'Back on the mainland,' Henry casually inquired.

'I'm not sure. How can I help you? I'm Mike,' and he brushed the question away.

'We are really just having a look. We want to take something back with us.'

'We have plenty to offer. Any particular distilleries?'

Henry looked around, and his eye caught a bottle on the top shelf. He stretched and took a bottle of Bruichladdich's bottling, 'Yellow Submarine'. The bottle was not in the brightly coloured metal tube.

'Ah, we keep the more expensive bottles in the back shop. No one wants to drop one. It would be a costly mistake, although that particular bottling is more sought after now because of its rarity. A great story behind it.'

'So I've heard,' and Henry placed the metal tube back in its place.

On the counter were several sample bottles of whisky opened and some small plastic thimbles on a tray.

'Can I try that one, Alan asked, and a sample was poured for him. 'Heavily sherried. I like that.' Once Alan had purchased the bottle, they left.

'A wasted trip,' muttered Henry as they wandered past the Coop.

'Very successful,' Alan replied, smiling. 'That's a beauty I will savour over the winter months.'

Hurriedly, they returned to their house as the rain started to sweep over Loch Indaal. Once back, they prepared to receive their visitors.

Gradually, the group assembled. First, Malcolm was punctual as usual, wearing chinos and a patterned jacket, the shoulders splattered with rain. He was smart as always, followed by Mick and Elaine, who came in behind him, huddled under an umbrella. Elaine was wearing an attractive red knee-length smock with short sleeves, appearing very content. Henry had been told why earlier. They settled together on the sofa, holding hands. Lastly, oblivious to the steady drizzle outside, Ronnie appeared in his trademark shorts and tee-shirt. Alan was busy serving tea and coffee, offering biscuits and bringing in extra seats from the bedrooms. Henry sat with his back to the window, taking in the scene, as was his way, observing how people interacted, watching for any tensions. Outside, the view was obscured by low clouds and a drizzle slowly intensifying, water droplets merging and running in rivulets down the patio doors. If the scene outside was bleak, the mood inside was just as sombre.

Finally, with everyone served, Alan sat down, motioning to Henry that he could begin.

'I want everyone to report back, and then we can discuss what we have found. There's quite a lot, although sadly, we've still not found Peter. But first, Elaine has something to tell us.'

Elaine cleared her throat. 'I visited Jenny last night. As you know, she is in a bad way, depressed. She is also pregnant.'

Malcolm looked up, surprised; Ronnie pursed his lips and sat back in his seat.

'I took her to the doctor today as no one had examined her, and I wanted someone to check her and assess her mental health. I went in with her to offer support. The doctor was very supportive, and they made arrangements to monitor her.'

'Thanks, Elaine, and congratulations to the two of you.' There was a brief pause before the others grasped what was said, and good wishes followed. The mood lightened, as Henry hoped, attempting to create positivity.

'Ronnie.'

'I have spoken to Jack. Fortunate timing, as he was about to go on holiday. He has checked the registrations for all the vehicles since the morning after Peter's disappearance and studied the CCTV footage of the car deck. Three white vans have departed the island, all of whose background is known to Jack – regular carriers with clear signage, none of which fits what we are looking for. That would suggest the van we are looking for is still on the island. He also searched for recent arrivals. A few were distillery maintenance, Kilchoman in particular.' Henry nodded, 'and a few he didn't know why they had arrived on the island. I also talked to him about white vans on the island. He could suggest a fair number, but he could discount most. He has made a big, but not exhaustive, effort, so there is still some uncertainty.'

'A worthwhile effort, Ronnie. We'll keep our eyes open.'

'I've also been checking while I have been out on the roads. I noticed a couple of unmarked white vans and noted their registrations. Pleased to share.'

'Thanks, Mick.'

'Malcolm.'

'I dug into Sir Angus's background and searched company records. As you would suspect of someone in his position, he is a director of several companies, some quite prominent, in the FTSE 100. He has pulled back a little on his portfolio in recent years, especially since he has been on Islay. Approaching retirement, I suspect he doesn't need the hassle. He has backed several projects on the island, including Shaun and Nora's Whisky Shop.'

'A finger in every pie,' muttered Ronnie.

'They run the business and are listed as owners. I tried to delve into their background. I'm afraid I could learn little about it or how they know Sir Angus.'

'Alan and I visited their shop this morning, but they are away for a few days. We spoke to a young man, Mike.'

'That's Jim Lawson's son,' Ronnie stated. 'Jim runs one of the distilleries. I think that Mike would like to follow in his father's footsteps. It's a summer job he has at the shop. Pity they are away. I'll try to speak with him and see what I can discover.'

'I was more successful in discovering the identity of our important visitor,' Malcolm said. 'It's Fred McIntosh, Red Fred as he is better known. To put it mildly, the cabinet minister for defence was one of the most surprising picks for that post. Talk about square pegs in round holes. He makes no attempt to hide his socialist, some say communist leanings. The defence chiefs of staff registered a formal complaint about his appointment and are not too keen on sharing sensitive information with him. I believe an understanding was reached with the prime minister. He has already ruffled a few feathers. He also enjoys a vibrant social life, parties, visits to festivals, and all the trappings of a capitalist society. Unmarried but has a hectic romantic life, including a duchess, I'm told. That's not what you might expect from a left-wing firebrand. McIntosh also enjoys fishing and shooting.'

'It must be Red Fred that I am taking out on *Casablanca*,' Ronnie stated. 'I had a visit from two security goons yesterday. They checked out my boat, installed some extra communication gear and ordered me not to touch on the pain of death. Two of them are going to accompany us on the trip.'

He paused for a moment. 'Red Fred, indeed, I might be able to use that for publicity purposes.'

'He arrives tomorrow at the airport. The local paper has been informed. There will be a photo shoot at one of the distilleries. No doubt he will receive a special bottling and a personal tour.'

'Thanks, Malcolm, more than we got, Alan,' he said, turning to his companion. 'Elaine, you wanted to add something.'

'Yes, when Peter didn't return, Jenny took Ben from his bed, and they drove around Islay in their vehicle searching for him. She drove to the lodges where Cash was staying, convinced that she would catch them out. The Porsche wasn't there, but a white van was leaving in front of Cash's lodge as she arrived.' Pensively, she added, 'Jenny said it was unmarked. I didn't inform her of the possible significance; it would have upset her even more.'

'I know the receptionist at these lodges,' Ronnie stated.

'How do you know Pamela?' Malcolm asked.

'There seems to be few people on the island he doesn't know,' added Henry, 'which is good for us, I suspect.'

'I met her at a party and had a brief flirtation. Ended when she refused to come over to Jura. We're still friends, and I can have a word. These are posh lodges, so there is bound to be CCTV. We might identify the driver.'

'Positive, do it.' Malcolm stated, 'It appears we have some catching up to do.'

'Island life didn't stop when you abandoned us', replied Ronnie with a big grin, 'life goes on.'

'I have something to add about Sir Angus.' Henry intoned. 'Sir Angus owns a farm at Saligo on the Rhinns. It is an unfinished project; the builders went bust. The farmhouse still needs work, and a cattle shed beside it is finished but empty. We didn't notice any sheep or cattle.'

'It's not listed as belonging to Sir Angus. I'll check it out. No white vans parked thereabouts?'

Henry laughed. 'Sorry, Malcolm.'

'The builders are all over at the Robinson's old farm,' suggested Malcolm. 'The new owners have demolished most of it and are rebuilding at pace. No shortage of money there. I bet that Sir Angus is frustrated. For Henry and Alan's benefit, Robinson's farm was at the centre of the drug ring run by McGory. Drugs were getting shipped onto the mainland via Islay. Peter, who knew Robinson's daughter, had a child, Jason, by her and got caught up in their machinations with terrible consequences. Neither Jenny nor Peter have fully recovered. Alison will fly over to be with Jenny for the next few days.'

'Let's sum up. We believe Peter is still on the island. We must search, ask questions, visit remote places, and increase our efforts. We need a breakthrough. Malcolm, continue to research Sir Angus. He may be innocent, just a social climber, but I am unsure. Ronnie, talk with Mike to find out what you can about Shaun and Nora. Mick and everyone keep checking for white vans, especially unmarked ones.'

At that, Malcolm's phone pinged, and he took it out. 'A message from my sister, Susie,' and he scanned the message.

'For once, Susie's timing is spot on. She has found the Porsche parked behind a deserted house on the shores of Loch Gruinart while walking the dogs.' Malcolm looked across at Henry.

'We need to get there, but it is a potential crime scene. Anyone got rubber gloves?'

'Plenty in my boot,' stated Ronnie.

28

Taking Ronnie's car with Malcolm in the front and Henry in the back, they headed for Loch Gruinart. The others stayed behind. Henry recognised the initial part of the journey from the day before, but soon after passing Bridgend, they turned right up a twisting, winding road before reaching the Gruinart Flats, where the barnacle geese winter. After the RSPB Centre, they proceeded up the side of the sea loch. Malcolm pointed out where his sister lived, and then a mile further on, Ronnie pulled over, stopping in front of farm gates beside a ruined cottage.

'This is a potential crime scene. Let me go on alone to check it out first. Ronnie opened the gate for him, handing him rubber gloves. The farm track led to a field where sheep grazed, the nearest sheep running away as he approached. Henry stepped along the rutted track, avoiding the puddles of water from the recent rain, and reached the rear of the house. There, tucked in, hidden from the road, was the Porsche. Two parallel furrows of churned mud indicated that it had been driven in recently. The other two watched intently as Henry tried the driver's door handle. The door was unlocked. Inside the car, it appeared clean and tidy. For a moment, Henry wondered if someone had valeted the vehicle, but then, remembering Cash, he knew she would maintain it in a pristine state.

Suddenly, the car alarm went off. A loud, high-pitched, repetitive hooting sound, growing in intensity, accompanied by the car lights flashing. Henry frantically searched behind the sun visor, looking for keys, but they weren't there. Stretching across, he opened the glove box, relieved to see the keys. Quickly, he sat in the driver's seat and inserted the key, hoping the engine would start and turn off the alarm, but with no success. Ronnie ran to the car, reached under the steering wheel, and located a switch, which he flicked. The noise stopped.

'Everyone on Islay will know that we have found the car,' Henry muttered, almost apologetically.

'It's an old car, probably didn't have a car alarm fitted as standard. My first car had a system like this,' Ronnie added.

'What I was looking for was any sign of violence, but I don't see any blood stains or tufts of hair or anything to indicate a struggle.'

By this time, Malcolm had joined them. 'No sign of her belongings. I'll also check under the bonnet.' Minutes later, having opened the bonnet, he shook his head. 'Everything has been removed from the car.'

'The fact that I saw the car at Ranald's farm and now it's here, suggests whoever brought it here has a good knowledge of the island. There also have to be a few people involved in driving the car, pick the driver up and so on. I imagine they have hidden it far from where they are staying. I would do that. If not, they will have heard the alarm. My ears are still ringing.'

'I have a small camera in the boot,' Ronnie began, 'which links to my phone. I don't particularly like leaving Casablanca unattended. My phone tells me if anyone goes near the boat, flashing a picture on the screen. I'll set it up; the battery will last a few days. If anyone returns to get the car, we'll know.'

'Good idea,' Malcolm agreed. Ronnie returned to his car to collect the camera. He set it up on a wall, partially concealed by a bush and checked the signal. 'The signal has much improved since you departed, Malcolm. You could work from here.'

'Don't think I wouldn't want to; I miss Islay, and so does Alison, but I would also miss the buzz in the editorial room as a deadline approaches. I am just a different type of adrenaline junkie from you.'

'Give me the Corryvreckan whirlpool anytime, with *Casablanca* cresting the waves.'

'And everyone being sick,' laughed Malcolm.

Henry observed their strong bond; each had chosen their own path. Wandering around, he could see nothing that would aid their quest. He turned back to the abandoned cottage. The door opened with a push, as some rubbish was trapped behind it, which he kicked away. The rooms were stripped of furniture, the wallpaper in the lounge peeling, ashes remaining in the grate. He noted that there was also an empty whisky bottle, not one of Islay's. The view from the window compensated for the gloom of the interior. There was a ruin of a church in the foreground. The tide was out, and sand bars were exposed in the loch. Farm buildings with a circular concrete silo and barren hills were on the far shore. Ronnie joined him and pointed out the church. 'What a setting. Catherine Robinson, Peter's ex and mother of Jason, is buried in the grounds of Kilnave Church. Peter hasn't been back to visit – too painful.'

'He sounds like a tortured soul.'

'He's been through a lot.'

Back in the car, Malcolm stated the obvious. 'Unless someone turns up, we are not much further forward.'

'Not quite true,' Henry explained, 'I am almost sure that their abduction happened when they were away from the car. So, the question is, why did they stop and leave it and then get into the van, driving it if Sir Angus is telling the truth. I believe Malcolm, the luggage was removed from the lodge later; otherwise, why go to the bother to visit it. You have to have confidence the pieces will eventually fit together. In this game, patience can be a virtue unless you are the victim or the victims at the centre.'

29

'Peter,' and Cash pinched Peter's arm. He responded with a jolt, and before he could respond, Cash muttered for him to be quiet.

'Somebody is walking about above us. Sounds as if it is only one person.'

Immediately alert, Peter stirred. 'Let's get ready,' he whispered and crawled towards the trap door, stretching as he moved, trying to loosen his limbs to remove the stiffness. Cash was more lithe, crawling towards the trapdoor with more ease. It helped that Cash was shorter and not so restricted by the low headroom, but she was also becoming more frustrated and angry with their continuing captivity. Meanwhile, Peter felt more claustrophobic as time passed, unable to stand up, panicky at times, and fighting to control his emotions. They had to be ready to grasp the opportunity to escape; more days in captivity and they wouldn't be fit enough to attempt to get out. The person above stepped on the trapdoor but continued on. Cash sagged in disappointment, beating the ground with her fists in frustration.

'I feel the same,' muttered Peter. He wondered how many days they had been held, worried he had lost track of time. The shaft of light through the trapdoor showed a very different Cash from before their capture. She was covered in dirt and grime, her face smudged with dirt, and her knees were grazed and bleeding. He was no different. Hungry and thirsty, struggling on a diet of sandwiches, the water peaty, as it so often was in Islay, the conditions were taking their toll.

The footsteps above had retreated when he heard someone shouting angrily. Peter pressed his head closer to the trapdoor, where he might hear more clearly what was being said, but he still couldn't make it out. There was real anger in the person's voice, yet it sounded familiar. He didn't feel sorry for the person on the receiving end if it was one of their captors, but they were certainly getting a rollicking. He wondered if things were about to change for them, his stomach tightening, concerned about their fate. Surely, people on the outside would be bothered about their disappearance by now, and Jenny would be even more fraught, which troubled him, knowing her present state of mind. Alarm bells should be ringing, people searching, and hopefully, the police involved. Then, that recurrent thought, Jenny would assume that they had eloped, so might friends. There would be anger amongst his loved ones. Ben would be picking up on it. What a mess and all avoidable. He cursed himself and glanced at Cash, who was studying him carefully.

'We'll get out of this somehow,' he said, but Cash moved back towards the corner without saying anything and huddled in the corner, wrapping a blanket around to keep out the dampness. He joined her without saying anything, head down, arms wrapped around his knees.

The shouting continued, and the person was walking above them again. The voice was loud but more legible. Suddenly, he realised who it was – Sir Angus. He moved position, going to shout out, when Cash grabbed him and whispered frantically in his ear. 'Keep quiet.' She wouldn't let go of him until the footsteps receded.

'I don't know what is going on,' she stated, 'but Gillies must be responsible, or why would he be here? How could he explain why he kept us imprisoned. More likely to get rid of us if we knew of his involvement.'

Peter absorbed what was said and thought about it.

'Maybe he owns the place; he has several properties on Islay. He might not know we are here, and we have just let him walk away.'

'Peter, he is not as nice as you think. Gillies uses people; people like him always do; it's his nature. The plans for the micro-distillery are shelved because he demanded too much control at the end. I'm sorry, but he was using your knowledge to get information about distilling. He would have ditched you once he got permission to build, even if it was on your land. He's ruthless. I have dealt with many people like him.'

'Why imprison us?'

'He must be involved in some way with what we saw. I don't understand, but I am worried. We've been brought to a place he probably owns and kept captive. There has to be a connection. If we get out of here, I will swing for him.' Peter sensed real anger in her voice.

30

The cul-de-sac was blocked off, and a police car parked across the road. Several police officers were searching the private gardens opposite the row of flats, poking in among the flower beds. Two police officers stood guard at the entrance to the flats in hi-viz jackets. Roddy could only imagine that the residents of the flats, who must be some of the wealthiest residents in Edinburgh, were less than chuffed at this intrusion into their lives. The officers, who Roddy suspected were of a similar age to himself, looked bored but still carefully checked their passes before letting them through.

'Nice antique,' muttered Imran as he spotted the lift, adding, 'I think we should take the stairs; it will be safer.'

They had reached the first floor when what they took to be a detective emerged from a flat. He had a distracted expression before turning towards them, wondering who they were. Automatically, they held up their security passes. 'I suppose you lot would want to join us,' but there was an edge to his voice, which both ignored. Brusquely, he pushed past them, heading upstairs in a hurry; Imran sidestepped him and almost toppled a plant pot perched on a small corner table before steadying it quickly whilst arching an eyebrow at his colleague.

'They must be panicking,' Roddy suggested, 'lots of pressure from above.'

On the landing of Reeves's flat stood another police officer, who again checked their identities and gave them rubber gloves and over-boots to wear. 'SOCO has been here and cleared the place, but put these on.' The guy appeared nervous as he recorded their names and the time of their visit on his iPad, fumbling with the keyboard and having to correct mistakes.

'Busy place,' he muttered as he opened the door to the flat. This death was a big deal; not often did one of the capital's most prominent citizens be found dead in suspicious circumstances. The floors had several lengths of plastic for people to walk on to avoid contamination of the crime scene. While SOCO may have departed, they carefully used them.

From the lounge came the harassed officer they had encountered on the stairs. This time, he engaged them more positively. 'CDI Ingram,' he stated, inviting them into the lounge, 'sorry to have been in a rush a minute ago, but this is, as you can imagine, a rapidly developing situation.' His face was gaunt, the close-cropped grey hair adding to the appearance of exhaustion. He was probably in his early fifties and didn't appear particularly fit, too long behind a desk.

A semi-apology, Roddy mused, but they had to work together, so it was a start. He continued. 'I'm the SIO; try not to interfere with my staff, who are still at work. I'm swamped, but I'll update you quickly.'

'One of Reeves's friends, a high court judge no less, alerted us. He was due to have a drink with him and rang the doorbell many times. Also tried his phone and was worried, as it was not like him. He asked the caretaker to let him in. Judges have a way of getting what they want,' he added. 'They both got a terrible fright when they found his body. The Judge contacted the paramedics immediately. Initially, it was believed that Reeves had had a heart attack as he was found slumped on the floor in this room. Paramedics concluded that he was dead and had been for several hours.'

'A neighbour also reported that images flashed on her phone from her video doorbell, which was more suspicious. One picture was of a young girl she had heard running down the stairs. I imagine that residents of this block do not permit running on the stairwell,' and he stared up at the ceiling to register his feelings with a disdainful expression. 'Like several other neighbours we interviewed, they had suspicions about Reeves's behaviour with women, especially young ones. Still, they liked the kudos of important persons being spotted arriving, something to talk to their friends about. "The first minister was here yesterday. I spoke to him, a nice man," he added, using a slightly higher-pitched voice mimicking one of the neighbours he had spoken to. 'Anyway,' he sighed. 'Thank goodness she used one of Amazon's finest products. We believe the girl is a local prostitute and are searching for her. But more important was the image of the man who walked down the stairs shortly after.'

Roddy and Imran nodded. 'That's why we are here.'

'You sent us a picture, several days ago, of a Paul Russell for the police to look out for. Our software matched the images. We are also analysing local CCTV.' Imran was pleased, glad that he wouldn't land the task. 'Russell headed towards the centre of Edinburgh after leaving. Our more sophisticated facial recognition cameras failed to pick him up at Waverley, Haymarket, or bus stations. He may, of course, have jumped in a car. That's harder to check, but the city centre has many parking restrictions. It would have been easier to head to Leith to drive off, but we are not assuming anything. It's a painstaking process,' and Imran nodded his agreement.

'We had Reeves's body removed, and the pathologist noticed a syringe mark on his back while conducting the PM. Tests are not back, but we suspect Russell must have injected him with a substance that would induce a heart attack. That's our hypothesis. We're checking his mobile phone records to see who he's been speaking to in recent weeks. You gave us Russell's fingerprints and DNA. We're doing the usual stuff.' Ingram stifled a yawn as he finished. Poor guy was tired, Imran believed. Given how well-connected Reeves was, many important figures would be concerned, not wanting their reputations tarnished, especially if there was a hint of scandal.

Roddy had warmed to Ingram, understanding the pressure he was under for a result. Once you had talked to him, he appeared more human than Swan.

'Any computers or listening devices in the flat?'

'We've checked for listening devices – we didn't find any after sweeping the flat. Nor a computer; Russell probably nabbed any laptop and took it with him. We did find an Ordnance Survey map down the side of the couch. It covered the Hawick area. There was a circle around the village of Denholm not too far from Hawick. A local team are investigating, going around houses showing photos of Russell and Reeves to see if anyone recognises them. It's a long shot, but we don't know the map's significance. It could even be a ploy to distract us.'

'Well, what can you tell me?' Ingram asked.

'We have been trying to find Russell after we received information, which, until our boss gives the okay, is confidential, I'm afraid. I am allowed to say that if he murdered Reeves, it's probably not out of character. It is vital that we find him, give his photo to the papers,' Roddy explained.

'There can be no public appeal or picture of him released,' Ingram responded firmly. Orders from the very top. The first minister was here last week. He doesn't want any association to be revealed. Ditto, several others. Can you not be more helpful.'

Imran glanced at Roddy, and Roddy replied. 'He may have been living under an assumed persona.'

'Bloody great,' the detective replied. 'So, we don't even have the correct name.' He changed tack. 'So why are you here? What are you looking for?'

'We are not sure.'

This time, Ingram's response was more profane.

'Sorry,' Roddy replied, 'but I am sure that Swan will communicate what he can when he can.'

'Not him,' Ingram growled, by now beyond exasperated. 'He won't tell you the time of day if you ask him. What is it with you guys? I have a probable murder investigation. Someone who is a VIP, connected to everyone. What was the motive? Who should I interview? Possibly half of the country's elite, who will all try and dissociate themselves from any connection.'

'I'm sure more information will come your way,' Roddy suggested, but knowing Swan, wasn't so sure, he felt sorry for Ingram.

Ingram shouted across to a colleague in the corner who was packing away kit into a case. 'We're finished in here, aren't we?' And the officer confirmed. 'Okay, start in here,' and he turned away.

Roddy moved across to a sideboard and examined it before pulling open the drawers, painfully aware that Ingram was watching him. He examined the contents of the drawers in turn, but Ingram was correct. What was he expecting to find? Imran had gone to an antique bureau and opened it. It was inset with leather and polished wood. There were letter racks at the back. Imran pulled out the letters in turn, noticing that someone had already dusted the letters for fingerprints. Imran studied them, but they were mainly invites and notes of thanks from those who had attended parties at his flat, some from well-known people.

Ingram turned on his heels and left the room, much to their relief. Imran pulled a face, and Roddy pursed his lips and breathed out. What could they find that the police hadn't, Roddy thought. The police had been very thorough.

With Ingram away, they worked quickly. Both worked around the room from opposite sides, meeting at the large window overlooking the Royal Botanic Gardens. 'What a view,' Imran said, a great place to watch firework displays over the Castle Esplanade.'

'Everyone would want an invite for such a fantastic view,' Roddy concurred. 'You can imagine the wine being distributed, the canapes. Maybe there were waiters. The great and good assembled. But he was only a university lecturer; how can he afford a flat and his lifestyle. I wonder if Reeves will turn out to be a Russian agent, working his way into the confidence of others, supported by Moscow. It's ironic if Moscow is buying food and drink for the capitalist elite. Anyway, let's keep searching. Let's see what's in the kist. It's the only thing in the room we haven't checked.' Roddy opened the lid of the kist. Inside were boxes of games. 'Must be for rainy days,' and he lifted the games. 'Monopoly. He must have concealed his communist leanings while playing it. I'll buy Mayfair and build a hotel,' he mimicked a posh accent. 'Up my rent, that'll teach you.'

Imran laughed, lifting up a game called Risk. 'I haven't played that in years.'

'And here is the chess set, another staple,' Roddy paused as he held it and then quickly flipped off the lip and let the pieces fall onto the rug beside the kist. 'I wonder how many pieces there are,' and he started to count.'

Imran caught on. 'There should be thirty-two pieces,' and he helped count.

'I make twenty-nine. I wonder what the missing pieces are?'

They laid them out in neat rows – Pawns in front, then the other pieces. A black King was missing and a black Bishop.

'They are the same type that I photographed in Petrov's house. This must be significant. And I know that Petrov had just received a package postmarked to Edinburgh. This must be the signal for him to be active.' Roddy took out his phone and photographed the pieces.

'Yes,' Imran countered, 'but why go and kill the person who sent you the chess pieces. It doesn't make sense.'

Roddy shook his head. 'We'll need to work on that later.' He picked up the box that contained the chess pieces and shook it. There was no rattle. 'We are also missing a white Queen. Is Petrov the only one that has been called into action?' That thought chilled them.

They put the chess pieces back in the box as Ingram walked in. 'You've found a chess set. How revealing. Nothing more? You've been a wonderful help,' he added sarcastically. 'While you've been playing chess, we can confirm Russell is the main suspect and its murder. Traces of a poison have been found in Reeves' body. Can't be sure which neurotoxin, but that will be confirmed later.'

'We've been thorough,' Roddy replied, 'but so far no clues.' Discovery of the missing chess pieces could be a red herring, and the police would have an excuse to ask more questions.

'We'll look at the other rooms, if we may.'

'Go ahead,' Ingram grunted, but they could tell he was less than impressed and left the room again. 'He wants to catch a murderer; we see a bigger, more complex picture,' Imran stated.

31

This time, it was different. Swan was here in person, and the overhead fan was working again – no coincidence, thought Roddy. It must be important.

Swan greeted everyone as they filed in, studying them, fixing his gaze on each person, probing them with deep-set eyes. Bill, Jean, Imran and Ash were all present. Jack was absent, being semi-retired. Roddy sat beside Swan who was casually dressed in a white tee-shirt and faded blue jeans. In the flesh, he seemed diminished in contrast to the figure who had appeared on the large screen on the wall. He was less threatening, less big brother, but Roddy wouldn't relax; that would be a mistake; Swan was the boss. Swan waited for everyone to settle, brushing his jeans with his hand, and Roddy realised he was removing dog hairs. That seemed very unlike Swan, almost human. Roddy smiled but only inwardly. He couldn't imagine Swan walking a dog or even having a life outside of work. Roddy viewed him like a school pupil would a teacher imagining that they disappeared into a cupboard at the end of the day.

'We are all here,' he began, and the people in the room stiffened, watching him closely. Swan smiled, appearing to relish the effect he had on them. 'Confirmation from the police, positive ID from fingerprints and CCTV, it was Paul Russell or, as we know him, Denis Petrov. I think that we knew that already. They are still working to identify the toxin, but Reeves was poisoned. They haven't yet released any of Reeves's phone records. They are still working on them, they say. We must find out who he was in contact with over the last few weeks. I will be pressing them. Little is being released publicly; the story they are spinning is that he had a heart attack. His death is too sensitive and has consequences for too many public figures. Neighbours might gossip about young women visiting him, but they won't want to broadcast the fact, might reduce the value of their property,' he added, 'so there will be an obituary in the Scotsman newspaper, and everyone will be saddened. At the moment, we don't know the whereabouts of Petrov. He didn't appear on the cameras at any station – train or bus. He might have driven off, but again, police are still searching CCTV footage.

However, Roddy and Imran have been busy; over to you.'

'Thanks, boss,' and Roddy began, hoping that didn't sound too casual. 'There was little we could add to what the police had done; they were very thorough, but it was a worthwhile visit, although it raises more questions than answers. At Petrov's house, there was a chess board, which I took a photo of and sent to Ash, given her obsession with chess,' and he avoided looking at her in case he blushed. 'Silly me hadn't noticed two extra pieces on the board – a black King and a black Bishop. We found a chess set at Reeves' house missing those pieces; the King and Bishop are both from the set we found. In the recycling bin at Petrov's house, I also noticed a small empty package, postmarked Edinburgh. The assumption is that Reeves sent the chess pieces to Petrov.'

'Hold on,' Bill said, 'he sent chess pieces to Petrov, and he returns the favour by visiting his house and murdering him. It doesn't make sense. Ordering his own demise.'

'Maybe Reeves didn't know what the consequence of his message would be,' Roddy replied. 'Maybe he was acting simply as a postman acting on orders from above. Reeves was almost certainly a sleeper agent who had excelled in his mission of infiltrating the higher echelons of society, passing back information to his masters back in the Kremlin. He acted as a postman on this occasion, probably unaware of who he was contacting. He may just have been following orders.

'A lot of assumptions in all of that,' Bill shot back.

'I agree,' Swan said, interrupting, 'but it's all we have. The chess pieces were a signal. Petrov left, we witnessed a brush-pass in the street, and he drove off on a mission, supplied with a car. Next, he kills Reeves. Reeves may have been in danger of being exposed and needed to be removed. We can only speculate. Roddy, however, you have more for us.'

'There was a further missing chess piece, a white Queen. It could be lost, or it could have been sent to another agent. This may mean we have two agents, two konservy on missions. They could cause a lot of damage. They won't have been called to duty for nothing. Russia invests a lot of money and resources in installing sleeper agents, using them only when it is vital.'

'Each chess piece could represent a life to be taken.' Swan paused before adding.' And whose lives are being threatened? We urgently need to know.'

The consequences caused the room to go silent as the implications sank in. Ash studied her laptop, Bill gazed up at the ceiling, and Jean examined her fingernails. Imran leaned back in his chair. Each had their own way of coping with bad news.

'I should add,' Roddy said that they found an Ordnance Survey map of Hawick stuffed down the side of the sofa. The small village of Denholm, not far from Hawick, was circled. Police have a team going around the houses in the village showing people photos of Russell and Reeves.'

'Thanks, Roddy. We'll leave the police to investigate the map's value, but it strikes me as a diversionary tactic. Anyway, we don't have the resources. I need to tell you about another event with a news embargo. A middle-aged male in Tomintoul has been urgently flown to Edinburgh, suffering from possible signs of poisoning. Indications are that it is Novichok or a close derivative. Does this incident involve Petrov or our other konservy? We need to find out. Imran and Roddy, I want you to drive to Tomintoul and discover what is happening. It is the highest village in the Highlands, I read on Wikipedia, above the Spey Valley. It would help if you left now, it's a four-hour drive, maybe longer. We need answers quickly before more damage is done. If they want to kill their own people, that is one thing, but what if they want to kill our own citizens. That is unacceptable.'

32

The journey took longer than expected; the A9, the main route north, was choked with holiday traffic, and they had to endure several tailbacks, frustrated by campervans and caravans. Once they left the road near Aviemore, they progressed quickly.

'I know this area,' Imran said, 'my grandparents had a shop in Elgin. They worked hard and earned enough to send my father to university. I owe them a debt of gratitude. They are both now dead. I wonder what they would make of my career. My sister and I had terrific holidays here, and I remember cycling to Tomintoul. I remember this part, the Bridge of Brown; it's hard enough for cars, let alone cyclists. It is strange to be back.'

'This is not a part of Scotland that I know. We tended to fly abroad to catch the sun.'

'You'll like the area.'

They finally reached Tomintoul. Immediately, they were aware of police activity, with several police cars in attendance. Roddy slowed and powered down his window, showing a police officer his security pass.

'First left, sir, and an officer will direct you.'

Roddy thanked him and drove down Conglass Lane to meet a road parallel to the main street. A blue forensic tent was erected outside a modest bungalow beyond a graveyard. An officer stepped from the pavement, holding up his hand. He checked their passes and directed them to park by the side of the road. A police inspector close to the bungalow broke away from talking to colleagues and came across. He glanced at their passes.

'I've been expecting you, lads. Glad you finally made it. Traffic on the A9 awful?' Both nodded in response. He shook their hands warmly, with a firm grip, and they noticed he wore rubber gloves. 'I have just put new gloves on; you can't be too careful. I'm Fergus McCrone. Pleased to meet you.' He was a giant man, easily six and a half feet, ramrod straight, with grey hair jutting from underneath his police cap, approaching the weary end of his police career, but astute and alert, thought Roddy. In some ways a bit like Swan.

'We have quite an incident here, not what we would expect in this part of the country. We know that a middle-aged man, Ricki Fraser, is seriously ill with suspected poisoning. Novichok, I believe, is suspected. He may not survive.' He studied the two of them to check that they appreciated the seriousness of the situation. Scientists from Porton Down arrived by helicopter last night and are still here. We can't go in until they give the all-clear. Mr Fraser staggered out of the bungalow and collapsed. A nurse in a neighbouring house came to his aid, suspecting that he was drunk, but could smell no alcohol on his breath. His eyes were glazed, breathing with difficulty, and she quickly phoned an ambulance. She is also in hospital but should survive. We were called and placed a cordon around the house. One of our forensic scientists put on a hazmat suit and bravely went in. There is a dead cat on the floor, which may be the source of the poison for Fraser, but that is speculation at the moment. The house's owner is Miss Sally Rundell, who lives on her own. Hasn't been seen for a couple of days. According to her boss at the Post Office, she is on holiday in Yorkshire with her sister. We are still checking that out. Locally, people think she is eccentric, living on her own with the cat and often seen practising yoga at the art installation at the local quarry, a viewing box.'

'My colleagues have been busy interviewing locals, and of course,

Mrs Fraser,' and he lifted his eyes to the heavens. 'She is a character, and while a God-fearing man, I can understand why he might be tempted to stray. Accuses her husband of an affair with Sally Rundell. Hell has no fury like a woman scorned. Worth talking to, however. There is also a possible lead from a Mr and Mrs Stewart, who narrowly avoided crashing into Rundell when Mr Stewart had to do an emergency brake on the road on their way home. They were furious with her. I can give you another couple of contacts worth following up. Our people have spoken to them, but it does no harm to have another word. I'll get PC Paul Shaw to show you around while we wait for results.' He beckoned over a young policeman and issued instructions.

The Inspector was certainly friendly, but, Roddy thought, very little escaped him. Having a policeman follow us around, he would know if we found anything.

'Where to first,' Shaw asked after being introduced.

'Give them a blast of Mrs Fraser,' McCrone suggested as he walked away, giving a large wink to Roddy.

'This way then, please. Call me Paul,' Shaw stated, and he walked then a few hundred yards to a small cottage beside the main road. As they approached, another policeman stood outside guarding the premises and rapped on the door. A small grey-haired woman opened the door.

'Have you not got enough answers,' she snarled. 'Oh, you better come in. My husband is a cheat, an adulterer, and has been seeing his fancy woman for at least a year. Always comes back with a smile on his face. Serves him right.'

'Sorry that you are so upset,' Imran began.

'Upset,' and she tossed her head, 'no, he's got what he deserved, and he won't be welcomed back.'

'What do you know about Miss Rundell?' Roddy asked.

'Little that's good. Shona next door once saw her up at the quarry, howling at the wind, making a right spectacle of herself. The woman has mental issues and should be locked away. Fancy poisoning her cat, how low can you go.'

After a few more questions, they left, asking Shaw to take them to the Stewart's house. They received a more convivial welcome and sat down in the lounge with the couple, who were very elderly.

'Jim got a real fright, it's not good for him. I was going to go around and tell her that she could have caused a serious accident. I never did it, I was too busy.'

'Aye,' Jim stated, 'it was an emergency braking that she did. I had to swerve to get past her. We could have been killed if another car had been coming along in the opposite direction. I saw her leave the car in my rear-view mirror and go towards a ruined cottage.'

'Maybe a call of nature,' Imran suggested, and Roddy glanced at him, wondering if he was being humourous, but there was little response from either of the Whites.

It was undoubtedly strange behaviour, Roddy mused, and why would someone stop so suddenly and then go to a ruined cottage. Shaw knew where the cottage was, but next was going to take them to Rundell's place of work, the Post Office in Aviemore.

It was late in the day when they arrived at the Post Office, and Rundell's boss Tom Paterson, was about to leave.

'My most reliable worker, I had to fight to get her to take a holiday. I hope that she's found.'

'Were all the security checks carried out on her,' Imran asked.

'Yes, we checked her background, birth certificate, passport, and financial records. All good, or she wouldn't have been allowed to work behind the counter.'

'What was her full name?' Roddy enquired.

'Sally Thomson Rundell. Came from near St Andrews, in Fife, I believe.'

'Do you know her date of birth?'

'I should have it somewhere.'

'You might have a scan of her passport?' Roddy added helpfully. Minutes later, they got the information. 'Can you think of anything unusual about her behaviour recently?'

'Only that she finally agreed to take a holiday. Just two days ago. I needed to make up holiday rotas and was putting pressure on her, but she wasn't keen, never was. The next day, she came in and asked to go away.'

'That's helpful, thanks.'

'Sudden call to action,' Imran suggested as they left. It fits. What is it she's being called to do that involves Novichok. Worrying.

The next stop was the Catholic church in Aberlour, where a neighbour had told the police she worshipped.

'Beautiful building,' Imran stated as they entered the church, crossing himself.

Father O'Hara, a tall man with long grey hair swept back from his face, was waiting for them.

'I can't picture her, certainly not a regular attender.'

Shaw showed a photo of Rundell to the priest.

'I remember her now. Came a few times several years ago. She asked to attend confession but never turned up. My impression was of a troubled woman with something on her conscience.'

They thanked the priest. 'Why did you cross yourself, Imran?' Roddy asked.

'I'm a Christian. My grandparents had to leave their home because of persecution.'

'You learn something new about your colleagues each day.' Imran smiled.

Roddy next asked for directions to the quarry and the viewing box. The quarry had not been in use for many years. They climbed up a steep path from the roadside and reached the metal cube, mirrored on the inside walls and exposed to the elements front and back.

'It allows you to get a good view up Glen Avon, not that you would know it today,' the policeman claimed. The two of them walked around as Shaw watched, but after ten minutes, Roddy shrugged. 'Can't see anything of interest, let's get back to the car,' and as they left, he took a few photos.

The final port of call was the ruined cottage. The chimney stack erect, like a lonely sentinel, a saltire painted high up on the outside. The rest of the building was in ruins, choked with weeds and brambles. Gingerly, Roddy stepped inside, standing in front of the hearth. He scanned around without much hope as Imran joined him.

'If it wasn't a sudden call of nature, maybe she was collecting the Novichok,' Imran suggested. 'As she passed, she saw some signal.' Apart from a few empty beer cans, there was little indication of what that could be. Roddy picked up a bunch of withered flowers. He saw a small, damp envelope on the ground and picked it up. No message inside. Probably family returning to their ancestral home, leaving a memento of their visit, and he placed the flowers on the ground respectfully.

'Here,' Imran exclaimed, 'someone has dragged this stone across the hearth; look at the bruised weeds and the scrape marks on the hearth.'

Imran stepped on the stone, studying the stonework above the fireplace. He reached forward and pulled on a square-shaped stone, pulling it out easily. 'Roddy, the stone is loose, and there's a space behind it. It might be a safe place to hide something.'

'Careful, there might be traces of Novichok.' Imran put on rubber gloves. 'Thanks for the warning.'

Imran stepped down from the stone, and Roddy stepped on it. Not being as tall, he struggled to see to the back of the cavity. 'Paul, get your guys over here; we might have found something. Have you got a torch?' Shaw suddenly appeared alert and handed over his torch.

'When fitted, the stone leaves a space at the back. I think it's recent. There are no traces of mortar like there are with the other stones.'

Shaw got busy contacting his boss. Meanwhile, Roddy wandered around the site with renewed interest, pushing back the strands of brambles which tugged at his clothes. 'Imran,' he shouted excitedly, and his colleague rushed to him. 'Look,' Roddy said, pointing at the ground.

'Wow,' Imran exclaimed, 'the missing white Queen.' Roddy photographed the chess piece. 'We'll leave it in position for the forensics' team. I believe we have identified the other sleeper, the eccentric cat lady and adulteress of Tomintoul, Sally Rundell. She is now on a mission and doesn't expect to be back, or she wouldn't have killed her cat.'

33

Ronnie drove through Bridgend and continued on the winding road towards Port Askaig. Just beyond a car park on the left, used by walkers, he turned right down a tarmacked road with passing places which ended just within woods overlooking the River Sorn. Here, six eco-friendly wooden lodges, complete with turf roofs, had been built in a large semi-circle with an office building in a similar style at the entrance to the development. Expensive cars sat outside several lodges and a boat on a trailer beside another.

Pulling over, Ronnie stopped in the visitor's parking space and walked to the office, noting several discreetly positioned CCTV cameras. Hopefully, they would have captured some of the events several nights ago. He was not surprised to be greeted by Pamela, sitting behind the counter, who had been watching his arrival on the monitor beside her desk. She was smartly dressed with a colourful scarf draped around her neck, held in place with a clasp showing the company's emblem, an outline of Islay. Pamela smiled as he entered. A cautious smile, wary of why he had arrived unexpectedly. Pamela flicked back her long black hair, studying him, a habit Ronnie knew only too well.

'Good to see you,' he began, apprehensive himself, 'sorry it has been so long.'

'Indeed, when you live on a remote island like Jura, so far from Islay, it must require a lot of planning to make the journey,' she replied waspishly. 'It is not as if you haven't got a boat if the ferry is cancelled.'

Ronnie held up his hands. 'Point taken.'

'No word of explanation, discarded like an empty whisky barrel left to bob about on the stretch of water that separates us, not knowing where I will end up,' she exclaimed, tilting her head to one side as she raised her eyebrows, looking questioningly at him.

Ronnie sat down on one of the chairs by the counter. 'Shortly after we spoke, Maria phoned me from Romania. She's not coming back. I haven't told anyone. Her life is now over there, looking after Hanna, and her dad is now unwell to complicate matters further.' He gazed at the floor, pausing before continuing. 'Maria asked for a divorce.'

'I know that you loved her. It must be difficult,' but the comment was spoken without any emotion, trying to hide her own hurt.

'Yes and no,' Ronnie replied. 'The stress of what happened to her sister changed her. Our relationship was never the same. I have expected this for some time. I got wrapped up in myself, and I should have let you know to ask for some space – sorry', he finished, looking at Pamela, awaiting a response.

'Communication, Ronnie, you need to talk to me, have confidence in me,' and there was still a hurt edge to her voice. 'Most people our age have issues. You know I have. We need to learn to trust again if it is to work.' Her expression froze; trusting makes you vulnerable.

'Can we try again?' Pamela closed her eyes and opened them, and he could see her eyes glistening.

'If you want to.'

'I do, and I am sorry.'

'Do you want a coffee?'

'That would be great,' and he visibly relaxed. 'How's Max?'

Before replying, Pamela switched on the kettle and added coffee granules to two mugs. 'He's settled at school, loves the teacher and has made friends. All happy there. Primary one is so important.'

'Still loves boats?'

'You know he does.'

'We'll organise a trip. It can't be this weekend. Some VIP from the south is flying in. I have to take him fishing.'

'I am sure Max can wait a few more days.'

'Did you know that Peter Meldrum is missing?'

Pamela appeared shocked. 'I saw him here last week, meeting that Elliot woman.'

'She's also missing.'

'You mean...' Pamela gasped.

'I don't think so; events are more complicated than that. We believe they are both somewhere on the island, last seen in a white van.'

'Not her fancy red car? We get many posh people here, some you like, some are cold. Elliot was cold, not unpleasant, just very business-like. Not Peter's type.'

'I agree, but they have been gone a few days. Last seen the night of the mysterious flare.'

Pamela turned towards the computer screen and touched a few keys. Signed, fully paid. Must have left very early; there was no sign of her the following day. I presumed she had gone for the early ferry. Poor Jenny hasn't been in good form recently.'

'Jenny was concerned that their relationship was more than platonic and drove here the night he didn't come home. She drove into the complex, searching for them and spotted a white van. Could you check it out on the CCTV footage?'

Pamela stopped, her hands poised above the keyboard and stared at Ronnie.

'I want to find my friend, but that isn't the only reason. I regretted that we had parted. Trust me.'

The clicking of the keys started, and Ronnie sighed with relief.

'Here we are,' Ronnie got up and leant across the counter, peering at the screen and leant close. 'There's the white van. Someone is getting out and going into the lodge. They must have the key. I wonder how they got it. Bags are being thrown in the front of the van. It's a woman by size and shape, but not Elliot; she's much taller.'

Ronnie watched as a Land Rover drove in as the van left.

'That's Jenny. Play it back. What type of van is it?'

They played the images back and forth. 'Freeze there.' After a few seconds, he added. 'I'm sure it's a Ford Transit. Sadly, there's no chance of reading the registration plate and no markings.'

'Have you involved the police?'

'Not yet,' and he explained who had been involved and their decision. 'The trouble is, would the police be interested.' He shrugged. 'People separate…' he stopped, realising what he was about to say. 'What's important is that they get back together,' and he gave an embarrassed smile, blushing slightly. Pamela touched his hand. 'You're right,' is all that she said.

34

Henry and Alan visited a few more distilleries in the afternoon, Caol Ila, Arhnahoe, and Bunnahabhain on Islay's east coast overlooking the Sound of Islay. The distilleries were straddled along the same minor road, busy with whisky fans, overlooked by the dominating peaks of the Paps of Jura. Views from the distilleries' still room by design were equally dramatic. Late afternoon, they drove back to Bowmore and stopped at Bridgend Hotel for something to eat. When they entered the bar area, sitting in the corner were Charlie and Drew, head down, talking quietly to each other. Henry observed Drew glance up and kick Charlie under the table, and Charlie's expression froze when he saw the new arrivals.

'Hi Charlie,' Henry called across the room. 'Can we join you for a minute? Do you want a drink?'

Charlie was surprised. 'Never thought you would ever buy me a drink, Mr Smith.' Their previous conversation at Kilchoman had raised questions in Henry's mind. What better time to ask them.

As they approached, Charlie pushed back a spare chair, and the detective sat down as Alan dragged across another chair.

'Oh, Mr Smith, I still get a shock when I see you, old habits,' and he smiled, exposing his missing tooth. He definitely was unsettled by their arrival, soon fidgeting with his long hair.

'Those days have gone now, haven't they?' Henry stated.

'You bet. I'm clean, reformed and enjoying retirement.' Maybe a little too eagerly, Henry thought.

'We're just popping in for a bit to eat and a glass of wine. We've been touring more of Islay's distilleries.' Henry was conscious of Drew observing him, restless and uneasy, not good at concealing his feelings, rubbing one of the tattoos on his arm as if trying to make it disappear.

They exchanged pleasantries with no one making a great effort, discussing the merits of the different distilleries before Henry plunged in. 'Drew, I found the place Gillies built near Saligo, out of curiosity. The guy appears to own half the island. When he has got the money, why is it unfinished?'

Drew seemed relieved by the question, pleased to speak, agreeing with Henry. 'Gillies fell out with the contractors. One day, he found poor Jim Semple sleeping on the job, hungover after a hard night and demanded that he be sacked. Jim was a big part of our team, so we went on strike to show solidarity, and he sacked us all. No changing his mind, and the contractor was stymied; there weren't a lot of labourers on the island. The contractor eventually went bankrupt. I wouldn't like to cross Jim, an ex-marine. He had to be held back from having a go at Gillies. Some say that the police even spoke to him after Gillies took offence at what Jim told him to do with his job.' The memory of what must have been an aggressive exchange made Drew smile.

'It was unfair; we had already put an almighty effort into getting his palace at Port Ellen ready. We had all worked hard for him for many months, and he treated us like dirt. Wouldn't believe the price of the materials, best of everything. Do you know that he has an air-conditioned wine cellar, dug out of the rock behind the house and another room designed to keep his fancy pictures, which he's not displaying at the correct temperature? Major excavations, no regard to cost.'

'Too much money,' Charlie added.

'Sounds like it,' Henry agreed.

Drew continued. 'Had to bring specialists from the mainland to complete some of the work, and they don't come cheap, and then he treats us like scum.' Charlie threw a warning look at Drew as he was getting het up, wanting him to calm down.

'It's how the other half lives. I have been in the Port Ellen house; it's very grand, but what was the point of the Saligo development?'

'His idea was to let cattle winter over on Islay. The mild climate means they develop faster, and farmers from the mainland are willing to pay a premium. He was going to buy land from local farmers, but that fell through, and the project wouldn't work without the extra fields. I suspect he deliberately fell out with the contractor to avoid paying.'

'Not a nice man,' Henry suggested, and Drew responded with a further tirade until Charlie intervened.

'I'm sure Mr Smith has often heard language like yours, but the barman won't be pleased.' Drew glanced at the barman who was drying a pint glass with a cloth and put his head down, scowling.

'So, who lives there?' asked Henry.

'A couple of men, maybe three, are employed as watchmen, not sure what they do, and they keep themselves to themselves. I've never seen them around the rest of the island.'

'They don't have a white van, do they?' enquired Henry hopefully.

Drew appeared puzzled.

'We had a run-in with a white van driver, almost drove us off the road near Kilchoman.' Lies could come so quickly, Henry mused.

'They run about in an old Audi.' Worth trying, thought Henry, now pleased that they had bumped into the pair.

'Do you still want a tour around Bruichladdich, Mr Smith?' Charlie asked.

'We would enjoy a tour,' Alan stated, speaking for the first time, pointedly not looking at his friend.

Drew cheered up, which surprised Henry. 'How about next

Tuesday at about 3pm? I'll have finished for the day. I'll speak to my boss. Turn up at the shop. I'm confident it will be fine.'

'I look forward to that,' Alan replied, making his intent clear.

Henry accepted, realising Alan was keen and that the trip hadn't turned out as planned.

'Give me your number in case we can't make it.' Drew scribbled it down on the back of an old betting slip he fished out of his pocket and handed it over.

'Did the horse win?' Henry enquired.

'Wasn't even placed,' replied Drew, picking up his pint and draining the glass.

35

Jenny reacted with delight as she opened the door to see Alison standing there. The two good friends hugged each other tightly.

'This is a surprise – a good one,' Jenny proclaimed, adding, 'Where's Dylan?' as they moved inside the cottage.

'With his doting grandparents, in Glasgow. Having a granny flat for them has been a bonus. I can watch out for my parents. They, in turn, are still fit enough to care for Dylan. He loves them. Dad is really good with him.'

'Sounds wonderful,' Jenny replied, appearing brighter, cheered by her friend's unexpected arrival. 'Allows us to spend time together. Herbal tea?'

'Of course.'

'I'll get it ready,' and Jenny entered the kitchen. Alison noticed unwashed plates and clothing stacked by the washing machine, ready to be washed. The house was a mess, and her friend needed help.

When Jenny returned, having pulled the cord to move back the vertical slatted blinds to let in more light, Alison was admiring the view from the conservatory over Loch Indaal. 'I do so miss Islay,' she stated. 'It will always be in my heart, what I know as home. The big city has attractions but lacks the big skies, fresh air and the sense of belonging,' and she laughed. 'Me getting too philosophical, at my age too. It's brilliant being back,' her enthusiasm made Jenny smile, which didn't go unnoticed by Alison.

They sat down beside each other. 'Malcolm's been telling me how difficult life has been. I'm here to help,' and she grasped Jenny's hand.

'Thank you,' Jenny replied, 'it's what I need.' Initially, the friends sat in silence, neither needing to speak. Then the dam burst, and they talked for hours, men, babies; no topic was out of bounds, as Jenny unburdened herself. Alison assisted Jenny as they tidied up the house together. 'I feel so much better,' Jenny stated, hugging her friend again.

'That's what friends are for. Malcolm and the others will get to the bottom of Peter's disappearance. He would never be unfaithful; he loves you and Ben. Every marriage goes through difficult periods. I'm frustrated, not angry, with the hours that Malcolm works – and we do argue. Night shifts are so antisocial, and I have to keep Dylan quiet while he catches up on sleep. He is so dedicated,' and she rolled her eyes, making Jenny laugh.

Looking outside, Alison said. 'The weather is brightening up, so it's time for a walk down at the beach. The fresh air will do us good, and Jodie will enjoy it,' and the dog's ears perked up.

Wandering from the house down the road to near the campsite, Alison could observe the positive impact that she had made on her friend's mood. Jodie ran around dropping sticks, waiting for them to be thrown as Border collies always do. As they reached the beach, Alison asked. 'Did you see the mysterious flare? You must have been the closest person on Islay to it.

'What are you talking about?'

Alison was incredulous. 'You didn't know about it? A large green flare on this beach lit up the sky a few nights ago. Quite dramatic, I believe. Many people saw it and thought it was an alien invasion or a meteorite. The switchboard at Malcolm's paper was inundated with reports. Don't tell me you slept through it.'

'Must have,' Jenny confessed. 'I go to bed early most nights and always pull the curtains tight shut in summer, or I can't sleep for the brightness.'

'Did you not spot the helicopters buzzing around for days after?'

'I did wonder what they were doing. I thought it was a military exercise. So, what was it?'

'The Navy lost some equipment, but we will never know for certain. They're very secretive.'

'A navy officer did approach the house, but I hid, not wanting to talk with anyone,' Jenny confessed.

'Jenny,' laughed Alison, 'the biggest news story for ages on Islay, and it passes you by.' She stooped and picked up a stick, throwing it for Jodie. Looking around, she added, 'I don't see any signs of whatever it was.'

Jenny was looking at the seashore, flicking seaweed aside with her foot, when Jodie stopped and sniffed, her tail wagging. Jenny held her hand to her mouth, grabbing Alison's hand and pointing towards rocks by the tide line. Among the seaweed where Jodie was standing, yards away, was part of a plastic casing from a mobile, bobbing about. 'That's Peter's,' she stated, reaching down and picking it up. Alison recognised the photo of Jason and Ben's faces from the remaining part.

'He's in trouble, and I've accused him of being unfaithful.'

Alison pulled out her phone and rang Malcolm.

36

Petrov gave a polite smile to the woman, casually dressed in jeans and a dark blue jacket. She sat opposite him shortly after the train left Waverley Station and pulled in his feet to give her more legroom. In her hand was a magazine, which she started to read, flicking the pages without any real intent to read them. It was almost like a mating signal, attracting his attention. After a few minutes, she placed the magazine on the empty seat beside her and took out her phone, studying it.

'Would you believe it?' Petrov raised his head from studying a leaflet he had picked up at the station to look at the woman. 'The ferry from Mull to Craignure has been cancelled,' she explained, responding to Petrov's gaze.

'When will service be restored?' Petrov replied.

'Not for a few days – propellor problem.'

'Is there an alternative route?'

'Yes, but I will have to change my plans.'

'That is a pity,' concluded Petrov.

There was no more conversation between them. Petrov sat hunched, baseball cap pulled down over his face, partly to avoid recognition but also because he was tired. The last few hours had been stressful since leaving Reeves's flat. Artyom had ordered that he stay in Edinburgh until told to leave. Petrov knew to always obey instructions, even if he didn't understand them, and he had spent time watching a Tom Cruise film in a small cinema to wait where he would be safe. He was amused by the film and knew it bore no relation to reality, but it passed the time, although he left before the end. Later, he stood on Princes Street and watched as a woman walked by, displaying a paper bag with the name of a boutique in Harrogate, which he took from her as she passed. The transfer was quick, and no one would have noticed. He went into a cafe, ordered a coffee, paid for it and sat down. Before leaving, he went to the toilet, changing his shirt and putting on a jumper. He emerged, appearing very different, much to the surprise of the barista behind the counter. It was time to get the train from Waverley. He now knew he had no further business in Edinburgh.

He had cautiously approached the station, hoping that what Artyom had told him about the cameras was correct and joined the train for Glasgow.

The train left Edinburgh behind, having sped through the suburbs and reaching the open countryside, passing the shale bings of West Lothian. Twenty minutes later, it entered a tunnel, and the woman opposite stood up, leaving her magazine behind. By the time the train had left the tunnel, she was waiting at the carriage door. Casually, he leaned across and picked up the magazine. The older man, opposite, seemed amused at his choice of reading material, but Petrov ignored him. There, on page six, was his next set of instructions. Nothing surprised him; nothing fazed him. The train stopped at Falkirk High, and the woman walked past the carriage window, ignoring him, her task completed.

For the rest of the journey, Petrov attempted to sleep. He was a light sleeper and was awakened, alerted by a change in speed as the train slowed down, descending through a tunnel before terminating at Glasgow Queen Street Station. There were a few police about as he alighted the train, but nothing appeared abnormal.

Walking quickly across the concourse, he left the station, crossed George Square and followed the directions he had been given to a Travel Lodge where a room had been booked for him.

He lay down on the bed and used the remote to switch on the TV. Flicking through the channels, he was pleased that Reeves's death was not mentioned. They must still assume it was a heart attack, but a good pathologist would soon discover otherwise, or they were withholding the information.

He had been taught to catch up on sleep where he could during his training, so after eating a baguette he had bought, Petrov showered and turned in. Tomorrow would be a busy day with an early start.

The early train to Oban left at 8.21, so he was up early, completing a series of physical exercises to ensure his body was ready. Petrov didn't bother with breakfast and reached the station and bought a single ticket for Oban and a newspaper. Approaching the gate, he heard an angry shout from behind and walked on, not thinking it was intended for him. However, he heard someone behind catching up and twisted around to see Claire's brother, Andy. Red-faced, slightly taller than Petrov, he remembered him from a party at his house that he had attended. 'Never again,' he proclaimed firmly to Claire as they drove home, 'he is a loudmouth, bigoted thug.' Claire, he recollected, agreed with his assessment; it was apparent they didn't get on. A fervent football supporter, bedecked, as usual, with a scarf in the team's colours, he followed his team all over the country. His team must be playing today, and they were leaving for the match. Now he was inches away from his face, and the last thing Petrov needed was a confrontation, anything that drew attention to him. A friend of his had joined Andy, ready to get involved. He glanced at his watch; the train left in ten minutes.

'Why have you abandoned my sister?' he shouted, speckles of spittle spraying Petrov's face from his pouting lips.

Remaining calm, Petrov replied. 'I haven't. I left abruptly, but I left a message,' which was a lie; he had no intention of returning. 'My phone was cut off because it was still in Helen's name, and she hadn't paid the monthly bill, but I'll be back in two days.'

'So why are you going to Oban then?'

'A personal matter that I would rather not discuss with you.'

'Speak to her then; she has something to tell you,' Andy quickly produced his phone, and within a few seconds, Petrov heard the ringing tone.

Taking the phone from Andy, he pressed it to his ear.

'Hi Andy, I'm just hanging out the washing. It's going to be dry all day,' she answered. Andy stood menacingly inches away.

'It's Paul here. I'm with Andy, who bumped into me; a bit of luck. Did you not get my message?'

'Paul, I'm so relieved. Where are you? Why did you go away?' her voice brighter, hopeful.

'There has been a misunderstanding. You've not got my message.'

'Paul, I'm pregnant,' she quickly stated. 'You left before I could tell you. The Doctor has confirmed it. Are you pleased?'

'That's wonderful,' Petrov replied, conscious that Andy was studying his face for his reaction.

'Wonderful,' he repeated, giving the thumbs up to Andy and grinning. Inside, he felt sick, an unneeded complication.

'I owe you an apology. Helen has been bugging me, wanting money she owes to a gambling company. Remember I told you about her problem.' Petrov was thinking fast. 'She was suicidal. I had to get to her immediately. I'm just about to get on a train to visit her parents and persuade them to get her support.'

Three minutes to the train left.

'I'll need to go. I'll be in touch soon, I promise,' and he handed the phone back to Andy, deliberately letting it slip. The phone fell to the concrete floor and smashed. Andy swore and instinctively reached down to retrieve it. Petrov ran to the ticket machine and fed in his ticket. Grabbing it as it emerged, he ran to the train, leaving Andy cursing in his trail. Out of the corner of his eye, he saw a station official walking smartly across to Andy and his friend.

The guard blew his whistle, and with a jolt, the train edged forward, reaching the tunnel at the end of the platform and pulling away in a minute. Petrov was flushed, out of breath, and cursing his bad luck. Noticing an elderly lady watching him, he drew a deep breath and smiled. 'Almost missed the train.'

So, Claire was pregnant, he hadn't expected that news. No wonder Andy was so angry, not that it took much to wind him up.

…

Jean opened the door to see Claire standing in floods of tears, a red silk dressing gown over her nightdress. Quickly, she ushered her into the lounge.

'I've heard from Paul,' she started between sobs before Jean could speak. 'He had to go away to sort out Helen's gambling debts. He still has to care for her; he's so kind. He was delighted that I am pregnant and will return in a few days.'

'Excellent news,' exclaimed Jean, although she didn't believe it, also curious why the listening devices hadn't picked up the news. The pathologist had found traces of a toxin in Reeves's body; he had been murdered. Jean had stationed herself here in case Petrov made contact.

Jean looked warmly at the poor girl, stroking her back as she sobbed. 'Excellent news,' she repeated. 'Where is he?'

'He was about to get on the train to Oban at Glasgow Queen Street Station. Andy bumped into him. Paul couldn't speak for long, and he was using Andy's, that's my brother, phone. We got cut off. I am so relieved I didn't want to bring up his baby alone.'

'I'll make you a cup of tea. When did he phone? Jean asked casually as she went to the kitchen and filled the kettle. 'Oh, two hours ago,' Claire shouted through. Jean sat down on a tall stool and immediately texted Bill. Time was of the essence. If he was on the train, the police could wait for him, but he would not be far from his destination after two hours. If they were fast, it might be the break they needed and could stop Petrov from causing more harm.

As the kettle boiled, she shouted words of encouragement to Claire. Her phone pinged and showed a thumbs-up emoji. Bill would be acting promptly. Jean readied the tea mugs.

Claire had settled, wiping her eyes with a handkerchief and smiled as Jean put down the mug of tea.

'The last days have been hell,' she said, 'not knowing where he was. Now, at least I have some hope,' and she patted her belly, 'for the both of us.'

'Do you know where Helen's parents live?'

'Not exactly, but he did say up north, so he might be going to see them.'

Jean knew that Helen had left the country weeks ago. She had to admire Petrov's quick thinking. Confronted with Claire's brother, he had managed to talk himself out of a tricky situation and placate Claire. Not to be underestimated, she considered. But where was he really going? And why.

Her phone pinged again. 'It's Bill, wanting to know if I need any shopping,' she lied.

Bill was moving fast, arranging a welcoming party for Petrov, assuming he was heading for Oban. The team could not make it there in time and had to depend on the local police. But to their advantage, Petrov didn't know that he had been rumbled.

37

Few people were on the train, consisting of only two carriages. Petrov could hear a rowdy group in the next carriage, which he could glimpse through the connecting tunnel. They seemed like a group of hill walkers with brightly coloured anoraks, backpacks and all the gear, using the train to reach the hills. Laughing and talking loudly, they were spread over several seats, some sipping hot drinks from flasks. In Petrov's carriage was the white-haired old lady, still clutching a shopping bag and a family with two young kids at the far end. The kids, occupied drawing with crayons on paper.

Petrov relaxed as the distance from the station increased. Cursing that he had bumped into Claire's brother. Still, he couldn't see how it would damage the mission. The scenery changed from urban to travelling beside the Firth of Clyde, with wading birds pecking on the muddy estuary shore with the tide out, revealing only a narrow channel for shipping marked by buoys, with views across the Firth towards towns on the far side. Then he spotted the volcanic crag, with its castle perched on top and sat bolt upright, realising why he was being sent this way. Flying in by helicopter, it was the landmark which would orientate the pilot. He allowed himself a smile.

'It's a long journey,' the old lady suddenly stated. She appeared more relaxed, her shopping bag on the empty seat beside her. Now, she had pulled out her knitting, and the click-click of her needles added to the steady rhythm of the train.

'Yes,' was all Petrov could reply, but eventually added, 'Beautiful scenery.' In Scotland, he knew that was often a good reply. Locals liked you praising their country's natural beauty.

'I'm visiting my brother in Oban; he is quite unwell.' Petrov noticed her suitcase that someone, presumably a porter, had put on the luggage rack above her head.

'I, too, am visiting family in Oban, but I have never travelled on this route by train before.'

'You'll enjoy the journey, especially if the clouds aren't down on the hills.'

The lady concentrated on her knitting, and Petrov looked out the window. The train lurched as it veered right, and the overhead catenary disappeared. Petrov now knew where he was. A loch appeared to the left as he passed Faslane, the home of Britain's nuclear deterrent. The train slowed as it navigated a tight S-bend. Petrov could picture the map in his mind.

He had trained on a mock-up of this site in his own country and could imagine the layout and his part in the operation. The *Spetsnaz* were trained to attack key positions; this was one of them in Britain. If any conflict didn't become nuclear, the *Spetsnaz* would swoop in by helicopter and try and destroy the facility. The troops and equipment would be concealed in a converted ship, foreign-flagged. Then, troops would disembark by helicopter to begin their attack. The irony was that he was now passing by the site without a weapon. He knew this was why he had been sent by rail, to remind him of his duty. As a *Spetsnaz*, he wasn't expected to survive long in battle. He was now on active duty. Don't forget the message. Petrov glanced across at the old lady, her head bowed as she knitted. She could never imagine who was sitting across from her.

The train stopped shortly after at Garelochhead Station, where a young couple got on. Below the track, down a steep embankment, was Loch Long, with more naval facilities, and to his right, Glen Douglas, where Britain's nuclear weapons were stored. High fences were strung along the trackside. The *Spetsnaz* plans were suicidal, he realised. The *Spetsnaz* were not the equivalent of the SAS, with their stress on individual endurance. It was a special force trained for surveillance, deception, and speed to disrupt the enemy. Unlike many Russian armed forces, the *Spetsnaz*, the 'tip of the spear', were trained to show initiative, where blind obedience was favoured over initiative by regular troops.

Beyond the station, the route ran parallel to the loch, and at the next station, the hill walkers got off, a noisy, excited group keen to reach the hills. Petrov noticed the old lady dozing, her head slumped. A loch appeared on the right-hand side before the train entered a long valley.

Petrov remembered the day that the colonel called him into his office. Expecting a disciplinary remand for some minor violation was the only reason the colonel usually ever asked to see any of his troops. Instead, he was surprised to see a small balding man in an ill-fitting suit sitting on the chair beside the desk, poring over Petrov's service history details. As he entered and saluted, the man studied him carefully.

The colonel didn't introduce the man but glanced at him, waiting for him to speak, appearing nervous.

'You have come to our attention.' Petrov kept his eyes ahead, still standing at attention, unsure if he was in trouble. 'We are going to train you in new skills, and you will serve the motherland and bring glory to your family.' Petrov knew to click his heels and agree; he had no choice. So began years of training, mastering English and learning to live as an Englishman or a Scotsman. He had an ear for dialects, one reason he presumed he had been chosen. There was a group of them, and he could remember their names, although all had since acquired British names. They were to become sleeper agents, settle in Britain and work their way in society to positions of influence, a long-term project. That thought reminded him of Reeves', who had apparently done so well but must have failed probably because of his dalliances with women. He knew the penalty for that; failure was not an option. Towards the end of his training, he was again taken aside and assigned a new role. You will lie low until your country needs you, he was informed. You will then carry out assassinations or other acts of sabotage in times of war or when your government requires it. The action had now started, almost a relief after years of waiting.

The train slowed as it reached Crianlarich, exposing another valley that ran at right angles. The sun played on the peaks to the north. Petrov imagined that this would be an excellent terrain to train in.

The old lady had sat up with a jolt when the train stopped, read the station sign and then resumed knitting. The family exited the carriage, and he didn't see anyone coming on.

Before long, the next station was reached, and he observed a busy village with cafes and a large car park, almost full. The route turned west, passing through narrow valleys, often tree-lined lochs, and close to a ruined castle. He appreciated the contrast between his homeland and its expansive, flat plains. In other circumstances, he would love to explore these hills.

The track bed then hung above the road, busy with tourist traffic; beyond the road was a loch, their companion for many miles. He heard a police siren and saw two police cars struggling to progress, flashing at vehicles wanting them to move over. The train kept pace with them as the traffic held them back. Petrov survived on his training and instinct. Some might feel that he was paranoid, but their presence suggested something was not right. Maybe they were going to the scene of an accident, but maybe not. Their presence made him nervous. He assumed they were heading towards Oban and didn't want to encounter them. Ahead, he noted a large cantilever road bridge, and the train's motion slowed. Petrov had been on the train for almost three hours. He glanced at his watch; fifteen minutes from Oban and Connel Ferry was the last station before the town.

Decisively, he got up, startling the old lady, who was slumbering again.

'This isn't Oban,' she declared. He smiled and pressed the open button, exiting onto a single platform with a Perspex canopy passenger shelter. Leaving the station, he saw a taxi parked on the concourse. 'How quickly can you take me to Oban?' he asked the startled driver.

'Probably, not as quick as the train you just left.'

'Never mind, do your best, and he brandished a few notes.'

'Okay, get in. I won't break any speed limits,' he warned.

'Do your best'. The taxi pulled out onto the main road behind. Petrov heard the wailing sound of a siren approaching. He was ahead of the police.

Petrov noted the driver watching him in the rear-view mirror.

'My girlfriend is waiting for me,' Petrov explained. 'I want to see how disappointed she'll be when I don't get off the train. Then she will turn around and spot me.'

'And you'll rush into each other's arms, just like the films.' The driver shook his head, not totally convinced. 'She must be some girl,' he stated. Petrov allowed himself to smile knowingly.

The road hugged the coast, taking a long way around, while the train headed inland. The taxi was not going to win the race. Behind the taxi, the police cars eventually appeared, and the driver pulled over, letting them pass. They were in a hurry, and the police looked tense. It might be a coincidence, but he was cautious.

Eventually, the taxi reached Oban, driving down a steep hill to a busy shopping precinct beside the harbour. The traffic was congested, and the vehicle slowed to a crawl. Petrov had memorised the street layout in the coastal town, knew where to collect the car he would use next, and asked the taxi driver to stop outside a Waterstones bookshop. Paying, he wandered along the street towards the station. His instincts were correct. The train had arrived to a warm welcome. Police cars were abandoned at the station, and several police officers were wandering around; two carried guns. Another officer was quizzing the old lady, who appeared bemused as she was led along the platform.

Petrov drifted into the shadows and made his way from the station. Now, he was worried. He had been outed. Thoughtful, he strolled towards a side street, where he knew to pick up a car. The car was unlocked, and he reached under a cushion in the back seat and collected the keys. He drove heading south. Whoever had found out about him would be disappointed to have missed him.

38

Petrov drove steadily, not wanting to draw attention to himself. Still convinced that the police welcome at Oban Station must have been for him, knowing that he now had to be extra cautious, but thankful that his instincts had been right. He would assume that the police were searching for Paul Russell, linking him to the murder of Felix Reeves. Petrov consoled himself that it had been only a matter of time before they were hunting for him. Whatever the circumstances – keep going and never give up. That message had been drilled into him.

The road south was windy, passing numerous sea lochs in an indented coastline. Half an hour into his journey, Petrov saw a sign for forest walks and drove into a car park a few hundred yards on. The weather was damp, a grey mist descending discouraged visitors, and the car park was deserted, with an overflowing litter bin in one corner. He parked the car against the conifers' sandy edge with the boot facing away from the road and got out. The infernal midges descended, and he swatted them away as he opened the boot, removing camping gear and a holdall containing clothes and rations. They had catered for his every need. With the boot cleared, he lifted the liner, exposing a metal lid he prised open. Inside was an oiled cloth, which he lifted out while checking no one was arriving. He carefully unwrapped it. As requested, a VSS Vintorez silenced sniper rifle and a 9mm GSh-18 pistol were inside. Petrov was familiar with both. He wrapped the weapons in the cloth again, lifted them out, and put them in a backpack which had been provided. The backpack was already heavy with magazines and bullets. Now, all he had to do was practice, ensuring his skills were still of a standard suitable for the mission ahead.

He slipped on the backpack, locked the car and followed the path away from the car park. The conifers were drenched with moisture, and spider webs were exposed on some branches. A mile up the route marked with red flashes, he stopped, sniffing the air, a nervous habit of his, and left the path, fighting through bushes, soaking his clothes until he stood at the bottom of a disused quarry. Skirting a pond filled with stagnant water, he worked past large stones left behind by the quarrymen until he found a suitable spot. After checking that no one was around, he unloaded his weapons and checked all the working parts. Satisfied that the guns had been well maintained, he took the sniper rifle, studied the sights, loaded the magazine and practised focusing on different objects, holding the wooden butt into his shoulder. Muscle memory-guided him. While best at short ranges, he favoured this rifle. Petrov would just have to ensure he got close enough to his victim.

Listening for some time before he was convinced that no one was nearby, he lay down, adjusting his position until he was comfortable and fired several rounds. Not pleased with his initial efforts, he reloaded and tried again; this time, the results were better, and he felt more relaxed. Likewise, he practised with the handgun. Finally, he put the weapons away and started to walk back to the car.

As he approached the car park, he heard people talking and stopped, hiding behind a conifer. Cyclists dressed in Lycra were unloading bikes from a bike rack on the roof of their car. Petrov watched them until they locked their car, mounted their bikes and rode off along one of the trails. It was better he wasn't seen. He quickly reached the car, stored away his backpack and drove off, feeling better that he still had the old skills.

Driving on, he reached Kilmartin village and took a single-track road heading south. There were only isolated cottages, bleak moorland, lochs, and low hills, not helped by the absence of sun. Half an hour into his journey, as the views were opening out towards the sea and what he knew was the Paps of Jura in the distance, he pulled off the road beside a metal gate at the beginning of a rough track to a white-walled cottage. A shiny metal chimney stood proud of the tiled roof. A wire fence surrounded the house, enclosing a mossy lawn to the front. In the nearby fields, sheep munched at the grass. On the sea side of the road was a boat shed painted white. Both buildings were of modern design. Petrov reached across the car to the glove box, removed a small pebble with a red cross, and shoved it in his pocket. He got out, aware that he was being watched by someone in the house, opened the gate, and walked to the house.

The door opened as he arrived.

'Olga,' he stated, smiling, trying to appear friendly. He had forgotten how small Olga was and her expressive face that struggled to hide her emotions. Petrov always considered her unsuitable, but few people were willing to make the necessary sacrifices.

'Denis,' she replied, eyes anxious, unsmiling. Eventually, she pulled the door further and let him in.

'I was told to expect you,' she muttered, indicating a cushioned seat by the log burner.

There was no pretence of a smile on Petrov's face now. 'What happened?' he asked as he sat down.

'Treachery,' Olga replied, her voice high with emotion. 'At first, I thought there had been an accident,' and Olga outlined what had occurred.

Petrov listened without indicating what he was thinking, studying the carpet.

'I reported the treachery immediately,' she concluded.

Petrov looked up, reading the fear on her face. 'You had no idea this would happen.'

'No, or I would have acted on it, told others of my concerns.'

It was what he expected, but it had to be rectified immediately. Olga's fate was of no concern to him.

'I will report back.'

'Please don't damn me,' she urged, a pleading note in her voice.

'That is for others,' he lied. 'My task is to clear up this mess,' and he stood up. Olga backed off.

He thought the woman was petrified and not up to the task, but he would leave her to reflect on what she did.

'I must go,' he stated, and Olga stepped back again, scared, as he brushed past her and left. He turned once as he walked back to the car, and she was still standing by the open door, her face ashen. People like her were of no use to the cause. As he reached the gate, he closed it behind him and placed the pebble beside the gate post, concealing his actions from her. It would only complicate the situation if she attempted to escape.

Olga knew her fate, but it wasn't for him to deliver; he had other urgent matters. A mile up the road, he stopped, reached into the glove box again, and pulled out an envelope. Inside was a ticket for a ferry crossing. He noted the time on the clock in the car. Petrov had to make the late sailing. A swift calculation indicated time was tight, and he drove faster, cursing that people could mess up so badly.

Petrov left the road he had travelled down before reaching Kilmartin, took a road running parallel to the Crinan Canal and rejoined the last stretch of the road to Lochgilphead. The road south to Tarbert was no better, and he was held up behind a vehicle hauling a caravan, which seemed oblivious to Petrov's presence. Impatient, he tooted his horn and flashed his lights. Eventually, on a straight stretch, the driver noticed him and slowed. Petrov went down a gear, put his foot to the floor, accelerated past him, and kept his speed up, reaching the top of the hill leading down to Tarbert. The latest check-in time was half an hour before the boat sailed, and he made it with minutes to spare, showing the attendant his booking confirmation.

'Thank you, Mr Jones, the attendant said, go to lane five.' For a split second, Petrov hesitated, not recognising the name used on the booking form. Then, he followed the attendant's instructions. The ferry had almost unloaded. Shortly after, the queue in front started to move, and he was directed onto the car deck. Leaving his car, he climbed the steep steps into the vessel's bowels, ate for the first time in what had been a long day, and washed the food down with coffee. He never noticed the cars that failed to make the ferry.

39

Roddy and Imran were shown into the interview room. They had driven fast to Oban after being told Petrov was on the train. They arrived at the railway station a couple of hours after the train had arrived without Petrov. The station area next to the ferry terminal on the Oban waterfront still had more police officers than usual.

After waiting for fifteen minutes, a police inspector came in to join them. He was probably early forties and already bald, slight in stature, with piercing blue eyes, and sat down opposite them, wiping his brow with a hanky.

'I'm Brian Matheson', and he extended a hand and shook their hands firmly.

'Sorry, we had a run-in with a prisoner on remand and had to restrain him. Now your Paul Russell,' and he fixed them with a knowing look as if to say we all know that is not his real name. 'He got off the train at Connel Ferry Station and then took a taxi into Oban. We have spoken to an elderly lady who travelled in the same carriage. She's enjoying her moment of fame and accurately describes Russell and saw him get into a taxi. We've traced the taxi driver, and he thought his story about surprising his girlfriend was unbelievable. The taxi driver dropped him off outside the Waterstones bookshop in Oban and saw Russell head towards the station. The driver couldn't turn around because the street was so busy and drove on. He then observed Russell walking away from the station, which he thought even odder, given the story Russell had spun. Something spooked Russell, who knows the police are probably searching for him. There was almost no one else on the train.'

Matheson paused, but neither Imran nor Roddy spoke.

'Okay, we can link him to the murder in Edinburgh, but you guys have a bigger agenda. You need to find him and quick. Am I correct?'

'Yes, but we can't say much...' Roddy began, but Matheson held up his hand.

'We are searching for him and studying CCTV. It'll take time, but hopefully, we can trace his route. Sit tight for the moment.'

'I can help,' Imran stated, 'I'm experienced in analysing camera images, and I have already spent hours searching for him in other locations.

'We are busy; offer accepted, but our coverage of the town isn't great,' replied Matheson.

'I'll check in with our boss to see if there are any updates,' Roddy added.

'Good lads, keep me posted,' he got up and left. Minutes later, a policewoman came in and took Imran away.

'Be sure to come back and visit me,' Roddy called out as Imran left.

Given the description the old lady and the taxi driver provided, the operative and Imran knew who to look for, but progress was frustrating. Two cameras were not working; one was very grainy. Imran scrutinised the footage of a camera close to an industrial estate. Still, he couldn't be convinced that it was the suspect. Petrov was proving elusive, probably trying to avoid the cameras; he was a shrewd operator, an elusive prey. Imran was gaining respect for him.

Roddy signed out and wandered outdoors; the contrast between the bleak interview room and the brightness outside was stark. Tourists and locals buzzed about; the streets were busy, some simply enjoying themselves, others going about their business. Roddy walked past the railway station, which was close to the police station and sat down on a bench by the water's edge, tempted to have an ice cream, when his phone rang. Glancing at the screen, he saw Swan's name flash up. Checking that no one was around, he accepted the call.

'The police have released Reeves's phone records,' Swan began, ignoring pleasantries. 'Reeves spoke with McIntosh, the UK defence minister, only days before he was murdered. This isn't very comfortable, given what we now know about Reeves. I've checked with the defence ministry, but McIntosh is away on a planned trip for the weekend to Islay. Petrov is in that general area. We can't take risks. I want the two of you to get across to Islay ASAP, and Ash will join you. She should be waiting for you at the ferry terminal. We need a presence on the island in case something happens. I spoke to the ministry and wanted McIntosh's trip called off, but his private secretary stated it was too late; he is travelling to Scotland as we speak and will fly to Islay tomorrow. Get moving.'

'Imran is searching CCTV footage searching for Petrov. I'll get him, and we'll head to the ferry now.'

'Good, Roddy. I want McIntosh safe to avoid any embarrassment to the intelligence services. In other circumstances, I would be pleased to remove him myself,' and with that curt announcement, he finished the call.

Back at the police station, Roddy collected Imran, who had failed to spot Petrov on the CCTV footage and bidding farewell to Inspector Matheson, they drove south, reaching Lochgilphead and continuing south on the A83. South of the Kilberry junction, they encountered a tailback. Police were on the scene and advised them to turn around and take the narrow, winding Kilberry road that would bypass Tarbert. Other drivers took the same action, and the narrow road quickly became congested. Frustrated, they lost time and finally arrived at the ferry too late. They watched the ramp rise as the ferry pulled away from the terminal.

As they turned around, Ash appeared in her vehicle, also too late.

'The accident delayed me,' she said, 'a tourist bus collided with a car on a tight corner.'

'Well, there's always tomorrow, and McIntosh doesn't arrive until then,' Imran added.

'But who will tell Swan.' And they laughed.

40

Ronnie was busy preparing *Casablanca* for his VIP. However, after meeting with Mike from the Whisky Shop, he updated Malcolm. The rest had gathered at Jenny's house as the long summer evening ended, the sun setting beyond the Rhinns casting a red hue over Loch Indaal. Alan stood by the open patio doors in the conservatory, admiring the view. Outside, the dusk chorus of the birds was starting, and there was a chill in the air. He closed the doors, using the cord to shut the vertical slatted blinds and joined the others. Having greeted her husband on his arrival, Alison made refreshments for everyone. At the same time, Jenny sat in the corner, brighter than Henry remembered on her last visit but still not very communicative, holding a twisted hanky in her hands. Ben was asleep in his bedroom.

'I spoke with Ronnie,' Malcolm announced, 'who has been to Mike's home. There was little he could add about Shaun and Nora. They keep very much to themselves – very private, and he knows nothing about their background. They live out at Sanaigmore, and he has never seen Sir Angus at the shop and was unaware of any connection. They are away on holiday and unsure when they might return. He did add that they know little about whisky and are just good salespeople.'

'We are no further forward with that line of enquiry,' Henry concluded. 'I've been down to the beach where the case of Peter's phone was found before I came here,' Henry added. 'To me, it puts a different slant on his disappearance.' He was trying to choose his words carefully, conscious of Jenny's presence. 'I don't pretend to understand how there could be any possible connection with the mysterious flare-up I saw a few nights ago, but I need to keep an open mind.'

'Smashing a phone is a deliberate act by Peter or someone else. If you were disappearing with someone,' Malcolm also chose his words carefully, 'why do that.'

Jenny was still slumped on a chair but following the conversation intently. Malcolm had filled her in on what he knew, including the sighting of Peter and Cash in the van, but not about Cash's earring or button being found. Henry and Malcolm decided that would be too traumatic.

'And why abandon her car and drive off in a van,' Henry added. 'I am beginning to believe that Sir Angus misled us. His reporting of spotting Peter and Cash in the white van put a slant on our investigations, pointed towards them eloping. He also offered to pay for me to investigate Peter's disappearance, making him appear a good guy trying to help. Since then, I have learnt a lot about Gillies, and none of it is positive. Could he be involved and stopping us from getting the police involved?'

'What is his motive?' Malcolm asked.

'Not wanting anything to disrupt his meeting with McIntosh would be one, hoping Peter will turn up eventually.'

'It's possible, or maybe something more sinister is going on,' replied Malcolm. 'If so, what?'

'Brick wall, no idea. I question if they are still on Islay, although all evidence suggests that is the case. I'm uneasy, and I think we should involve the police.'

'Okay, Henry, but what do we say.'

'They have been gone too long, no sightings. Car found abandoned, can't trace the Ford Transit.'

'They would have to interview Sir Angus. His status probably makes them reluctant, especially with McIntosh's arrival.'

'We are going around in circles, and they are still missing,' Alan stated bluntly, finally speaking out. 'Go to the police. How long must we wait?'

Henry had begun to appreciate his friend's intuition but glanced towards Jenny to see how she was reacting. Jenny also did not want the police involved. He understood why they had not gone to the police, but now it was different.

'I know I haven't been myself. I'm still not, if I am honest. I was too angry with Peter; his actions were the final straw for me, but Elaine and Alison helped me. The discovery of the broken case from his phone on the beach alarms me. He would never throw it away. Remember, he ran into trouble at Machir Bay before. I thought something like that couldn't happen again, but now I'm unsure. It's a nightmare; who has taken him?'

'It can't be McGory or his associates; they're dead or in prison,' Malcolm added quickly, trying to console her. 'We know that the Navy searched the area where the phone casing was found looking for lost equipment. I don't know if they found what they sought, but I'll ask more questions.'

'Go to the police,' Jenny stated. 'I appreciate all your efforts and friendships, but we must find him before...' and her voice tailed off. Everyone could complete the sentence. The emotional edge to her voice convinced Henry.

'I don't like admitting defeat, but we should listen to Jenny. I'll go to the police station first thing tomorrow.' He looked at the darkening sky outside. 'I suspect that no one will be at the station right now, and even if they are, there is little they can do tonight. We are on Islay, after all.'

Alison indicated she would stay with Jenny, and the others left.

41

Petrov had studied the map of Islay on the ferry to reinforce what he already knew. As the ferry glided up between Islay and Jura, he noticed the rugged barrenness of the two opposing shores and the scree-lined peaks on Jura. He appreciated the solitude of wild places and enjoyed his company with little need for socialising or companionship. Helen had been to him a partner; they had had a working partnership with both having a commitment to a cause, which was more important than any personal feelings. These reflections made him think of Claire, carrying his baby, and how she has been different. Petrov was contemptuous of Western values and always felt like a stranger in a strange land, a phrase he had heard often. Claire had somehow made him do things where everyone else had failed. He was too cynical to think it was love, but he did wonder how he would have been as a father. Not very good, Petrov mused. He would soon be gone, returning home, so any such thoughts were quickly dismissed.

When the ferry docked, he trooped down to his car with many others, impatient to get off the vessel and onto Islay. He sat in his vehicle to be directed and waited to get allowed off. Petrov was in a convoy of cars heading up the steep incline from Port Askaig and was content to take his time. With a photographic memory, he could tie in place names with the maps of Islay he had studied. Eventually, the convoy, now reduced in number, reached Bridgend and the turn-off for Port Charlotte, which Petrov ignored for the moment. Then, he was driving along the shore of a loch with a village in sight. Lochs would always remind him of Scotland, and the landscape was not too dissimilar to some areas of his homeland he had encountered on training expeditions, including the infernal midges.

Bowmore was small, with the landmark round church at the top of the hill. He slowed down to study the shops, and then he was up and past the church. Petrov scoffed at believers. There was no meaning in life, only atoms and molecules and by some crazy coincidence, life had begun. You obeyed the state and placed responsibility in its hands to look after you. Sometimes, and he was one, the state selected you to follow instructions and defend its interests, whatever the consequences.

Now driving towards Port Ellen, he carefully examined the airport, deserted at night. Fifteen minutes later, he arrived at the campsite, spoke with the owner and having paid for the overnight stay, he found a place among the sand dunes at the end of a long stretch of sand. Petrov pitched his tent, took out a small stove, and soon boiled water for coffee. As he sipped the coffee, the sun was setting, and he pulled on a fleece against the breeze from the loch.

Petrov was pleased to have reached his destination without snags but remained vigilant. What he was about to do would change a lot of lives. That made him think about Olga. Despite being puzzled that Petrov had left her alone, she knew her fate and still realised that the price for failure was death. He was disappointed in her meek acceptance. However, the powers directing him wanted him here, allowing someone else to deliver the final blow. Poor Olga, he remembered her well from training, and now their paths had crossed in a foreign land far from home.

With the sun finally setting, Petrov crawled into his tiny tent and made himself comfortable rehearsing what he had to do next. Greed and betrayal had consequences, and the state could never let anyone imagine they were beyond its reach.

42

Sally Rundell was tired, having driven all day. Tomintoul was far behind. Aviemore, Fort William, Oban, she had seen them all. Now they blurred into one long image, like a reel of film, a never-ending stream of images. Outside Fort William, she had driven up Glen Roy as instructed. Climbing a winding road to an empty car park at the top, a viewing point without any view on this day, thick clouds capping the hilltops. On the opposite side from a tourist board with information about the history and geology of the glen was a Citroen van, white, streaked with dirt, unremarkable. She parked her car beside it and transferred over her few belongings, careful with the small package containing the vial which she placed under the passenger seat. There was a packet of wipes in the van's passenger seat, and she used these to clean her own car.

She heard a twig snap in the bushes beside the car park, and a bush moved; a bird flew up in the air, startled. Someone was watching her, as usual. Probably waiting to drive off in her car once she left. For a second, she wanted to shout out. 'I can see you; you're caught,' but that was not playing the game and wouldn't win her Brownie points.

Another piece of her past was left behind, a feature of her unravelling story. In many ways, she was glad; now there would be a resolution, no longer living in never-never land waiting for the call. The tension she lived with was ending for good or bad, and Rundell didn't really care about the outcome.

Some people could quickly settle in a foreign land and assume a new cultural identity, but Rundell now realised that wasn't for her.

Living with strangers was difficult, but the surveillance made life so challenging. Was that customer in the Post office, wanting to send a parcel, or was it someone checking how she was doing? Had her accent lapsed, did she show signs of stress or simply someone using the service. Did the woman sitting across from her in the café scrutinise her to check if her manners were British enough or was she was simply a lonely person looking for company? All sleepers were watched; she was told in training to get used to it.

Then, there was more intrusive inspection. On several occasions whilst out, someone had broken in and gone through Rundell's possessions. Nothing was ever taken, but it was as if her life was being itemised, degraded to check the purity of her existence. Even in deepest Scotland, the tentacles of the state could reach her and make her feel uncomfortable. "You might think you are alone, but you never are," they told her in training. It was a statement of fact but also a threat. And Rundell resented it.

Training had been challenging, and there she stopped, refusing to expand her train of thought. She knew where it would lead and refused to go there, especially now. Once the task was completed, she could go home.

She was south of Oban, on a winding road, sometimes coastal, at other times inland, views frequently masked by conifers. Suddenly, she felt overwhelmed by exhaustion and wanted to pull over to rest. 'You must keep going,' another message drilled into her because you might not start again if you stop. 'Failure was not an option.'

Rundell reached Kilmartin, which she knew meant 'church of Martin' from her time in Scotland. Break a rule, she decided and stopped in a café for a strong coffee, which revived her. Feeling better, she continued to head south, the road becoming narrower, the loch to her left dazzling in the sun, and each bush came complete with a long shadow. Rundell stopped on the crest of a low hill and saw ahead a white cottage with a boat shed on the opposite side of the road. The dwelling was secluded, with access to the sea, and she understood why it was chosen. A car was parked beside the cottage at the end of a rough driveway.

So, Olga was in, she thought. Probably waiting in fear. Rundell released the handbrake and drove slowly forward, not desperate to complete the task. Driving past, she noticed a red skirt on a washing line wafting in the wind. She remembered that red was always Olga's favourite colour, a part of her identity not lost. It was possible still to be you, even if it was only a minor victory. A mile on, Rundell turned the van around and returned to the cottage. Parking the car at the gate, she opened it, noting the stone Petrov had left – guilty. By the time she had walked a few yards, Olga was standing at the door, watching her, arms crossed.

Rundell reached her, and Olga pulled back wordlessly, letting her enter.' You are my second visitor today,' she eventually said. Without asking, Rundell sat down where hours before Petrov had sat.

'I tried my best,' Olga began, and Rundell felt empathic, understanding her situation. Sadly, there was only one outcome. Rundell fingered the wire loop in her pocket, stopping as she saw Olga noticing the movement.

'Who else was here?' Rundell enquired, more to make conversation.

'Denis, you remember him.'

'Denis Petrov?'

'Yes.'

This was where her training was helpful. Remaining calm, Rundell stood up, and Olga backed off. Moving swiftly, Rundell closed the space between them, the wire loop exposed in her hand. Olga almost seemed to resign herself as the noose was cast over her head and tightened. Olga made a gurgling noise, then tried to fight, as at last self-preservation kicked in, but it was too late, and she sank to the floor.

This had been a late addition to her mission, no chess piece delivered, just instructed to eliminate Olga for her failings. Rundell held Olga in contempt, having been a witness during training to what took place; she made no comment, too frightened to respond, a one-time friend who had failed her. The Novichok was for a couple in Lanarkshire, traitors who had endangered the lives of many brave people – tartan Skripals. Now, it had other uses.

43

The three of them were at the ferry terminal just after six in the morning, now sharing one car, to book for the crossing to Islay. They had managed to find accommodation in Tarbert and skipped breakfast, knowing they could eat on the vessel. As they arrived, they were warned of a problem with the sailing. The MV *Finlaggan* loomed above the pier, the bow doors firmly shut as they were directed to a holding lane. Suddenly, skipping breakfast did not seem such a good idea. Ash sat in the car, her fingers drumming on the steering wheel, while the other two checked their phones for updates.

Eventually, they were informed of a delay, a problem with the ramp doors, but the staff member appeared confident of a quick resolution. There was nothing they could do but wait, frustrating as it was.

...

Early next morning, Henry climbed the steep, narrow road from Shore Street and, reaching the top, turned left on Beech Avenue towards the Police Station, retracing his route when he called on the Soutars. When he visited them, the Police Station, almost opposite their house, appeared practically deserted. Today, as he suspected, the scene was different. The low white flat-roofed building was a hive of activity. There were two police minibuses outside, as well as two police cars. Fred McIntosh knew how to draw a crowd. One of the minibuses had police inside waiting patiently. The other was empty, presumably having disgorged its passengers somewhere.

Henry used the disabled ramp to access the building and was about to enter when the door opened. Out came a police inspector, who immediately stopped.

'Henry,' she stated warmly, 'good to see you. What are you doing on Islay and entering a police station? I thought these days had gone.' Lena was a good head shorter than Henry but full of energy and drive. Henry had encountered Lena at a particularly gruesome murder scene when she was a young constable, unfazed by what she witnessed. He had marked Lena down then for a successful career and had been proved correct. Still young, her blonde hair neatly plaited, only some fret lines at the side of her eyes suggested ageing.

'Police Superintendent Marshall,' using her title deliberately with a warm smile, 'I don't think I have had the opportunity to congratulate you yet.'

'All down to the encouragement of people like you,' she responded.

'Over here to keep Red Fred safe?'

'You're not meant to know about his visit.' Some police officers would have attempted to deny that someone was visiting, but Lena was not one. Refreshingly direct.

'Islay does not usually require such a turnout,' and he waved his hands towards the minibuses.

'You haven't answered my questions.'

'Islay part holiday, part business. I now have a small company searching for missing people. It keeps me busy.'

Lena touched his arm briefly, 'So sorry to hear about Mary. You've had a tough time. Life can be so unfair,' and her compassion extended beyond her sympathy for Mary.

'Who are you searching for on Islay, or is it just the perfect dram?'

'I've tried a few, but I must do more research. Sir Angus asked me to come over,' and her eyebrows arched. 'A private family matter. He also asked me to find out the whereabouts of Peter Meldrum, a local man well-known on the island. That's why I'm here. Sir Angus told me or implied that he had disappeared with a woman, a business associate. It's been several days, and while I feel he is still on the island, I am becoming concerned.'

'Not a good day to report it, Henry. We are so busy waiting for the Defence Secretary to arrive after his visit to Faslane this morning. The ferry has also broken down, hence the empty minibus. What are your concerns?'

'Missing too long with no contact. There were signs of trouble at the site of their last sighting, and we found the broken casing of Meldrum's phone on a beach. Her car has been found after being moved around the island by people unknown. I believe that Sir Angus may have misled us accidentally or otherwise.'

'Your gut feeling?' she asked.

'He and Cash, his associate's name, are in trouble.'

'Speak to the duty officer. Leave your contact details, and I will try to speak later,' she replied, but we are too busy now.'

Marshall left him and walked to the minibus full of police, and as she did so, the door of the police station opened again.

Chief Inspector Arthur Rogers was the opposite of Marshall and immediately recognised Henry.

'I thought you were banned from police stations.'

'I have the duty of any citizen to report a crime.'

'Pity you didn't live up to these standards,' Rogers stated, full of fancy braid and self-importance.

Please help me, Mary; Henry prayed as his blood pressure soared.

'I have never doubted my standards,' Henry replied, failing to hide his irritation.

'Too late, the police do not accept corrupt practices. You were fortunate to be allowed to retire early.'

'That's your opinion; as usual, you haven't bothered to find the truth.' Henry knew this wasn't helping his quest for help, but his wounds were still raw.

'I have more important people to deal with than washed-up cops,' and Rogers strode past Henry, barking out an instruction to the driver of one of the police cars.

Henry spun around and marched off, trying to control his temper. It was not his first run-in with Rogers, who, to Henry, epitomised the worst type of police officer. His duty was to find the missing persons, not rake over old injustices, and he had probably failed.

...

Petrov was up, staying inside his tent, not wanting to be seen. Pulling back the flap of his tent, he studied the beach. As the early morning plane approached the airport, he watched it land through binoculars. Habits were entrenched, especially on duty. However, he had work to do, and he left the tent, returned to his car, and drove off, heading towards Bowmore.

Petrov drove to the distillery in Bowmore and up School Street, leaving the road beyond the distillery and taking a short coastal path overlooking Loch Indaal, leading to Battery Point. There in the bushes was a supermarket carrier bag, the handles tied with string and pushed in under the bushes so no casual person would notice it. He grasped the bag and retraced his steps, almost bumping into a lone walker sampling the air, clearing his head. The two of them exchanged a brief smile, and Alan walked on.

...

The ramp doors opened, and the ramp was lowered, with flashing lights and bleeping noises. The waiting area had filled up with vehicles. The loading marshal directed vehicles according to how they wanted to fit them. Ash drove slowly, parked behind a car, and they all got out hungry, heading towards the restaurant. Already, a group of policemen were ahead of them in the queue. They finished eating and sought a quiet spot to talk. Huddled over a laptop, they read Swan's update. McIntosh had made an early morning visit to Faslane, an excuse for the day out, Roddy felt, and was travelling on to Islay by a Chinook helicopter. Roddy glanced at his watch. McIntosh was about to leave the naval base.

Swan had alerted others of his suspicions, and there would be heightened security. Still, such warnings were frequent and given Islay's isolation, how would an assassin get away. The authorities would pay lip service even to Swan, claiming he was covering himself, the likelihood of anything terrible happening next to zero.

There was no update on Sally Rundell, who had not been found. Her boyfriend was still recovering in hospital but likely to survive at least until he went home to his wife. The news about Reeves' death and Ricky's Novichok poisoning had been successfully suppressed. The thought of Petrov and Rundell having been activated troubled them. Who were their targets? Reeves was already dead. Who would be next?

...

Henry returned to the house, disappointed with himself and angry with Roger's manner. It hurt him deeply how his career had ended. Hadn't helped Mary, who he felt was still by his side, always loyal.
Alan was waiting as he walked in and listened as Henry unburdened himself. His companion was sympathetic. 'We'll find them by ourselves,' he stated, but Henry was unsure. Later, he phoned the police station and left his details, realising in his anger he had forgotten.

...

The confined loading space at Port Ellen was crammed with waiting vehicles as the ferry turned into the pier. The unloading began, and Ash drove off, studying the sat nav, before declaring, 'I'll manage to find Bowmore; only two roads lead to it. Islands have advantages.' They drove past warehouses and the tall building that housed the maltings, already encountering Islay's vibrant whisky industry.

As they drove past the airport, they saw several police cars and police guarding the gates and the security fence, several with dogs on leashes. In the sky above the runway, rapidly approaching, the sun glinting on its metal surface, Imran saw a Chinook helicopter growing in size as it reached the airport. Police cars headed towards it as it hovered. Imran wound down the window and the engine noise could be heard.

'Mr McIntosh is arriving,' he shouted, not that the others needed to be told.

...

Petrov scrutinised the arrival through his binoculars. Beside him lay the latest instructions. He put down the binoculars and studied them again. Something was missing, and it didn't make sense. He was now on his own; success depended on him. He packed up his belongings, took down the tent and took his things to the car. As disciplined as ever, he carefully packed his belongings in the boot before driving off.

44

The Chinook settled on its six wheels, and slowly, the rotors stopped spinning. A Mercedes drove up and parked a safe distance from the helicopter, followed by an unmarked Jaguar. Further back was a police car. As the engine noise subsided, the ramp at the back was lowered, and two crew quickly descended the ramp as a welcome party assembled on the tarmac. The crew members saluted as a diminutive figure emerged in camouflaged overalls, still wearing his helmet. He returned the salute of the crew and turned, knowing exactly where the press photographers were positioned with their long lenses focused on him. Fred McIntosh waved towards them and hoped to see a good action photo in the following day's papers.

Looking around, the Defence Secretary saw the welcoming party arrive and approached them, removing his helmet and tucking it under his arm. A lone piper started playing a slow march, the drone of the pipes providing a loud backdrop, competing with the dying noise of the Chinook's engines, making conversation more difficult. The Lord Lieutenant for the area introduced the welcoming party. McIntosh shook hands and smiled broadly, wanting to appear enthusiastic. Inside, the Defence Secretary felt tired after an early start. The journey had been uncomfortable, and the noise and the blustery conditions enroute had made him queasy. He wanted formalities over quickly.

Before disembarking, he had glanced at the briefing notes provided for him. Civil servants appreciated when their ministers absorbed the information provided and mastered the brief, but McIntosh frequently disappointed them. CI Rogers was irritated when he asked if he was chief of policing on the island, replying that this was only a tiny part of his area. McIntosh smiled and walked on.

Fred McIntosh was small and sensitive about his height, annoyed when one paper described him more like a skelf than a stick. He noted such comments, and the journalists responsible were unlikely to have access to interview him.

Waiting at the end of the line was Sir Angus, who smiled broadly, proffering a hand. 'Good to see you,' Sir Angus stated, his grip tight, the hold lasting for a few seconds.

'Once the formalities are over, we are going for a light lunch and a tour of a local distillery, the one you suggested,' Sir Angus added. 'A special bottle has been laid aside for you.'

McIntosh almost purred. He needed a break at the end of a demanding week with mounting criticism of his appointment and decisions. Earlier at Faslane, he had endured a presentation about Britain's nuclear capability. The commanding officer wished to stress the importance of the deterrent. That had been deliberate, he knew, given his known opposition to nuclear weapons. The staff at Faslane didn't like him, and he didn't care.

His security officers watched while he entered the Mercedes with the Lord Lieutenant and Sir Angus. He usually hated talking to local worthies, and on the face of it, McIntosh would have wanted away quickly from the Lord Lieutenant with his plum tones and thin moustache, but Sir Julian was a great character. Pleased to talk about Islay's whiskies, of which he appeared expert and with amusing tales, the journey to one of Islay's newest distilleries overlooking the Sound of Islay passed quickly. The other knight in the car also joined in providing an aperitif from a hip flask, which they all shared. The security officer in the front looked away. The peaty whisky soothed his throat, the flush of alcohol relaxing his mood. On arrival at the distillery, another piper played him in, the public enjoying a meal in the restaurant recognising him, some nudging each other, pointing him out as he walked to a private dining room.

Poached salmon, a pleasing lemon tarte with fresh cream and Mcintosh was ready for a personal tour. Listening as the tour guide explained the intricacies of the distilling process, his attention was frequently drawn to the view of the Paps of Jura from the still room, a stunning feature which distracted many. The tour finished with a tasting, the presentation of a special bottling of cask strength whisky finished in a rum cask, and the obligatory photos. McIntosh weaved back to the car, Sir Julian departed, and the party drove off. He even had a short nap in the time it took to drive to Sir Angus's house at Port Ellen.

At the house, he admired the view over Port Ellen before Murdo showed him to his room, with only one phone, a direct line to the servant he had just met. In his London flat, he had three phones: one for personal use, one for governmental business and one if there was a security crisis that he had to deal with. Outside in a Ford Galaxy, they had the means to receive calls from the Prime Minister and the defence ministry via the secure satellite system installed temporarily at the house. McIntosh relied heavily on his permanent secretary, whom he respected, to ease him and keep him informed. Others watched out for him twenty-four hours a day around the house's gardens and hills. A police car blocked access to the house. He was cocooned by a security web which was restricting, but he accepted came with the job.

He showered, freshened up and walked to the lounge. Murdo noticed his return and, in minutes, had provided coffee just the way he liked it. Sir Angus re-joined him, muttering about avoiding whisky at lunch, and the two sat down to talk.

Sir Angus was a social climber, and the Defence Secretary was a big catch. McIntosh might drop a comment about a new contract going out. Sir Angus's team could then make an educated guess as to who might win it and buy shares accordingly or advise clients to invest. They had been talking for about an hour before one of his security detail was shown in by Murdo.

'Sir Alan is on the phone, Sir. It's pretty urgent.' McIntosh excused himself, puzzled as the morning briefing had not highlighted any concerns. He sat in the rear of the Ford Galaxy and took the satellite phone.

'Fred here,' he stated, still mellowed by the whisky and trying to sound informal.

'Defence Secretary, good afternoon.' Sir Alan was never one to ignore formalities.

Slightly irritated, McIntosh said curtly, 'What is it? I am on Islay.'

'I know that, Sir, but intelligence has informed me of a possible threat to your life.'

'Oh,' was McIntosh's only response, surprised by the turn of events.

'On Islay,' he added a second later. 'Who?'

'The intelligence services have been tracking a couple of Russian sleeper agents who have suddenly become active. We believe one was responsible for the death of Felix Reeves, whom you talked to last week.'

McIntosh stayed mute.

'The other was responsible for using Novichok in a Highland village.'

McIntosh had been informed of both incidents during briefings and was pleased that Reeves's death had been hushed up as a heart attack. The other incident troubled him; no one wanted another Skripal, though the victim had been an innocent man whose only crime was to have an affair with the suspect.

'What's the latest development?' He was intrigued and a little concerned by now.

'One of the sleeper agents, identified as Denis Petrov, is heading in your direction, and Swan, you know him, believes he is trying to reach Islay. As usual, there is a mixture of facts and conjecture, but you can never be too careful.'

'I understand.'

'Security and the police have been informed and are searching for Petrov. I'll update you with any developments. Please listen carefully to any security advice given.'

'I will,' he replied

Returning to the lounge, Sir Angus noted his demeanour.

'You're frowning, Fred. Can't get away from the responsibilities, can you.'

'High offices of state are demanding,' he replied, unable to share the information he had received with his friend.

'Murdo,' Sir Angus shouted, 'more coffee.'

'We're on an island; we're immune from the problems you get on the mainland,' Sir Angus added as if reading McIntosh's mind.

McIntosh stared out the window, hoping that was the case, wondering why anyone would want to kill him, especially a Russian. Indeed, one or two columnists had hinted that he might be a Russian sleeper, a modern-day Manchurian candidate, given the two years he spent in Moscow as a student. During his time there, he knew he was being watched and surprising even himself; McIntosh had avoided honey traps, knowing the direction he wished his career to take. Despite his left-leaning tendencies and his disdain for the class-ridden British state, his eyes had been opened during his stay to the reality of communist rule, the corruption, the overbearing state, and the shortages. He never wanted to return.

However, he also hated nuclear weapons, thought them obscene, had little time for the armed forces, and was surprised to be appointed to his position. The machinations and the Prime Minister's manoeuvring were a master class in deception, and he had learnt a lot from observing him. 'Sink or swim,' the PM stated with no attempt at finesse. 'In politics, you often have to find ways of reconciling different beliefs. The armed forces won't like you; you must work hard to impress them. Succeed, and you will grow, fail, and become another embittered backbencher.' One day, the experience would be helpful if he progressed and he was highly ambitious.

But not if he was killed. The consequences of his death would be so severe; how could it be worth it to Russia.

'You are worried,' Sir Angus suggested, studying him. 'Remember I have booked a fishing trip for later. Ronnie, the owner, is a good guy, and I know that your security has prepared the boat. It would be a pity to miss the opportunity.'

McIntosh thought for a minute. He would be safe in a boat floating off the coast on a remote island. Surely.

'Leave as soon as I have dealt with a red box?' he asked, and Sir Angus's face lit up.

'A couple of hours at sea, a spot of fishing, and back for dinner and another couple of whiskies. What could be better?'

45

'Sir Angus, Ronnie is here,' Murdo announced, showing Ronnie into the lounge.

'Thank you, Murdo,' and Sir Angus rose from the couch to greet his visitor.

'Sorry about the change of plans, Ronnie, but needs of the state, I am afraid. The Defence Secretary has a red box to deal with.'

Sir Angus saw Ronnie glancing towards the window, where a man dressed casually in a green tee shirt and mauve trousers stood eyeing Ronnie. Even from a distance, the man's stare was unnerving, the scrutiny intense.

'Oh, this is Lee, part of Fred's security team,' although he hesitated, unsure how to describe him.

'Pleased to meet you,' Ronnie stated, accepting the host's invitation to sit down. Lee walked a few steps towards the pair and sat down, producing a map from a briefcase on the sofa beside him.

'Security for Fred is essential, and intelligence has raised a concern,' Sir Angus explained, now understanding why Mcintosh had been alarmed when he returned from the security car.

'I need to go over the plans for the fishing trip,' Lee stated, unfolding the map and spreading it out on the coffee table.

Probably mid-fifties, Ronnie thought; once red-haired, but now only streaks of the original colour, it appeared that he had little time for social niceties.

'Please show me the route you are taking,' the accent was Irish, although it had been anglicised over many years.

Ronnie bent over the map and pointed out the Oa. 'Starting at Port Ellen, we'll head for the Mull of Oa and the American Monument, give a bit of background history,' he checked that Gillies thought that a good idea. 'There are many coves, caves and sea arches to brighten the trip, and some good places to fish – mackerel, pollack and coolies mainly, nothing dramatic. I don't know if the Defence Secretary is interested in bird life, but we will probably see at least one sea eagle and other birds of prey. I intend to stop opposite a ruined farmhouse there,' he finished. 'Probably the best fishing spot.'

'I drove around the Oa earlier to get a feel for it. Lots of places to hide,' Lee suggested. 'We don't have time to ensure it is all safe. We work with what we are given.'

Ronnie shrugged. 'Very few people live there, and only one road in to check. Safety is usually my concern, not security on my trips.'

'That I understand, but we can't be too careful. The type of person I encounter doesn't usually take the roads. The Defence Secretary is a high-profile target.

You have a RIB?' Lee enquired, changing the subject.

'Yes.'

'Can we hire it?'

'Of course. I brought it over from Jura because you guys are guarding *Casablanca*.'

'Have you someone qualified to use it?'

'My friend, Mick Soutar.'

'We leave in two hours. Can he make it?'

'I'll phone him and check immediately.'

'Please. We'll place two men on board the RIB, equipped with binoculars and weapons. They will go ahead of your boat and check out the terrain from the sea. You will stay off-shore until we call you in to allow you to start fishing. As I said, we have a team already checking out the land. I'll make sure they have a look at the ruined farmhouse.'

'Ranald lives at the farmhouse, a bit eccentric. He has a shotgun, probably used for shooting rabbits.'

'We'll speak to him.'

'Harmless,' Sir Angus suggested. 'The farmhouse belongs to me, and I tolerate his presence. I doubt if he could hit anything with the shotgun. And I don't imagine he would have any motive to attempt to shoot Fred.'

'We will check him out, nevertheless,' Lee replied.

'My life is uncomplicated compared to this. Remind me not to go into politics,' Ronnie stated, but Lee smirked, expressing emotion for the first time. 'Some people take a lot of looking after,' and Ronnie knew he meant McIntosh.

'Good, all is settled then. I will accompany the Defence Secretary on the boat,' Sir Angus stated.

'I will join you with one other,' Lee added, addressing Ronnie.

In the study Sir Angus had allowed him to use, McIntosh peered at a briefing file on a suspected coup in Africa involving a terrorist group. Too much information, and he still had a dull headache from the whisky at lunchtime, which made concentrating hard. Since there was little requirement for military intervention, he signed it off, expecting the Foreign Office to deal with it diplomatically.

Sitting back in his chair, he remembered the earlier security alert. His mood changed, it was simply another scare, and he never forgot that his security team made a living from watching him, justifying their existence. Having finished his tasks and bored, he closed the red box, called in his defence detail to take it away and headed to his bedroom. There was time for a shower and a nap. Now, he could relax, enjoy the trip and look forward to a few more whiskies on their return.

…

Imran, Ash and Roddy sat bored in Ash's room in a Bowmore hotel.

Since their late arrival on Islay this morning, they had reported to the police station as instructed and spoken with a female police inspector, who apologised that her boss was welcoming the Defence Secretary to the island and was unavailable. Despite urging the police to watch out for Petrov, there appeared to be little urgency. A call to Swan had brought a McIntosh security team member to the station, and he promised to deal with it. So they sat frustrated, having drunk too much coffee, Ash busy on her laptop, Imran reading a book, and Roddy studying a map of Islay hung on the wall.

There was a rap on the door, and Roddy was the first to respond, opening it to see Inspector Marshall standing there. 'Hi,' she said as Roddy ushered into the room. 'I've been to a briefing meeting. Sorry you guys were missed out, but I volunteered to update you.' Ash stopped typing on her keyboard, Imran stretched and put down his book.

The Defence Secretary and Sir Angus are going on a fishing trip this evening accompanied by security, fishing around the coastline of the Oa,' and spotting the map on the wall she indicated the area. 'Your bosses' info about Petrov has shaken them up.'

'Good,' replied Roddy. 'Anything we can do?'

'You requested to study the CCTV footage from the ferry. The ferry is due in at Port Askaig within the hour. I've arranged for you to check it.'

'We'll be there.'

...

Petrov had taken the back road towards Bowmore and turned onto a rough track, a few miles along, which led into the hills. The track was stony, and much of it had been washed away. He had to navigate over large stones, which forced him to slow down to give the wheels enough grip. Ahead was an abandoned house, now roofless, birds perched on an exposed rafter, lifting off as the car approached. Near the house was a gully with a stream running through it, with bushes on either side. Leaving the track, he drove the car as far along as he could, the underside scraped by rocks and bushes scratching both sides of the vehicle. Getting out, he pulled a camouflage sheet from the boot and covered the car with it. After a few minutes, he was satisfied and removed his belongings from the car. He went to the ruined house and searched for a stone marked with chalk. Underneath, in a waterproof wrapping, he found a small package. He ripped open the package and exposed an envelope. Inside was a sheet of paper with the instructions he required. The instructions were concise. Ahead lay a long trek. Energised by his actions, he studied the terrain and plotted a route.

46

A few people had gathered around Port Ellen Marina, attracted by the vehicles lined up by the pier, consisting of a Mercedes and several Land Rovers with tinted windows topped and tailed with police cars, indicating that some personality had arrived. As McIntosh got out of his vehicle, he worked those watching as if he was at a political rally, despite one of them hurling abuse until a policeman had a quiet word in his ear. A woman wanted a selfie, which McIntosh was happy to provide. He paused on the pontoon beside one of the blue utility pods, put his arm around the woman, and smiled at her phone. Good or bad didn't bother McIntosh; not being noticed was worse. Lee and another minder introduced as Chris scanned the crowd impatiently, urging McIntosh to board the boat. Despite being requested not to wear a khaki jacket and camouflage trousers, he had ignored them. 'It identifies you as a target,' Lee explained patiently, but McIntosh would not remove them.

The pontoons stretched from the shore into Loch Leodamais, and the berths were crammed with yachts tied up with the gentle lapping of the water, causing some to bump against their moorings, tethering ropes creaking. Providing a sheltered haven for boats traversing the west coast of Scotland, the landing fees and crews provided a valuable source of income to Port Ellen. The small gathering around McIntosh comprised mainly of the yachting fraternity, who tended to their vessels; there were not many locals about. Port Ellen was primarily built around the loch. It was an idyllic scene on a beautiful evening, the low sun making the houses on the bay's far side stand out, recessed windows golden. Some cottages had even lit peat fires, tendrils of purple smoke rising slowly.

Sir Angus steered his guest towards Ronnie's boat. Eventually, McIntosh climbed on board, not before turning and waving towards those who remained. Chris was now on board, helping him to embark. Murdo, who was accompanying the group, handed over a hamper and a cool box to Ronnie as he clambered on board, followed by Lee. Ronnie's other boat, a RIB, waited out to sea by the ferry terminal, its engines frothing the water, with more security on board scanning the scene.

Casablanca was looking its best, Ronnie thought proudly, washed with the metal work, highly polished and awning extended to the rear. Lee gave the nod, and Ronnie started the powerful Yamaha 150bhp engine. The water was whipped up, and they followed the RIB into Kilnaughton Bay. Sir Angus took no time to point out to his guest his house perched on the hillside and further over, near Port Ellen, low white warehouses containing many whisky casks.

Directly ahead was a tall square lighthouse, Carraig Fhada, its white paintwork gleaming in the sun. Already, Sir Angus was in full flow. 'It's the only square lighthouse in Scotland. There is a tragic story behind it, built by Walter Frederick Campbell in memory of his wife Ellinor, who died aged only thirty-six.' Ronnie caught Lee's gaze, and they exchanged knowing looks. Sir Angus, puffed up, was going to try and impress his guest. It was to be a long trip.

Once out of the bay, Murdo opened the cool box and extracted a bottle of champagne, prising off the cork, which hit the awning and landed inside the boat, the contents of the bottle bubbling over the neck. The two men sitting at the rear clinked glasses and sipped their drinks. The others watched, their radios crackling as information passed between the boats and shore. As requested, Ronnie piloted the vessel, keeping the prescribed distance from the land. Mick steered the RIB, hugging the coastline, his shipmates scrutinising it with binoculars.

On this tranquil evening, the Kintyre peninsula was clear. Rathlin Island and the coast of Northern Ireland were visible to the south. The two vessels made steady progress, with the two guests increasingly relaxed. The two security personnel remained vigilant, Lee in the cabin beside Ronnie, who gave a running description of the cliffs and ravines out of habit. Lee remained largely silent. Murdo was unwrapping canapes and platters of salmon and prawns to feed Sir Angus and his guest.

After twenty minutes, Ronnie pointed out a ravine and mentioned it as a place where he had had success fishing before. Lee turned to the pair, drinking at the stern at the rear, shaking his head.

'I don't think they are that interested. An expensive exercise to feed his ego,' and Ronnie could only agree. At least he was getting paid a healthy fee with the bonus of the RIB being used. McIntosh's security had to endure long hours.

Lee spotted colleagues on the cliff top near the American Monument, radioed them, and heard a message back. 'No issues.'

'You're uptight,' Ronnie suggested.

'You can never relax,' Lee replied, lowering his voice. 'Someone like him, he motioned towards McIntosh, 'is unpredictable. He has no clue about the dangers facing him. What he fails to understand, or maybe doesn't care, is the danger he places others in.'

Ronnie nodded. As the vessel navigated further around the coast, it encountered the swell in Loch Indaal. Conversation between Sir Angus and McIntosh had paused, both having stopped eating or drinking. Murdo stood hand on the guard rail, impassive.

'There's the farmhouse; the best fishing is off-shore. Time for distraction therapy,' he said to Lee, then he shouted, leaving the cockpit. 'Time for fishing, gents,' and plucked the rods from their rubber cups and wandered to the back of the boat. He noticed Lee on the radio, and the RIB moved closer to the shore. That's going to disturb the fish, he thought, but does it really matter. He pulled back the awning to give more space for fishing.

Ronnie patiently added bait to the hooks for them. Sir Angus proved a competent fisherman despite having drunk a lot. McIntosh fumbled, but surprisingly, having finally dropped the hook into the water, he got a nibble and excitedly called out. He hauled in a mackerel and dropped it into a steel pail. In half an hour, the steel pail was filled with fish, and the two men decided to stop, satisfied with their efforts.

The sun was beginning to set behind the Rhinns, the sky was darkening, and a breeze was chilling those on board. 'Time to head back, Sir Angus?' Ronnie hinted. Lee was studying the farmhouse from which shone a solitary light, never relaxing. On the track close to the farmhouse stood one of their Land Rovers, headlights on.

…

'There he is,' exclaimed Imran, and the others crowded around the small screen in the backroom of the police station. 'That's him; you'll get a better view when he reaches the top of the stairs in a minute. No doubt. Petrov is on Islay as of yesterday.'

Inspector Marshall had managed to obtain CCTV footage from the ferry company for recent sailings. Imran, with his usual patience, had been searching through the images.

They huddled around the small screen confirming the sighting.

'He got out of a Ford Focus, grey in colour,' Imran added.

Roddy was searched through the car manifest. 'The car belongs to a Mr Jones. Ash alert Swan.'

Inspector Marshall left the room, issuing instructions, returning a few minutes later.

'I have informed McIntosh's security and ordered a search for his car. One of my colleagues will contact hotels and all places offering accommodation, including campsites. We should find him or his vehicle with the extra resources on the island for McIntosh's visit. He's had time to settle in, maybe go into hiding, which is unfortunate. We assume his arrival is due to the Defence Secretary's trip.'

'Could there be any other reason?' Roddy asked.

'I don't think so,' replied Imran, 'but you are correct; we can't assume anything.'

'I'll keep you posted,' Marshall stated, leaving the room.

'Good type,' Roddy asserted, 'better than her boss.' They all agreed.

'I'll inform Swan of developments; his intuition has proved correct again.' And Ash got busy on her keyboard. A team would be visiting Mr Jones's stated address within the hour, not expecting it to be anything other than false.

...

'Are you sure?' Lee exclaimed, speaking into his personal radio, and even Sir Angus and McIntosh looked his way, breaking off their conversation.

'Confirmed sighting of Petrov on the island, Chris.' Lee paused for a second before turning to Ronnie. 'Take the boat further out, now,' he commanded.

'Defence Secretary, can I speak with you,' motioning for McIntosh to come to the cabin.' Close your ears, Ronnie,' he added and then huddled with McIntosh. Ronnie picked up little of their conversation.

'...so, we head back now.' McIntosh nodded and resumed his seat at the rear. 'Put up the awning, Chris. Sir, don't sit at the back; come into the cabin, there is more protection. McIntosh hesitated. 'That was an order, sir. Now.' His voice was sharp.

Ronnie noticed the RIB manoeuvring to position itself between the shore and *Casablanca*, presumably receiving the same message.

Suddenly, there was a crack over the still night air, and Ronnie, looking towards the shore, noticed a flash. Sitting facing the cabin, Sir Angus fell forward, collapsing on the deck, knocking over the pail of mackerel. Ronnie turned away as bits of his brain splattered around the confined area. Murdo screamed and dived to the deck as Lee grabbed McIntosh, hauling him to the floor and lying on top of him. Chris reached the radio and shouted a coded phrase. Ronnie went full throttle, heading out to sea. The RIB was turning, churning up the ocean, ready to follow *Casablanca* further out. Sir Angus's body was lying surrounded by the dead fish.

On the land, the Land Rover was reversing up the track at speed, the beam from its headlamps rising and falling as it traversed bumps in the track bed.

Lee pushed McIntosh inside the cabin and pulled shut the door. 'Stay there,' Lee ordered and don't move. I have no doubt someone has tried to kill you but got your friend instead. You are fortunate; Sir Angus was in the wrong place.'

'Is he dead?'

'Yes, no one survives getting their brain removed, even you,' and he quickly left him in the cabin.

A short time later, a helicopter, lights on, lifted off the airport tarmac at Islay and headed towards them. Word would have reached London, and the defence department would be in full response mode. The Prime Minister would be alerted, and other NATO allies. Word would spread quickly, and until a reason was found, countries would raise their alert level. Islay was suddenly the focus of the world's attention.

...

Marshall burst into the room but spoke calmly. 'Sir Angus has been shot. He's dead. McIntosh is unharmed. Someone shot him from the shore.'

The three of them stared back, absorbing the information. 'McIntosh must have been the target. He was lucky,' exclaimed Ash, standing up and for once abandoning her keyboard.

'I don't know if Petrov fired the bullet, would he have made such a mistake having got so close.' Imran suggested, but no one else was listening.

47

Murdo repeatedly retched over the side of the boat, and when he stopped, he curled up in a foetal position, distraught, on one of the side benches. He stayed huddled up in denial of what had occurred. After a few minutes, he attempted to compose himself, sat up, wiped his mouth with the back of his hand, and carefully positioned a blanket over his boss before standing up and bowing his head. A moment of reflection whilst all around there was frantic activity. Already, a helicopter was hovering above *Casablanca*, the down draught making it hard to move on the boat, the noise making communication impossible. A winchman was lowered, and Chris grabbed him by the legs as he reached the boat. With a final calculation that they were safely out of range of any rifle, Lee hauled McIntosh from the cabin. The Defence Secretary was ashen, his mouth opening and shutting like one of the mackerel spread out in front of him. He closed his eyes as he took in the scene, blanking it out, shivering. The crewman and Chris fitted him with a life jacket and fastened the collar under McIntosh's arms. A hard helmet was placed on his head. The crewman attached himself to McIntosh and signalled to those waiting above. The pair rose jerkily together before becoming free of the boat. The helicopter increased height as the defence secretary and the crewman swung back and forth, with no time for a steady ascent; this was an emergency evacuation. Hands reaching out to haul McIntosh in as he reached the machine. Once inside, the helicopter tipped to the side and sped off toward the mainland.

'At least he's safe,' muttered Chris; both he and Lee appeared relieved that he had gone, and presumably, they were no longer under imminent threat. 'No doubt we will all face an inquisition before too long,' he added. The authorities would want to know how it happened and who was responsible. With a dead body in front of them, there were a lot of questions to answer, but the members on board the *Casablanca* were more concerned with returning to Port Ellen.

'Head back, Ronnie, as quickly as you can,' Lee commanded. Murdo was on his knees, ignoring the blood and gore, throwing the mackerel overboard, trying to give dignity to the body underneath the blanket. Water, mingled with blood, was swilling about on the deck, and Murdo attempted to scoop some out with the pail.

By now, the RIB was close by, holding a position between the *Casablanca* and the shore, providing protection like a destroyer protecting an aircraft carrier, ready to take any incoming fire.

'Ronnie, you saw a flash on the shoreline as the rifle was fired. Point out the position.' Lee demanded.

'To the left of the farmhouse,' where light still shone in an upper window. 'Maybe close to the barn in the farmyard.'

Lee conveyed the position to the team on shore. Their Land Rover could be seen approaching the farmhouse at speed.

'A small detachment of SAS are on standby at Islay Airport to be called on in an emergency. They'll be here shortly. Murdo, have you any coffee left in the thermos flask?' Murdo, ashen white, nodded.

'Good, try and give everyone a sip of the coffee. It will help revive us.' Lee explained. Murdo seemed pleased with something to do and got busy as Lee retreated into the cabin area for more privacy.

'They're taking McIntosh to the Queen Elizabeth Hospital in Glasgow for a check-up. He'll be okay. We'll get quite a reception back at Port Ellen. Be prepared for lots of questions, and they won't be gentle; too much is at stake. If a foreign power had done this, there would be all hell to pay,' Lee concluded.

...

The mood inside the police office was tense and subdued. Rogers had been roused from his bed in a local hotel, and he appeared flushed and flustered, struggling to exude an air of authority. Marshall, meanwhile, was trying to get a grip on the situation, calmly issuing instructions. Islay had only a few resident police officers; the rest had arrived from the mainland without local knowledge. The only local cop on duty was pointing out on a map how to block off the Oa. Lack of familiarity and night-time made the task more difficult, even though there were few access points. Rogers was too aware of his position and unwilling to listen to local advice. Marshall looked frustrated, raising her eyebrows at Roddy and shaking her head. As instructed, a minibus of police officers left the station to block all exits from the Oa. Whoever had shot Sir Angus surely could not get far.

The three intelligence officers sat in one corner, unsure if their presence was welcomed. Ash had informed Swan, who wanted them to help if needed, but he knew in times of crisis that not everything dovetailed. An egotistical personality could derail efforts, and Roddy began to suspect that Rogers was not up to the task.

...

The security team were approaching the farmhouse when they heard another crack, and simultaneously, the light in it went out. The driver slowed down as they got ready to abandon their vehicle. There was another shot, and one of their headlamps was hit. Quickly, they left their Land Rover, and the three officers dispersed, crouching low, taking different approaches to the dwelling, each armed and in contact through earpieces linked to their radios.

'There he is, one of them spoke fast into his radio. 'Over by the barn, heading towards the wood.'

Armed only with Glock pistols, the distance was too far for accuracy. One of them ran towards the fleeing figure, and as the distance closed and holding the pistol in both hands to steady herself, she fired. The target staggered, reaching down to hold his calf, but adrenaline drove him on and using his rifle as an emergency crutch, he reached the edge of the wood. In seconds, there was a flash, and a bullet whistled past them, too high to be any danger but sending a strong signal that they had to be careful. They received a message on their earpieces. 'Hold your position; help is on its way. The suspect will not get far.'

Carefully, they manoeuvred their position around the farmhouse, and with other two covering their colleague, the woman who had fired at the suspect raced towards the farmhouse and reached the porch, staying low. Inside, she switched on her torch and surveyed the scene inside.

The hall was deserted, and she pushed open a door which led into the kitchen. The kitchen was empty, a high three-legged stool tipped over, dishes drying by the Belfast sink, a mug on the wooden table. Carefully, she flung open a door which led into a lounge area, sweeping the room with her Glock. No one was in the room, a TV on, muted, she recognised the characters from a soap opera. Then she heard a groaning noise from upstairs and ran up. On the landing was a figure sprawled on the floor. Scanning the person with her torch, she saw a pool of blood slowly spreading from the area of his chest, staining the carpet. Kneeling down beside him, she quickly messaged the others. Her fingers searched for a pulse on his neck, but it was very faint. One of her colleagues rushed into the farmhouse and was soon by her side. She shook her head as he crouched down beside the body. The man was too far gone; breathing stopped as they knelt beside him. The man murmured a 'Hail Mary' and crossed himself. Both stood up, shaking their heads, reporting back on the radio.

Outside, a helicopter was hovering, and in the moonlight, they watched as four figures rapelled towards the ground, rucksacks dangling from them. The transfer to the ground was over in seconds, and there was a flurry of activity as they reached it and dispersed. In minutes, one of the figures reached the farmhouse.

'One dead upstairs, from the look of him, probably lived here, no jacket, just the clothes he would wear around the house. The person we were chasing fired at us and left, running into the woods. Somehow, I think I shot him in the leg.'

The man replied, 'Well done,' and underneath his camouflage paint, he smiled. 'Only one? Possibly injured, most likely, the marksman who took out the person on the boat. Stay here, and we will try to locate him,' he added, and then he was gone. The two security personnel left in the house watched from the side of an upstairs window. Already, there was no sign of any of the new arrivals who had already merged into the night, hotly in pursuit.

An ambulance soon arrived along with a police car, and soon the farmhouse was lit up. Police sharpshooters positioned themselves at the edge of the wood. 'It's Ranald,' one of the ambulance crew stated as they edged him down the stairs on a stretcher, 'he occasionally used to come in for a drink in Port Ellen.'

...

'Another victim,' Marshall declared as she entered the backroom. 'His name is Ranald, and he lived at the farmhouse, quite well-known locally. He had been shot in the chest, and the culprit was seen running towards nearby woods and was possibly wounded. Police and security are at the scene, and the SAS lead the search.

McIntosh is safe in Glasgow.' Roddy felt that Marshall was also updating them.

...

He was slowing down, the leg stinging. The bandage he had put on, failing to cope with all the blood, stained bright red. This was not part of the plan. He would struggle to reach the cove now where his gear was positioned. A swim across Loch Indaal was not possible in his state. Aware of the helicopter, he knew the search had begun, and possibly the highly trained SAS he had watched were already trying to trace his path. Keeping up the pace until the pain was too severe, he paused. Ahead, he could see an unlit cottage. He hoped it was unoccupied and he could make a stand there. A hostage or hostages, however, could be a valuable card. Hobbling he left the cover of the trees and reached a porch. The door was unlocked, and he pushed through. A bright searchlight beam was playing over the ground, maybe half a mile away. A dog started to bark, and with surprise lost, he put his shoulder to the inner door, which flew open. The dog continued to bark more frantically, prancing around him but responded quickly to his outstretched hand. A light went on in the bedroom. He drew his pistol and leant on his rifle. The door opened, and a woman screamed.

Pointing his pistol, he told her to be quiet, or he would shoot the dog. She began to tremble, rubbing her bristling hair, her mouth opening as if she was about to scream. Waving his pistol, he turned it towards the dog.

'Please don't shoot her,' she stated, her voice dry, fading, and quickly called the dog towards her. He was aware of another door opened slightly. 'Tell your friend to come out, now,' he snapped, and another woman emerged. He gestured for her to stand beside her friend, glad that the dog now appeared under control.

'Sit down,' he growled, aware that he was light-headed; he perched himself against the back of the sofa. The second woman was more composed. 'Go to the kitchen, boil water, put it in a bowl and bring it to me with towels,' he ordered. The leg was hurting, a stabbing pain; one lucky shot and his mission had changed to survival. 'No tricks,' he added, 'or your friend gets it.'

The other woman was strange, muted now, spaced out, the trauma too much.

'What's your name?' he asked the other woman as she returned. She was calm and composed, unlike the other one.

'Alison,' she replied, remembering that somewhere she had read to be friendly in hostage situations, and she smiled.

'Take off the bandage, carefully,' he added, the pain etched on his face as he cursed his wound. Holding the pistol steady required an effort, but Alison was aware of the barrel inches from her face. A glance told him the bullet had left a deep groove, raw and sore in his calf. He writhed as Alison bathed it, dried it and rewound the bandage.

'You'll need a doctor,' she suggested, but he dismissed her statement, waving the gun and indicating that she move back. The other woman troubled him, incredibly tense, with a glazed expression. Alison placed a comforting arm around her. 'You'll be okay, Jenny,' Alison said, trying to comfort her. The helicopter was getting closer. 'Shut the blinds,' he ordered Alison, who got up and pulled the vertically slatted blinds shut, checking the key in the lock. As far as she could tell, it was unlocked.

'We wait and hope no one comes searching,' he stated, adding, 'switch off the lights.'

There was a bumping noise from the bedroom that Jenny had come from, and a small boy appeared, holding a toy.

'Come here, Ben,' Jenny shouted, panicking, her chest heaving. 'Don't you dare harm him,' she added, on the verge of hysteria.

Alison grabbed the small boy and brought him between Jenny and her.

'Oh, please don't touch him,' Jenny screamed.

'Tell her to be quiet,' he growled, 'or else. Now, everyone settle down.'

48

The pier lights were on at the ferry terminal as Ronnie brought the *Casablanca* towards the pontoon, followed by Mick Soutar guiding in the RIB. Police had stopped people from reaching the vessel and ordered those on their boats to stay inside. Ronnie scanned the crowd, noticing Pamela anxiously watching – that was a silver lining. Word travelled fast on Islay, and all the nocturnal activity from the airport must have brought out the curious. Malcolm was also there; a news story always attracted him, and this was big. There were several flashes as photographs were taken, pictures which would be on the front pages of tomorrow's papers. As they berthed, two police officers erected a screen to stop gawking.

A police sergeant and a man in plain casual clothes stepped on board, and the sergeant ushered Murdo off, past the screen, and Ronnie heard a woman screaming, 'Your safe.' Shortly after, he saw Murdo and his wife, Fiona, being eased into the back seat of a police car, which sped off.

Both Lee and Chris knew the man who remained on the boat. He didn't introduce himself to Ronnie but knelt, lifting the blanket and peering underneath. 'Crack shot, Lee.'

Lee murmured in agreement.

'But who was the target. If our sniper friend is that good, why did he hit the wrong target, or did he.'

He turned towards Ronnie, still without introducing himself. 'We'll need to impound your vessel whilst our enquiries are ongoing.'

Ronnie had expected that. 'We better get the SOCO on. Ronnie,' and he squeezed Ronnie's shoulder, 'you have been through a lot. We'll interview you tomorrow. Stay on Islay tonight. I believe someone is waiting for you,' and he indicated towards the group gathered on the shore. Edging towards the front was Pamela. Lee, Chris, you know the drill, we're going to base ourselves in a local hotel. The island police station is too small.'

'How's the search going?' Chris added.

'No result yet, but Sarah winged him, we believe, so he shouldn't get too far, and the SAS are on his tail. We'll get him.'

Ronnie left the boat with a final glance at Sir Angus's covered body as booted and suited officers climbed on board. Not a task he wanted, he mused. Beyond the screen, Pamela waited, hugging him as he reached her.

...

The man was sitting on the sofa, obviously in pain; at times, his eyes drooped, and he fought himself awake. The two women sat quietly; he told them gruffly to shut up if they attempted to speak. Fortunately, Ben had gone to sleep in Jenny's arms. Maybe he believed it was all a dream. A helicopter was circling overhead, and through the slatted blinds, they saw a searchlight slowly surveying the ground. Alison had been late in going to sleep and had messaged Malcolm, who had replied. She heard her phone pinging, but she suspected he would think she had gone to sleep. So, no help there.

Suddenly, there was a hard knock on the door. Jodie started barking and then growling as Jenny told her to be quiet. The man froze. 'Go to the door; if I think you are acting suspiciously, I will shoot her and the boy.' He moved out of sight.

'Sorry to disturb you, especially so late at night, but a dangerous man is on the loose. We've come to warn you to lock all doors and report anyone you see acting suspiciously.'

They heard Alison reply, 'We've not seen anyone.' The police officer looked beyond Alison. 'I see that you are still up. Anything wrong.'

'No, Ben, my friend's little boy has toothache; we'll soon get him back to bed with some Calpol.'

'Sorry to disturb you. Please lock all doors and keep windows shut.'

'We will, officer,' and as he turned, she mouthed 'help'.

The officer paused briefly and turned away. As he walked off, he turned again, a puzzled expression on his face. Alison raised her eyebrows at him before shutting the door.

'You did good,' the gunman stated, waving his handgun for her to sit down. He reached into his pocket, took out a strip of white pills, and pushed out a couple of tablets. He swallowed them quickly without water, his gaze not deviating from the women.

'Will I get you a glass of water?' Alison asked. He nodded, and she got up and brought him water, which he gulped down.

'Is there anything else you need?' Alison was trying to engage him in conversation.

'No,' and he looked around the room, his eye fixed on the wedding photo of Peter and Jenny.

'Who are they?' he questioned, his expression changing, puzzled.

'That's Jenny,' Alison replied, and at the mention of her name, Jenny raised her head.

'The other one?'

'That's Peter,' a slow smile enveloped his face, and he shook his head.

'Why do you ask?' aware that Jenny was more alert following the conversation.

'Nothing,' he growled, 'just passing time. Now shut up. Don't try to be friendly. I know your game.'

Jenny blurted out. 'Do you know my husband?'

'Shut up,' he snapped and rubbed his leg as a spasm of pain made him grimace.

Jenny's eyes were darting back between Alison and the gunman, hungry for a response.

'Do you know where he is?' she asked, unable to contain herself.

He laughed at her and told her to 'shut up' again.

...

Marshall felt trapped in the claustrophobic room at the police station, wanting to clear the space which was not fit for purpose on this occasion. Islay police station was not designed for major incidents. Outside, a catering van had arrived, offering hot drinks and sandwiches.

She suggested to Rogers that she would go to the roadblock set up at the Oa and take control. Rogers was pleased to get rid of her. He hated those that showed him up, '…and take them with you,' he added, pointing to Roddy and the team. Inspector Marshall commandeered a police car, driving herself and invited Roddy, Imran and Ash to join her. They would help identify Petrov, who was being hunted down as they drove. Likely wounded, he would be a dangerous prey. The SAS were doing the dirty work, but the police were needed to keep the public at bay and reassure them.

They reached the roadblock on Port Ellen's outskirts before the campsite junction. Marshall powered down the window to talk to the officer, who approached the car. Several officers were standing about. The officer stiffened up as he recognised her. 'Good to see you, Inspector,' he stated.

She drove a few yards and stopped, pulling over to the side of the road. The others got out and joined her. There was a hint of dawn to the east, and they stood around, the air cool, Imran stamping his feet. In the woods, he noticed an armed officer lurking.

'Good, I'm here to take charge. The others are intelligence officers who I vouch for. They can identify the suspect.' Marshall walked about speaking to the officers, appreciating that the night was long.

She briefed the intelligence team. 'Down that road is the campsite that Petrov used on his first night on Islay. It is located among sand dunes. Over there is Sir Angus's house, all lit up. They'll be in shock. Specially trained officers are on their way. At the moment, we have two officers guarding the place.'

'Do you know much about him?' Roddy enquired.

'Not a lot. I met him. Usual rich type, charming but ruthless, I suspect.'

'Not likely to be assassinated.'

'I wouldn't have thought so.' It had been a long day, and she was tired; her conversation with Henry Smith had been long ago, but eventually, it surfaced. 'I was talking to an ex-colleague this morning who reported a missing person,' and she had to reach into her memory to recall the name - Peter Meldrum. I suggested he speak to the desk officer and we would check up later. He mentioned Sir Angus funnily enough, claiming he was not too popular. I always respected Henry. I will follow him up when I get a chance.'

From the direction of Port Ellen, they heard a car approaching at speed. Marshall stepped out from the side of the road, holding up her hand to stop the vehicle. The car braked sharply, and she went quickly to the driver.

'Sir, you were driving too fast.'

The bespectacled man apologised. 'Sorry, Inspector, but I must get to my wife. She is in danger,' Marshall sensed the alarm in his voice. 'She's staying with a friend and her child in a cottage beyond the campsite. I'm worried the man who shot Sir Angus might reach them.'

'The SAS are on his trail, and we have warned everyone to stay inside and lock doors.'

'I've not had a reply from her, which is most unusual.'

'Give me your details.' Malcolm got out of the car. My name is Malcolm Baxter,' and he handed over his business card. 'My wife, Alison, is staying at Jenny Meldrum's cottage, up a rough track from the campsite.'

The name instantly registered, and out of the corner of her eye, she saw Roddy standing nearby, also clocking the name.

'Let me check,' she walked smartly to an officer sitting in a Land Rover, and they talked.

Returning to Malcolm, Marshall said. 'It's okay, our officers visited the cottage this evening. Everything is fine.' Except it wasn't. The officer who had visited the cottage had noted Alison's silent cry for help. The search helicopter had hovered over the house and picked up heat signatures for three adults and a child. The cottage was now surrounded, their approach complicated by a dog, who would bark if he detected strangers.

'We have your contact details. If we can let you through, we will phone. I would suggest going home.' Marshall didn't like deceiving the man, but she didn't want an overwrought husband barging in.

Malcolm was not reassured. 'I have sent an initial story to my newspaper. Anything I can add?'

'Not whilst the operation is in progress, but I will update you when I can.'

He got back in his car and turned it around. He drove back towards Port Ellen and turned left, the road that eventually led onto the airport road. There, he stopped to ponder on what he would do next.

Marshall had noted the surname Meldrum and was left wondering why Jenny's husband was missing and if it could link to current events.

...

Henry Smith was having trouble sleeping. He hated it when he was stuck, making no progress in a case, and felt personally responsible. In the morning, he would attempt to speak with Marshall again. He had awakened when a helicopter passed overhead. When he got to the toilet, he spotted searchlights over the Oa and wondered what was happening. But there was little he could do. Returning to bed, he struggled to sleep, but eventually, he dozed off.

...

The ambulance arrived at the roadblock as the early morning sun streaked the clouds above red. It stopped as requested. Marshall spoke to the driver and explained the situation. She returned to her car with the others and edged forward, positioning herself in front of the ambulance. Then Marshall waited. Ahead, she heard the powerful throbbing beat of the helicopter rotors coming nearer, crossing over them and heading towards the campsite. The radio burst into life. 'Go, go,' her driver put the car into gear and turned towards the campsite road. The ambulance followed behind.

From the woods overlooking the road, Malcolm watched what was happening, having abandoned his car and headed back on foot. In dismay, he saw the local GP's car following on behind the ambulance. Now, he was very concerned. There was no choice. He ran towards the cottage as fast as he could

Ahead, the encirclement of the cottage was complete. The plan was being put into action. Hopefully, the dog would not alert the inhabitants to the presence of the SAS. Lives depended on it.

49

The helicopter swung away as if heading along the coast, still searching. Inside the cottage, the gunman relaxed, breathing out, and then he winced as the pain intensified. 'Do you want a coffee?' Alison enquired.

'Black, sugar, no funny tricks.'

'You can watch me,' she replied.

Alison got up carefully, leaving the kitchen door open wide and filling the kettle from the tap in the sink. A head popped up below the window as she stood at the sink. Alison only just managed to stifle a scream. The face was streaked with camouflage paint, and he wore a black beanie. Immediately he put his finger to his mouth. He pointed up while circularly moving his finger, and she guessed he wanted her to wait until the helicopter returned. Then, the soldier made a gesture as if he was going to insert a key in a lock. 'Yes,' she mouthed, conscious her mouth was very dry. Seconds later, he had gone. Her heart was beating fast as she placed a mug on a tray with a coffee jar, sugar bowl, and teaspoon, returned to the room and placed the tray beside the gunman, returning for the kettle. The man managed a frown and watched as she made him coffee. Glancing down, Alison saw that his bandage was soaked in blood again, and his hands trembled as he sipped the hot drink.

Jenny was clinging to Ben, who was still asleep in her arms. That was both a surprise and a relief.

'Can I put him back in his bed?' Alison asked.

The gunman barely nodded, but she took it as affirmative, lifted him from Jenny's arms, and carried him to his bedroom. Kissing him sweetly on his forehead, she covered Ben with his duvet. One out of harm's way, she hoped.

The coffee appeared to revive the gunman, and she cursed that fact, but how would she have known that the cottage was surrounded if she hadn't gone to the kitchen. Alison was in a territory where there were no easy solutions.

The wounded man looked up as the helicopter drew near again, the noise in the room intensifying, the mug and coffee jar vibrating together as the machine reached overhead, and Jodie began to bark then howl.

'Put the dog in with the boy. The dog is doing my head in.' Alison obliged, though Jodie kept barking, then growling as she left him.

In her seat, Alison gauged the distance to the patio doors, knowing they were unlocked. What if there was no one there, or vital seconds were lost, and the gunman managed to kill Jenny or her. Alison was sweating, an image of Malcolm forming in her mind – what would he do without her. What about Dylan? From an early age, Alison had always had a strong faith, though in recent years, that had lapsed in practice. Squeezing her eyes tight, she prayed to Jesus. Opening them, she decided to be bold. Although she doubted he was sleeping, his head was down. All it needed was a quick sprint to the patio doors, throwing them open. She tensed, and then he looked up, staring directly at her as if he could read her mind, but his eyes looked distant.

'It will soon be gone,' he murmured, lifting his handgun to the sky.

Alison forced herself to appear relaxed and smiled, covering her ears with her hands. His eyes drooped again, and then she was up and racing to the door, almost tripping over his feet and attempting to pull the door open, her hand caught up in the vertical slats of the blinds. While feeling for the handle, Alison's heart lurched as it didn't move, and she remembered to lift it first. Behind, he could hear him stirring, reacting. Yanking down the handle and pulling it, the door slid open, and cold air flooded in. She was pushed aside as a soldier hurtled in, surveyed the scene and fired three times in rapid succession as the wounded man attempted to respond. The silenced weapon only made a quiet phutting sound.

Alison screamed as more bodies ran in, weapons ready. She dared to look at her captor. He was slumped, blood soaking his clothes – dead. The first soldier rushed into Ben's bedroom and quickly checked it. 'All clear,' he shouted as Jodie ran out barking furiously. The helicopter was rising up, the thrum of the rotors receding. Echoing calls came from other rooms.

A young man took her by the arm and led her outside. Later, she told Malcolm he was so young that he thought he was a boy who had run in. Jenny was awake from her almost comatose state and immediately shouted for Ben. A soldier brought him through in his arms, and she grabbed him and hugged him tightly.

A police inspector came in, followed by Dr Khalid, the local GP. He glanced at the dead man and shook his head. Jenny repeatedly sobbed and screamed, 'Where are you, Peter?' The GP put his arm around her and eased her onto the sofa before opening his case. Seconds later, he injected her; initially, Jenny resisted the effect of the injection, but she became more relaxed very quickly. 'Jenny will need to go to hospital,' the GP stated. The paramedics, who were standing outside, came in and escorted Jenny out.

'I'll look after, Ben,' Alison replied and took his hand, and they followed Jenny out. As she left, the soldiers were examining the dead man's weapon, ignoring him.

Outside, the police were restraining a man she instantly recognised. 'Malcolm,' she shouted, and the inspector turned around with surprise as the two hugged, tears flowing down her face. They hung together for a few minutes, emotions raging. Ben touched Alison, and she jumped. They had almost forgotten him, Alison feeling bad. Beside Ben was Jodie, her tail wagging.

'I think we have got us a pet,' Malcolm added.

The police inspector left the room, still surprised at how Malcolm reached the house, calling on Roddy and the others to accompany her.

'Petrov is dead,' she informed them as they reached the patio doors. 'I need you to formally identify him,' but there was uncertainty on her face.

Roddy looked at the slumped figure, turned to Imran, and shook his head. 'That's not Petrov. I have no idea who he is.' Imran confirmed Roddy's statement.

'Who is it, then?' Marshall asked.

'I've no idea, but it is definitely not Petrov.'

The young soldier who had helped Alison and was obviously in charge stared at them.

'Are you sure?' he queried, sharing the concern on Marshall's face.

Ash chipped in. 'I have also studied pictures of Petrov. This is a different man.'

'This complicates matters,' Marshall replied. 'So, who is the man we have just killed,' and she paused. 'And where is Petrov.'

'If Petrov is still on the island, what will he do next.'

'I better report to Rogers, and I hope you guys have some answers when I return,' and she coughed nervously.

50

One of the captors approached the trapdoor, and the bolt was slid back. The trapdoor was opened, lifted, and crashed on the ground, exposing the cellar. Peter could see the man's boot, caked in mud, and heard him choke as the smell from the spilt contents of the pail reached him. 'Heads down,' he growled out of habit. Cash was poised, her face grim, streaked with dirt, as she glanced towards Peter.

Peter jumped on the upturned pail, grabbed the man's boot, and pulled. The man staggered but quickly recovered balance as Peter hung on both arms wrapped around his boot. The man kicked out with his other foot, narrowly missing Peter, but this seemed to unbalance him, and he landed heavily on his back. With surprising agility, Cash was clambering out of the cellar but got trapped by her captor, who grabbed at her, leaving her legs dangling in space. Quickly, she grabbed his leg and bit hard. The man roared, but Cash kept biting, receiving a flailing blow on her face. By this time, he was on the floor with Peter tugging him towards the cellar entrance. Assailed from two directions, the man lashed out randomly. Cash squirmed between the edge of the opening and him as Peter dragged him towards it. Peter pulled the man's other leg into the gap and bent it up, unbalancing him. Again, the man roared as Cash started to punch his face, and when that had little effect, gouged at his eyes, making him release his grip. As he tried to fend Cash off, Peter yanked harder on the leg while still trying to bend it further, forcing the man into a more vertical position and edging him closer to the cellar entrance. It was a grim tug of war until Cash manoeuvred behind him, sticking her fingers in his eyes more forcibly. He screamed, and Peter pulled more of his leg over the wooden edge, twisting it again as he did so. Cash released him and jumped on his other leg, causing him more pain and pushing him, but the man was robust and enraged. Frantically, Cash looked around for an improvised weapon and spotted a pile of discarded wooden staves at the entrance to the building, a few yards away. She ran and grabbed one as Peter hung on determinedly. The effects of confinement and lack of food were telling, and he couldn't see what Cash was now doing, thinking that she had run off, his energy levels waning.

Cash grabbed the wooden stave and ran back; the man spotted her but could not free his leg, which Peter still hung onto grimly. He swore using words Peter didn't recognise, cursing Cash as she approached. He writhed and twisted but could not free himself from Peter's grip. She swung the wooden stave, and he fended it off with an arm but yelled as it hit him. Cash repeatedly tried, landing more blows until she connected with his head. For the first time, his body momentarily slackened. Then, Cash drove it into his body using the stave at its blunt end. He yelped, momentarily stopped resisting and finally, Peter could drag his body over the edge. As he frantically tried to balance, Cash lashed out again, and Peter finally managed to pull him down into the cellar, where he landed on top of Peter. Peter kicked out at the man, freeing himself and desperately tried to pull himself up and out. With one leg on the cattle shed floor, he felt the man grabbing at his other leg, their positions now reversed. He shouted to Cash for help. She took the wooden stave and lashed at the man's clinging arms and body as he rose up like a bloodied monster rising from the depths. The more he exposed himself, the more the beating from the stave was effective until he finally released his grip on Peter, who hurriedly withdrew his other leg and staggered onto the floor of the shed, scrabbling over to the trap door, lifting it up and letting it fall shut. Still, there was pressure from below as their captor attempted to raise the trapdoor until Peter jumped on it and Cash rammed the bolt home. There was frantic banging and roaring from the cellar.

They looked at each other, bruised and cut, but Peter grabbed her arm and yanked her towards the entrance, gasping for breath as they reached it. The cold night air shocked them, making them draw breaths, and they headed towards a sand berm they saw outside the barn, which surrounded at least two sides. To their left was a farmhouse lit up. They heard the muffled sound of the trapped man shouting for help from behind.

'Russian,' Cash stated, adding, 'with a good vocabulary for the obscene,' between gasping for air.

Peter took in the information, and then he commanded. 'Over here,' and they staggered towards the sandy ridge. The sand berm was fairly recent as patchy grass sown struggled to establish itself. The ground underfoot was soft as they ran up, holding them back and adding a nightmarish edge to their escape. Once at the top, they ran down the other side, using the loose sand to break their descent.

Peter gasped for breath and looked around, trying to locate where they were. All around was a sandy strip, and he could detect sea air, but it did not help much on Islay. Then ahead, he saw the distinctive of Dun Bheolain beneath the starry sky, which some likened to the Sydney Opera House with its ridged appearance, like an Armadillo.

'Saligo Bay,' he uttered. 'I know where we are,' he smiled encouragingly at Cash. 'Now I have to decide which direction to take.' He thought quickly, turning towards the farmhouse that would take them onto the road that wound around the shores of Loch Gorm, Islay's biggest inland loch. Memories of another nightmarish night-time trip chased by McGory's henchmen were etched on his mind. He shook his head in despair as Cash looked on worried, urging him to make a decision recognising the vulnerability of their position.

Too exposed on the road, he finally decided.

'Head for the hills; they won't expect us to go in that direction. We can reach Sanaigmore, the next bay along and get help.' Decision made, they started walking fast, both now too drained to run after their exertions. Peter heard a door slamming over the still night air from the farmhouse. He pulled at Cash's arm and urged her on. Peter pointed towards sand dunes and heard waves roaring on the shore. They dived into the sand dunes as a torch beam began to search for them, playing across the flat ground they had just left. The torch beam was some distance off. Hidden in the sand dunes, they were more aware of the cold breeze from the sea, and Cash was shivering.

'Are you okay?' he asked her.

'Like you a bit battered. Our captor was powerful and determined.'

'And Russian?' Peter queried.

'Ex-military with a rich vocabulary.'

'So, what is he doing on Islay?'

'Up to no good. He was one of the men who grabbed us the night we were captured. I didn't get a great look at him; after all, he was wearing a balaclava, but I remember he had an unpleasant, sweaty odour.'

'This brings back horrible memories for me. There is a loch over that hill. I was chased around it.'

She held out a comforting arm to Peter.

'Anyway, I survived, and we will do it again. No time to dwell on the past.' He parted the clumps of marram grass and looked out, careful to keep his head low. Now, two men were standing on the sand berm, searching for them; the second one had been released from the cellar, as he was hopping about and rubbing his head, someone with a grudge.

'We can't stay here, we'll die of exposure in our state. If we head along the shore, there are plenty of rocks to hide behind. Then we can edge inland to the right of these cliffs and reach Sanaigmore for help.'

They kept low until they reached the shore and then worked their way between the rocky outcrops, often slick with seaweed. It was hard for two people in their state, and they had to stop frequently. As the distinctive rock formation loomed in front, Peter led them inland, where the ground was covered in rough grass and bracken. Finding a path made progress quicker, and they eventually climbed higher. The farmhouse was now lit up, and Peter saw a vehicle, headlights on, covering the terrain between them. He nudged Cash and pointed it out.

'They'll have to abandon their vehicle quite soon and try to find us on foot.' Cash nodded and determinedly walked on.

Suddenly, an intense light shone around them, directed from the top of the vehicle, and again, they were forced to pause their escape and crouch in a shallow gully. There was shouting, and they heard a man running up the path, torch in hand. Instinctively, Peter pushed Cash closer to the ground, and the man passed them by. Because he was ahead, they couldn't continue. They lay there for some time until they heard footsteps returning, and the man, slower this time and with a torch directed at his feet, was seen reaching the vehicle. On the other hand, Peter had noticed a gun.

Giving him time, they carefully got up stiff from the cold and rejoined the path. They saw the vehicle turning around. They stopped near the top; Peter scooped up ice-cold water from the edge of a small loch and drank it. Cash joined him.

Looking around, Peter spotted searchlights crisscrossing the sky to the east, like light sabres joined in a duel and the first hints of dawn. Alarmed, as night provided cover, he led Cash, who was now shivering, her arms wrapped around her body, along the path, relieved as the gradient changed heading down. Shortly after, they reached a vantage point above Sanaigmore Bay. Stopping again, he surveyed the bay. One house had lights on, but the farm buildings, many abandoned, and the Art Gallery that he knew were all in darkness.

'The house looks like a possibility for getting help, but we won't take any chances. I am not sure why it has lights on at this time. At worst, one of the farm buildings can provide cover until people arrive to open the Gallery.

Cash was too tired to respond, but Peter helped her onto her feet and got moving again, their muscles aching from the blows they had received and both shivering with cold.

51

Peter and Cash hid behind a rocky outcrop, looking over Sanaigmore Bay as dawn streaked the sky to the east, bringing what had been dull outlines to life. Narrower at the mouth, the bay expanded its rock-lined shores in a horseshoe shape, giving way to a sandy beach and sand dunes. In front of them was a cairn commemorating a shipwreck, if he remembered correctly, then the dwelling, a two-storey modern build with farm buildings beside it, some in ruins, extending to the long single-storey Art Gallery with a pitched roof. The Gallery was a good outlet for Jenny's paintings, and the owner was friendly, but it would be hours before she arrived. The problem was they needed help now as they were cold and wet, Cash shivering and inadequately dressed. In the circumstances, it was going to be a long wait.

The curtains were drawn at the house, and the light he had noticed earlier was now switched off; probably someone had gone to the toilet, he thought. While thinking about the next steps, Peter saw a pickup truck, headlights on, driving at speed down the twisty, narrow road to the bay. On top of the cabin was a spotlight, so he reckoned it was their captors, and instinctively, they kept their heads down.

The truck braked hard in front of the house, churning up the grass in front of the house in his haste, and a man got out, limping and walking with difficulty to the front door. It had to be their captor, relieved they had not gone to the house. An outside light came on, so the driver was expected, and he was ushered inside quickly. Having had such an arduous journey, Peter was dismayed that the people in the house and back at the farmhouse they had left were somehow connected.

Neither was in a good state, and a long walk to the road that circled Loch Gorm was challenging. And they might encounter the pickup or some other vehicle searching for them. He had gambled on the route over the hill, and it hadn't worked out. Glancing at Cash, he reckoned she would need more of her feisty spirit to survive the next few hours.

More lights were now back on at the house, and he watched as the man with the limp emerged, walking again with difficulty back to the pickup. In a minute, he drove off, and Peter breathed a sigh of relief as the rear lights receded.

'We need shelter,' and Cash stared back, and he could tell she was struggling. The bay in front of them was a scene Peter was familiar with from childhood, a breath-taking view with islands on the horizon on a clear day. He had swam from the sandy beach often in better times. He reckoned they could slip from rock to rock, avoid being seen from the house, and reach one of the farm buildings to hide.

A noise from behind distracted him, and he turned to see what he believed was their other captor walking along the path, head twisting and turning, searching for them. He would be level with their position in a few minutes, and they would be exposed. Mind made up, he gripped Cash's arm gently, pointing towards the figure approaching and motioned for them to move. Shifting their position without being seen was not easy. Still, fear of discovery drove them on, and they worked their way down the slope, reaching the beach where large boulders shielded them. The tide was almost in, the waves covering their feet before receding. Quietly, he explained his plan.

Slowly, they crouched and worked their way from boulder to boulder, hoping not to be seen, leaving bold footprints in the soft sand that was unavoidable. Soon, they drew level with the house, but a moss-covered stone wall, topped with a rusting iron single-strand fence, provided cover. Buoyed by the progress, they reached a sandy dune, opening up to a sandy gully which hid them as they passed below the house. Above them was a large brick building, once a shelter for cattle; now, out of sight of the house, they ascended a steep bank and dropped inside the building through a frameless window. There was a rotting bale of hay in one corner and a van, the front of which was draped in a large tarpaulin with a trailer beside it. Peter immediately recognised the van, and as he pointed it out to Cash, she stepped back, not wanting to relive the horror of their abduction days before.

'I think we should move on,' he added. Peter glanced out of a brick-framed window with the rotting remains of a wooden frame and stiffened. Someone was approaching, and he motioned towards Cash. He relaxed slightly when he recognised Shaun from the whisky shop, then changed his mind. He could only have come from the house. Did he live here? Was Shaun involved in this? Peter decided not to take the risk and pulled Cash beside him as they moved between the van and the wall, attempting to hide.

Shaun appeared to walk past the brick opening at the far end as they shrank out of sight. Suddenly, Shaun twisted towards the van. 'Peek a boo, Peter, out you come,' he stated. They froze. 'And bring Cash with you.'

'Come on, hurry up,' he added impatiently. They stood up as Shaun entered the building, a smile playing on his face. 'You've led us a merry dance,' he stated, his Irish accent more pronounced than usual. 'Time you came inside and talked to us.'

In his hand was a handgun. 'I'm the friendly face,' he warned, 'some of the others are not the nicest, and you have upset some of them. Be polite; remember your manners with this lot.'

Shaun pointed his handgun towards the house as they stepped from the false security of the former cattle shed. 'We spotted you making your way along the beach. Too colourful a dress, Cash, even if it is streaked with dirt.' The front door was open, and he could see someone lurking there. Taking Cash's hand and offering her support, they walked before Shaun. As soon as they reached the front door, hands hauled them in, and the door was immediately slammed shut behind them.

52

Malcolm had updated Henry by phone earlier on what he knew. He told him he was now caring for Alison and their new family additions at his dad's house. The events had surprised Henry, and Sir Angus's death was a mystery. Was he indeed the target, or was it the bumptious McIntosh? The investment manager had no doubt made enemies, but killing him was a powerful statement. Malcolm had added that the man who had been tracked and killed appeared foreign, so in his mind, he ruled out Jim Semple, the bitter ex-marine who hated Gillies. But he would mention his name to the police. If the gunman was foreign, it raised all sorts of questions. Who did he work for, and what were his motives for killing Sir Angus - crucial questions needing answers. Questions of national security also loomed large. Was the killing the start of something bigger? If an unfriendly power had sanctioned the killing, then goodness knows the consequences. And all done here on a remote Scottish island, which would now live in infamy and be known not just for its whisky. Henry poured himself more coffee but was disturbed by a knock on the door. He quietly shut Alan's bedroom door as he passed his sleeping friend.

Lena Marshall was standing outside, her face etched with exhaustion, a group of three people beside her – a red-haired man with a straggly beard, a tall Asian man with a long, bushy beard and a tall black woman with braided hair.

'Can we come in?' Lena suggested, 'You'll know what has

happened,' and Henry grimaced, 'and we have some questions you might be able to help us with.'

Intrigued, Henry pulled the door wide and led them to the lounge.

'Time for coffee?' he asked, 'none of you appear to have slept, I suspect.'

'Coffee would be good,' and Henry got busy.

'I take it you have heard?' the police inspector added.

'Malcolm phoned me. Bit of a mess.'

'An understatement. My colleagues are from intelligence,' she continued. 'This is Roddy, Imran and Ash.'

'Make yourself at home,' and Henry invited them to sit as he went to prepare the hot drinks.

'Inspector Marshall,' and he gave her position in front of the others to show respect, 'we have been in major incidents like this before, but probably not with so many political ramifications.' Lena was being tested, he felt, but coping.

'They have taken fingerprints and the DNA of the gunman and are searching databases. And keep this to yourself. They have also found diving gear stowed away in a cove on the Oa. The assassin intended to swim across Loch Indaal and escape. It was carefully planned, and he knew where to find his victim, so he must have had inside information. A lucky shot winged him, and he was forced to change plans. You have met Jenny several times, so you can imagine how distraught she was when a gunman arrived at her front door, reviving memories of past traumas. She was highly agitated and was calling out for her husband. Jenny's now getting help and support. You've had a lot of contact with Sir Angus recently and can best describe his mood and movements and your dealings with him.

I also know that Jenny's husband and business partner, Cash, are still missing. However unlikely, we must consider any possible connections between their absence and last night's events. You appear to know much about them from what you told me yesterday and are worried about their safety.'

Henry noticed the others checking him out, assessing him, no doubt aware of his background. That was a cross he was always going to have to carry. Enough about the cross you carry is designed to be just right, not too heavy or too light, that was too simplistic to Henry. Without Mary easing the load, his cross was overwhelming.

'Our friend, Arthur, is flapping about,' Lena added, raising her eyebrows, 'fortunately, more senior help is coming. When further help arrives, I will want attention paid to those who are missing,' and the look she conveyed convinced Henry that Rogers would not consider any issues raised by Henry. The biased, ignorant fool, Henry thought.

'I can imagine,' Henry replied, sipping his coffee and picking up another biscuit before remembering to pass the opened packet around.

'He doesn't know we are here, would disapprove, but you mentioned Sir Angus's unpopularity. My colleagues here would like to investigate this with you, and since they report to a different boss, they have more freedom.'

'I'll do what I can.'

'I knew you would, Henry. Keep in touch.'

Marshall finished her coffee and got up, leaving them a weary figure, but that was the nature of police work. Everything tended to land on your plate at one time. You had to prioritise and yet keep an open mind.

Henry turned to the three who were left. 'I'll start at the beginning,' and explained how he was contacted and instructed to investigate a family issue and then support Jenny by finding her missing husband. Sir Angus was going to pay, 'which might be an issue now,' he added wistfully.

'I might have gone to the police about Peter Meldrum's

disappearance, but Sir Angus was dead against it. He said the family wouldn't want the publicity. Jenny did agree, her mental health fragile, to say the least, and difficulties in the marriage,' and he explained the background and Jenny's state of mind.

'The clincher was Sir Angus claiming to spot Peter and Cash in the front seats of an elusive white Ford Transit van and expressing the opinion they appeared happy. I was expecting to find the pair in a love nest. Now I know he didn't want anything to upset the planned visit of McIntosh. I went back and quizzed him about the sighting after I found Cash's earring and button at the site he mentioned. That suggested trouble to me, but he couldn't explain it and didn't change his story. A lover's tiff, he hinted. If it was, it didn't bode well for their relationship.'

'I should mention we were burgled, and that doesn't happen often in Islay, and my notebook was photographed. Whoever it was used the information to send a false message to a person on the list claiming to be Peter Meldrum and basically stating he was alright. I was a bit more suspicious after that. Someone was trying too hard to convince me that the couple were okay.'

'We decided to go to the police when Alison, Malcolm's wife, and Jenny found Peter's phone case smashed on the beach near their home. That again suggested something untoward had occurred. Lena was prepared to hear my story about them missing, but her boss, Chief Inspector Rogers, stopped it. He doesn't like me, but that is another story.' Henry paused, taking time to admit why he had delayed contacting the police. 'I'll be honest, I didn't want to deal with the police,' he confessed, 'or at least some of them after the way they treated me. I was right. Rogers dismissed me out of hand, but Lena is more open-minded; we've worked together in the past.'

He explained what also worried him: the disappearance of Cash's Porsche, its discovery at the farmhouse and subsequent removal to a place beside Loch Gruinart after it had been spotted. That required organisation. Who did the removal?

'It all sounds as if Peter or the people behind his disappearance didn't want you getting involved. That surely couldn't be Sir Angus because he employed you.'

'Good point, Imran.'

Interrupting Henry, Roddy stated. 'Did you know Ranald, the occupant of the farmhouse, was also killed?'

'No, I didn't. Good grief,' replied Henry, shocked, 'Malcolm can't have known.' Henry frowned, tapping his finger against the tabletop as he tried to work out the implications of this latest news. The others waited.

'Why kill Ranald?' Henry queried as he started to crystallise his thoughts. 'Was he in the wrong place at the wrong time? Or was there a link to Sir Angus?'

'This could change everything,' he finally announced. 'Ranald allowed the people who had taken the Porsche to keep it at the farmhouse. It had been removed within two hours after we saw it on our boat trip. I thought of him as eccentric, and Sir Angus gave the impression he was harmless, finding a living where he could and allowed to use the house with his permission – an act of kindness. Ranald knew about the car and was probably paid to hide it. If he was killed, maybe it was because he knew too much and might expose the group behind the shooting of Sir Angus. We have a possible link between the two killings. Someone has something to hide. That might suggest that Sir Angus was the intended target after all. Everyone would think McIntosh was the intended victim. Ranald also described the woman who took the Porsche. Alan, my companion, later thought it might fit the description of Nora, who works in the local whisky shop. But that's very tenuous,' Henry added. 'I would trust little Ranald said.'

Alan, who had now appeared was making breakfast for himself and had heard some of the conversation, agreed.

'I should introduce you; this is my brother-in-law, Alan, who has been a great help and extremely patient for someone who only came to Islay to sample the whiskies.'

'Would either of you recognise this person?' Imran asked, producing a photo.

Henry shook his head, but Alan took the photo and examined it closely. 'I saw him at Battery Point retrieving a carrier bag from under a bush yesterday.'

'A dead drop?' Roddy suggested. The terminology didn't need to be explained. Everyone had watched John le Carre films.

'Petrov,' Imran blurted out, adding quickly, 'forget the name.'

'Maybe he is the case officer?' Ash contributed.

'Could be,' Roddy replied.

Henry liked the team; they worked together, no one attempting to better the others.

Ash pulled out her laptop and got busy. 'Our boss needs to know,' she explained, 'and Lena.'

There was a knock at the door, Alan got up, and Ronnie came in, puzzled by the group in the room.

'They are working on the case along with the police.' Henry explained. Ronnie's recent experience with intelligence officers like Nick meant he didn't ask any further questions, nor was he over-friendly.

'I've been grilled, so will everyone else, and have you seen the morning news. Everyone from the American President to our PM is very concerned. McIntosh has appeared on the screens expressing grief that his good friend Sir Angus was assassinated but refusing to speculate that he was the intended victim. When the daily newspapers arrive, his face will be on each one. He'll love it. They've impounded my boat for the moment, but I can still use the RIB, so business continues, thankfully.'

Imran leant forward towards Ronnie. 'Please talk us through

what happened. I know that you will be asked many times, but often, something extra comes to mind.' When Ronnie finished, Imran thanked him. 'Who would know about the trip?'

'Lots of people. Those at the marina in Port Ellen, all the security, Mick, who sailed the RIB, but he wasn't aware of who was on the trip until he arrived.'

'Let's consider Nora again,' Imran requested. 'She works at the Whisky Shop?'

'Yes, Shaun and Nora's Whisky Shop in Bowmore,' Henry replied.

'A woman possibly fitting Nora's description takes the car away from the farmhouse on the Oa.' Imran stated.

'Yes,' said Henry, seeing where this was going.

'We better check them out,' Imran suggested.

'They are off the island and have been for a few days. I spoke to Mike, their shop assistant,' added Ronnie.

'We still need to check them out, visit their shop, pay a visit to their house and see if they are back,' Roddy suggested.

'I agree, the whisky shop is around the corner, up from the Coop.' Henry stated. 'Do you fancy a trip to Sanaigmore, Alan, where they live? No distillery, but there is an Art gallery. Just have a look around. A preliminary visit before a more formal one from you or the police.'

'A different type of culture. Might be good for me, and I need to take Hazel something back which is not liquid.'

'I'll update, Lena,' Ash added.

Ronnie's phone pinged as they spoke, and he took it from his pocket. He called to Henry. 'Are these your friends Charlie and Drew having a nosey around Cash's Porsche?' The group gathered around the screen as Henry confirmed their identity, watching Charlie open the car door. The alarm went off, and quickly, Charlie reached down and switched it off.

'Experienced,' Imran suggested.

'Very, but not very good. I encountered him many times in the course of my career. He was good for my arrest statistics. He claims he is on Islay to visit his daughter and her partner, the other person we are viewing.'

Imran smiled. 'They've lost interest anyway and are moving away.'

Henry declared, 'That sums Charlie up, 'always looking for unlawful gain. His son-in-law appears cut from the same cloth. When you contact Lena, you might suggest they bring in the car for safety.'

53

Petrov had made it to a ruined cottage at the edge of the Gruinart Flats at the end of Loch Gruinart and decided to rest. It had taken him the previous day and overnight to reach this point, mainly trekking over moorland with woods giving him cover for short breaks. He now had regained his fitness and sharpness, he felt, something he struggled with when he was living in Glasgow. Everyday living didn't give him the scope to go for long hikes or tone his karate skills since nothing could be allowed to draw attention to himself, marking him out as different. Occasionally, he would tackle a long-distance route but complete it in a few days, while most people would struggle in a week.

The cottage had been deserted for many years, its earthen floors trampled now by cattle and sheep, turned into mud by the rain seeping through the holes in the roof. Petrov found a dryish corner and sat down, hauling his large backpack towards him. Sipping from his water bottle, he nibbled on an energy bar and ruffled his hair, wiping the sweat from his brow. Minutes later, he felt composed and reflected on his journey.

The first part had been challenging across the moorland, exposed and vulnerable, careful to avoid being seen, which lengthened his journey. There were few houses or roads to cross, but he avoided any contact, keeping well away from places where dogs might be alarmed by a stranger's presence. Woods provided more security, but near the road from Port Askaig, people walked dogs along forest tracks, and he hid from them. Carefully, he crossed the road, skirted around a large house and sheltered in a small outcrop of trees, taking time to rest.

As evening fell, he waited to cross more moorland. He saw to the south helicopters, their searchlights scanning the ground, performing some macabre dance. Someone is in trouble, he mused. Maybe a missing fisherman or a walker fallen off a cliff. For the rest of the night, he noticed planes arriving and leaving, lots of activity at the airport, suspecting something more dramatic had occurred.

Petrov rationed himself to one energy bar, drank more water, and took in his surroundings. The package would be somewhere, and eventually, he found it taped under the kitchen table, annoyed he hadn't noticed the small chalked mark left as a sign. Removing the plastic coating, he found a small radio and more instructions. The instructions were simple, and he was pleased he had reached this place with easy access to his destinations. He never met those who left instructions and resources for him and probably never would. Still, he was proud his nation had penetrated enemy countries and could deliver a support network.

The radio was a small transistor, nothing fancy, but he switched it on, tuning into the BBC. As he listened, he understood the flurry of nocturnal activity over Islay's sky. An assassination attempt on the UK Defence Secretary on this island was a dramatic event. His mission was now more complicated; he was surprised it was not to be abandoned. It was imperative he wasn't exposed, or people would link him to the attempted assassination and cause problems for his country. His superiors had faith in him; he would deliver. He felt a surge of patriotic pride, given the responsibility to save the day, the lone hero against all odds.

It was too early to move, so he settled down, but not before he checked his weapons, ensuring they were ready. Then he rested his head on his rucksack and permitted himself to snatch some sleep.

54

The text message was blunt, which was Swan's style. A Royal Navy Land Rover will pick you up from Morrison Square, opposite the Coop. Be there in ten minutes.

They were about to leave Henry's house, and Roddy updated the others as they went.

'Message from Swan; he has sent a vehicle for me,' and he shrugged. 'A bit of a mystery. You get the good bit, a visit to the Whisky Shop,' and made light of his excursion, but inside, he was puzzled.

'Let us know where you're going,' Ash commanded, appearing baffled, and Imran looked thoughtful.

'If I can,' Roddy replied.

They covered the short distance to Morrisons Square and hung about, sitting on a bench almost opposite the Whisky Shop. Shortly, an RN Land Rover appeared beside the church at the top of the street and drove down the hill. Roddy stood up and motioned to the driver, a naval rating who got out and confirmed Roddy's identity. Roddy got in and was whisked away. The two left behind shrugged.

'Who knows what Swan gets up to,' Imran commented as the Land Rover disappeared around the corner at the church.

'I have to take you to the airport, where a Chinook is waiting,' the rating explained. Fifteen minutes later, the vehicle was allowed onto the airstrip and drove to a waiting Chinook with the rear ramp down. The landing strip was busier than usual, with tents pitched over by the perimeter fence and several vehicles, primarily military.

As he walked up the ramp to the Chinook, to his surprise, sitting in one of the metal frame seats was Swan, helmet on, his expression dour as he pointed to the seat beside him. Roddy was strapped in and given a helmet. With the rear entrance closed, the din rose appreciably as the twin rotors lifted the Chinook off the ground. Swan turned, giving Roddy a thumbs up, and put a finger to his lips. The mystery continued.

The Chinook swiftly left Islay behind and crossed the Sound of Jura, and then Roddy was aware of it losing height and then a bump as it settled softly on the ground. The whine of the rotors eased, and the ramp was lowered, and Swan and Roddy got out in the middle of a field, a white cottage a short distance away with water beyond. Parked close to the house were several police cars and an ambulance. The building was a short distance back from the road, and between it and the sea was what appeared to be a boat house. One of the crew members ushered the pair of them towards a waiting policeman, all instinctively ducking. Roddy and the Inspector immediately recognised each other from their meeting in Oban.

'Inspector Mathieson,' Roddy stated warmly, shaking the policeman's hand. He introduced Swan.

'Your friend Paul Russell has been active again,' he declared sternly, fixing them both with piercing blue eyes.

'We now know him under a different name,' Swan contributed.

'Interesting. A messy business. The woman who lives here – Jean Scott was the name she was using,' and his expression conveyed that he didn't believe that was her real name, 'was discovered by a friend this morning, having failed to meet up with her as arranged. Jean Scott was dead when her friend arrived, and sadly, her friend is quite traumatised by what she discovered. It wasn't an easy death. Her body bears all the signs of torture. SOCO are in there just now. Maybe let them finish before we go in.'

'Russell's fingerprints have already been identified, along with the bloodied fingerprints of Sally Rundell. Whatever the motive, the poor woman struggled and suffered grievously. I have witnessed many a murder, but this ranks amongst the worst. Whether she was being punished or some dire secret was being extracted, I don't know, but the killer is a nasty piece of work. The sooner this person is apprehended, the better.'

'But I would like you to see this first,' and the Inspector led them from the cottage across the road towards the wood-slatted boathouse. 'No boats inside, and we were only checking for bodies, and we almost missed it,' he said, issuing them with rubber gloves. Opening the side door, he showed them in. At the entrance, two wooden doors hung above the sea level and inside, the water lapped against the interior. To each side and to the rear was narrow decking and metal rungs for tying up boats, and a long pole with a hook was suspended on the far wall. The Inspector pulled on a cord, and light flooded the inside.

Mathieson waited, wondering if they would spot what his men had noticed. Roddy moved forward, eased up a section of the panelling, and placed it against the far wall.

'Good boy,' the softly spoken policeman said. 'When our officers noticed it, it hadn't been replaced correctly.'

They peered inside the void now exposed.

'Wow,' Roddy exclaimed. The exposed space was far more extensive than expected, at least doubling the size of the boathouse, and was lined with concrete. There was extensive wiring and sockets and a stack of what appeared to be batteries charging up, red lights on, hooked up along one wall. There were several electrical panels, one showing a small greenlight and several dials and digital displays.

'Quite a treasure trove. We traced the cabling back outside, and whoever did this tapped into the electrical supply for the area. The clever bit is that it is constantly used at a low current to charge up batteries. I don't think the electricity company would notice. The panelling can be removed to create extra space to hide a small vessel.' Mathieson stood back and let the others inspect the space. 'Jean Scott's fingerprints are everywhere, along with some others, so she knew all about this, probably was the caretaker.'

Roddy gave Swan a sideways glance and waited for his response. Swan examined the batteries and the display units.

'This is a significant find, Inspector. I am most grateful for your diligence. I can't reveal what has been discovered, not a hundred per cent certain myself, but the technology is Russian. We've uncovered assets an unfriendly state is using to spy on us. I can say no more. Others will be here soon to conduct further analysis. Please let no one near here until they arrive. Now, I wish to see the body.'

'I'll provide plastic covers for your shoes when we get to the cottage. Come this way.'

Inside the cottage, SOCO was finishing off, the body still lying on the floor, covered by a plastic sheet. The Inspector pulled the cover back to reveal the body. Roddy felt the acid burn at the back of his throat as he struggled to keep down his last food. The woman's eyes were bulging, her mouth open. It was clear she had been tortured.

'A brave woman who didn't reveal her secrets easily,' Roddy stated as he swallowed hard.

'Or a very frightened one,' Swan declared. 'Thank you, Inspector; I've seen enough.' Roddy was relieved to turn away and leave the building and gulp in the fresh air outside, attempting to steady himself.

'Never easy,' Swan suggested, almost kindly, and he led Roddy aside.

'The poor woman suffered grievously, and I suspect we'll discover she is Russian when we research her background. Something has gone wrong, and this woman has borne the consequences. Why it had to be so brutal, I don't know.'

'Sally Rundell's fingerprints were smeared with blood, so she probably did it, not Petrov.'

'A reasonable conclusion, Roddy. We also know Rundell has access to Novichok, and I wonder why she didn't use it. After all, she used it on her lover.'

Roddy stood quietly beside Swan, not wishing to interrupt his thoughts.

Finally, he turned towards Roddy, biting his lower lip and placing an arm on Roddy's shoulder.

'Before we get back into the helicopter, we have much to discuss; I believe I know what is happening.'

55

The hands that grabbed Peter and Cash pulled them roughly inside, and Cash stumbled, falling against the arm of a chair and landing on her knees, winded. Peter instinctively went towards her but was gripped firmly from behind, unable to move. Shaun stood by the door, gun in hand. In the corner, Peter was shocked to see Nora observing the scene as if she was watching a movie – disconnected, her black hair contrasting to her white face, a woman under pressure and uncomfortable. Little made sense. He knew the couple, talked to them, gave some advice about pricing rare whisky, never imagined another side to them, and wondered what their role in all this was.

The handgun in Shaun's hand was a statement, so both were heavily involved. There were three others, including the man who held him, and the others didn't appear disconcerted by his weapon. They were, however, more openly hostile. He couldn't see the man who held him with a painful grip, arms pinned behind him, breathing down his neck, reeking of garlic. The other two were stocky, one completely bald, his white woollen jumper making him appear like the Michelin man, the other grey-haired with a nose that had been broken and twisted to one side, no stranger to violence.

'Help Cash to the sofa, and both sit still,' Shaun commanded, and the powerful grip was released. Cash was sobbing quietly, traumatised. Peter could now see the person who had gripped him, tall, younger than the other two, brown-haired with a long beard. He recognised two of them from the night he was seized.

'Don't try anything funny,' Shaun stated. 'You'll wish you had remained in the cellar. It would have been a lot easier. We could have released you or let someone know where you were. Now you know about us and have also upset Eriks. He will be the only person pleased to see you both when he returns,' looking at his watch, which suggested Eriks's return was imminent.

The grey-haired man gestured for the gun, and Shaun handed it over. The three men then started talking heatedly, in a foreign language, pointing at their captors, ignoring Shaun and Nora. Cash sat head bowed, but Peter looked around in horror, not understanding a word but knowing the men were very angry.

Nora stood up and crossed the room to Cash. 'She needs to wash and have something to eat. So does he. Will it make any difference, and they will be more biddable.'

The grey-haired male understood English and grunted, turning to the others, and a further debate ensued. The man with the beard who had held Peter so firmly appeared annoyed with the other two. Shaun shuffled his feet uncomfortably.

'Shut up,' yelled Shaun, 'and I told you before speak in English. Nora, take Cash to the bathroom. Everyone else pipe down. We're almost there, let's not lose it now. We need to hold our nerve.'

The bald man stomped off to the kitchen, and Peter soon heard the kettle boiling. The others sat down, keeping a wary eye on Peter, and quickly talked animatedly to each other, still not in English.

'You've caused a lot of trouble,' Shaun told Peter after a brief silence. 'Why were you so nosey. Couldn't you have driven on?'

'A big fireworks display, not far from my house. A boat burning, yes, I was curious, so would you have been.' His aggressive tone briefly alarmed the man with the beard. 'What the hell was it?'

Shaun didn't reply, noticing the others had stopped talking; the person who had returned from the kitchen was also following the conversation.

'It's you who will suffer for being so inquisitive,' he stated, his accent heavy.

Having let Cash shower and then given her a jumper, which swamped her, Nora brought Cash back into the room, leaving her to be watched by others. Nora soon returned from the kitchen with a mug of tea and a sandwich.

'Shaun, you let Peter have a shower,' and grumbling, he led Peter to the bathroom, keeping an eye on him. The hot water was refreshing as he cleaned himself, but it also identified the bruises and cuts on his body, which stung. Shaun only gave him a couple of minutes before turning off the water.

'Towel yourself, quickly.' On his return, a cup of tea and a sandwich awaited him.

'I'm not sitting here all day watching them; tie them up and shove them in another room,' the grey-haired man demanded. 'And warn them not to make any noise,' and he ran his finger across his throat to emphasise the point.

Shaun nodded, returned to the room after a few minutes with a clothes rope still in its packaging, cut a length off and tied their hands together. 'No tricks, now.' He led them away upstairs, pushing them into a bedroom. 'No shouting or I'll gag you.' Shaun bound the pair to the metal frame at the bottom of the bed. He pulled heavy curtains across the glass doors, which led to a Juliette balcony, before leaving, blanking out the blue sky, heightening their sense of being confined.

To Peter, this brought back too many memories aboard McGory's boat, off Mull, with Jason. He struggled to contain himself; this time, he couldn't think of a solution. Taking deep breaths, he eventually opened his eyes to see Cash studying him.

'We are in trouble,' she began.

'Really,' Peter answered sarcastically.

'One of them stated Sir Angus was dead.'

'Sir Angus dead,' Peter queried, shocked by the news.

'Yes, shot last night while out fishing in a boat with the Defence Secretary.'

'That'll cause a stink and explains all the searchlights and helicopters buzzing about last night.'

'One of the group killed him, and they believe that he was in turn killed by the SAS. They are very twitchy, frightened they will be exposed. They are in lots of trouble. The men are Russians and already up to their necks in trouble, having stolen something from their government.'

'It's good Russian is one of your languages.'

'And several other languages. I even spent some time in Moscow. By their accent, these men come from somewhere east of the capital. They're leaving tonight; a boat is coming to collect them. Shaun and Nora are going with them. We're not; they'll kill us since we can identify them.'

Initially, Peter was stunned, and then he swore it helped release a little tension.

'The boat-like thing we saw is going with them. They are going to make a lot of money from it.

I recognise the grey-haired man; I believe he is called Daniil. He and the bald man surprised me as I stood by the Porsche and hauled me into the back of their van. They keep talking in the room about a fugu, which means a puffer fish in Russian, but I don't understand what they mean. They're frightened of the Russian state coming after them, though they are Russian themselves, so they must have stolen the boat from them. Maybe it is some spy vessel. It was fancy with all its solar panels and rigging on the mast; it looked strange with burnt-out fairy lights. It's probably still in the van, though you think there would be little left after it flared up so brightly.'

'They transferred us to the front when they loaded it into the back. And still had the bald-headed one in the back pointing a gun at my head to keep me quiet,' Peter stated, 'making me drive. We stopped at Duich Lots when the thing in the back shifted position and pushed open the back doors, and you surprised them by trying to run away.'

'I didn't get far. Oh, I wish we had not stopped to look and just driven on. You would be safe with Jenny, and I would be on holiday.'

'So do I,' Peter replied, 'I'm sorry for the mess I got you into. I thought I would only be a moment, and it was close to the house, so I wanted to check what it was and phone the coastguard if needed. The bearded guy was using a fire extinguisher to put out the flames. He was startled when I appeared, the flames almost out. Suddenly, he whipped out a handgun and pointed it at me. I couldn't believe it. If we get out of this, I am staying away from beaches forever.'

Cash briefly appeared puzzled, probably not fully understanding Peter's previous history.

Peter paused before continuing. 'What gets me is how Shaun and Nora are involved. I was shocked to see them, although Nora was uncomfortable. We have got to think our way through this – third time lucky.'

Cash closed her eyes and muttered something under her breath as if she was praying.

'I have an idea, but let me think it through first.'

56

'Let's pay a visit to Sanaigmore,' Henry suggested after the others had departed, keen to discover what was there and whether the Byrnes were home. So, on roads now familiar, they drove down towards Machir Bay. Then they turned right, and just beyond a red telephone box, they turned right again, following the road down to Sanaigmore Bay, a new part of Islay to them. The condition of the road deteriorated as they approached the bay. As they neared the small settlement, they passed a stone memorial inside a low stone wall. Henry spotted a new house and then drove past farm outbuildings. In the fields around were cattle and sheep. At the end of the road, they reached the gallery.

'No prizes for guessing which house Shaun and Nora live in, and it seems there are people there,' Henry concluded, noticing peaty smoke from the chimney, 'but let's have a walk and then visit the Outback Gallery and not appear too curious.' A few cars were parked close to the gallery, but they found a place.

The air was fresh, and they spotted the now familiar Paps of Jura in the distance, peeking over the horizon. After changing into walking boots, they went through a gate towards the beach. Henry strolled towards the sand dunes at the end of the beach, far away from the house, sheep running away, bleating as he approached. The view was clearing, and they could see islands further out to sea. Having edged down among the sand dunes, Henry lay down, made himself comfortable, took binoculars from his pocket, and started examining the house.

He spotted washing hanging on a line behind the house and noted blinds pulled down in some rooms. Two of the upstairs windows had Juliette balconies, black metal frames with double glass doors behind. Offering the binoculars to Alan, he stated. 'People are living in the house, can't say who.'

Alan quickly handed the binoculars back. 'Someone has just come out, walking towards one of the outhouses.'

Henry quickly refocused. 'A guy with a white jumper? That's not Shaun. He's gone into the largest of the outhouses. Not too much more to tell from here,' Henry suggested, 'time to visit the Gallery.'

The gallery was quite busy, a family sitting at one of the tables having tea and cake whilst a few others were studying the pictures on display or flicking through the racks of prints.

'Something for Hazel?' Henry queried, taking Alan's order for coffee and cake and seeing him work his way around the displays. Henry was no art expert. Most of the frames at his house contained photos of the family, Mary and the boys over the years. Jenny's type of painting did nothing for him. He sipped his tea, enjoyed forking lemon drizzle cake into his mouth and forced his mind from thinking about Mary. Eventually, Alan joined him, and Henry ordered more tea.

'So, what did you get for Hazel?'

'A watercolour of Machir Bay by a local artist.'

'That's excellent,' Henry exclaimed, studying the picture, 'the artist shows the remains of the wrecked ship's boilers beautifully caught in the evening sun and reflected in the pools of water beside it,' Henry stopped, surprised by his sudden eloquence.

Leaving the gallery, they carefully put the picture, now gift-wrapped, in the back of the car and walked towards the memorial. It commemorated the tragic loss of the *Exmouth of Newcastle*, a boat carrying emigrants to the New World from Ireland. It was woefully overloaded, driven off course by a fierce storm and shipwrecked with around two hundred men, women and children lost. While Alan read the inscription, Henry pretended to but instead focussed again on the house, wanting as much information as possible. They walked back towards the gallery and noted that the front groundworks were incomplete and saw many muddy imprints. The people inside, whoever they were, were keeping themselves out of sight, but that proved little.

The next stop was the outbuildings. Some had been reroofed with metal sheeting fixed onto old brick walls, some of the structure possibly dating back to the war. At this time of year, the cattle were all out in the fields. Glancing in, he saw the first one was empty, a layer of mud and glaur clinging to the concrete floor, puddles where the roof leaked. The next building was the one the person from the house had briefly entered. It was bigger, had frameless windows, and the wind whistled through the building. A hay bale was rotting in the corner, and then tucked in behind the front wall, out of sight from the road, was a van covered by a tarpaulin, a trailer beside it. Henry quickly reached it and partially pulled back the cover – it had to be the elusive white Ford Transit. He immediately took a photo of the registration plate and let the cover slip. It wasn't the time to peek inside the van, and Peter and Cash would be elsewhere by now. So, Sir Angus had said something of the truth, but Henry was still unconvinced he told the whole story

Seconds later, he joined Alan again, hoping no one in the house had seen his slight detour. 'Keep walking. The van is in there. We have now a definite link to Shaun and his wife. Take your time so they don't suspect anything,' he cautioned Alan. They reached their car, removed their boots, and Henry reversed the vehicle. 'Don't look at the house as we pass. Let's get away and hope no one saw us.'

57

Just as Henry and Alan returned to their accommodation and were letting themselves in, he noticed Ash and Imran getting out of their car, parked along the street. They had been waiting for them.

'Can we talk?' Imran asked as he reached Henry.

'Of course, in you come,' Henry replied, opening the door.

'We've been to the Whisky Shop. Little is happening there. Shaun and Nora were not there, and Mike, the assistant, thought they were still off the island.'

'Someone is at their house. I've just been to Sanaigmore, and there was at least one person living there who looked Eastern European. More importantly, I believe I found the missing white Ford Transit. It was concealed under a tarpaulin in a farm building nearby. Can you check the registration for me?'

'Yes, of course,' Ash replied.

'Maybe someone has taken over their house, or there is a possible link between the couple and the disappearance of Peter and Cash.'

Imran's phone pinged, and he took it out. 'Lena says they've finished interviewing Murdo Evans, Sir Angus's butler, and he states Sir Angus was outraged when he returned from a visit to his farm at Saligo Bay last week. He wasn't sure what upset him, but he was furious, unlike Gillies.'

Henry interrupted. 'I know he had a fallout with the builders, but they have long gone. The house at the farm is incomplete.'

'Our boss is not so sure it was a political assassination and wants us to follow up on any leads. You seem to share his doubts, so here we are. Lena felt you could be useful in helping us.' Ash explained, 'and it got us away. Rogers is still fixated that McIntosh was the intended victim, and politically, it is vital to discover if there is a connection. Let's hope not.'

Henry stated. 'I've walked past the farm he owns there. I know where it is. Shall we check it out?'

They left quickly and headed for Loch Gorm, stopping outside the gates that led to the beach. Alan got out and opened them, ushering the car through and past the remains of wartime installations.

'Beautiful, unusually shaped hills,' Ash commented as she looked north towards what Henry had been told were known locally as the Opera House rocks, according to Malcolm. Ahead lay the house and the empty cattle shed beside it.

'It's thought as many as three men lived here despite the house being unfinished. They drive an Audi, but I don't see any car. Maybe they've gone out.

'Very quiet, where are the birds,' Alan commented.

'It does seem very quiet,' Henry agreed.

The house still appeared empty and unfinished as they reached it and parked the car. Henry wandered outside, the white harling gleaming in the afternoon sun. The dormer windows were covered in sheets of MDF. Weeds were sprouting around the bottom of the downpipes. Round the back, two concrete steps led up to the kitchen, and Henry immediately noticed dark patches on the steps.

'Quickly here,' he shouted as he reached the steps, bending down. 'Blood,' he stated, and the others caught up and stopped beside him. The door was partially open. A bloody, smeared trail led into the kitchen.

'Imran, you know the drill. Carefully enter and see where the trail leads.'

Avoiding the blood as best he could, Imran worked his way in.

'Someone has been shot here in the hallway, there's blood,' Imran shouted, adding, 'and I suspect a bullet embedded in the wall. The body's been dragged out.'

'Okay, Imran, I'm coming in. Alan, the fewer people inside, the better. Stay outside. Ash, check your phone signal; we must call the police.'

Henry joined Imran and pointed to the stairs, where there was more blood.

He glanced at Imran. 'Another shooting upstairs, and a body dragged down. I think we're looking at two people having been shot.'

Imran edged his way upstairs. 'A pool of blood on the landing and a bullet hole in the wooden floor,' and he worked around the two bedrooms and bathroom. Still no sign of anybody. A sign of commotion in the first bedroom; the metal framed camping bed has been overturned, and the sleeping bag and blankets scattered.'

'I think they both have been hauled outside.'

Henry's mind was whirling with too many questions, hoping it couldn't be Peter and Cash. Back outside, he looked around. Marram-covered sand dunes were close, and ahead was the cattle shed. He walked to the cattle shed; strip lights were still on inside.

He remembered they were on the last time; it seemed Sir Angus wasn't concerned with his electricity bill.

Henry sniffed the air. There was a foul smell. Not so much decaying bodies but human waste. Puzzled, he searched the cattle shed, noticing blood on the ground stretching towards a plastic sheet. Henry grasped it and hauled it away. Underneath was a trapdoor, and his fingers pulled back the bolt, and he lifted it just as Ash and Imran reached it. There was a pungent stench, which made him and the others gag.

Imran produced his iPhone and used it as a torch, kneeling at the edge and ducking his head inside the cellar.

'Two bodies inside, both dead and male. Shot. Besides them, there are many empty sandwich wrappings and an upturned pail, which I think was used as a toilet. I'll go inside,' and he dropped down, forced to crouch, covering his nose with a hanky.

'Both men shot in the back, a bit messy. Some people have been kept here given the empty food wrappings and empty bottles of water. In the corner, hold on,' and he shone the light into the corner. 'Snatches of a dress. Paisley pattern.'

'That's what Cash wore when I saw her at the restaurant. This is where they were kept captive. But they're not here now, and the car has gone. Ash, call the police and let your boss know. We should have a wee look around,' Henry continued, pausing as Alan appeared very pale.

'Never nice, Alan. You go to the gate and wait for the police to arrive.' Alan was pleased to leave the scene, and as he wandered away, Henry added, 'We still haven't found the missing pair, but we know where they were held, and someone has come along and murdered the two staying here, who were probably looking after them. So, either they escaped, the murderer has taken them, or someone else has got them, and the murderer is elsewhere.'

'Roddy mentioned a person called Petrov,' and both Imran and Ash pulled back, unwilling to confirm.

'Okay, you can't tell me, but the name sounds Russian, and those two down there are probably East European. There has to be a connection.'

'Logical,' Imran stated, and he started to look around the cattle shed and quickly outside, wandering over to the nearby sand dunes.

In the distance, Henry heard a police siren approaching. Minutes later, through the gate came several police cars, stopping at the house. Henry wandered over.

Rogers bustled out of the first car. 'What are you doing here?' he demanded of Henry.

'Still searching for the missing couple. It appears they were being held underneath the floor of the cattle shed for several days. Either they have escaped, or someone has taken them elsewhere, but their two captors have taken their place.'

'Get him away from here,' he shouted, 'contaminating a crime scene.'

Henry shrugged and walked towards his car.

From the last vehicle, a familiar face appeared – Roddy and, beside him, a man with the most deep-set eyes and bushy eyebrows, who quickly covered the ground between them. 'Henry,' he queried, 'I'm Swan. I would appreciate a chat with you. Later at your house?'

Henry agreed. Looking back, the Chief Inspector was barking instructions. Lena was staying by the door of the car she had arrived in. Trampled by incompetence, he thought as he started the car and drove slowly towards the gate where Alan was waiting, still ashen-faced. They had to pull over as they drove back to let an ambulance pass.

…

Hidden in the hills overlooking the crime scene was Petrov, disappointed that his victims had been found so quickly. Still, he only needed a few more hours to complete his mission. Again compulsively, he checked his weapons.

58

Ronnie had berthed at Craighouse, on Jura, when he received the call on his mobile. A woman wanted to hire his boat to take her from Tayvallich, a small village on the mainland opposite part of the way up Loch Sween, to Port Askaig. He had frequently completed this regular crossing, covered by his passenger licence. Cautiously, he checked the weather forecast; she wanted to travel in a few hours, and the outlook was calm. Some people didn't like travelling on the RIB, but she appeared keen and assured him she was a good sailor. She offered cash and an excellent rate. Despite being tired, he accepted, not knowing how long *Casablanca* would be out of commission; the money was helpful. He did have friends in Tayvallich, but they had moved on to live with their son in Perth.

Early afternoon, he set out on the twenty-mile journey and allowed an hour, given the tides. Port Askaig also suited him since Pamela would pick him up later from there. He arrived on time and saw a woman standing by herself, clutching a holdall, a woollen hat pulled down over her face, partly covering her long hair. He waved as he pulled the RIB up against the small concrete pier, tying the boat up as she approached.

'Lily?' he queried, and she walked quicker towards him.

'It is so good of you to do this,' she responded, 'I missed the Islay ferry, and I don't want to disappoint. It's a special birthday surprise for my sister.'

'They'll certainly appreciate the effort you've made.' To Ronnie, Lily appeared tired, and as he took her arm to take her on board and the sleeve of her anorak slipped up her arm, he couldn't help but notice bruises and minor cuts. He helped Lily onto the RIB, showed her a seat, gave her a life jacket and clipped her in.

'I live in London and was knocked off my bike,' she stated, noticing her exposed arm and Ronnie looking at it. 'It could have been a lot worse. That's partly why I couldn't travel with the others although they have my luggage. I can't let down my sister and our friends.'

'I'm pleased to oblige. You'll need the anorak and hat once we reach the open sea.'

'I realised that, and before I forget, here is your money.' Ronnie smiled and pocketed it. The evening with Pamela was about to be even more memorable.

The noise of the engines and the wind made conversation sporadic. Once they left the shelter of the loch and reached the Sound of Jura, there was a swell, but Lily sat still unperturbed. Most passengers commented on the Paps of Jura and the panoramic views, but Lily sat mute.

The early thirties, Ronnie thought, maybe older when he noticed the hints of grey. A determined lady, he concluded.

'How did you get from London to here?' he asked.

'I hired a car,' she replied.

'So, will you need to travel back.'

Hesitation showed on her face in response to his simple question.

'No. A friend will pick it up for me. I know the area and have connections here,' but as she spoke, Ronnie was not convinced. However, he had enough to contemplate and think about, so he let the conversation drift.

Over an hour later, he guided the RIB up the Sound of Islay against the tide, the vessel rising and falling with the waves. Lily's eyes were shut; not sleeping, he believed, but meditating, her arms splayed out to each side.

'Here we are, he shouted as he approached the quayside at Port Askaig, manoeuvring the boat close to the lifeboat. Pamela stood on the quayside, and as he cut the engines, he threw her the rope.

Lily waited until Ronnie motioned her to get up, and he helped her step off the boat as Pamela reached out and helped her onto the pier.

'Good journey?' Pamela asked.

'Yes, a lifesaver,' she replied. 'I didn't want to miss my sister's birthday.

'I'm taking Ronnie back to my house. Do you want a lift?'

That was greeted with a big smile. 'Wonderful,' Lily replied, squinting at her watch.

'Is the Bridgend Hotel on your route?'

'You're in luck. Just wait a minute.'

A short time after the vessel tied up, Pamela drove up the steep hill away from the pier, Lily sitting in the front. As they reached the hotel, as Pamela parked the car, Lily got out quickly, hanging onto her holdall.

'Thanks,' she said and waited as Ronnie clambered into the front and they drove off.

'Strange woman,' Ronnie declared and, looking in the wing mirror, noted she was still standing. Once the car had disappeared, Sally Rundell left the hotel, crossing the bridge over the River Sorn and turning sharp left at the road junction.

59

Nora entered the bedroom, bringing sandwiches and mugs of tea, crouching and placing them carefully on the floor. The strain was showing, her eyes bloodshot and with a blank expression, she was exhausted. Peter mentally vowed he would never eat another sandwich if he got out of this. At least this time, it was freshly made and not days out of date.

Cash started speaking. To Peter's ears, she was talking too fast, but he always thought that if the person was speaking in a foreign language. Nora was bemused, not understanding a word, turning to Peter, wanting an explanation.

Cash stopped. 'You don't understand Russian, do you?'

Nora shook her head. 'I thought it might be Russian; it sounded like them downstairs.'

Cash's face softened. 'Does Shaun?'

'No, maybe a few words, he should by now, but he is not good with languages.' Cash was relieved to hear that.

'I speak fluent Russian and understood what they were saying when we were downstairs. You are both in big trouble.'

'How?' Nora replied, her eyes narrowing, very suspicious.

'Because some of the time they were talking about how they would kill you,' and Cash paused, waiting for the message to sink in.

'I don't believe you,' she replied defiantly, stood up and stepped back sharply from the food and drink she had brought.

'We'll be first, but you won't make it off-shore. Either here or in one of the empty buildings. They want your share. You are no longer of any use to them.'

'You're trying to stir up trouble and to think I'm trying to be being kind.'

'Yeah,' Peter stated, 'making our last hours easier. I understand and appreciate what you are doing, but it doesn't change what Cash has told you. You are also in trouble. The grey-haired Daniil is greedy. Nikolai and Sergei are the same, and all are ruthless and playing a high-stakes game. They know their own lives are at risk.'

The fact that Peter knew their names impressed Nora, confirming Cash had been listening.

'Has Shaun used a gun before,' Cash queried.

'No,' Nora replied, 'well, once during a robbery, but he served time for that.'

'It didn't go well.'

No, he fired into the ceiling of a bank to frighten people.'

'Has he practised since?' Peter asked.

The silence told its own story.

'Speak to Shaun and warn him, for your sake.'

'Leave the door open,' Cash suggested, 'we'll keep you updated. We'll keep quiet; they won't know we're listening in.'

Nora studied their faces, left, turned briefly to look at them, and walked out. Both waited, relieved when Nora didn't shut the door completely. They heard her footsteps receding down the wooden stairs. The distance from the bed, where they were tied, to the open door was only a couple of feet.

It wasn't perfect, but Cash could hear snatches of conversation from downstairs, which could be helpful. More importantly, they had planted a seed of doubt in Nora's mind.

Eagerly, they ate the sandwiches and drank the lukewarm tea.

Half an hour later, Shaun appeared angry and red-faced, slamming the door shut.

'What are you two up to, frightening my wife,' he demanded.

'I speak fluent Russian and spent time in the country. I know what they are saying, and they are stringing you along, especially Daniil. Whatever you've stolen must be valuable, or you wouldn't have taken us prisoner. The men downstairs want to sell it on, and with the Russian state on their tracks, they want a big slice each. Do you really expect them to share it? You're in above your heads. You've been used.'

Shaun raised his hand, wanting to swipe it across Cash's face, but lowered it, scowling.

'You'll be dead first.'

'I hope you get consolation from that.' Cash was staring right into his face. Shaun flinched, turning away. 'Will they shoot you together, or will you watch Nora die first? She added coldly. 'Get out when you can.'

Cash was pushing it, and Shaun was getting angrier, his breathing noisier. Suddenly, he spun around and stormed out. Again, he left the door open. His footsteps reverberated down the stairs.

'Well done,' Peter said.

'Better from me; few men will hit a woman. He would have probably thumped you.'

Cash slumped against the bed frame, exhausted. Peter read the red digital numbers on the bedside clock. It was 7pm. The last of the cars from the gallery had left hours before. Jim McKenzie, the farmer, would probably be up to check his flock, and maybe a romantic couple would venture down to the bay later. It would be a few hours before dark this time of year. By midnight, all would be quiet.

He closed his eyes and reran how he had ended up in this predicament. Who wouldn't have stopped to find out what was going on? Then, he grasped the consequences of his simple action. That inevitably led to thoughts of Jenny, Ben and Jason, and he wondered if he would ever see them again. Opening his eyes, he saw Cash leaning forward, listening intently to loud voices from below. As he didn't want to distract her, he looked around the room, noticed a door presumably leading into an ensuite bathroom, and studied the wallpaper and the framed print on the wall. He realised it was an early print of Jenny's and welled up. Things had been difficult between them, but he still loved her.

Sometime later, Shaun appeared with fresh mugs of tea; he placed them in front of them and knelt down close. 'What were they saying?' he asked, a softer, more conciliatory edge to his voice.

'They're expecting the boat to arrive off-shore at midnight. A boat will come ashore, and they will haul the fugu, whatever that is on to it. There won't be room for you. Run if you can, while you can.'

Shaun studied Cash's face intently and stood up.

'Why did you kill Sir Angus,' Peter asked.

It was Peter's turn to be scrutinised by Shaun's fierce gaze.

'Gillies knew too much. He guessed we were behind the flare-up and that we grabbed something from the shore and threatened to report us. Gillies also worked out we had kidnapped you. He demanded we leave both properties and the island immediately and release you. He would have exposed us and spoilt our plans, but he wanted McIntosh's visit to be over first. Too much effort has gone into this operation. Unfortunately, McIntosh was arriving with all his security detail, or we would have left earlier. However, that diverted attention from us as everyone assumed McIntosh was the target.'

'It won't take long to work out. These people are ruthless and,' Peter pointed downstairs, 'killed someone who stood in their way. Tells a story, doesn't it.'

Shaun shrugged. 'I would say you have more problems than me,' he answered defiantly, checking the knots.

'Are you and Nora still useful? Can you use that gun, or was it for show?' Peter persisted, building the pressure.

'They have already lost one of the team; will one or two more make a difference,' Cash added.

Shaun stomped out.

Peter shrugged. 'High stakes. We'll have to wait to find out if our plan works.' Cash closed her eyes and lowered her head.

60

They had sat talking for an hour, discussing events from the afternoon and earlier. Henry's theories were plausible, and Swan now believed McIntosh was not the target. Sir Angus had been killed, most likely because he would tell others what was happening at Saligo and Sanaigmore. With the information Swan had discovered on his short visit to the mainland with Roddy, it was all beginning to make sense. While he trusted Henry, he wasn't yet ready or able to share what extra he knew.

Henry was surprised when Swan accepted the offer of a whisky. 'I noticed the bottle of Lagavulin,' he had said and wasn't for putting his hand over the glass to stop Henry pouring. 'It will be a long night,' he added by way of excuse and smiled dryly, refusing water. 'Sometimes whisky is better than coffee.' Then Henry poured a large whisky for himself.

Swan sat back in his seat and studied the lapping waters of Loch Indaal, barely breaking against the patio outside.

'I like Islay,' he stated, 'always have. I spent my honeymoon many years ago here when facilities were less sophisticated, let's say. Now here I am back, the conditions very different.'

The last thing Henry had expected was a philosophical Swan. He had garnered something of his reputation from being beside Ash, Imran and Roddy these previous days. They had utter respect for him, if not a little fear. Now, he sat, looking out at the loch, strangely vulnerable.

Swan had dismissed his team, told them to rest, and invited

himself to Henry's holiday let. Alan had excused himself, enough drama for one day and had gone out to meet Ronnie.

'I read the report on your dismissal from the police. I get access to all sorts of reports; don't be offended.'

Henry was surprised but sipped his whisky, conscious Swan was studying him.

'A load of rubbish,' he stated, facing Henry straight on.

'I exposed corruption among more senior officers. Never an easy thing to do. Those above me closed ranks, and I managed to save my pension. The whole scenario was very stressful, especially for my wife.'

'I'm sorry,' Swan stated with surprising emotion.

'My wife died young, cancer. I have never really got over it.'

Now, that was candour. Henry sat up.

'I know about Mary. You are in the early stages of grief. Bear with it. Everyone is different. Also, I hear you were a bloody good cop.'

'Speaking to Lena?' Swan smiled.

'Dealing with staff is so important. I know I am distant and a hard taskmaster at times. Each of them has their strengths and weaknesses. Did you have to confront your children, and I am being very vague?'

'No, problems don't go away,' Henry replied, thinking of his two sons and realising Swan was referring to his team members.

'Thank you. I wanted reassurance,' and lifted his Lagavulin, sipping it. 'They say the style of a whisky distillery changes over time. Here on Islay, there is a lot of discussion about the peat they use. It's a few years since I sampled the sixteen-year-old, and it's still wonderful. Maybe a little less peat, more delicate?' he raised his glass again, swirling it gently, smiling. 'Maybe I need to do more research.'

Henry hoped he had helped Swan, whom he instinctively liked, whatever his problem was. They were interrupted by a knock at the door.

'This should be Imran,' Swan said, glancing at his watch. When Henry opened the door, Ronnie stood there, a shy Pamela at his side.

'You're too late; he has gone ahead of you. I think he is very thirsty,' and they laughed.

'We were held back as a woman wanted desperately to get across for her sister's birthday party. Got me to pick her up from Tayvallich.'

'That will defray the loss of business from *Casablanca* being impounded,' Henry replied.

Henry was unexpectedly aware of Swan by his side, and Ronnie was slightly startled.

'Please, could you describe this woman?' Swan asked directly, not waiting to be introduced.

'It's okay,' Henry stated, 'Swan here is very involved in the whole business with Sir Angus,' and realising he didn't know Swan's first name.

'Better still, here's a picture,' Swan said, showing Ronnie a photo on his phone.

'That's her,' Ronnie replied, 'isn't it Pamela?' and his partner edged forward, agreeing.

'Did she give a name? Not that it really matters.'

'Yes, Lily.'

'I know her better as Sally, but close enough. Where did you leave her?'

'The Bridgend Hotel.'

'When?'

'An hour ago, we've been to Pamela's first. That's when I phoned Alan...' but his voice trailed away as he saw Swan's reaction.

Swan was already phoning, walking back into the house.

'I don't know the importance of what you just confirmed to him, but it has been significant, judging by his reaction. We'll probably never know how important it is. Thanks for meeting up with Alan; I appreciate that.'

When Henry returned inside, Swan was still on the phone. Finally, after a few minutes, during which Henry tried not to listen, Swan put his phone on the table and picked up his whisky, sipping at his drink again as he sat down.

'Henry, that was a breakthrough. While I can't say too much, we have been searching for Sally, an extremely dangerous individual. Lena is sending a team to the Bridgend Hotel immediately. However, I doubt our visitor will be there. There will be a hunt to find her. Unfortunately, a good number of the police have returned to the mainland. Henry, you are still bound by the Official Secrets Act?'

'Of course.'

'The police station is still overcrowded, and that man Rogers is still there. Can we use this room as an annexe?'

'Be my guest. There is also still more whisky if you wish.'

'Perfect. I hoped you would say that. Imran is on his way and will set up a laptop for us.' Turning to the wall-mounted television, he added, 'We'll get a better picture on it.'

Shortly after, Henry showed Imran into the room and watched as he set up a laptop and connected it to the TV on the wall. The picture was fuzzy and then became pinpoint clear.

Henry sat transfixed at the images on the screen. Swan sat beside him. Both were watching pictures from a military drone hovering over Sanaigmore.

'We've been searching for two Russian sleepers. The first one is called Petrov, probably in the hills overlooking the bay. I believe he killed the two men we found this afternoon. The second Sally Rundell, I don't know her Russian name, is the woman who has arrived on the island and I expect to join him. We have an armchair seat to the action; we're too old to get involved directly. Please don't speak as the PM, Defence Secretary, and others will join the live stream soon. Don't worry; the SAS are on their way as we speak. I wonder what they will find at Sanaigmore Bay.'

Imran was now wearing an earpiece. 'There has been a delay,' he stated. Helicopter problem. They will be another hour.' The clock on the wall read ten o'clock.

Swan grimaced. 'They're cutting it fine,' he replied, pushing his dram to one side.

61

Shaun revisited them an hour later, checked the knots on the rope and promptly left before anyone could attempt to engage him. Downstairs had been quiet; maybe they were resting, and Cash had drifted off to sleep, her mouth slightly open, almost snoring, an undignified look for her. Peter had fought the tiredness and knew from previous experience what it meant to live on the edge, waiting for the action to start like a cancer patient waiting for the surgeon's report to arrive — live or die. Maybe if the two of them kept quiet, they might be forgotten. Peter knew some considered him naïve, but he was not that naïve. It was just wishful thinking. He knew Jenny was hurting but regretted they hadn't been connecting. The boys would be devastated, and Jason, still an outsider in some ways, would be on his own again. He struggled with his emotions before forcing them to one side. Experience had taught him that if he was to survive.

Hours later, he heard Daniil call out downstairs, and everyone appeared to be arguing within minutes. Peter looked to Cash for an explanation. Immediately aroused from dozing, she was absorbed and motioned to leave her alone and let her concentrate. He heard Shaun shouting. 'What's wrong,' and was told to shut up. Shaun started shouting and swearing until there was a loud crack, and he heard something like a chair crashing and a scream from Nora.

Cash turned quickly to Peter. 'Eriks and Aleksandr have not returned, nor can they be contacted by phone. We know Eriks, good if he is missing, and Aleksandr must be our other captor. They're worried as they need to move the fugu to the beach and need all the muscle they can get. Can't understand what's wrong. Two of them want to go and find out, but Daniil is unsure. They don't have much time. Shaun interrupted at the wrong time, and someone hit him.'

'That last part I worked out, but what is a bloody fugu?'

Cash shook her head in frustration. 'It must be the small boat we saw, all charred. I can't believe it is worth anything, especially all this trouble.'

Both were now fully awake as activity increased downstairs, increasingly tense. Orders were being issued, and Cash listened intently. 'They're eating something before leaving, giving the others extra time to arrive. Peter heard the front door shut and, in the still night air, heard someone walking outside, a stray sheep bleating as it was disturbed. The clock showed eleven, the bright figures like harbingers of doom. The Ford Transit was started up, the engine noise magnified by the walls of the outbuilding it was parked in. He heard it being manoeuvred out of the farm building. There was more noise from downstairs and then footsteps on the wooden stairs. Both held their breath as the door swung fully open. Daniil stood there clad in black, his grey beard and hair framing his face. He studied them momentarily, checked the ropes that bound them, spoke gruffly, and even Peter understood that he was swearing.

He left, slamming the door behind. 'What did he say?' Peter asked. 'Russians know how to swear, but the gist was we are pests.' Peter's stomach flipped; was that a ray of hope? No final decision yet on their fate. Seconds went by, and they heard Daniil calling on Shaun from downstairs. They waited, and nothing happened. Outside, the noises appeared more distant, and Peter became aware of a cold draught under the bedroom door.

'I think they have gone,' Cash muttered.

'For the moment,' Peter replied. It was a miracle he escaped from the clutches of McGory, on Jura, whose leering face was forever imprinted in his mind, as he leaned forward, holding the glowing metal tube with tongs until suddenly he was blown away. It needed another miracle now.

...

Outside, Petrov was moving, stealthily working his way down the hillside, his movement covered by an encroaching sea mist, blurring the contours, chilling the land. An assault on the house, he had decided early on, was too dangerous, as he had no idea of the numbers inside. He had counted three men leaving the house and then a couple hanging back, almost trying to edge away. After the long wait, he was stiff and uncomfortable but watched as the men went to the outhouse and saw the van emerge with a trailer attached. On the trailer was the fugu, a boat-shaped craft, which, as he expected, was blackened on the top. They had to be stopped; his nation's secrets were being stolen into the arms of those who would sell it to the highest bidder.

Having driven as close to the beach as possible, the men disconnected the trailer from the van and attempted to drag it onto the shore. Creeping past the outbuildings, Petrov was dazzled by a motion-activated security lighting flooding the area around what he saw was an Art Gallery and pulled himself sharply back around a corner of a building. The couple had triggered the lights, and he dropped to the ground, peering around the corner after the lights went out. Having observed the couple close up, he couldn't understand their presence other than it must be their house. They stuck together and appeared fearful, not sure what to do.

Carefully, he retraced his steps and positioned himself closer to the beach. Petrov could see the men struggling to move the fugu, cursing as they dragged it on the trailer towards the water's edge.

Close enough to hear them curse their missing colleagues in a language he understood. A torch was switched on to work out what was holding the trailer back, and one of them started loosening a stone and prising it out of the sandy surface. They attempted again, and the trailer edged a few more inches forward. They were all sweating, consumed by their efforts, an easy target.

'Shaun,' one of them shouted, 'we need your help,' Shaun eventually appeared apprehensive. 'Help us push,' he was instructed as he joined them, leaving his partner alone. Petrov was now close enough to see them, their faces streaked with sweat, an aura of perspiration around them. They had reached the sand yards from the water's edge. A trickle of water from a stream undermined their efforts, making the sand soft, and eventually, they stopped.

'Far enough. Nikolai, collect the bag from the house,' and Nikolai, nearest the house, walked back towards it. Petrov took his chance and followed him. Nikolai passed the woman standing by herself, arms wrapped tightly around her, saying something he couldn't make out, and then walked towards the house. As he reached the end of the farm building closest to the house, Petrov's hand reached out and grabbed him by the neck, pulled him inside, covering his mouth, as he slit his throat. Warm blood pulsed over Petrov's clothing. As the blood flow stopped, Petrov lowered him to the ground and dragged him further inside the building before dropping him unceremoniously.

One down, he mused, quickly retreating from the body, wiping his hands on a clump of grass and then wiping the blade of his knife.

After ten minutes, those left at the trailer were becoming impatient, wondering where their colleague had gone.

'Nikolai?' the leader demanded anxiously, his shout dispersed by the patchy mist. 'Sergie, fetch him, find out what the delay is.'

'Okay, Daniil, maybe he has gone to the toilet,' but the attempt at humour fell flat.

Petrov was crouching, waiting, having pulled back twenty yards behind a low brick wall, ready to fire his VSS Vintorez silenced sniper rifle. Tightening his finger on the trigger, he jumped as his body was illuminated, followed by a sharp crack, and a bullet hit him, lodging itself in his thigh. Petrov felt dizzy, the pain intense. He almost dropped his rifle but immediately flopped to the ground to try and protect himself. Twisting around, he spotted a boat appearing from the mist, a searchlight now probing the area, a figure beside it moving the light scouring it, searching for where he had gone. Petrov had not expected support to arrive for the group so quickly. Squirming beside a rocky outcrop, he fired back as the boat beached, and a man at the prow pitched forward onto the beach. Immediately, several others jumped out of the vessel and scattered. He let off another shot, which missed and then pulled back. His leg was bloody, and he checked the wound, grimacing as it felt as if the thigh bone was fractured.

Crawling away, he made for the house where he could give himself first aid and find a defensive position. He used his rifle as a crutch for the last few yards and hobbled inside, shutting the door behind him. Glancing back at the people who had arrived, no more than three, he reckoned, not counting the one he had shot, not sure what to do. Five-to-one odds were not great before adding in the couple.

...

Peter and Cash were alarmed by the gunfire but remained tied to the bed frame and each other with ropes around their wrists. They heard someone enter the house.

'Drag the bed towards the ensuite; the worst they can do is shoot us. There might be something in there we can use to cut the ropes.' Cash responded immediately, and tethered together, they attempted to haul the bed, first towards the bedroom door, pulling it out from between the bedside cabinets and then dragging the bed to the side towards the ensuite, a distance of only two yards, but the bed was large and not on castors. It was also heavy, and they were both in a weakened state but desperate. The bed started to move, scratching and squealing on the wooden surface. They heard a shot, and a bullet passed through the floor, narrowly missing them, absorbed by the mattress. Sweating and out of breath, they pulled the bed closer to the bathroom door, and although neither could stand up, Peter used his foot to move the door handle down and kick it open. The wash hand basin was on the opposite wall. Other than soap and a towel hanging beside it, the bathroom was empty. Another bullet missed them, hitting the bed's metal frame and ricocheting away. Cash screamed several times and stopped and then whispered. 'Whoever it is will think he has hit us.'

Peter swore quietly and then saw a bathroom cabinet on the wall beside him. Lying on his back, he tried to kick it off the wall, kicking out at it repeatedly until it was beginning to be prised off. A final kick and it fell down, a foot away, on its front. A bullet passed through the flooring, close to Peter and smashed the wash hand basin. This time, he screamed, hoping to satisfy the person firing that they were no longer a threat. They held their breath, but no one came upstairs, and suddenly, there were many shots fired from outside that were returned. Whoever had fired at them now had other targets. Cash took over and attempted to slowly drag the bathroom cabinet towards them with her foot, trying not to make a noise. Precious time was taken as they managed to turn it over and slide the glass front open together. In the dark, they rummaged about inside and found an open razor. Peter grabbed it and took out the razor blade, cutting himself as he did and started sawing at the ropes.

Below them, they heard more shots, and return fire shattered their glass doors leading to the Juliette balcony, the glass fragmenting and falling to the floor, scattering glass everywhere. They heard someone moving about downstairs and more shots.

Peter was busy sawing at the rope which bound Cash's hands, trying not to cut her. The strands began to fray, and finally, one coil was cut through. Cash's wrist cut as it parted, blood oozing out.

'Keep going,' she said, drawing a deep breath and grimacing.

The firing intensified from the house and from outside. A scream echoed through the night air. A spotlight played on the house, and another round hit the bedroom wall.

Another coil of rope was cut through, loosening some of the bonds and allowing Cash to move her hands. She took the razor and started working on the rope which bound them to the bed frame. It finally parted, and they were free from the bed frame. Working on the remaining rope that bound them together was now more straightforward. It parted, and the rope fell away from Cash's hands. Immediately, she worked on the ropes binding Peter's hands, which were cut through quickly. They rubbed their hands, massaging them, Cash sucking at the wound on her wrist and reaching for the towel to staunch the blood flow.

Outside, the firing had stopped. Voices were raised. 'They're leaving,' whispered Cash. Impulsively, they hugged each other, but their joy was short-lived. Peter froze as he heard someone at the window attempting to climb in. Cash saw his face and stopped. The curtain was pulled back, and a shadowy figure entered the room very slowly. The person's breathing was laboured and heavy, the footsteps light on the floor. A torch beam flashed around the room, and slowly, somebody crossed the room. Cash bit her lips, trying not to scream, as Peter held his breath. The bedroom door was pulled further open, and more light swept into the room. They were conscious of a presence, pausing probably peering towards the bed, but then stepping outside onto the landing. They waited as the person slowly made their way down the stairs.

'Shall we attempt to escape? The person must have used a rope to get in.' They waited a minute as the footsteps retreated down the stairs and then clambered over the bed and towards the curtains, which were sagging and looked out. A boat was drifting yards from the shore. From a helicopter overhead, a spotlight illuminated the mast and bow of the boat. People were writhing on the beach and the vessel. They watched someone fall into the sea screaming before drifting out of the beam. The scene was confusing as gunfire had ceased.

Cash grabbed the rope held onto the metal of the Juliette window by a grappling hook. Looking at Peter, Cash clutched the rope that reached the ground and, with his support, climbed over the metal frame of the Juliette balcony and started to shimmy down the rope, her feet kicking against the wall. Once down, she motioned to Peter, and he joined her. They ran towards the nearby hill, diving into a ditch beside a track.

...

Petrov was in pain; having found a towel to wrap around his leg, he lay to the side of a window, cursing that the group were escaping with the fugu. Adrenaline was pumping through him, but the pain was overpowering him, and the thought of failure gripped him like a steel corset.

He heard a creaking sound from behind and edged around to see a figure emerging coming down the stairs. His fingers gripped his handgun, and he lifted it shakily.

'Who is there?' he croaked.

'Someone from your past,' the voice replied in Russian. Petrov knew the voice but struggled to place it.

'Zoya.'

'Oh Zoya, so good, I am in trouble, a bullet smashed my thigh.'

'You are in a lot of trouble, Denis.'

'I know.'

'No, you don't. I haven't come to help you but to kill you slowly.'

'I don't understand. We need each other to get out of here.'

'Put down your gun. Now,' she demanded.

Petrov hesitated, and Zoya fired, knocking the gun from his hand and breaking one of his fingers with the force.

Petrov yelped and stuck his hand in his armpit.

'What are you doing, Zoya?' he screamed.

'Getting revenge for my sister, Clara. Remember the day in the woods at our English training village. Clara was in trouble; she had tried to run away but was caught. Brought back. The commander insisted on an example being made of her.'

'She was doomed.'

'You stood up and demanded she be executed. No one else did.' The anger in Rundell's voice was palpable.

Petrov wiped the sweat from his brow.

'I thought it was a test. Please believe me,' he pleaded.

'Even when they brought in the mobile crematorium. You lie,' and Zoya moved closer, kicking the handgun into the corner away from Petrov, snatching his rifle, and flinging it across the room. Petrov was in too much pain to offer any resistance.

'You grabbed her, helped feed her into the incinerator, and shut the door. She was alive, screaming for mercy. You burnt her alive. I still hear her screams every day. My sister burnt alive, and you turned and smiled at me that day,' Zoya fired again, hitting his other arm.

'No, Zoya, mercy please,' he screamed.

'They'll kill your parents.'

'No. Mother died several years ago. I received news a few days ago that my father has now died. My family no longer exists.'

'They will get away with the fugu and get the acoustic recording of the Trident submarine,' Petrov screamed. 'Russia can use it in the event of a war. Their submarine will be more easily traced. Even though the fugu has been damaged, the recording will still exist.'

'I now no longer care.'

Zoya stood over Petrov, ignoring his rants and fired again. Petrov slumped, squirming in agony. Then, another shot into his good leg. Petrov screamed as the door burst open, and a stun grenade was thrown in. The concussive force of the explosion disabled them. Zoya heard footsteps running down the stairs and fired again towards Petrov and then was cut down in a hail of bullets.

...

Swan watched the drone footage, wearing headphones with an attached microphone and saw movement cease around the boat. He spoke into his microphone. 'Tell them to avoid the boat, repeat, avoid the boat, she's sprayed it with Novichok.'

Henry appeared stunned.

An acknowledgement came back, and Swan told the others. 'Petrov and Rundell are dead. A team has picked up the missing pair on the hillside. They managed to escape from captivity – safe but in a poor state. A couple have also been picked up and held in custody. I believe it is the Irish couple.'

'Thank God,' said Henry with some emotion as Swan relayed the information, reaching for the whisky bottle and pouring himself a large dram. Swan had not touched his whisky in several hours.

Swan relayed another message. 'A yacht, the *Marianna VI*, has been boarded inside territorial waters by the Royal Navy. They were preparing to receive the fugu. The Navy has been busy turning away a Russian fishing boat, a spy ship hanging about.'

'What the hell is a fugu?' Henry queried later as they shared another dram.

'A Russian wave glider, a surface vessel of very low profile, sent in to record the acoustic signatures of boats passing by, especially submarines. Radar will not detect them; they sit there soaking up acoustic traffic. They captured the acoustic signature of a Trident sub despite us using a surface vessel to follow the Trident in to try and mask the sub's signature. We only have one Trident at sea at a time. If the Russians knew its signature, they could follow it, and our nuclear capability would be compromised in the event of a war.

'High stakes.'

'But we stopped them.'

'And Peter and Cash are safe?'

'On their way to hospital as we speak.'

Swan removed his headphones and pressed a switch, and a familiar voice spoke to the room. 'A successful mission. Thanks to all involved,' Henry recognised the voice of the Prime Minister.

'It's all over,' said Henry.

'I wish it was,' replied Swan, and his body sagged back into the chair. 'I wish it was,' he repeated, his face ashen, 'but it never is. There is always another attempt to attack us.'

62

There was a palpable tension as Swan entered; his face was chalk white, his eyes red and bleary, making him appear ghoulish. He, like the others, was exhausted. Bill and Jean acknowledged his arrival but kept their heads down. Ash sat bolt-up, staring at her laptop screen, clicking away while Imran fussed over his laptop. Roddy avoided everyone and sat in a world of his own.

'A successful mission,' Swan started, having to clear his throat. ' The Russians had been deprived of vital secrets but at some cost. Many dead litter a beach on Islay, including the crew from the boat who came ashore.

'We rescued the wave glider, and once it was de-contaminated, we retrieved the recording. The acoustic signature of the Trident sub was clearly recorded. Steps will be needed to avoid this occurring again. The Russians were using the wave glider to listen in on our activities. Our side also uses wave gliders; indeed, the Americans were world leaders in developing the technology they initially used to monitor humpback whales in Hawaii. Inevitably, a military use was found for them, and the Russians copied it.'

'For those who don't know, a wave glider, like a surface drone, has a boat part, and underneath and tethered to it is a small sub with fins, which convert the up and down motion of the fins into forward thrust. They move very slowly. On the surface, they are almost unnoticeable, and with the solar-powered panels on the boat providing power, they act as a listening station, soaking up any acoustic noise from passing vessels.'

'Our nuclear submarines pass through the North Channel between Scotland and Northern Ireland before disappearing into the Atlantic, a pinch point where they are vulnerable to being picked up and followed. It's an excellent place to seek out our subs and alert the Russians because they are almost impossible to follow once in the depths of the Atlantic. The information gained from the wave gliders, or fugu, as the Russians call them, could enable our subs to be identified, tracked, easier to follow, and eliminated during conflict. The consequences could be grave for our nuclear deterrent.'

'Using our own shores to operate from, the Russians could hang around longer, and it is believed that the fugu found had new features, including a fine mast structure draped with what looks like long strands of tinsel. It's these which caught fire. Being based here, they could be brought in for servicing, which helped them. On board was a recorder; onshore, the information could be downloaded. This wave glider didn't directly communicate with satellites; we might have picked up transmissions, but could send short bursts of messages to the shore base if it identified the signature of one of our nuclear subs. Operating from the Scottish coastline meant they didn't have to use spy ships to drop off the wave glider. We track their spy vessels and sweep areas they have visited to try and find wave gliders.'

'The boathouse in Argyll was the base, and one of the operatives realised the value of the information gathered, alerted interested parties and started an auction. A team was set up on Islay to help to exploit the recordings. The operative, the man with the long brown beard in the photos of the deceased, tried to direct the fugu into Loch Indaal, where a welcoming party was waiting. Fortunately for us, something went wrong. The underwater part probably got snared and pulled off because it was not found. The boat glided with the tide but caught fire as it hit the beach. Ultimately, a Royal Navy frigate apprehended the yacht waiting offshore in territorial waters to take the wave glider away. The crew were mainly Chechen, funded by a mafia group. It is worrying they are moving into such areas.'

'How did Gillies and the Byrnes fit in?' Bill asked.

Swan acknowledged the question.

'Sir Angus Gillies had gotten entangled in the situation, although he may have thought their mission was drug related. He was being blackmailed by the Irish couple, the Byrnes, who had already fleeced him for the Sanaigmore house and forced him to set up a whisky shop for them. But Shaun Byrne became greedy when approached by an intermediary who promised even greater riches if he helped them out. He was seduced, allowing them to use his house and a nearby property owned by Gillies. Shaun and Nora are singing their hearts out, glad to be alive. Seemingly, Cash, one of those held captive, spoke fluent Russian and persuaded the couple they were for the chop. Cash admitted to us she had made it all up. We haven't told them yet.'

'Shaun Byrne background is interesting. He was in prison in Dublin for a failed bank robbery. In the same cell as Sir Angus's son from an earlier failed relationship. Together, they conceived of a plan to blackmail Gillies. The son, Kevin McKenzie, died of a drug overdose in prison. Shaun continued with their plan, contacted Sir Angus on his release, and proceeded to blackmail him. Sir Angus must have been convinced to shell out so much of his money on the Byrnes. Sir Angus had employed our friend Henry Smith to investigate his son's background, so maybe he was becoming suspicious. The police are still investigating why he was so generous to the Byrnes.'

The group leader, Daniil, believed Sir Angus knew they had kidnapped Peter and Cash was angry and might be about to expose their secrets, so had him killed, taking a risk that everyone would think McIntosh was the intended target, hoping they could depart once the initial fuss had died down.

We did enough,' which was big praise from Swan Roddy thought, 'to identify the sleepers in time. Felix Reeves, you will have realised, was also a Russian agent who had got dangerously close to the political elite, moving in the same social circles as the First Minister and the Defence Secretary. We had suspicions about him for some time and managed to get him to switch sides; he wanted to stay in the country, and his behaviour with prostitutes was troubling his bosses, so he was vulnerable. He was starting to be productive for us, revealing the identity of Petrov.'

'Reeves was also used as a postman to pass information to sleeper agents. However, those who controlled Reeves became aware he had switched sides. Just as we learned about Petrov, he was sent to eliminate Reeves. How ironic that his alert to Petrov ultimately led to his own death. Petrov was then sent to Islay as the Russians had found out about their missing fugu and the betrayal of one of their operatives.'

'We believe Sally Rundell was also a Russian sleeper working independently of Petrov. She used Novichok by smearing it over the boat, which killed all the crew. She was unlikely to be given the Novichok for that purpose, and it is probably not ideal for spraying on a vessel, as it would probably wash off quickly.'

'More likely, the Novichok was intended for another target, which worries me. We have no idea who, but we don't want another Skripal incident. Possible targets have been warned, and some moved to different safe houses. However, I believe she was diverted to kill the Russian agent in charge of the operation at the boathouse, leaving Petrov to reach Islay more quickly. Rundell brutally tortured and murdered the woman at the cottage and then hopped over to Islay. I wonder if she found out information from the woman that made her change plans. Before spraying the Novichok, Rundell grabbed a grappling hook and rope from the boat and used it to access the house and attack Petrov. The rest is speculation, but she appears to have had a grudge against Petrov. One of the SAS lads saw her shooting Petrov repeatedly as he entered, her face almost demonic, as if she was torturing him and she made no attempt to defend herself. Almost suicidal, inviting death.'

'I expect everything will calm down for a few weeks, at least. The Russians have been damaged, a network they invested a lot of time and money in at least partly destroyed. Petrov and Rundell lived off-grid, with no fancy technology, alerted using simple spy craft and fed information by dead drops, which suggests a strong network. We need to find who the spymaster is. Our work never stops.'

Ash interrupted. 'I believe Sally Rundell was Zoya Popova. I have positive identification. She had a sister, Andreeva. They have been identified in a group photo while at college studying the English language. Both dropped out of sight about the same time, and no further records exist. They might even have been in the same line of business.'

'That an interesting thought, Ash, thanks,' Swan replied. 'I wonder where Andreeva is today.'

63

Jenny was in a private room, heavily sedated, a nurse beside her monitoring her heart rate. As the nurse stood up, a doctor and Peter slipped in. Peter crossed the room, sat on the seat vacated by the nurse and took Jenny's hand, caressing it.

'I'm back,' he stated. 'I was being held captive. There is nothing between Cash and me. Never was. It is you I love.'

Initially, there was little response, and then Jenny's eyes opened.

'It's you. Where have you been?'

'It's a long story, but the important thing is I am back.'

Jenny tried to lift her head, and her eyes opened wide alarmed. 'Where is Ben? Jodie?'

'All safe. Malcolm and Alison are taking care of them.'

Jenny ran her tongue along her lips, which appeared parched. Peter offered her a sip of water, which she took, sitting up slightly to swallow.

'Where are we?'

'In Glasgow.' Jenny accepted this without comment. Her eyes rolled, and her eyelids closed. The doctor shuffled about to interrupt them when Jenny spoke again. 'You appear thin, and why is your face bruised?'

'That's for another day,' Peter responded, kissing her gently on her forehead.

He felt battered and bruised but lucky to be alive, but he knew this could never happen again if he could help it. Islay was spoiled for him, and he was sure Jenny must feel the same. They still had some of Catherine's money. There were possibilities.

...

Henry woke the following day with a headache, the events like a bad dream playing out in his mind. At least Peter and Cash were alive, no doubt traumatised, but the joy of survival would keep them going. The incident he viewed on the screen was like a movie, the drone footage surreal, but real lives had been lost, a high body count, some by Novichok. He knew how governments worked; the news would be suppressed, a fake situation created to deny people access until everything was cleared up.

Alan had returned late from his outing with Ronnie and was still asleep. Busying himself in the kitchen, he was frying bacon when the door was rapped. Pulling the frying pan off the plate, he opened the door.

'Come in, Lena, do you never sleep?' but his expression was sympathetic. He knew the strains of a big case. 'Fancy a bacon sandwich?' and glancing at her watch, Lena accepted.

'I could murder one and a coffee.'

'Have a seat, and I'll serve you quickly.'

'So,' Henry began as he placed the plate of food and mug of coffee in front of Lena.

'Somethings I can't tell you,' she replied, 'Peter and Cash are safe – bruised and battered but alive. Peter has already flown to Glasgow to be with Jenny. Cash has booked into the Islay hotel and is probably getting pampered and manicured. She is a tough, innovative lady. We'll interview her again today, and then she can go. I doubt she will ever want to return to Islay. Shaun and Nora are in a lot of trouble but are alive and in custody. Shaun was blackmailing Sir Angus.

Whilst in Mountjoy Prison in Dublin for a failed bank robbery, he met up with Kevin McKenzie…'

'Sir Angus's illegitimate son.'

'The same one. In doing time for drug offences. A bitter man, so it seems, and they spoke about Sir Angus a lot and concocted a plan for when they were released. It seems Lesley, Kevin's mother, died in mysterious circumstances, and they would make it out that Sir Angus had her murdered. Before they could start, Kevin died of a drug overdose, but the seed was planted in Shaun's mind. We'll do a cold case review of Ms McKenzie's death because Sir Angus was worried enough to pay out. I've asked for the case notes to be reread, and there were suspicions at the time that a hitman was involved but not sufficient evidence. The letter you saw must have been written by Shaun. Maybe Shaun was becoming greedy, wanting more money or else Sir Angus had had enough. Sir Angus was a smooth character, but fear drives people, especially if they can afford the means.'

'Thanks, Lena. How is your boss?'

'He's back on the mainland, boasting about saving the world.'

'All by himself,' and Henry rolled his eyes.

Lena smiled as she stood up. 'Take care, Henry, it was good to catch up.'

64

After all the events of the last few days, Henry and Alan stayed on to properly relax and visit the last few distilleries they hadn't been to. On Tuesday, their last full day on the island, they intended to take Drew up on his invite for a personal tour of Bruichladdich. They arrived, drove through the gates, found parking in the courtyard, and entered the shop, asking for Drew. The shop assistant seemed uncomfortable and asked them to wait. Henry and Alan looked at each other, Henry not totally surprised that there was a problem. A more senior assistant arrived minutes later and explained Drew no longer worked there but offered a tour.

They accepted and enjoyed the post-tour dram. While savouring the dram and nosing it as suggested, Henry noticed a bottle on one of the shelves – Yellow Submarine.

'How much is it?' he asked.

'That much,' he replied, but it was cheaper than the bottle in Shaun and Nora's shop.

'It's very rare.'

'I'll take it,' Henry replied impulsively, thinking it was highly appropriate from what he had witnessed a few nights previously. Alan appeared surprised but pleased.

'It will appreciate in value, sir.'

'We'll drink it tonight. It means something to us.'

Later, pleased with his purchase, they drove down to Machir Bay, and as he parked the car, his mobile rang. Taking it from his pocket, he answered it.

'Lena here. Just thought you might like to know. Two people claiming to be your friends were stopped for speeding through the small village of Keills going to the ferry.'

Henry thought for a second. 'My friends?'

'Well, one claims to know you well.'

'Charlie Smith. What has he been up to?'

'There were several expensive art pieces in his boot.'

'Don't tell me. They've robbed Sir Angus's house.'

'You would make a good detective,' Lena answered, laughing.

'He'll never change. My proud family name is besmirched again.'

'Wish them all the best. I have no sympathy. If Drew had stuck to the original plan to show us around Bruichladdich, they might have succeeded and not be caught in a speed trap.'

Henry briefly explained to Alan what had happened as they crossed the sand dunes and reached the beach. The tide was far out, not a drop of wind, no one in sight.

'Left or right?' and Alan pointed left, and they walked towards the rocks and cliffs at the far end. Halfway along, Henry noticed a couple coming down the hill track towards them with their dog.

'That's good news,' he stated, and Alan appeared puzzled.

'It's Peter and Jenny holding hands, no less. A good sign.'

Henry waved as the couple got nearer, and Jenny waved back. Jodie raced towards them and gave them a friendly welcome, nuzzling against Henry.

'Good to see you,' and her smile was brighter. Quickly, she explained who Henry was.

'Thanks for your efforts and being persistent.' The bruises had begun to fade on Peter's face, and Henry noticed a bandaged hand. Still, he was recovering, and Jenny was cheerier, more colour in her face, a sparkle in her eyes.

'I'm delighted to see you both,' and he couldn't help but hug them, surprised by his sudden rush of emotion.

'This is such a beautiful place,' Henry continued, his voice catching. Mary would have been pleased Peter and Jenny were a couple again.

'Always will be,' Peter replied, 'a special place,' and he turned and smiled at Jenny.

Acknowledgements

My special thanks to my wife Christine and Scott for their support and encouragement and to Mike Clayton for editorial support, typesetting, cover and book design.

Cover image -
the view from the Oa across Loch Indaal to the Rhinns of Islay

WS - #0125 - 241024 - C0 - 197/132/18 - PB - 9780993340048 - Matt Lamination